Ryan, Mary.

Summer's end.

34116753

$23.95

DATE			

SUMMER'S END

Also by Mary Ryan

Whispers in the Wind
Glenallen
Into the West
Mask of the Night
Shadows from the Fire

SUMMER'S END

Mary Ryan

St. Martin's Press New York

A THOMAS DUNNE BOOK.
An imprint of St. Martin's Press.

 For information, address St. Martin's Press, 175 Fifth Avenue, New York, N.Y. 10010.

Library of Congress Cataloging-in-Publication Data

Ryan, Mary.
Summer's end / by Mary Ryan.
p. cm.
"A Thomas Dunne book."
ISBN 0-312-14427-X
1. Man-woman relationships—Ireland—Fiction.
2. Friendship—Ireland—Fiction. I. Title.
PR6068.Y33S86 1996
823'.914—dc20 96-1423 CIP

First published in Great Britain by Headline Book Publishing

First U.S. Edition: May 1996

10 9 8 7 6 5 4 3 2 1

For my sons
John and Pierce

ACKNOWLEDGEMENTS

As usual I pestered many people for help and information and would like to express my gratitude to the following:

My friend, Breda Ging, who gave me a guided tour of the Inns of Court in London, and furnished me with books about the Temple; Robert Neil, Barrister-at-Law, for his generosity with his time when descended on in the Temple, and for an inspiration from which I have had the temerity to borrow; Ilona Scott, my former neighbour, now living in Ottawa, who sent me enough research to make me regret that the book is not set in Canada; Ian and Pat Williams of Cambridge who so kindly fed me and patiently answered questions; Katie Kahn-Carl for coming up trumps at short notice; my gentle agent Bob Tanner, who inspired in me the idea of writing a love story in the first place, and my editor, Cate Paterson, whose enthusiasm and constructive criticism spurred me on. Finally, my gratitude to learned copy-editor Yvonne Holland who had the tedious end of things and who did a splendid job.

Mary Ryan
Dublin, March 1995

. . . like nothingness or empty space,
The place beyond which there is nothing
Face to face.

Mark Patrick Hederman, *African Hymns*

Prologue

Sometimes I see her as a child.

In this vista of the past I am sixteen and Helen is eleven. She is alone in the dappled avenue. I watch covertly from the yard gate, see her run and leap at the overhead branches as though she would propel herself from bough to bough. There is a breeze and high above her reach the beeches are sighing. Her tangled hair is down her back. Small breasts are pushing at the cotton of her summer dress. Her skirt is too short – she is growing fast. Her legs are brown; there is a dark scab on one of them; her bare feet are in scuffed brown sandals. She turns at the gate, studies me calmly, gives me the ghost of a smile. Her face, to my surprise, is beautiful, although her smile is a child's quirk of the lips. In later years, she will say that in this, our first meeting, she felt a *déjà vu* certainty of our complicity like 'a memory of the future'.

PART I

Chapter One

I was very small when we came to Ireland. My earliest memory is of the stairs in our house in Blackrock, which I negotiated on my bottom. When I retreat to this hazy safe haven of so long ago, I hear my mother playing the piano, see my father offering a piggyback, know that Rachel is within howling distance and that James is throwing toys at me through the landing banisters. I know that I am small, but I also know my power.

As I grow I will learn that my parents are Canadian, my father from Ottawa, my mother from Quebec. These places will mean nothing to me – although I see them pointed out to James on the map of Canada, (which is on page eleven of his school atlas) – even though the map of the city itself with the great bridges spanning the Ottawa river is spread before me on the kitchen table.

My father, a diplomat, had been posted to Ireland in 1941, about a year after I was born. He came, he often said afterwards, with no great joy. 'A little inward-looking country on the fringe of the Old World, riddled with religious and economic monomania – what was there to rejoice about in being stuck in a place like that?'

'Weren't you even curious?' I once asked him.

'No! As far as I was concerned the place was poor and the people thought they could make a virtue of provincialism. I suppose I was disappointed in not getting London and ready to vent it.'

'But you were a diplomat, a being without vices!'

He laughed. 'Don't you believe it.'

'Did you hate it?'

He raised his eyebrows in his quizzical way. 'Ireland? After two months I loved it so much I would have stayed there for ever!'

'Why?'

He sighed. 'I was a man in Ireland. Everywhere else I was merely a suit.'

The house in Blackrock was rented for us by the Canadian High Commission and was run like clockwork by Rachel 'Jewish on me grandmother's side' O'Mahony. Rachel came from the Liberties, the oldest part of Dublin, and was fiercely proud of her Jewish blood. She had an accent like some arcane tongue, but was a good cook, able to conjure up occasional delicacies notwithstanding wartime rationing. My father found her amusing, but she established a strange rapport with my mother, although the two women were as different as they could be, one rotund and garrulous and the other icily elegant and somewhat remote.

There was a field across the road where my brother James and I played, and not far away was Marsh Park, our school, where we were mesmerized by the headmaster, Father O'Toole, who was known as The Tool and sometimes as The Buffalo. That my father should have sent me to a Catholic school was not something that struck me with wonder. The place was near, my friends were there and my father had become so Irish that he had absorbed the ostensible indigenous dismissal of everything contrived. Besides, he was a secret agnostic like my mother.

My best friend was Kieran Fitzgerald who lived a few doors away. Kieran was a handsome boy. He had brown hair, hazel eyes and an early fascination with wheels. 'Whees', he used to call them and had a favourite, a tiny rubber thing, which he would clutch for days on end in his three-year-old fist. I managed to prise it from him one afternoon and promptly lost it in a hole in the garden wall. Kieran screamed and tried to demolish the wall. Being three myself I joined him in bawling and Rachel had to come and pour lemonade on troubled waters. She tried to fish the wretched 'whee' from its new bed in the masonry with a stick, but without success.

When we went to school it was soon evident that Kieran was one of the best in the class. He took to sums as though he had invented them; he was good at reading about the cat and the mat and the bat and the hat, and he progressed quicker than the rest of us to Rita and her shop. He became the class star, as popular as he was clever.

I was a poor student. An introverted child, I liked to paint and draw, and my 'rabbits', with which I had a love affair before I discovered elephants, were frequently pinned to the wall. 'It's hard to assess him,' I heard Miss Sweeney tell my mother in the *sotto voce* used by grown-ups when discussing present children. 'He's very quiet in class, but you can see from his drawings that the mind is working away; he puts in all the incidentals . . . and he likes animal . . .' and she produced my latest offering with apple trees, well burdened, and emerging from the foliage, the two ears of the inevitable rabbit.

Kieran had scorn for my artistic endeavours – 'Rabbits don't live in trees, you eejit; they can't climb!'

'They can so,' I insisted. 'I once knew a rabbit who could.' This was not entirely true as the animal in question had had to be assisted. But, having saved face, I learnt the power of scorn, the safety of orthodoxy, and all my rabbits ever after remained sadly earthbound.

The truth was that I was a little in awe of Kieran. He was the only child of academic parents and he spent mysterious summers somewhere in the mountains, in a holiday home belonging to some relatives. He would tell us about it – an old house belonging to his uncle Tim and used as a summer retreat. When I was eight, not long before we left Ireland, this uncle married a widow with a three-year-old daughter called Helen. They came from Dundalk, just south of the border with the Six Counties.

One summer Sunday, having pestered my father to the point where he sighed and said it would be a drive anyway, he agreed to see if we could locate this fastness, which was supposed to be an hour's drive from Dublin. So we journeyed into the mountain wilderness to the south of the city, a place my father loved. The sky was clear with a few desultory clouds and the wonderful moorland was vivid with purple heather and fresh green bracken. We drove for hours, up and up along a narrow tortuous road with the vale of Glencree stretched out below us and the two Sugar Loaf mountains blue in the distance. We left Glencree behind and found some reasonably flat stretches of tarmacadam, surrounded on both sides by desolate heath merging into the mists of more mountain, but there was no sign of a lake except one inaccessible and forbidding tarn down a stony incline. My father then discovered that he had forgotten his map and, of course, there were no signposts. In Ireland divine inspiration was virtually a prerequisite on a journey of any length; road signs were only good for the stretch to the next crossroads where there might be no signposts at all. My father had a theory that this was deliberate, designed for the purpose of developing ingenuity and imagination, and was the principal reason why the Irish were so inclined, as a race, to poetry and mysticism.

James moaned intermittently throughout the journey, in a private lugubrious monotone, 'We are doomed . . . to go around in circles for all eternity.' I giggled and kicked him and he thumped me in the ribs and soon we had a good fight going, he pinning me to the back seat. James always said he was the 'dominant bull' and insisted on the subservience due to this status from his younger brother. He was four years my senior and a great deal stronger.

'Stop that,' my mother said, looking back at us with her 'you'll-hurt-that-child' expression.

'Can't we go anywhere without you two at each other's throats?' my father demanded irritably. We knew perfectly well that he would let us wrestle until we were blue, but that it genuinely upset my mother. 'I'll put the two of you out on the road if there's any more tussling!'

James sat up. 'Aw, Dad, you wouldn't do that . . .' His voice assumed a hurt and plaintive note. 'Your only babies?'

My parents laughed in unison, my father despite himself, and my mother with the silver chuckle she reserved for James's witticisms.

'Some babies!' my father said, glancing at his two small sons in the rearview mirror and then at my mother in one of their rare moments of sudden intimacy, which I felt, but without understanding. In such moments I sensed their grown-up *entente*, the memory they had of a mysterious time before us and, of something even more mysterious, the events precipitating our arrival into this world.

We drove through the Dublin and Wicklow mountains, but we failed to find Lough Corrloch. We stopped to ask direction of an old fellow cutting turf and he looked up at us from under his peaked cap, gathered his brows suspiciously when he heard the Canadian accent, approached the car, and asked in the kind of careful voice that would have done credit to any susser-out of fifth columnists, 'Now where would ye be from?' We might have been the redcoats in disguise and he wasn't giving anything away.

My father laughed heartily as he drove off.

'Someone should tell the old geezer that the war is over,' my mother said, clicking her tongue. She was pragmatic in all things and her sense of humour, except where her children were concerned, was generally retrospective.

Kieran's father dropped in that evening, something he did quite frequently while his wife and son were away in the mountains. I was dying to tell him that we had tried to find Lough Corrloch, but my mother gave me a look which quelled me. I understood immediately that she did not want him to know that we had searched for it out of curiosity. Professor Fitzgerald drank whiskey, talked about his brother Tim and the latter's new wife Drusilla and her little daughter Helen the child of her first marriage – 'her husband, an old friend of Tim's, was killed in an accident,' he said, and added that really we must visit Lough Corrloch sometime, that it was an interesting old place, a grand place for the holidays.

'It's an old gamekeeper's house, built to serve a hunting lodge owned by the Malcolms, an Anglo-Irish family who left during the Troubles. Tim inherited it from an old cousin who worked for the Malcolms. It's held under a ninety-year lease from the Malcolms at a peppercorn rent; the Malcolms have let the grazing to a neighbouring sheep farmer and boarded up the Lodge. Tim can't modernize the house because of the terms of the lease. So they rely on lamplight and candlelight and draw water from a well.' He paused, as if suddenly suspecting that foreigners like my parents would find these deficiencies either risible or distasteful and then added almost defensively, 'Well, Breda and Kieran love it . . . And I find it a wonderful place to relax.'

'Is the lake deep?' I asked, casting aside the *Dandy*. It was James's comic, but he was out at his secret poker school. He had even invited me to join him; but much as I would have normally jumped at this rare honour I wanted to hear about the mysterious place in the mountains.

Now Kieran's father looked at me over his glasses. 'They say it's bottomless!'

I straightened, imagining what this portended. Did it come out at Australia? Was that possible for something to come out at the other side of the world?

He smiled at my expression. 'Of course they'll say anything. Would you like to visit?'

'Oh yes . . .'

'Well, talk to Kieran when he comes home and we'll try and arrange something.' He turned to look at my parents. My mother smiled politely and sent me to the kitchen to bring in another siphon of soda water. But when I came back Professor Fitzgerald was leaving.

I pestered my parents after that, but fruitlessly.

'I don't like the sound of that lake,' I heard my mother tell my father when she thought I wasn't listening. 'You can't supervise children all the time. And you know what Dan is like . . . into everything! And as well as that, no proper bathroom . . . it's not hygienic.'

So, my longing was at that time in vain.

When I was nine my father was finally posted to London. He had served two four-year terms in Ireland and was, in the view of the diplomatic powers that were, ripe for greater things. I came home from school one day and my mother broke the news.

'We're moving to London. Your father heard this morning.'

As always she was calm, but I sensed the anticipatory tension in her, the pleasure which was all the more intense because it was contained.

She regarded me for a moment, lifting her eyes from her shopping list. 'Well, aren't you excited?'

My mother was beautiful. When she felt strongly about something her eyes, normally blue-grey, became almost violet. Now she turned these wonderful eyes on me and gazed on me dispassionately. I stared at her, speechless, like someone confronted by a spectre. I knew a change was likely – I had been warned often enough – but, like the certainty of death, I had never quite believed it.

'For keeps?' I demanded when the dismay allowed me to speak. 'Is that what you mean?' For some reason I was acutely aware of the light from the garden and the scent of the roses in the big Wedgwood bowl, the room fragrant with Mansion House wax. I heard Rachel thumping pots and pans in the kitchen.

'Nothing, darling, is "for keeps". But we will stay in London until your father is posted somewhere else. Aren't you glad?'

'No. I think it's terrible. I'm not going!'

My mother sighed and her eyes became cold. She had never been able to tolerate displays of emotion. It was something she shared with James, her favourite son, this dislike of the anarchy waiting at the heart. I am certain now that this stemmed from a personal intensity which she fought all her life to control. Perhaps my father was not great enough, perhaps he had not space enough, to encompass what she could have given him. But her terror of emotion translated as distaste, and may have been the reason why, in the end, he left her.

'You have to go.'

'No I don't.' The panic mounted as the full realization of what she had said sank home and I fought the tears.

She shrugged. 'Where do you think you will stay?'

I thought desperately. I thought of St Aidan's, a children's home in Dun Laoghaire, which had recently featured on the wireless news.

'I'll stay in St Aidan's . . . the orphanage.'

She frowned and, as recollection dawned, laughed suddenly. 'Daniel, I'm afraid you can't. It's not as though you're some kind of waif. They only take orphans.' She watched my struggles for self-possession with an unwilling tenderness. 'You see, we'd have to die before you could go to St Aidan's . . . Do you want Daddy and me to die?'

It was too much. The tears spurted and in a moment she had me in her arms. I was aware of her perfume, of the powdered feel of her face, the gentleness of her body, of the loose lock of her ash-blonde hair which brushed my forehead, of the deliberation of her half-amused concern; as though she had opened a chapter in her childcare book entitled 'What to do when your child is upset'.

'No, I just don't want to go to London. Why can't I go to boarding school? I could stay in Ireland then . . .'

My mother's correct sympathy changed to exasperation. 'You know how your father feels about boarding schools! He thinks they're a last resort, and there are perfectly good schools in London. For heaven's sake, darling,' she added with some asperity, 'it's only a hop across the duck pond. We'll come back to visit; you'll see Kieran . . .' But I hated her amusement, hated the cool appraisal of my fraught emotions, and tore myself from her arms.

Later, in my room, James came to comfort me. He was obviously buoyed up with excitement and, for once, did not tease me, but he nudged me gently with sardonic superiority.

'London will be fun, you mollusc. Think of all the things we can do. What are you making such a fuss about? It's a great big city and there are simply billions of things to see . . .'

James had inherited my mother's pragmatic streak. He was thirteen and could even remember Ottawa. Occasionally he repeated my parents' stories of the scale of things there, such as the Rideau Canal linking Ottawa to Kingston and becoming, in winter, the world's largest skating rink; Gatineau Park, the wilderness on the city's doorstep with one of the highest densities of beavers in the world; the winter darkness for months on end and the unimaginable cold. He knew that there really were other countries out there; that they were not just configurations in the school atlas, or a grown-up conspiracy like Santa Claus – something I privately suspected, on the basis that, so far, I had had no proof.

Of the two of us James was the sophisticate, the man of the world. 'Don't you want to see Tower Bridge? Remember – the one I made with Meccano? You can travel down the Thames and there are trains running around the place under the ground. Can you imagine that? It'll be great . . . !'

I knew I was beaten. We would go to London whether I liked it or not. I suffered in advance the partings and the nostalgia, the loss of home, school, friends, Kieran, The Buffalo, everything known, everything hated, everything loved.

When my father returned from his office in Merrion Square he came up to my room where I was pretending to do homework, lying on my bed with my face blotched with tears.

He put his hand on my shoulder. 'Nothing lasts,' he said. 'But because it has been, it cannot be lost. And it's so easy to come back.'

He asked me for my atlas and showed me the Irish Sea and the short journey from Dun Laoghaire to Holyhead. He traced with his thumb the train journey to London. I knew he was sad too, although I also sensed in him a certain gratified ambition, but because he had recognized my pain, I found a measure of peace.

Kieran came to say goodbye. 'I wish it was me,' he said. 'You're lucky. Jeepers, I'd only love to go. There's the wax-works and the

War Museum . . . and the Science Museum . . .' His eyes had a dreamy faraway look.

'Will you come back and stay with us when you can?' his mother asked me, having shaken hands with my parents and wished them Godspeed. 'You'd be as welcome as the flowers in May!'

I brightened, nodded. 'And Kieran can come to London, can't he, Mummy?'

I saw Kieran's eyes light up. He glanced at me sideways with a grin, the sudden lightening of the face which, with him, was always full of charm.

My mother nodded, laughing. 'Any time he wants.' She turned to him and added, 'Just put your toothbrush in your pocket.'

Mrs Fitzgerald studied our new address which my mother had written down for her. 'Chelsea,' she said. 'That's nice . . . very central.' The word rang in my head; I thought it sounded wonderful; 'Chelsea' like 'Shell-sea' – the shell of the sea. Maybe we would be near the sea, which was only a walk of some fifteen minutes from where we lived in Blackrock; maybe it would not be so different after all in this place with its romantic name. I looked around me at the hall full of trunks and boxes, tea chests; the cream distempered walls bearing forlorn rectangular marks where the pictures had hung; the house already echoed, as though it too were saying goodbye.

At first even the light in London seemed different. I hated the huge city to which I had been transplanted, partly because I had been determined to hate it, and partly because all the sense of loss I had imagined from a distance came, in fact, to haunt me. On our first Sunday as Londoners my father took both his sons on a sightseeing tour. I was already used to the red buses, but I was struck by the size of everything, Big Ben, the Houses of Parliament and most of all by the river, where we watched for a while the pleasure cruisers and barges plying the stretch between Tower Bridge and Westminster. So many people, crowds of them, and underlying everything the muted throb of a city so much vaster than anything I could have imagined.

The house in Chelsea, in Walton Street, was elegant, a white stuccoed terraced house with black wrought-iron balconies on the first floor and a basement where Rachel was installed; but there was no sea nor shells, just polite, ever-present traffic.

James was sent to the French Lycée in Kensington and I went to prep school. I would get up each morning like someone destined for the firing squad, for, in a sense, that was what was in store for me. The class bullies had singled me out. I was small for my age; I spoke with an Irish brogue. They called me 'Paddy' and occasionally 'dirty Irish'.

'Eat your breakfast, young man,' Rachel used to say in exasperation, while I stared at the porridge, sick with nerves. 'Yez can't go to school on an empty stomach.' She would then appeal to my father: 'He hasn't eaten enough for a robin,' adding with characteristic hyperbole, 'the child will die!'

My father would ask, 'Everything all right at school, Dan?'

'Yeah, fine . . .'

'Are you sure?'

'Yeah, 'course I'm sure!'

I was destined to fight it out with Nigel Hanson, my number one tormentor, a boy a bit bigger than me and possessed of a truly breathtaking superciliousness. The fight took place in the laneway behind the school and I came home bruised and bloodied.

My mother was out and Rachel gave a shriek when she saw me, and rushed off for the Dettol. 'Oh dear, oh dear, what will your mother say?' She dabbed with the cotton wool and whispered conspiratorially, 'Did you win?'

'No.' I grinned painfully while I considered the drawn sword embellishing the Dettol label. 'But he won't bother me again.' I held up my torn knuckles. 'I broke his brace.'

'Good man yourself,' Rachel muttered under her breath and then compressed her lips like a woman who'd said her bit.

When my father returned he took one look at me and asked, 'What was it about?'

I shrugged. 'It was Hanson. He kept slagging me . . . I warned him . . . I warned him at least twice . . .'

'You're new,' he said. 'It's a rite of admission to the tribe.'

'They think I'm Irish.'

He sighed. 'That would be unforgivable.'

'Why?

'Several reasons . . . And they genuinely can't understand their neighbours, don't even realize how much they need them.' He laughed at my expression and added, 'Without the Irish the English would die of respectability within two generations!' He smiled. 'I'm quoting Shaw . . . But they might leave you alone if they know you're Canadian; Canada is in the Commonwealth. Why don't you tell them the truth?'

'No!'

I was surprised by the vehemence of my response. Let them think I was Irish. Anyway it was true; being homesick, I felt that I belonged to Ireland in ways I could not fathom. It was only my blood and genes, mere accidental baggage, that could claim a different inheritance. My father regarded me with parental whimsy. 'They'll make you pay.'

I clenched my puny biceps. 'I'll make them pay!'

He smiled at me with love.

My first school report was disastrous and my father took me aside for some angry parental remonstrance. When I told him I couldn't see the blackboard I was packed off to an optician and the upshot was that I became the proud owner of a pair of spectacles. They were miraculous, those spectacles, for the world of books and blackboards became overnight not only visible, but crystal clear. Thus was dispelled my notion that numbers and letters were faint and nebulous by nature, as though they inhabited a fog.

An eagerly anticipated letter came from Kieran in which he enclosed a snapshot, taken, he said at Lough Corrloch. It was a picnic photo, Kieran standing beside a lake, looking grave. Nearby a woman with dark hair was seated on a rug. She was watching a tiny girl in knickers who was digging at the white sand of the shore. The child had corkscrew curls, the fat little tummy of babyhood and seemed absolutely absorbed in her engineering works.

It was my first glimpse of Helen.

Poor Kieran, I thought; a yukky little sissy to mind. I could imagine her noise and how spoilt she must be. It almost made me glad that I had never managed to visit Lough Corrloch. When, finally, I did get there I was sixteen, and Helen was on the verge of adolescence, but that was for another day.

Chapter Two

Rachel acquired two kittens, two tabby things. She was smitten by their milky blue eyes and their aura of innocence. 'They were a present, Mr Smart-Ass,' she told James. She did not tell my mother about them: 'Sure can't the two of yez keep a secret? What harm are they doin'? I'll give them away when they're a bit bigger . . . sure the size of the craythurs is pathetic!' She kept them in a biscuit tin in her room, nicely bedded down on an old vest and she fed them drops of milk and biscuits.

'What are you going to call them?'

'Their names is Minky and Jinky,' Rachel said. She glared at us, seeing our ill-suppressed laughter, and added defiantly, 'Them two names is grand and classy!'

James sniffed and examined the two furry morsels who were now active, running around the floor after a ball, their little erect tails as stiff as aerials.

'Stinky and Sneak would be more like it,' he said in a reasonable voice. 'Either could respond to either name, thus saving energy.'

Rachel was indignant. 'Jamsie McPherson, may God forgive the wicked tongue in you.'

Rachel had her room in the basement, next door to the kitchen. Behind the kitchen was a room overlooking the garden, where my father had installed a snooker table. This became our haunt, the place we brought our friends, the place where a new poker school was established. I was now regarded as old enough to participate on a regular basis, largely because my pocket money swelled the pot. We would lie on the floor under the snooker table and deal the hands. Rachel didn't bother us. But one evening the kittens, now much bigger, escaped from her room and came dancing into the snooker room through a chink in the door.

'Scat!' James said and threw his useless hand of cards at them. The kittens retreated with James in hot pursuit. One of them ran up the basement stairs and was quickly followed by the other. My mother was in the hall greeting the Canadian High Commissioner as the two kittens, propelled by their initial enthusiasm, slid towards her along the parquet. At least this was what she told us later.

'Oh, glory be to God,' Rachel moaned, coming out of the kitchen in her starched white apron. She was carrying a tray of canapés and stared after the two waddling kittens as they negotiated the final step at the top of the basement stairs. 'Herself will have me guts for garters!'

'Go and get your filthy cats, woman,' James ordered, coming out of the snooker room and eyeing the proceedings with delight. Rachel, at a loss for once, turned to me and I saw the genuine horror in her eyes. I had never paused to consider her vulnerability, but I saw it now. I put down my poker hand – two pairs, the only half-decent hand that evening – and ran up the stairs, scooping up the kittens from under the feet of my parents' guests, while my mother directed a look at me which left me in no doubt as to the content of the morrow's breakfast conversation.

'They're mine,' I told her next day. 'I got them from a boy in school. Can I keep them?'

'No cats!' my mother said. 'I can't stand them!'

'Please, Mummy . . .'

My mother had the notion that Rachel was a fount of common sense. This was one of the reasons why she had asked her to come with us to London. Now she turned to her: 'What do you think, Rachel? It wouldn't be fair on you. I mean there's bound to be the occasional problem . . . are they even house-trained?'

'Sure if the child has his heart set on them, ma'am, what harm?' Rachel said with alacrity. 'Cats is very clean animals. I'll look after them – see they don't give trouble.'

'I don't want to see them upstairs again,' my mother said, looking at me sternly. 'If I do, they go!'

'Yes, Mummy.' I glanced at Rachel and she winked at me from behind my parents' backs, pulling down one whole side of her face in conspiratorial camaraderie.

James sat there gravely, spooning egg. Then he said, 'If Dan can have two smelly little cats, why can't I have a pet? It's not fair!'

'You can have one each,' my mother said.

James glanced at Rachel. 'Uggh . . . can't stand the little beasts,' he murmured. 'Why can't I have . . . you know – something with a bit of brooding passion?'

'Like what?' my father asked, looking up from his paper and fixing his teenage son with amused eyes.

James assumed his innocent look. 'I was thinking of a python!'

My father smiled grimly and resumed his reading.

'You're a true blue, a real brick,' Rachel told me afterwards, giving me a hug and a Rolo tube. 'And don't give any of them sweets to that brother of yours. He was the wringin' divil who sent them cats up the stairs.'

I put the sweets in my bedside locker. But the 'dominant bull' had ways and means of discovering my treasures and when I came back from school they were missing.

'You took my Rolos; where are they?'

'Where do you think, you miserable cretin?' He patted his tummy, gave a contrived burp. 'What are you going to do about it? Naa-naa, naa, naa, na.'

But James was not really unjust. Although he liked to play the satrap, his conscience never let him get away for long with his excesses. He approached me later and told me I could have 'black tax' in exchange. This meant I could beat him up without retaliation. He waited, tensing, but black tax was a commodity so valuable that I always saved it for a rainy day.

About a year after our move to London I began my love affair with the city.

Walton Street was near Hans Place where the Treaty between Ireland and Britain had been discussed before it was signed and I often wandered around to have a look at the hall door of number 22 and imagine that romantic personage Michael Collins darkening the doorway. But despite all this, my links with Ireland were becoming tenuous. I was ten years old and had succumbed to the charm of the great imperial city to which I had been transplanted. London, as James had pointed out, had everything.

And I was Rachel's pet, a distinction which I shared with Minky and Jinky. Nothing was too good for me. She took me to sail my boats in St James's Park on Saturdays, to see the Changing of the Guard, Madame Tussauds; she even sacrificed her day off to me. She never gave away her two kittens; they were grown now and had a bed in the garden shed for show purposes and their real one in her room. Her conversation centred on them, weren't they lovely; do you know what Jinky did . . . that cat is so clever! The other poor divil is a dote, but a bit of a slob . . .

I learnt to escape Rachel and her eulogies about her bloody cats; I would wander away on my own, taking the red buses, journeying to Westminster, and back to find an angry housekeeper. 'Where were you? I'll tell your mother if you do that again!' I knew this was an empty threat; since the Day-of-the-Kittens there was some kind of compact between the two of us. She didn't squeal on me and I didn't squeal on her.

I wrote to Kieran to tell him about Hans Place and Big Ben and his reply brought nostalgia with it, although it was only to do with what the class clown, Fuggy Murphy, was doing and how The Buffalo had caught him red-handed. Then he wrote, 'Aunty Maeve is going to London for the Easter holidays. I'd love to go with her!'

'Can Kieran come to stay?' I asked my mother. 'His aunt is coming to London at Easter. He could come with her.'

She glanced at Rachel. 'I suppose so, darling. If Rachel doesn't mind the extra work.'

'Sure 'tis no bother in the world, ma'am,' Rachel said expansively. She turned to me. 'I suppose he'll have the spare bed in your room?'

So my mother wrote to Kieran's mother and extended the invitation formally and I confronted James triumphantly when the invitation was accepted.

James was sardonic at the news. 'You mean that numbskull Fitzgerald; what will you do with him? Tie him to the railings and offer him up as a sacrifice?' and he gave a rendering of what he regarded as a proper incantation for a blood sacrifice. 'And what if he should require a pig to warm his bed? Have you thought of that? Piggy's presence would, doubtless, disimprove even your room!'

I knew he was remembering an 'Irish' cartoon we had recently come across in an ancient edition of Punch – poor old Paddy in bed with a pig – which had filled me with ire, and him with paroxysms of laughter.

But my father did not understand. His face darkened. 'What sort of talk is that?' he thundered. 'Have you forgotten the happy years you spent in Ireland? You didn't learn that in the Lycée!'

James was crestfallen. 'No. I didn't.' He hung his head in mock contrition. 'I'm really sorry, Father.'

My father glanced at my mother. She seemed unimpressed by the exchange, as though she found it too tedious to remark on. Indeed I had become aware of the increasing distance between my parents, the politeness, the way my father would glance at his wife as though he expected something she could not, or would not, give, and turn away, his disappointment hanging in the air between them. My mother seemed strangely oblivious to this increasing distance, as though she saw marriage as a unchanging constant and not as a dynamic.

It took years for this hope of my father's to wither; he would look up when she entered the room with a kind of stubborn anticipation, but it would soon become apparent that her concern was for the flower arrangement, or the shopping list, or the novel she had been reading, or, most of all, for the piece she was rendering on the piano. He would sit and listen to her play and compliment her afterwards and she would smile and say, 'Thank you, darling.' We all knew how she had given up a career as a budding concert pianist to marry him, and I suspect, he felt a certain guilt because of it. There was a hint of passion in her playing which I never saw translated into her domestic life. And, although my father would listen and hand out compliments, his fragile expectancy – the hope of joy, or other small, unexpected blessing lying in wait beyond the call of duty – would dissipate and die. I have often thought of the expression 'not all there' as absolutely appropriate for my mother at this time. She was perfectly sane, of course, but she was never 'all there'; she had managed to stifle the fluid, unconsidered element of her own vitality virtually out of existence.

Easter came. Kieran alighted from the train in Euston, a freckled boy of eleven, taller than I remembered, but still in short trousers and wearing matching jacket, and grey V-necked pullover. His handsome face shone with eagerness. He scanned the crowd, saw me, said something to the woman behind him and then rushed down the platform, pulling himself up at the last moment with just a hint of surprise and sudden diffidence, as though it had suddenly occurred to him that old assumptions might no longer have the same currency.

But he recovered his poise. 'Dan!' he said, sticking out his hand. I grasped it.

'Good to see you,' I said, feeling the words to be inadequate, feeling the unbidden lump in my throat. I felt as though the intervening time had gone, as though we were back on the Blackrock pavement with conkers in our pockets and the trees of Marsh Park behind us in the sunlight.

'You've got big . . . and you sound English,' he said with his old infectious grin, as though he had caught me out in some amusing peccadillo, and then he added, 'When did you get the specs?'

'Recently.'

I heard the rootedness of his voice, the way the tongue embraced the consonants, became aware, for the first time, that my own voice had changed, that I had learnt to touch words with cool, detached inflection.

I shrugged. I was suddenly self-conscious, conscious of my voice, of my new spectacles, feeling myself different, seeing myself with his eyes as someone who had become unaccountably alien, with a height change, face change and voice change.

'But I like English accents,' he added magnanimously, 'they're funny! And I like your specs as well.' Kieran was one of those blessed mortals who assume, as a matter of course, that whether they like things or not actually matters.

He turned then, introduced his aunt, a woman in a tweed suit, who was shaking hands with my mother. She took my own hand gravely, said she had heard a great deal about me, and then the two women moved down the platform, followed by us children.

I did not think I was a child then; I felt I was on the brink of the adult world, being over ten, which was the watershed. Little did I know how the watersheds would shift ever after.

That night we looked down from my room at the desultory traffic.

'London is the biggest city in the world,' I said.

'No, it isn't. Tokyo is!'

'Well, it's the biggest city in Europe!'

Kieran conceded that this was true, adding, 'Can we go to Madame Tussauds tomorrow?'

'Rachel will take us. I'll ask her.'

'Can't we go on our own?'

I hesitated for only a moment. I hated to seem attached to Rachel's apron strings. 'OK. We'll have to sneak off, though.'

I changed the subject, asked him about school and heard the update on all the news. Fuggy Murphy had left. He had concocted a gunpowder of sorts and had stored it in his desk with interesting results; his parents had been invited to seek alternative academies for him.

'Poor eejit,' Kieran said, and I heard the admiration. 'You should have seen The Buffalo!'

'How did he find out?'

'Someone threw a lighted match into the desk during RK, just as oul' Rooney was going on about hellfire. Cripes, the smoke! Everyone was coughing; we all had to get out of the room.' He paused, shook his head. 'It was great!'

I was mute with envy. None of the desks in my new school had been blown up. But I knew something even more impressive.

'There's a museum near my school with the skeleton of a dinosaur! A brontosaurus!'

Kieran looked at me with a grin and a sardonic raised eyebrow. 'Go on! Those fellows were so big you couldn't fit their skeletons anywhere, except somewhere en-normous. Anyway the bones wouldn't last this long – only fossils.'

'Well, maybe it's a fossil, but it takes up the whole entrance hall, which is simply huge,' and I raised my arms above my head to emphasize the point.

I had Kieran's undivided attention. His eyes widened. 'Oh jeepers,' he breathed. 'When can we go there?' Then he turned to look at me suspiciously. 'How do you know it's a brontosaurus?'

'It is! I read about them in the *Wizard*.' In those days my only voluntary reading material consisted of the weekly *Beano*, *Dandy*, *Hotspur*, *Rover* and *Wizard*. Rachel bought them for me and my perusal of them absolved me, in my own mind, from more serious reading. I was perfectly aware that my guest was widely read, had an inquisitive mind and I was desperate to hold my own with him.

'Oh yeah . . . I read that one too,' he said.

It was only on the tube the next day that I thought again of the strange house in the valley where Kieran spent his holidays. In thinking about it, in imagining the lake, the surrounding mountains, I was beset with a longing for Ireland, a homesickness. I imagined the silence, the wind stealing across the heather, the clear sweet song of the lark. I glanced at my companion. He sat rapt in delight, watching through the window as the train charged into South Kensington.

'I wish we had the tube in Dublin,' he announced. 'I'd go round on it all day!' Then he told me that I was a lucky blighter and I nodded modestly, quite willing to appropriate as my own all the wonders of London.

We had fun that day in the Natural History Museum, examining the brontosaurus, and many of the other offerings in their glass cases. I was astonished at the breadth of my companion's knowledge. I realized in a dim sort of way that he genuinely was a born scientist, while I was merely a hanger-on, someone who got a thrill of sorts from the thought of dinosaurs and great blue whales, but had little interest in their insides, or in insects, birds, or indeed in any of the marvels of evolution. But my business was to entertain and I followed Kieran from one hall to the next, from one exhibit to the next.

Closing time came. When it was announced Kieran turned to me with his eyes alight with daring. 'Tell you what,' he said breathlessly, 'let's hide. We can always get out a window later, or something!'

I was secretly horrified. I thought of Rachel who did not even know where we were.

'No, we have to go home. They'll be worried!'

'No they won't. Only Rachel, and we'll be back in plenty of time for supper. Let's do it . . . I dare you . . .'

I looked at Kieran and sensed his perspective. If I refused this dare I was lily-livered, no longer fit to be his friend. If I refused this dare he would no longer be my friend and I might never get to the valley with the lake.

'Where do you want to hide?' I asked dubiously.

He drew me down behind some glass and wood exhibition cases and there we stayed while the attendant checked over the hall. I held my breath, expecting his footsteps, his loud remonstrance – 'And what are you two doing here then?' – but instead he moved away and we heard his departing footsteps down the staircase.

After a while all sounds in the museum ceased. We heard voices bid each other good night and then there was silence. The light of evening still played through the window blinds, but the bones on exhibit now seemed ghostly and full of malevolence, as though aching for the life which had deserted them. We went out on to the balcony overlooking the main hall and peeped over the balustrade, but there was no sign of life.

I felt the panic rise in me. I suspected at once that the likelihood of our being able to get out before morning was remote. Kieran did not seem perturbed. He went to one of the windows, pulled back the blind, looked down into a series of small yards at the back of the building. He tried the window, but it was secured.

'What are we going to do?' I demanded. 'We'll be stuck in here for the night. And I'm starving. And we've nowhere to sleep.'

'Come on, Dan,' he said. 'It's early yet; we'll think of something. This is an adventure!'

I went to the windows on the other side, looked out on the front gardens and the locked gate, rapped at the pane to draw the attention of people passing on the street, but they were far away and did not notice. Kieran grabbed my fist. 'We'll be in trouble if they find us. Let's deal with this our way!'

He began to run down the great stone staircase to the hall with the brontosaurus. The museum echoed; Kieran forgot caution and began to whoop, Indian fashion. I followed him, swept up suddenly in this extraordinary freedom, in the lordship of this huge palace of the past.

But as the evening deepened and the shadows filled the museum, the fossilized skeletons, the stuffed gibbons, chimpanzees, assumed a terrible dimension of their own. Like Dracula, they were empowered by sundown. They became our enemies; they followed us, waiting for us to drop our guard; they hid behind the turn of the corridor, lurked in every dark nook we passed. Worst of all, the stone simian creatures clinging to the Romanesque-style arches above the main hallway, seemed to have taken on life; they swarmed silently down towards us, like so many demons hot from hell.

We found a niche under a staircase, where we sat against the wall near the public lavatories and talked in whispers. Even Kieran's sang-froid seemed to have had the chill taken off it. I knew he was glad of my presence, or maybe it was that my terror communicated itself, but we shared a toffee bar with the fatalism of condemned men.

'Where are you going for your holidays?' he asked at one point with an effort at normality.

'I know where I'd like to go,' I blurted. 'Lough Corrloch. Do you think I could? I've often thought of it!'

Kieran sighed. 'Uncle Tim doesn't like strangers in the place. It's just for the family.'

Later, being frightened of the darkness, we had the bravado to sing and our singing, if such it could be called, was heard by the curator who had returned to his office. He initially threatened the police on us, but when he saw what he had, and that we were very scared indeed, he drove us home in his car instead.

My parents were both at home and half out of their minds with worry. They had reported our absence to the police. My mother said nothing, but she put her arm around me in a silence so intense that I was afraid she would burst into tears. I was more terrified of her tears than of my father's wrath, because the latter was to be expected, but the former would be so abnormal that my map of reality would have to be redrawn.

My father berated us soundly, but with such thinly disguised relief that Kieran and I grinned at each other when we were hurried up to bed. Rachel brought us sandwiches and milk, but other than directing a look at me which was intended to fill me with contrition she said nothing at all, keeping her lips tightly compressed to evidence how profound was her ire.

Kieran and I talked for a long time that night. Initially we were full of sheepish mutual congratulation, and then we fell to reminiscing about Marsh Park. I knew Kieran was avid to tell the class how he had met me again and how we had got ourselves locked into the Natural History Museum.

He reached for his bag and got out some photographs of the class, taken the year before. I was able to pick out the person of the banished Fuggy Murphy, and others whom I remembered well. He produced some snaps of Lough Corrloch which he had brought with him, he said, because he thought I might be interested. I saw an old stone house, and a young girl petting a small dog. 'That's Helen,' he said.

There was a picture of his Uncle Tim in profile against the wilderness behind him. 'He looks a stern old fellow,' I said.

'Oh, he is and he isn't. But he's sick a lot – something wrong with his old ticker. He used to be a teacher but he had to retire. He loves the lake; he knows almost everything, is always reading; you should see all the books he has; the place is full of them.'

'What will happen to Lough Corrloch when he dies?' I asked.

'I don't know. I suppose he will leave it to Aunty Dru – or to Helen. He has no children of his own!'

'He might leave it to you!'

'I wouldn't want it!'

'Why not? It's a great place.'

He hunched up his shoulders, taking back the snapshots and returning them to their envelope. 'Ah ... just a feeling I have. Sometimes I think it's not a lucky place – at least not for me!'

'Why not?'

'Don't know ... Just a feeling!'

'What about Helen?'

'Helen's a pest,' he said. 'She's always hanging around me. She has no one to play with when they go to the valley. She used to be allowed to bring her friend Christine, but not any more.'

'Don't you like her?'

'Who? Christine or Helen?'

'Helen.'

'Like her? But she's a girl ...'

'But if she's such a pest, why do you visit Lough Corrloch, especially as you feel it's not a lucky place for you?'

He pondered this for a moment. 'I've always gone to the valley,' he muttered. 'It's just the way I spend the summer. Besides, I can get heaps of books read while I'm there, and do experiments.'

'What kind of experiments?'

'Well, dams and things like that. There's a stream and a river and a pool, as well as the lake. And I can go fishing with Uncle Tim ... there's trout and even pike. I'm not tied to Helen, you know! She's just a little brat.'

The next day Rachel miraculously recovered her voice.

'I thought me poor heart had stopped,' she said, shaking her head at Kieran. 'I thought ye'd have more sense,' she hissed at him, 'traipsing off with this fella and giving everyone a terrible fright!'

James overheard all this, looked at Kieran with supercilious amusement, and then announced when he was out of earshot, 'Well, your old friend is a good influence anyway! Never knew anything like the chagrin and gnashing of teeth your little escapade caused. I must try it myself!' He lowered his voice in fraternal admonition. 'But the parents are none too pleased. You would both be well advised to do a bit of grovelling.'

Kieran had, in fact, gone to apologize to my mother, which pleased her, and when I presented myself with my excuses, I received parental absolution.

Our escapade improved Kieran's stock so much with my elder brother, that he made a real attempt to be nice to my guest and I could see that he was gradually won over by my old friend's quizzical charm.

Kieran went home the following week and although we wrote to each other regularly I did not visit him in Ireland until his uncle died and I was finally allowed to visit Lough Corrloch. This was six years later and I was grown, as I thought, and Kieran too was in long trousers, deep voiced but with the same grin, and as opinionated as ever. The six years had flown; we had kept up our friendship through long anecdotal letters and Kieran had come to see us in London each year, had even been allowed to take time off school to be with us for the Coronation. He always asked me back to Dublin, but something cropped up every time to prevent my taking up this invitation. Once it was appendicitis; on another occasion my father took James and me to Canada where we visited relatives in both Ottawa and Quebec. Another summer my mother took both her sons to Paris, a trip I couldn't bear to pass up.

When I finally returned to Ireland at the age of sixteen everything seemed to have shrunk – the streets, the buildings, even the expanse of the bay.

Kieran and his parents met me at Dun Laoghaire and we drove to the mountains. His parents enquired after mine and asked after James. I told them that he was studying Medicine.

'That'll be one doctor with the smoothest of bedside manners,' Kieran's mother said. 'Even as a tiny fellow he had a bit of the grand gentleman about him. I used to think he would follow your father into diplomacy!'

'James always wanted to be a doctor,' I said. 'He's thinking of specializing in paediatrics.'

En route the Fitzgeralds talked about the sad death of Kieran's Uncle Tim from a heart attack, and how they tried to help poor Drusilla, and how Kieran had agreed to spend some of his holidays with them again, so that they wouldn't be alone at Lough Corrloch. Helen had insisted on coming, because her stepfather had loved the place so much.

'Anyway, I'm going to Paris for the last three weeks of next month,' Kieran confided. 'I'll be staying with some people the parents know. So a week or two in the sticks won't hurt me!'

It was night as we came down into the valley. The sky was cloudless and the stars twinkled with a clarity I had never seen before. 'Look, there's the Plough,' Kieran said, and his father stopped the car so we could get out and have a look at the heavens. But it was chill on the hillside and we clambered back inside after a moment and set off again.

'It's like going down a wall!' I whispered to Kieran, realizing how steep the incline was. I watched the headlights pick up the curving road, the grass verge and the heather and the sudden gleam from the retinas of one or two sheep.

Suddenly the posts of a gateway materialized and I saw the yard of a old cut-stone house, the shabby doors of what might once have been stables, and then the back door of the house itself opened and we were greeted by an effusive woman who told me I was very welcome.

It was on the following morning, having breakfasted on bacon, eggs and homemade brown bread, having chatted to Aunt Dru, my hostess, and Kieran's parents, who were going back to Dublin but who had lingered to talk with her, that I finally made my escape out of doors. I crossed the yard, found myself in the avenue and, for the first time in my life, came face to face with Helen.

Chapter Three

'Hello.'

I laughed and walked towards her along the avenue. I was acutely aware, for some reason, of the holly to one side, the sound of the wind in the boughs, the colour of the climbing dog roses on the left, the wonderful shifting kaleidoscope of sunburst and shadow. In later years I would realize that she always had this effect on me, made me aware that I lived, that I partook of everything, colour and scent and sound. She moved dexterously, the quaint charm she possessed already apparent, her dark red hair spilling untidily around her. This was the pest Helen. But for a mere pest, she possessed presence such as I had not encountered. It was tied in with her youth and the imperious way she examined me. I tried to think of something appropriate to say and fell back on condescension.

'Hello, Tarzan!' I said.

She was beside me now, regarding me with polite curiosity, but as soon as I spoke she gave a contemptuous and half-disappointed laugh.

'Don't be silly!' but she flushed. I knew immediately that she saw my badinage for what it was. From my perspective I was a man. I felt the patina of my manhood, the uncertain longing for its recognition.

'I'm Dan . . . Kieran's friend from London.'

'I know,' she said politely. 'You came late last night. I heard the car.'

I nodded, remembering the face at the window, the white nightdress, the sleepy eyes staring down into the yard, which the headlights had made as bright as day. 'I saw you at the window,' I added, privately piqued that she did not by gesture or diffidence confer on me any acknowledgement.

She stood regarding me for another moment, said gravely that she had to go and walked away. I looked after her, my confidence dented, uncomfortably aware that I had been weighed and found wanting. She pulled a twig from the hedge, absently, as though she had already forgotten me and I saw there her hands were grubby and her nails bitten to the quick. But as she turned into the yard she paused and directed a steady look back, narrowed her eyes and called mockingly: 'Tarzan was a bit of an eejit, you know!'

I laughed, surprised and oddly glad that this girl had offered a response. 'I was not comparing your brains . . . just your energy.'

She stood for a moment, calmly regarding my approach and then, with a toss of her untidy mane, turned into the yard.

Kieran appeared a few moments later. He was tousled and yawning.

'Was that Helen?' I asked.

He looked back, yawned again. 'Who else? Has she been bothering you?' And when I shook my head he added eagerly, 'Would you like to see the valley?'

I wanted to ask him about the girl, but contented myself with following him, being curious anyway to see the place. The mountains were around us, but it seemed so small and private a valley, a place almost hidden, that it reminded me of a story by F. Scott Fitzgerald in which a family had found a diamond mountain that they kept safe from the prying eyes of the world.

Kieran and I left the avenue and found ourselves on the road. It was an unsurfaced track, full of stones and potholes. I could see that, on one side, it led up the side of the valley to join the main thoroughfare, itself a narrow artery between Slea and Glendockery; on the other side it wandered further into the valley.

Now in the open, clear of the trees which surrounded the house and bordered the avenue, I was better able to see my surroundings.

My sense of being enclosed was compounded. Except for some flat fields further down at the bottom of the vale near the lake itself, which were so well cropped by sheep that from the distance they resembled a golf course, the sides of the valley rose quite precipitously; the mountains seemed to gather themselves around us. I looked from one slope to the other, from the heather-clad sweep rising to my right, which was dotted with sheep, to the other side where a long thicket of deciduous trees clothed the foot of the mountain. I smelt the smoky pungency of the gorse, which bloomed around us everywhere in brilliant yellow glory.

'This is wonderful!' I exclaimed. 'You never told me it was like this. It reminds me of something I read by Scott Fitzgerald – or of Doone Valley.' I glanced at him when he didn't answer, 'You remember *Lorna Doone*?'

Kieran turned his hazel eyes on me, grinned. 'I didn't read it,' he said flatly. 'What would I be doing reading sentimental old codswallop like that?'

I tried to find a fitting answer to this put-down but he continued in his pragmatic voice: 'This is a U-shaped glacial valley. The glacier swept down here, gouged out this space between the mountains, left a spate of moraines and a lake.' He glanced at me and smiled. 'Are you coming?'

'Lead on, Macduff.'

I followed him to the left, along the road which was dusty with one of the rare dry spells in an Irish summer. We came to a stile.

Kieran gestured straight ahead, along the path of the boreen.

'The lake is in that direction, but I want you to see something here,' and he crossed the stile. I scrambled after him and he followed the overgrown path beyond it, which hugged the side of a stream. The water was low, but it sang and whirled about the rocks. We followed its course for a few minutes until, turning behind a heather-covered bluff, the stream opened into a pool.

It was a naturally formed swimming pool, an irregular limestone basin measuring approximately twenty square feet. It was in a sheltered and private spot, guarded by two moraines, a pair of huge boulders which stood like sentinels at the furthest end, and it was sheltered also by the rise of the land around it. I saw that the stream did not actually flow through this pool, but simply fed it from a small fork while it disappeared underground.

'We bathe here,' Kieran said. 'It has parental approval.'

'But what about the lake?'

'That,' he said with a wry smile, 'does not, I fear, carry the parental blessing. It's about two miles away. Come on, I'll show you.'

We retraced our steps to the boreen and followed it. It rose for a little while and then, as we crested the top of its rise, we saw before us the sward of the valley sloping down to the banks of a fast-flowing river and beyond that the still waters of Lough Corrloch.

The lake was dark blue, almost indigo, and behind it the mountains rose in deeper hues of blues and greens. There was a small shore which I recognized from the snap Kieran had sent me all those years before, where a tiny Helen had dug the sand; bushes grew quite close to the edge and there were clumps of reeds through which the water rippled. About half a mile away to the left, quite close to the shore, I saw the chimneys of a house and, in front of the house, virtually on the edge of the lake itself, a small white building, resembling a temple of love, a structure exquisite in its classical perfection and utterly incongruous.

'What's that?'

'Which, the house or the gazebo?'

'Both.'

'The house is the hunting lodge, built by Sir Henry Malcolm early in the last century. The gazebo is a monument to his son who was drowned in the lake.'

'What happened to him?'

'It seems he was a keen fisherman. One day he went fishing from his boat and that was the end of him. He was never seen again. Some said the fairies took him; others that he was drowned and his body sucked down to the depths of the lake.'

'Which do you believe?'

He glanced at me with his quizzical grin, the look which was always accompanied by infectious merriment in the eyes. 'What kind of a half-eejit do you think I am, Dan? He was drowned, of course, fell out of his boat. He probably couldn't swim, and there are a few interesting currents out there!' He gesticulated with his hand towards the expanse of water before us, on which the light was dancing. 'Do you want to see the boathouse?'

'Of course.'

He moved away to the right. The boreen had petered into a narrow track which was marshy and overgrown. The boathouse was hidden from view by a spur of rocky land. It was a small stone edifice, built right on the shore. The boats had, evidently, once been stored in the front section, for it had a stone slipway leading down to the water.

But there were no boats now, nor any sign of them. I went around to the back, stared at the door and the dark window.

'Can we go in?'

'No,' Kieran said equably. 'The door is locked.'

I tried to peer through the filthy window, noting the rotten frame. 'It would be easy to get in. The wood of both door and window is rotten!'

'Who'd want to? Anyway,' he added, 'there's an old story that the dead boy will return to curse anyone who uses his boathouse. He kept his fishing tackle there!' He turned an almost avuncular, freckled face to me and his tone changed from one that was slightly nervous, to one that was contemptuous of shibboleths. 'So now you know!'

'Can we visit the Lodge itself?' I asked, pointing back towards the chimneys around the northern side of the lake.

'Sure. Only it's boarded up. The Malcolms never come here now. They live in England. But their heir, funnily enough, is said to be an American, although no one has ever seen him.'

We got to the Lodge by retracing our steps to a stone bridge over the river and taking a small path which led to the northern shore. Eventually, this brought us to the stables of the Lodge, a small cobbled area with dilapidated looseboxes for four horses, and a coach house. The Lodge itself was on the other side of the stables, through a stone archway.

It was a beautiful house, low slung, with big windows, well shuttered. The paint had peeled on the door and on the window frames; the gutters were leaking in places, and had deposited ugly rust stains on to the stuccoed walls. In front of the house was an overgrown forecourt which led to a long driveway This was the front access and, like the back entrance which served the old gamekeeper's house, it wound back up the side of the hill to the main road. Beyond the forecourt a grassy lawn, on which a few sheep were grazing, sloped to the shore. It was here that the gazebo, which we had seen a little earlier, was built. I approached it with wonder; a classical love temple in the middle of one of the most remote places I had ever been in, a touch of Attica in the Celtic Twilight. It was built of marble, with Corinthian columns supporting a curved roof. Inside it, on a plinth, was a marble urn. The plinth bore the legend, 'SACRED TO THE

MEMORY OF JASPER MALCOLM, 1815–1829'. Beyond it the lake whispered and the blue mountains enclosed it all.

'He was only fourteen,' I said.

'Was he?' Kieran echoed without much interest. He craned his head to read the dates and added, 'You're right!'

'Can you swim?' he asked me as we made our way home.

'Of course. My school organizes lessons for us!'

'I can't,' Kieran said conversationally. 'Funny, isn't it? No swimming lessons at our school, you know.' He chuckled. 'Just work!'

'But the sea is so close to you in Blackrock.'

'It may be all right for a quick dip, but it's freezing, old fellow.'

'What about Helen? Can she swim?'

'Not really.'

'Does her friend visit the valley at all?'

'What friend?'

'I thought you said her name was Christine.'

'Oh, Christine – no. Poor Chris!'

'Why "poor" Chris? Did something happen to her?'

Kieran walked to the steps surrounding the gazebo and sat down, motioning me to do likewise.

'I'll tell you what happened to her, but you mustn't say anything to Helen.'

I nodded and waited, and then he told me that Helen and Christine had been fast friends since babyhood, and that one day, about two years earlier when Helen was nine, Christine had been killed in a road accident.

'It was one of those stupid things . . . the girl had come out of her ballet lesson, saw Helen across the road and ran to join her. She didn't see the car and the driver couldn't avoid her.'

'Was Helen very upset?'

'She didn't speak for two weeks; she didn't cry, but she changed, became introverted. My uncle was very good to her. He used to take her on walks in the hills, give her books, talk to her about all sorts of things. She became very precocious, had to be moved up a class in school and was at the top of that! It was as though she was trying to compensate, or to achieve some mastery over circumstances. When my uncle died six months ago Aunt Dru was very worried about

Helen, afraid that she would go back into the strange silence she had when Christine died. But she took his death better than expected, although she was very cut up. I think the old man had been preparing her for it. But don't mention it to her. Don't rake up the past.'

When we got back to the house it was almost lunch time. I saw that the car belonging to Kieran's parents had gone.

'They had to get back to Dublin,' he said. 'I said goodbye before we left.'

The scent of soup met us as we trudged up the avenue, making my mouth water. I watched Kieran's long strides and wished I were as tall as he.

'Where did you two get to?' Mrs Fitzgerald asked as we came in the open kitchen door. Helen's mother was wearing a wrapround apron and was standing by the range. She was the quintessential Irish matron, the good housewife, the concerned mother. Helen was setting the table and glanced at us. I saw, with some relief, that she had washed her hands. She had also had her hair plaited and now sported a pair of white ankle socks. She seemed civilized somehow, different from the proud little savage of the morning.

Kieran sat on the chair inside the door and took off his wellingtons, putting on his shoes. I followed suit, aware of the eyes of the matron upon me and, for some reason, I felt that she was comparing me with her handsome nephew. She gave a half-glance at Helen, as though wondering whether she, too, had noticed how different we were in height and looks. But Helen was putting out the cutlery and ignoring us.

It began to rain during lunch. The first pattering was heard against the window, and the room became dim. Without the intermittent shafts of sunlight it seemed gloomy, although the fire glared through the bars of the range. We ate the barley soup in virtual silence.

'What would you like to do this afternoon?' Kieran asked.

'What are our options?' I asked, indicating the rain.

'Well, we can read; I've a great book I want to finish. Or we could play chess, or play cards – are you any good at poker?'

I glanced at Helen, somewhat surprised that he had not adverted to her, had not included her in his deliberations. It was as though she lived in another dimension, or was too young to understand what we were talking about. I turned to her, saw her green eyes fixed on Kieran.

'What about you, Helen?' I asked, aware that she was perfectly *au fait* with the matter under discussion, and that excluding her was downright rude. 'Would you like to play cards; there's loads of things we can play besides poker.'

'I can play poker,' Helen said calmly, 'but I wouldn't mind a game of chess!'

Kieran looked at her indulgently. 'Is my liggle Helen interested in chess?' he asked with an laugh. 'I would have thought it would bore her stiff!'

I listened to the first conversation I had ever heard between these two. They had known each other for years and still Kieran did not know that she liked to play chess. He exhibited an avuncular indulgence towards her in tone and manner, covering, perhaps, the impatience I remembered hearing in his voice in London six years before when he had referred to her as a pest.

Helen did not reply, but she smiled as though she liked the status of his 'liggle Helen'. She looked at her mother who raised her eyebrows.

'No it wouldn't,' Helen said. 'It wouldn't bore me stiff.'

'I'll play with you,' I offered.

'OK.'

'Do you know how?' Kieran asked her with affable condescension. 'Do you know the rules and the pieces?'

'I have a fair idea,' Helen said drily.

'Fine,' he said. 'Dan can play liggle Helen and I'll play the winner.'

So, a little later, Helen and I lay on the rug before the drawing-room fire with the chess board. Kieran had gone upstairs for his book and he did not return for some time. The beautiful girl before me gazed at the board with fierce concentration and I played the worst chess game of my life. The game inspired some kind of passion in her, for she lost the remoteness, even the hauteur, which I had encountered that morning in the avenue. Instead she began to treat me like an old friend. At one point she said, 'Dan, are you sure you want to make that move?'

'Yes,' I said automatically; 'yes.'

When my queen vanished from the board my opponent murmured with a triumphant smile, 'Dan, you are letting your ambition cloud your common sense.' I have often thought about it since, the clouding of sense by ambition. Maybe I should have sensed the undercurrents then, revised, before it was too late, the ambition that was about to overtake me, that would consume me for years. But life is lived forwards and understood only in retrospect.

Kieran came back just as we were finishing the game and I was trying to make my poor king dodge the inevitable, until I could do so no longer and he was well and truly cornered and checkmated.

Helen gave a triumphant shout. 'Check . . . mate!'

'Well done,' I said ruefully. 'You play well.'

Kieran stood looking down at the board. 'You let her win!' He smiled at Helen, who bridled.

'He didn't *let* me win, did you, Dan? Now I have to play you, Kieran.'

Kieran groaned.

'That's what you said,' Helen insisted.

Kieran glanced at me, put his book down and took my place on the hearth rug. I sat on the couch and watched, while pretending to read a *National Geographic* magazine I had picked up from the shelves beside the fire. The pair on the rug seemed a little incongruous – the youth with his long legs sticking across the carpet and the young girl, legs bent at the knees, hands propping her face.

Helen returned to her intent concentration on the board. Kieran assumed an attitude of almost lordly certainty, which gradually fractured and became disbelief. Helen was making mince of his game and I cheered her silently from behind the pages I wasn't reading, oddly glad for the dent it put in Kieran's assurance. The game was over quickly and she looked up, flushed with victory.

'Now maybe you'll believe I can play,' she said flatly to her erstwhile opponent, grinning like an imp. But Kieran was not amused. He challenged her to another bout.

This time the game was slower, but after a few preliminary skirmishes the momentum began to swing in Helen's favour. Kieran's men, his pawns, a bishop, a knight, were soon lost. She was building a war machine to wipe him out. Her opponent realized what was happening and his brow furrowed. I saw Helen glance at him and then her game began to falter and she lost with such speed that I could not understand it, throwing away obvious opportunities until he said gently and with some covert relief, 'Checkmate, my liggle one.

'Never mind, you can't win them all,' he added as he put the pieces away in their box. 'But you certainly showed Dan a thing or two! And me also – your first game wasn't bad, even though I wasn't concentrating.' He leant towards her, closed his eyes and smiled in a charmingly condescending shake of the head. He looked very handsome and very winning.

'Beginner's luck,' Helen murmured modestly, plainly delighted with the notice and throwing me a look which was tantamount to conspiracy.

But why the conspiracy? I wondered afterwards. Was she seeking my help in the wooing of my friend? Because, young as she was, she was wooing him, although whether she knew it or not was another matter. She always turned to Kieran, followed him with her eyes, sued for his approval. My approval, on the other hand, was patently of no consequence whatsoever.

'Where did you learn to play chess like that?' I asked her *sotto voce* when Kieran had gone upstairs to his room.

She muttered something about playing her stepfather. 'He was great,' she said. 'He knew everything,' and to my consternation her eyes filled with tears.

'I never met him,' I said, thinking of the stern-looking bloke I had seen in the snapshot, 'but I was sorry to hear he died.'

Helen struggled with her emotion, wiped her eyes impatiently with the back of her hand. 'We used to go for walks in the hills. He gave me books . . .'

She excused herself and went upstairs.

I was left alone in the drawing room. It was a typical Victorian room, high ceilinged with cornices, with a marble fireplace and dividing doors to what would have been the dining room if it had been used. I had already had a glimpse of the dining room, with its bare boards, half empty except for stacks of books piled against the walls.

But the drawing room was more hospitable. There was an old Indian carpet, an upright piano, a set of bookshelves reaching to the ceiling, a chesterfield couch and some armchairs, an old gramophone on a table in the corner, and under the table a box of records.

Mrs Fitzpatrick came into the room, sank into an armchair, took out her knitting and asked me to put a few more sods on the fire. The turf was in a creel by the hearth and I obeyed her, conscious of the aromatic smell of the peat and the way the smoke puffed out a little as the new fuel kindled.

'Is there anything I can do to help?' I asked, knowing that she had spent the hour after lunch in some culinary exercise in the kitchen. Her cheeks had a high colour from the heat of the range.

'Well,' she said, 'we're running a bit low on water. You could ask Helen to show you the well and you could fetch some more if you don't mind! It's stopped raining now!'

Water from a well! I knew the house was without running water. I had already visited the outdoor privy, but had not adverted to the real logistics. I remembered that there were barrels of rain water near the back door. This, presumably, would be the water for washing and the well water was evidently for drinking.

She went into the hall and called her daughter, and in a few minutes I was walking between two buckets which Helen had fetched from the pantry, together with a length of rope which was kept on a peg. The sun had come out and the day had warmed up again.

'The well is down here,' Helen said, guiding me along the length of what had once been an orchard. We came to a number of short planks laid side by side and Helen removed them, to disclose a dark, stone well shaft, with moss growing at the upper edge. Looking in I saw the gleam of still water far below.

'You have to throw the bucket in – upside down,' she picked up one of the buckets and hurled it down the well with a laugh, 'like this!' The bucket hit the water with a reverberating splash. My guide handed me the rope. 'You have to haul it up now!'

I obeyed, and the bucket, more or less full, came up the well shaft. It was not easy work, because I had to straddle the well and pull the rope in slowly in case the bucket impacted on the edge of the shaft and spilt the water.

This operation was repeated a second time and then we replaced the planks over the opening and made our way back to the house, I straining with the weight of the full buckets and secretly trying to impress Helen with my musculature.

Kieran was in the kitchen when we came in. 'Ah,' he said, taking one of the buckets from me and leaving it on the raised stand in the pantry, 'I see you are getting acquainted with country life!'

That first evening of my visit to the enchanted valley I bathed in the pool with Kieran. This was the pool he had shown me earlier, the formation which nature had cut into the living rock. Mindful of his confession that he could not swim I thought I would try to teach him, but Helen came along, laughed when she saw us, suddenly stripped to her knickers and joined us without waiting for an invitation. She dived down into the brown mountain water and emerged triumphant, glistening, her plaits undone and streaming over her shoulders, the water running down her chest and its soft contours, the nipples a little swollen with burgeoning womanhood. I felt overwhelmed, and watched her covertly. She turned to look at me frowning, as though suddenly aware that she was having an effect beyond reasoning, like an alchemist who had stumbled on a formula not of his making, had touched the spring of magic beyond personal understanding. But there was total trust in her gaze, as though this magic was something in which all of us shared, and which she knew none of us would injure. The valley around was redolent of evening; the shadows were long, although the sunlight still blazed on part of the west-facing scarp; a few sheep could be heard bleating; it was like Eden or some kind of Arcadia.

I glanced at Kieran, but he seemed oblivious of Helen as though she were just a kid who was taking up precious space in the pool. Then Mrs Fitzgerald appeared, calling her. Her voice sounded strident as she came in view round the heather-covered bluff and told her daughter to come home at once, and I heard her as Helen obeyed, picked up her clothes and followed her, remonstrate in whispers, '. . . half-naked in the pool with two young men. You're developing, you know. You're not a child any more!'

Helen did not look back at us. But she studied the ground and shivered as she walked away, her wet knickers tugging at her slim hips, her body language suddenly full of uncertainty. I felt that Mrs Fitzgerald was a serpent who had entered Eden and brought with her the end of innocence.

After supper we sat and read around the fire. The lamps were lit and the curtains open to the gathering dusk. The sounds came to us through the window, the staccato bleating of the sheep, the barking of a sheep dog in the distance, the whisper of the wind in the trees. I let the peace subsume me. There was no radio here, no electricity, no intrusion by the machinations of modernity. At ten o'clock Helen made cocoa, then fetched a toasting fork and we toasted bread before the fire, spreading it with butter and homemade apple jelly. When we had cleared up, we took our respective candles to light us up to bed. The light flickered on the walls and the stairs and Helen's chirp of a laugh warned about the hole in the stair carpet.

That night I studied my face in the mirror. The candlelight made it mysterious, or plain grotesque, depending on where I held the flame. I took off my glasses and saw my own myopia reflected back at me, large pupils, tired eyes. But my face, I told myself, even if not actually handsome at least had regular features, and I stared at my mouth which my mother had described as 'strong'.

'What's a strong mouth, Mummy?'

There had been an amused sigh. 'One that isn't weak, darling . . . you know, all miserable with indecision.'

There was a scattering of pimples on my chin. I thought of Helen and rubbed soap into them before turning in, knowing, because I had checked, that Kieran hadn't a single spot, and wishing that he wasn't so perfect.

I stayed for a week in Lough Corrloch. I learnt the calm to be had in a place where one day followed another with only gentle rituals to fill the time. There was work to be done, turf to be carried in from the shed, meals to be prepared, washing up to be done – and we all shared it. And we youngsters read and talked and walked into the valley and up the surrounding hills. We were sent on errands to fetch milk and eggs from the Grehans, the people who had the grazing of the valley for their sheep. Their cottage was on the road, not far from the back gate, and the three of us negotiated the climb there and back without mishap. The summer air was sweet and the larks rose from the heather with sudden swooping flight and breathtaking song. I never saw anyone about in the valley itself, except Mr Grehan, whose spare form could occasionally be seen in the distance as he checked on his sheep. I had time too to walk alone into the mountains, and when I was up high enough, to wonder at the seeming eternity of summits across the valley, as they stretched, bluer and mistier, into the distance.

On the third day of my stay we cycled into Glendockery, pushing our bicycles up the hill to the main road. It was a long ride, eight miles. Once there we visited the grocer's and the post office and the butcher's.

In each of these emporia, where both Helen and Kieran were evidently already well known, I was introduced, 'This is Dan McPherson from London,' and made a fuss of.

Was I of Irish extraction? No, Canadian, I said. But I had a Scottish name? Well, my father's people came from Scotland. 'He's really a Dublin man,' Kieran announced sententiously and explained how this had arisen and there were cries of, 'Oh, were you living in Dublin for eight years, sure you're a native so!' There were long conversations with Mr Gaffney the grocer, Mrs Cafferty the post mistress and Mr O'Beirne the butcher, and any customer who arrived joined in the chat. I was asked about London, and whether I was still at school, and what I wanted to do when I left, and whether I was enjoying my stay in the valley. ''Tis a grand place for a holiday, and please God now the weather will hold . . .'

I said I hoped it would and Kieran made everyone laugh telling them how I took to the hills with a book and was not seen from morning till night. Helen smiled at me half apologetically. As we were leaving Mr Gaffney took a block of ripple ice cream from the freezer and cut us a huge slice each, sandwiching them in wafers. We went off licking our free ice creams and later ate our sandwiches sitting on the base of a monument in the middle of the village. This was a stone basilisk, a demon with good old satanic wings, and the inscription said that it had been erected in 1824 to Sir Henry Malcolm 'by his grateful tenantry'. Kieran laughed at this.

'What's so funny?'

'Have you forgotten your Irish history, old fellow?' he asked with a twinkle. 'Don't you know hypocrisy when you see it?'

As we cycled home I pondered on the effect Kieran had had on each person we had spoken to. Their eyes were glued on him as they listened to what he said. It was clear that Helen was regarded as the pretty child and I as the interesting stranger, but Kieran had held them with every gesture and syllable, with his amusing and deliberate pronouncements, and he had, I realized with more pique than I cared for, held Helen too.

In the days that followed I learnt how to milk a cow – courtesy of Mr Grehan, who was milking one day when we arrived at his place – light lamps, trim wicks and luxuriate in a strange solitude of the spirit. Kieran became absorbed in a project he had devised, something to do with magnets. He was trying to build his own variation of an electric gun, originally designed by a German scientist by the name of Zipplemeyer. He had improvized by using a piece of old railing as a kind of arrow. He called it a Magnapult – a catapult powered by magnets – and tried to interest me in it, but I preferred, as he had been quick to point out in Glendockery, taking long walks around the lake, and up the surrounding mountains. There I would sit with a book and dream.

On one morning, from my seat in the shadow of a boulder not far from the lake, I saw Helen walking alone along the path to the shore. She sat down on one of the rocks near the water and gazed upon its expanse, her chin on her hand. I scrambled down the side of the hill to join her. She turned and saw me coming, waved and called with the clarity of sound that always obtains beside water, to be careful. I reached her side and we sat together for while, throwing pebbles and twigs into the lake.

'I love it here,' I said. 'It's like Eden!'

She looked at me curiously for a moment. 'But Eden had a serpent!'

I conceded that this was true. 'Well, like Robinson Crusoe's island, a place cut off from the world.'

She smiled. 'But even there the cannibals came. I'm reading it at the moment!'

'Are you telling me there is evil no matter where one goes?' I teased. 'What possible malevolence could intrude on this enchantment?'

She sighed loudly. 'Don't be silly. There's only Mam and Kieran and you and me!'

Then she questioned me about London and I asked her would she like to visit and she said she would but that her mother would never let her go.

'Why not? If you went to visit a family who would look after you, wouldn't that be all right?'

'She would still say I'm too young!' Helen dropped her voice and added confidingly, looking at me from her calm green eyes, 'You see, she's overprotective. I've lost two fathers!'

'Yes,' I murmured sympathetically, 'but you won't always be a child!'

She turned to look across the lake. 'That's true. I can't wait to grow up!'

After a moment I asked, struck by the isolation of her long summer solitude and forgetting Kieran's admonitions, if she were lonely. 'Don't you miss your pals?' I asked. 'A summer is a long time to spend on your own.'

She stiffened, got up, moved a distance along the shore. I followed, remembering only then Kieran's advice, contrite that I had somehow struck a bum note. But when I saw her face I knew that I had done more than that. Tears were spilling silently. I put out my hand.

'I'm sorry, Helen . . .'

She sat on a boulder, put a forearm across her face, as though to ward off any overtures. 'I'm a jinx,' she sobbed. 'You don't understand.You don't know that my best friend died because of me . . .' and she crumpled down on to the sand and struck it with her fists. 'I killed her!' she screamed through her teeth, while her breath came in gasps and the ferocity of her grief astonished and moved me.

The lake took up her agony, echoed it to the mountains. Tears started from my eyes. I hunched down beside her at the rock and was silent, instinctively immobile, letting her vent this storm, humble before the most violent expression of feeling I had ever witnessed.

She pounded the granite boulder, slammed her fists into the sand, and then, when she was exhausted, leant over and put her head on her limp arms.

Still I did not speak. The water lapped against the shingle. Except for the whisper of the lake, the silence had returned.

I lay beside her, pulled her against my shoulder. 'Helen,' I said against her hair, with as much authority as I could summon, 'it was an accident. Let it go . . . It's time to let it go.'

She drew herself into a sitting position, wiped her face with my proffered handkerchief. Her hands were trembling. After a moment's silence she said without turning, as though I had caught her out in some shameful peccadillo, 'Don't tell anyone.'

'My lips are sealed.'

She smiled shakily, added, after a moment, in a voice that was even and grave, 'Will you be my friend?'

Something wrapped itself around my heart. I looked at her, at the down on her cheek, at the light on her hair, at the intensity of her profile which was staring into the water, at the fingers with their bitten nails, crumpling the white, sodden handkerchief. 'Of course,' I said. 'Of course I will be your friend . . . Would you write to me in London?'

She hesitated for a moment. 'OK.'

'I'll write back to you.'

Again she hesitated. 'Don't, or at least only at Christmas or something. Mam wouldn't like it . . . And I'll be going to boarding school in the autumn and they read all your letters there. But I'll write to you and tell you the news.'

I read desultorily on my last evening, aware that I hated leaving this place. What did it have that I loved so much? I know now. In a place without any distractions except its own unearthly beauty, where immediate human values are the measure of all things, one is thrown back on the joy of simply being alive. There is something fundamentally dynamic too in being responsible for creating one's own entertainment – in games, cards, books, conversation, wit and laughter. But there was more than this.

I watched the tableau around the fire. Helen's red hair, washed earlier and loose on her shoulders, had the firelight playing on it. She had recovered from the morning, but I felt strangely privileged to have had a glimpse of the forces struggling in her soul. I saw that she was still reading *Robinson Crusoe*, watched her engrossed expression while she read. Now and then she lifted her head and looked at Kieran and then at me, meeting my eyes with private camaraderie. I felt as though I had been admitted into some charmed circle, and rejoiced in secret. I felt that I knew Helen and that she knew me in ways that surpassed words or explanations. We had found each other. I could not evaluate nor understand this; the communion felt natural; I had no means of knowing its rarity.

When I glanced at Kieran I saw him sitting back on the couch, oblivious to everything except his book, his long legs stretched out in front of him, his immersion patent. Mrs Fitzgerald read and knitted at the same time and occasionally made little gestures of annoyance if she dropped a stitch. They were present, but not on the level of mutuality in which Helen and I were present. On some level only Helen and I were in the room.

On the day of my departure Kieran and I were both driven back to Dublin by Helen's mother. Helen came too. I was to catch the boat to Holyhead from Dun Laoghaire and we arrived there early. Kieran and I amused ourselves by running up and down the pier in an exuberance of animal spirits. Helen sat on a stone bench in the shadow of the old bandstand and gazed out at the harbour and I came to sit beside her.

'Did you enjoy your stay?' she asked me.

'It was wonderful,' I said earnestly. 'I've wanted to visit Lough Corrloch since I was a child.'

She seemed surprised, even touched, by my enthusiasm. 'I suppose it's nice to get away from a big city like London! You must come again. We're there every summer.'

'I would like to very much.'

'Kieran will let you know when he is coming,' she said, and then we walked to the ferry and I thanked my hostess and took my leave of her. Helen held my hand shyly and gave me a conspiratorial smile. But her eyes travelled back to Kieran as though for approval, and as I moved beyond the ferry gate I looked back and saw him walking away with Mrs Fitzgerald. Helen was behind them kicking the pleated cap from a lemonade bottle before her with the toe of her sandal. She turned for a moment, searched for me with her eyes, gave me a grave, half-puzzled look, before she smiled, turned back and followed them.

Chapter Four

All the way back to London I felt more like someone banished into exile than the wanderer returning home. After the solitude of Lough Corrloch the crowds on boat, train and station platforms seemed to belong to some purgatorial dimension. London itself had a touch of Dante's inferno, with its milling millions, the stressed urgency of its population, the stridency of its commerce, the dusty roar of its great life. At the bottom of my heart I heard the contrasting whisper of wind across the heather and murmur of water among the reeds.

I took a taxi to the relative calm of Walton Street, put the key in the glossy black door, let myself into the cool interior and was greeted with a hug by Rachel who was polishing the hall. 'Yeh got a bit o' the sun anyways,' she said after she had inspected me. 'Are yez hungry? Come down to the kitchen and I'll fix yez a bite!'

'I'm not hungry, Rachel; thanks.'

'Well, yeh'll have a cup o' tea anyway!'

I followed her to the kitchen, wondering where everyone was. 'They're out,' Rachel said, as though she had read my thoughts. 'Yer mother's at the hairdresser's and James is in Paris.'

'What's he doing in Paris?'

'He went off with some of his university friends, some job or other . . . Then they're goin' to Italy, if you don't mind.'

'Good for him,' I murmured. I remembered that Kieran was also going to France in a day or two and wished I had known about James, so that he would have a contact. But Kieran, on second thoughts, would already have plenty of contacts. Kieran was like gravity; people were drawn to him. I had pondered on this for the first time during my sojourn in the valley, and in the end was forced to the conclusion that he had two extraordinary features – he was attractive in some way which was not quantifiable and possessed, at the same time, a total disregard for everyone else. This disregard was never expressed as such; he would treat you as though you were the most important person in his life and in the next breath make you feel that you were invisible. This made for fascination. He was a human version of the flytrap. People fell for his charm, which he could focus to devastating purpose. And then, because they had already invested themselves in relating to him at all, they wasted time trying to penetrate the wall of his indifference, led on all the while by an occasional acknowledgement full of good fellowship.

I was no different from everyone else. I loved Kieran, but now I had also come to resent him. Most of this had to do with Helen. When I tried to rationalize why I should care about a little girl, whom I had only met recently for the first time, I found no convincing answer.

Rachel made the tea and as soon as I smelt it I felt ravenous. I had had little to eat during the journey, except for some sandwiches which Mrs Fitzgerald had made for me. Rachel put some biscuits and a cheesecake she had made 'specially for yez' on the table. She sat down with me and asked, 'Well, how's the ould sod?'

'Great – at least Lough Corrloch was. It's an amazing place.'

I described the valley to her, found a pencil in my pocket and drew her a little map on the back of an envelope containing Helen's home address in Dundalk.

'But what did yeh do? Weren't yeh bored?'

'I milked a cow, brought in turf and water from the well, and cycled into Glendockery for groceries. I traipsed up to the top of the valley to collect milk and eggs and I walked in the mountains and read in the heather!'

'Glory be to God! Milkin' cows! Bringin' in the water! Readin' in the heather! And did that make yez happy?'

'I have never been so happy in my life,' I said truthfully.

I heard my mother's step in the hall, heard her voice. 'Rachel,' she called a little anxiously. 'Did Dan come home yet?'

I ran up the kitchen stairs to meet her. She had her silken blonde hair newly coiffed, was wearing a taupe, princess-line dress with three-quarter-length sleeves, white peep-toe sandals, and seemed like one of those ethereal beings who graced the cover of *Vogue*. She embraced me carefully. I suppressed the initial urge to hug her; but this might have upset her coiffure or her couture and so I pecked her proffered cheek dutifully instead.

'Did you have a nice time, darling?'

'Super,' I said.

'He was milkin' bloody cows and the lord knows what else!' Rachel intervened from the kitchen door below us. 'Milkin' cows and bringin' in turf and water, I ask you! What kind of way was that to treat a guest, and a boy who's been used to nothin' but the best? I ask you!'

My mother gave the small pained smile she reserved for Rachel's diatribes. 'He looks well enough on it!' she commented drily, drawing me out of earshot and into the dining room. 'Did you enjoy yourself?' she asked *sotto voce*. 'I hope you didn't do anything silly. How is Kieran? What were his relatives like?'

I told her about Mrs Fitzgerald and Helen and said Kieran sent his best regards. I also said, in as dry a tone as I could muster, that I had done nothing 'silly'.

She laughed, as she always did when she sensed that I was piqued. 'Don't mind me, darling. I was just worried about that lake. When you're a mother your children are always children!'

'I've grown up, Mummy,' I said.

The smile left her face. 'Have you indeed, darling?' she murmured. 'That's very nice. Well, bring up your bag and unpack. We're having supper at seven.'

I think it was that evening that my father asked me what I wanted to do with my life. 'Live in Lough Corrloch' was on the tip of my tongue, but knowing this for an impossibility, I mentally vetted the professions. I had a precise enough mind, for all my longing to escape precision; I was intrigued by solutions; I wanted to understand the system which held every citizen in the palm of its hand. I was afraid of powerlessness.

'Law,' I said.

He glanced at my mother, clearly pleased. 'Good man.'

That night I took out the small bits of flora I had brought home from my sojourn in Ireland – a few pieces of heather, a small stone from the lake shore and a small circlet made of dried grass which Helen had wound idly on the day we had sat by the lake, after her confrontation with her suppressed grief over the death of her friend. I put this on my little finger and then placed it, and the other small mementoes, into the Black Magic casket in which I kept my treasures.

Time began to freefall, O levels, then A levels, swirling towards the future as though, once it was reached, Time would stop and let us all simply be. The years of longing for the end of schooldays disappeared and the end of schooldays came, looming faster and faster as it drew nigh. As I walked across the yard of the Lycée on my last day I was full of a kind of disbelief, a sneaking nostalgia and, at the same time, a jubilant expectancy at the prospect of embarking on adulthood and autonomy.

The greatest part of this new autonomy was Cambridge, where I had applied to St John's College. I had passed the entrance exam, had walked through its ancient front gate, beneath the carved coat of arms of Lady Margaret Beaufort, nervous enough to get sick. I was accepted, however, subject to my A level results.

St John's was magnificent. Architecturally beautiful, redolent of a privileged past, it was one of the richest colleges in Cambridge. It represented the next stage, the place where I would put on the mantle of adulthood, free myself from adolescent constraints, seize the world.

I had been back to Lough Corrloch twice after my first visit and on each occasion no one had been in residence. When I went to stay with Kieran in Dublin, on the two successive summers after my visit, his father drove us to the lake in the mountains, but, on each occasion, the house was shuttered. We had walked to the lake, taken the small detour to inspect the pool, but without the life which had been in the house the atmosphere was wanting.

'They don't come every summer now,' Kieran said. 'That's why Aunt Drusilla didn't ask you again. I think she finds the place too lonely.'

'How is Helen? Do you ever see her?'

'Sure. Whenever they're in Dublin they call in.' I waited for him to go on, and when he showed no signs of doing so I asked if Helen had grown.

'Yeah, I suppose she has,' he said, regarding me thoughtfully with a lopsided grin. 'She's a bigger lump of a girl than she was!'

I had her letters. They had begun about two weeks after my first visit and continued for a while. I wrote to her each Christmas, but only once did she acknowledge receipt of these missives and, after a while, her own letters stopped.

Kieran himself came more and more frequently to London – Easter, summer, even for a few days after Christmas one year. He always invited me to Dublin, but if I could not go to Lough Corrloch, or if it were boarded up, I had less and less interest in making the journey.

I began to forget what the place had evoked in me. The sixties were not far off and London was swinging. In Liverpool a small group had begun to make pop music history. I met Chantal, a sultry French girl, at the Café des Artistes in Radcliffe Gardens and fell sensuously in love.

But all was not well with my parents. My father had given up his touching, half-beseeching, attitude to my mother; she had, evidently, fallen from the pedestal where he had placed her. The years of his hope had ended; he no longer looked to her to endorse his life, to give him the love he craved. He became increasingly abrupt, cold and detached, and eventually moved into the spare bedroom. I thought for a while that it would all blow over.

James said it was a lovers' tiff. 'That pair need each other,' he informed me with his usual sardonic assurance; 'he needs what she can't give and she needs him needing it!'

I knew that we would have to brace ourselves for a sea change when I saw my father, one Friday evening, going into the Garrick Theatre in Charing Cross Road with a strange woman on his arm. I tried to see her face. Her back was towards me and she was inclining towards my father as though he contained the sum total of the world's wonders, and laughing with him over some shared joke. Her laugh was low and melodious, full of genuine mirth. And he laughed back and looked at her with bemused happiness. I tried to guess her age, sure that she was younger than my mother because her laugh was so fluid. I was full of hatred for her and for my father. I felt as though the ground had moved under my feet, as though an old fault line was ominously opening and the cataclysm was upon us.

I did not go to the party I had set out for that evening, but went home to Walton Street instead. My mother was there and looked up at me over her reading glasses.

'I didn't expect you back so early, Dan,' she murmured, studying my face. 'Is everything all right?'

'Of course!'

'Your father is working late,' she said. I sensed in her the desire to talk about his increasingly late homecomings, needing reassurance. I also sensed in her the immediate assessment that all was not well with me, that I was hiding something from her.

'Are you sure you're all right? You're looking a bit pale.'

I was saved from replying by Rachel's appearance with a tea tray. My mother liked to take tea at ten o'clock and then she would read for an hour before going to bed.

'What are yez up to?' Rachel demanded. 'I thought yez were off to a party?'

'I came home.'

'A young fella like you to be missin' a party! Are yez all right in the head?'

Sometimes Rachel's certainty that any action outside her anticipation had its roots in a disease of the brain grated on my nerves.

'For God's sake – can't I come home if I want without you giving me the third degree?' I hissed, leaving the room and finding my own.

I threw myself down on the bed and studied the posters on the walls – the underground system, the varieties of whales, a cartoon of Bugs Bunny, a display of different types of machine guns and an old framed etching of a lake scene in Scotland, with a boat by the shore. This made me think of Lough Corrloch. I reminisced for a while and then got out my Black Magic box and unfolded the letters from Helen.

Dear Dan,

I hope you're keeping well. Boarding school is like the army. We have to get up at 6.15 every morning and it's simply freezing. Then we go to the chapel for Mass and then have breakfast and then we have classes. There's a half-hour for lunch at one o'clock followed by another half-hour playing hockey and then we have classes again. At half-past three we have a cup of tea and a bun and then we have an hour's hockey lesson with Miss Toohey who keeps screaming, 'Lift those hocks,' and then study and then prayers and then supper and then half an hour's recreation and then more study and then bed at nine. What do you think of that? We are not allowed to talk indoors except when spoken to, or during recreation. Even at meal times we have to keep silent until Al Capone (Mother Teresa who is 'Mistress of Schools', which simply means she's the bloody headmistress) rings a little bell and then we can talk for ten minutes.

Katie Doyle in my class secretly took out her cabbage from the refectory in a paper bag because she had found a slug in it, but Mother Teresa noticed it because it made her pocket bulge a bit and now she has to eat it for tea! (The cabbage not the slug!)

We have confession every Saturday. Katie is in love with the priest and tells him she has bad thoughts. He doesn't know they're about him.

Kieran sent me a card for my birthday. Does he write to you? I wish he would write to me.

How's London? I would love to see it sometime. Mam comes to see me every month. She has met a doctor and is going out with him. I thinks she likes him a lot. It makes me feel very insecure, because there's no reason why he should want me.

Do you ever think of Lough Corrloch?

That's all my news.

Love, Helen.

PS I'm sending this letter out with a day pupil because you're supposed to hand up all your letters unopened so that Mother Teresa can read them. If the day pupil's caught you'll never get it and I'll be for it (and so will the day pupil)! So if I'm expelled you'll know why!

There were more letters, each shorter than the last.

Thanks for your Christmas card and your letter. I'll be going back to school on the 8th. We're doing the Inter this year. Sometimes I think how nice it would be if you and Kieran were to visit the school. Kieran told me all about his stay with you in London. It sounds lovely.

I got my green ribbon last term (it's the first step to becoming a

Child of Mary; you have to ask all the nuns if you go up for it and if one of them says no you can't and have to try again the following term. It's their way of keeping us on our toes, because it you don't have a ribbon appropriate to your class you're regarded as substandard, some kind of pariah).

Kieran sent me a funny Christmas card, with Santa Claus who had a big red nose arrested for drunken driving. Mam isn't seeing the doctor any more (his name was Hughie). I'm glad.

Best wishes, Helen.

But while I read these, the thought of my father with the strange woman kept intruding and I put the letters back in their box. I wondered if she were a whore, that woman who had looked at him with such intimacy. But there had been a certain carriage to her, a way of dressing and moving, which made me doubt it. And her laugh had been low and conspiratorial, the laughter of someone who knew the humour of her companion very well and shared in it.

I had seen the women of the night strutting their stuff in Piccadilly and had often wondered what it would be like to go home with one of them. I could not afford it, of course, and the thought scared me; after all, what would I say to them? Would I be able to do it? Would it be terribly thrilling, this partaking of the fleshpots without ever having to look back over my shoulder? Now I wondered if my father did IT with her, the woman I had seen him with outside the Garrick. The thought of it was alarming and breathtaking, as though all the parameters of my whole life were up for re-evaluation.

I put away my box of letters and took down the photograph I kept hidden in a book on my shelf. This was from a magazine which had done the rounds among my male peers in school. The girl had breasts like melons and a bottom like a great peach. She was all softness and coyness and smiling invitation. I put her under my pillow, undressed, and then I got into bed, took her out again from under the pillow, stroked her for a while before I drummed my life force into her, or rather into the fantasy of her which uncurled in my brain.

As I lay back my mother's step could be heard on the stairs. I was trembling with spent passion and turned off the light. She knocked and came into my room. 'Dan,' she whispered, but I did not stir and she thought I was asleep. She left, shutting the door very softly and I felt her loneliness for the first time, the great fearful void in her, the vacuum within which she hid her heart and soul.

I did not sleep for a long time and lay awake listening to the sounds of traffic in the street. I was waiting for my father's steps on the stairs. But it did not come, although I heard James's lighter tread at about half-past one.

My father did not come home that night, but he arrived around noon the following day. I was upstairs and I heard my parents' voices in the drawing room. They were low and I knew that something very serious was under discussion. It felt as though the very air in the house was aware of the tenor of this conversation, for everything was muted, the whole house, walls, floors, ceilings – listening. Rachel's radio was not to be heard from the kitchen. James slept late as he always did on Saturdays, but I went into his room and sat on the end of his bed. He surfaced, but he did not tell me to clear off. He sensed immediately that something strange was in the offing.

'What is it, Dan?'

'They're talking! It's serious!'

He accepted this as though he knew exactly what I meant. He said nothing, but sat up as if he were listening, although there was nothing to be heard except the flat murmur of voices.

'I saw him with a woman last night,' I whispered. 'They were going to the theatre. He was out all night!'

'Does Mummy know?'

'I didn't tell her I saw him.'

'It doesn't necessarily mean anything!' James said. 'What did she look like?'

'The woman? I didn't see her face, but she had dark hair and she was laughing. He was laughing too.'

James sighed. 'She might have been an old friend.' He shrugged. 'But even if she was a whore – it's not the end of the world. You needn't think that Mummy goes in for . . . you know . . . that sort of thing, and he might be getting a bit desperate!'

'She must have gone in for it at one time,' I said drily. 'They must have done it at least twice!'

James threw me a wicked glance, laughed. 'God, you're a card.'

James got up, went to the bathroom, and I went downstairs to the kitchen, passing the drawing-room door en route. I stood in the hall for a moment, hoping to catch something of what they were saying. The voices within were dangerously quiet; my father sounded pragmatic, my mother subdued. Then I heard her say in a raised and acid voice I had never heard her use before, 'And I suppose your whore has no compunction about breaking up this family?'

'She's not a whore,' my father said. 'And you were the one who broke it,' he added, raising his voice. 'You broke it. Years and years of your indifference broke it. I can't live as a support system and nothing else. You're ripping me off . . . I'm living a lie.'

Then I heard her say in an uncharacteristically small voice, 'I do love you; I have always loved you!' She said it with difficulty, as though the admission would be enough to deflect the course my father had embarked on. But when he didn't answer she went on, 'I gave up my career for you, for this life of diplomat's wife, always smiling, always saying the right thing; I've had years of being the bloody mannequin on your arm, the prop without input, the cipher in the background! Did I have to wear my heart on my sleeve for you? You know perfectly well what you mean to me. You knew it from the way I gave you my life.' She paused. 'I'm not one of those ill-bred women who are always flaunting their feelings . . . like emotional fishwives!'

There was silence for a moment before my father's tormented voice answered, 'How was I supposed to know what you felt? With you everything had to be nice, sanitized! Everything had to have the harm taken out of it in case you were, as you put it, an emotional fishwife! If you would share nothing of yourself how was I supposed to know what you thought, or wanted, or what emotions, if any, you possessed? You didn't give me your life! You spent your life alongside mine, but you gave nothing. You were afraid of letting your guard down, of taking emotional risks. Well, nothing grows if you can't take risks. Without risks, without some small modicum of passion, relationships die!' Then he added, 'It's too late, Anne! It's too late. I can't even help it. You see, oddly enough, I am not in my gift!'

When I went into the kitchen Rachel was out. She generally went shopping on Saturday morning. I looked out of the window and saw Minky and Jinky sitting in the sunshine and yawning at each other, showing wicked fangs – the reality, as I always reminded myself, under all that fur and cuddles. The aubretia – violet and mauve and white – was creeping down the side of an ornamental urn in the patio. The grass, mown just two days before, was neat with its crew cut. But I knew that nothing would ever be the same again.

In due course my father's voice called us and James and I went to the drawing room. My father looked pale and his face was set. My mother was white and her eyes seemed to burn, but she was, as ever, rigidly in control.

He sighed as he looked at us, came and put a hand on each of our shoulders. 'I have something to tell you, boys. Sit down.'

We sat, stiffly, like two dummies. I felt my mouth go dry, my tongue sticking to its roof.

He looked at us for a moment and then he said very slowly: 'I won't be living here any more. I wish there was some other way of telling you this, or of making it sound better. I am not deserting you, or your mother. But I will be living somewhere else, and with someone else. I don't expect you to understand, until you are a lot older and have learnt more about life. Come to me whenever you want. I'll always be there for you and I would like to see a great deal of you.' He looked from one of us to the other, as though, for a moment, he hoped for clemency.

'I hate you,' I said. My words dropped like stones into the silence. My father simply bowed his head, glanced at James, who only stared at the carpet without speaking, and then he left the room. As he did so he said to my mother, in a toneless voice, that he would collect some of his things and would send someone around for the rest of them. He went upstairs and after about ten minutes we heard him walk down the hall and out the front door. I went to the window and watched him load a bag into the boot of his car, which was parked across the street.

'This will do nothing for his career,' James said. He looked at our mother, who was still sitting bolt upright, with the same glassy expression. 'Are you all right, Mummy?'

She turned to him as though she were deaf. 'What? Yes, yes, of course.' Then she got up and slowly, like an old woman, fumbled for the door knob and made her way upstairs.

Later, James and I heard the noises from her room, the sounds of her grief, the wrench of the wardrobe door, the clatter of clothes hangers and the thump of my father's clothes being shovelled out of his wardrobe and the crash as she broke his mirror. When the sounds subsided we pushed open the door and found her lying on the floor amid the mess, blood seeping from a myriad cuts which she had made to her face with the broken mirror. They mixed with her tears so that her face ran with blood and water and was reflected in the fractured pieces on the floor like in a bloody kaleidoscope. She could have been a figure from a Greek tragedy and anything more unlike my normally contained and ice-cool mother I could not have imagined. The passion at her heart was abroad at last, but it fed only her destruction.

James, her favourite son, lay down on the floor beside her and held her in his arms. I backed away. I knew I could do nothing. She had kept me at arm's length too long for me to have known how to comfort her.

I went to the landing. Rachel had just come in and she was making her way upstairs.

'What kind of a racket was that I just heard?' she demanded. 'What have the two of youse been doin?'

'It wasn't us, Rachel. It's Mummy!' She stared at my ashen face. 'Daddy's left her,' I whispered, 'and she's taking it very badly!'

Rachel pushed past me and went straight to my mother's bedroom. James stumbled out, weeping, his clothes and hands streaked with his mother's blood. Rachel stared at him aghast, as though he had murdered her. She ran into the room and then turned to the two of us standing in the doorway. 'Go away,' she hissed, before she shut the door firmly upon us.

Chapter Five

My father's departure took place in September. In October I went to Cambridge. From now on I would be my own man; I wore my short undergraduate gown, had a room in the College, ate dinner in Hall and felt a life opening to me which promised independence. But I was hag-ridden by the spectre of my mother's suffering, which I could do nothing to alleviate and thanked God that James was still at home with her in Walton Street.

King's Cross station became a kind of gateway to the holy land, the place where I was free, where I could be myself. Home was the place where my mother brooded and for a long time after my father left the atmosphere there was dark and gloomy and fixated. Even Rachel lost her bounce and I half expected her to hand in her notice. But she stayed, looking a little grim and anxious, and trying to make my mother focus on doing anything at all in order to shift her perspective from her sense of betrayal.

'Don't choose misery,' she would say to her. 'Sure yer loaded down with talent, so yez are, ma'am, so take yer life in yer own hands!'

She would polish up the rosewood piano, the Broadwood concert grand which had followed us from Dublin, lift the lid and occasionally touch the keys, as though trying to reawaken my mother's oldest love, but to no avail. My mother would not play. The piano remained silent, and, in its silence, somehow accusing.

The trouble was that my mother had no idea how to take charge of her own life and, I think, that but for her housekeeper, she might have become seriously unbalanced. She began to talk to herself, to whisper conspiratorially that she knew what they were saying about her on the radio, and when she mentioned my father it was with such yearning that I had to turn away. I could not give her the emotional support she needed, not because I did not feel for her, but because, on the subliminal level where such matters are settled, she did not really relate to me, thinking perhaps that I was too young for empathy or simply too crass. So she withdrew beyond the point where I could ever reach her, leaving me in a limbo of the spirit which I took pains to conceal. In the absence of parental sympathy my feelings would simply have been risible.

James knew what to do, how to embrace her, touch her shoulder with filial love, listen with eternal patience to her diatribes and to her terrible silences. I suspected that her yearning was more for the past, for what she had, at one time, projected as the golden future, more than for my father himself. Rachel was wonderful; she would put in her oar when my mother embarked on some bitter invective, say something about her cats, whom she knew my mother barely tolerated, and somehow keep matters earthbound.

On one of my weekends home I went to see my father in his new abode, an apartment overlooking the river at Westminster and was introduced to his new lady, Kelly Winthorp, an American. She was a divorcee, as dark as my mother was fair, with brown eyes and thick black hair. She was not much younger than my mother, did not strike me as either beautiful or particularly sexy, but she welcomed me cordially and with a nervousness which I found touching in spite of myself.

My father was happy. It was evident; he had a glow to him, a relaxation. That he felt guilt at his happiness was also clear, at least to me. Kelly left us alone together and he asked me about my mother.

'I think she's going mad!'

He started. 'What do you mean?'

'She's very strange in herself, very withdrawn, never even plays the piano any more. She talks to herself; she thinks she features in radio broadcasts and that there are spies putting listening equipment down the chimney. She never goes out. Rachel looks after her, but only for that . . .'

My father looked stricken. 'She needs help! She should see someone – a psychiatrist. A shrink could help her to get everything into perspective.'

'If I suggest it she asks me what precisely I think is wrong with her, says she's perfectly fine and that there was a time when sons showed some respect! Then she goes off and stares in the mirror and fingers her scars.'

'What scars?'

I had wondered if James had told him, but it was clear that he had not. His loyalty to her would not have permitted it. I knew that he had seen my father for lunch one day, but that, when my father had refused to return home, he had declined other invitations. I was, therefore, the first of his sons to visit my father's new home.

'The day you left she cut herself. She broke your mirror. She has lots of small facial scars.'

My father's eyes filled with horror, then his expression became glassy and his mouth set. If I had thought that imparting this information to him would have brought him home to us, I had mistaken my man. He had severed the old bonds, and while he still loved my mother with all the ties of their shared existence, he was plainly impatient of any hint of what he regarded as hysteria.

'That is not like your mother,' he said. 'She always abhorred "emotional fishwifery", as she called it. What can I do?'

'You could come home!' I suggested hopefully. 'You married her, after all, for better or worse!' I knew that this would get him where it hurt. I hated him at that moment, resented his intransigence and longed for his pain.

'Dan,' he said after a moment, 'you won't understand this, but there was something so fundamentally wrong with the relationship between your mother and me that the terms "better" or "worse" are inapplicable. Before something can become "better" or "worse" there must be something there to begin with. I thought there was; I was so in love with her beauty and her grace that I would have believed anything to have possessed her. I thought that love and patience made things happen.' He sighed. 'But they don't, at least not when the control of the situation is in someone else's hands! Love wilts without reciprocity. It becomes impossible for you to express . . . what you feel . . . when there is no emotional space in the other person to receive it. And time only compounds the problem; you watch your life tick away while everything you have to give stays bottled up and useless.'

He glanced at me as though to assess the level of my understanding. 'It's a kind of death in life,' he went on. 'It's not her fault, but it's not mine either.' He frowned, running his hand through his hair. 'The worst aspect of an unsuccessful marriage is not so much that you don't receive from it, but that there is no room for you to give!'

'You mean a sort of emotional constipation!' I offered with as much sarcasm as I dared. 'I thought fathers were above that kind of slop!'

He looked at me with a sad smile, as though I had said something very young instead of something very insulting. 'Fathers are human, as you may yet learn. What do you want me to do – other than go back?'

'You should just drop dead,' I said, rising and leaving just as Kelly entered with a tray of coffee and biscuits.

Kelly put the tray down on the coffee table. 'Stay for some coffee,' she said, pronouncing it 'cawfee', which got on my nerves. She tried a smile. 'I would like to get to know you properly.' She had a soft voice, sounded kind and a little diffident. I could not bear the prospect of her 'getting to know me properly'; the very idea of her tentative familial liberties made me nauseous. I thought of my mother at home, how she referred to this woman as 'your father's whore'. The presumption of her in assuming any iota of my mother's place inspired me with black rage. I pushed past her muttering, 'I don't consort with whores!'

I glanced back at the door to see how she was taking this *coup de grâce*. My father had started angrily to his feet but Kelly had her hand out to restrain him and I saw on her face, as she looked at him, an unspoken caution, in which there dwelt patient love and understanding. I had expected her anger; I had hoped for a biting retort. I stumbled out the door, feeling suddenly like some kind of barbarian, to have handed out words like knives before I knew the calibre of the enemy – or whether there was any enemy at all.

The tube provided the necessary breathing space, bringing me all the way out to Cockfosters and then eventually down to Wimbledon while I tried to sort myself out, while I thought of my mother and my father and his new establishment, thought of how the unthinkable had happened and must be faced and survived. Finally, when I had worked out the turmoil in my brain, I went back to Knightsbridge.

It was evening. I went straight to the drawing room and told my mother: 'I've been to see Dad and he won't come home. I think you'd better shape up, Mummy. You're only hurting yourself.'

She was sitting staring out of the window and idly picking at the sleeve of an old grey cardigan, unravelling threads and pulling them, so that the sleeve ruched up. She radiated loneliness. I saw the grey at her temples for the first time. Not that she had suddenly gone grey – there had been silver threads glinting among the pale blonde for years – but only that suddenly it seemed to matter. I saw how gaunt she had become.

'Did you see his whore?' she demanded in the monotone which now passed as her speaking voice.

'I met Kelly. She's a bitch . . . a real tart; she made coffee, but I refused it. Uggh. You won't catch me drinking her concoctions – eye of newt and toe of frog – you just wouldn't know . . .' I glanced at her, saw that I had got her attention.

'She's triumphant in stealing your man!' I went on. 'A real cheap second-rate cow, without a moral between her and kingdom come! Dad will soon be sick of her!'

My mother frowned and straightened a little self-righteously. She stopped picking at the threads in her sleeve. Her face lost its faraway focus and concentrated on me. She was clearly avid for more.

'Is that what you want to hear?' I hissed at her. 'In actual fact she seems a nice, moderate, loving person whom you'd probably scare to death. I was horribly rude to her. Dad finds peace with her; he can relate to her. I think that's why he stays. They understand each other. I think you were too complex for him, Mummy. Complexity is your problem, it's what you have to deal with. You can do something with it and or let it tie you up in finer and tighter knots until you are completely mental and they do actually come and take you away! Stop bottling up what is inside you; it's a force you have to loosen or it will destroy you.' I glanced at her to see if she were receptive, but her face registered nothing, and I went on. I didn't care if she ordered me out of the house; I had something important to say and I wanted her to hear it.

'OK, so you invested your life in Dad, or in your notion of him, or in your notion of marriage, or in other people's notion of your marriage; well, take it back and reinvest it in yourself! There's no one talking about you on the radio; no one is listening at the windows or bugging the bloody phone. The whole of London does not wake up in the morning wondering how you are, anxious for your suffering. No one gives a damn. The parameters of your life are set by you!'

I had prepared my speech on the tube and had committed myself to its delivery, but inside I wanted to weep. What I was saying was so removed from anything filial that I had to force myself to continue.

'There's no use trying to control Dad by being miserable. It won't control him, and even if it could, it would be a temporary measure built on his pity. Is that what you want from him? Pity? Could you bear it, Mummy? Could you endure it?'

I stopped. I saw myself in the mirror, reading the riot act to my mother, my mother who had been young until recently, but who was slumped in the armchair like an old woman, her face covered in small, pink scars. If James, who always treated her with kid gloves, who gave up so much of his time to keep her company, had been there to hear me, I think he might have killed me.

I waited for her response with trepidation, but there was only a long silence. I became afraid that she was gathering her ire and that I had precipitated another terrible scene like the one she had indulged in when my father had left, but instead, after a few preliminary sudden intakes of breath, she began to laugh. Her laugh, genuine and melodic, gathered force. She laughed until she was spent, leaning back against the chair like one exhausted, and then she drew a long breath, put up her hands to her hair and said, 'Go on, clear off. You'll make a good barrister!'

I left, aware that I had shaken her up a little. But I had the forlorn suspicion that she had laughed because, in my presence, she was too proud to cry. She did not know how I loved her, how I longed to hold her, to join my grief with hers.

After that, however, things began to change. At first it was the occasional scale on the piano and then it was Chopin and Liszt and Rachmaninov and soon the house rang with her music on a daily basis. When I came back at weekends I found her playing as I had never heard her play, with a passion let loose and sweeping everything before it. Rachel crept around smiling, making scones and lemon meringue pie and all sorts of things my mother had suddenly taken a fancy to, as she set about regaining the weight she had lost. The two of them had long conversations in the kitchen, like conspirators. My mother never went out at this point, but wore a dressing gown all day.

'Yer comin' along,' Rachel said grudgingly of her playing. 'If yez can keep that up they'll be sittin' outside on the pavement to listen to yez!'

When my father finally called unannounced, about three weeks after I had been to see him, he entered a house which was echoing with music. He came, he told me afterwards, out of duty, fearful that he might find his wife in the kind of withdrawal I had depicted, but instead he had not encountered any reason to trouble her at all. Hearing my mother play, he motioned to Rachel not to disturb her, but sat in the hall and listened. Rachel told me later that he sat with tears in his eyes and then smiled and nodded to himself and went away.

Kieran came for his annual holiday. He was now a student at University College, Dublin, reading Chemistry and Biology. He had fulfilled the promise of his childhood and adolescence, had grown to be taller and better looking than I, and his charm was, if anything, more laid back.

'Your mother is a bit of a genius,' he opined on his first morning. I found him sitting on the stairs that first day following his arrival, his face wearing an expression of awe. The tempestuous notes of Liszt's Hungarian Rhapsody Number 1 could be heard from the drawing room. 'No one except a concert pianist can play like that!'

'She used to be one,' I said, 'or rather an aspiring one, before she married Dad!'

'Did she?' Kieran raised his clear hazel eyes to mine. 'A waste of talent all these years!'

'She had me,' I said. 'And James. It wasn't a waste . . . not of her time!'

He smiled at me quizzically. 'Well, it's good to have a disinterested opinion.' He ducked as I took a mock swipe at him.

'What happened to her face?' he whispered a moment later.

'It's a long story . . . an accident. But she'll be fine. The scars are shallow and a plastic surgeon is to have a look at them.'

'She's some woman,' Kieran said admiringly, as the arpeggio gathered force and the notes crescendoed. 'She's full of fire!'

For a moment I wondered if he fancied my mother and I looked at him closely. He was nearly twenty years old, tall, handsome, winning, with a clever brain and a lazy charm that seldom failed. But the very thought was disgusting. She'd eat you for breakfast, dear boy, I told him silently. Don't even think about it!

James joined us. Despite his early propensity for baiting me about Kieran he had himself fallen victim to his charm and the two of them had become fast friends and spent a great deal of time together. Secretly this miffed me because Kieran was my friend; it was as though he had been my personal find and I had some property in him. I knew, at the same time, that all of this was childish so I tried to ignore these promptings.

One evening after supper I brought the conversation around to Ireland.

'Do you ever go out to Lough Corrloch now?' I asked Kieran.

'Not often. Nobody goes there much any more. I think they find it too lonely. There was a tenant for a while, but it didn't work out. No one nowadays will put up with the absence of mod cons for very long.'

'How is Helen?'

'I knew we were getting around to that!' James said, with his most irritating drawl. 'That kid certainly made an impression on him! How many years is it now since he saw her? And still he hasn't forgotten her!'

I wanted to tell him that he was jealous because no one girl had ever 'made an impression' on him for very long, but I kept quiet.

Kieran turned frankly curious eyes on me. 'Ah, Helen is grand. She did her Intermediate this year.'

'How did she get on?'

'Results aren't out yet, but she's a clever little thing and will do fine.' He paused. 'She always asks after you! She's quite tall now . . . quite grown up.'

I tried to imagine her, but the image of the young girl in the avenue, the prepubescent child in the pool, ousted any intruder. I heard the water lapping and the small voice, still tremulous from crying, asking, 'Will you be my friend?'

'I'd love to go back to Lough Corrloch,' I said. 'Is there any chance of an invitation?'

It was the first time I had asked straight out. Kieran shrugged, raised his eyebrows. 'Helen and Aunt Dru will probably spend some time there next summer, if you want to fish for an invitation. Helen is going to France this year. There's some exchange programme organized by her school, and a little French girl will be coming to Ireland next year as her guest. Why don't you wait till then?'

'And they'll be staying in the valley?'

'Of course. The little Frenchie will have to be entertained, let her see life in the rough! You know what the French are like – can't get enough of *la vie sauvage*.'

'Is that what you thought of the lake – *la vie sauvage*?'

He turned his unsentimental eyes on me. 'Well, it was, wasn't it – wild after a constraining fashion? Plenty of chores, hardly enough time to read! And poor little Helen tagging around after one everywhere!'

'She didn't tag around everywhere after me!' I said.

'But you were a stranger! She's always tagged on to me – probably trying to make up for her solitary childhood. That's one of the reasons why Aunt Dru sent her away to school – to force her to meet girls her own age. She's convinced Helen never got over the death of her friend. I told you about her . . . Christine.'

'Yes.' Then I added, thinking of the lake and Helen in that long overdue storm of tears, 'Do you think she has got over it yet?'

'Of course she has,' Kieran said pragmatically. 'She isn't one of those silly females full of emotional mush!'

'That school of hers sounded like Alcatraz! She wrote to me about it!'

'Girls' schools are dumps; prepares them for life, can't have them expecting too much!' He looked at me with his open teasing smile. 'Proper order too! Otherwise the damsels would run amok and what price then the fibre of the nation?'

I was often taken aback by Kieran's semi-fundamentalist pronouncements, particularly as he always delivered them with the same smiling mien, eyebrows raised at the obvious. Sometimes I wondered if he actually meant them.

'Don't be so pompous, old man,' James interjected sleepily. 'It's bloody boring. Sometimes I'm surprised you didn't take the cloth!'

Kieran grinned. He looked at me and winked.

'How'd you do in your exams?' I asked him.

'Grand!'

'What does that mean? A grand scrape or a grand triumph?'

'He came second in his class,' James said with a yawn. 'He didn't come first, so he's no bloody use!'

We heard my mother's step on the stairs. She came into the room. 'Who's no bloody use?' she demanded with a twinkle. 'You'd better not have been discussing my playing.'

Kieran rose to his feet. 'Mrs McPherson,' he said with a gallant bow, 'your playing is inspired.'

Mummy smiled. 'Don't be trying your blarney on me!' she said archly.

I stared at her in surprised delight. She was dressed in one of her lovely frocks. Her hair, which had grown during her illness, was swept up in a French roll. She was my mother restored, but without the brittle quality which had always been her hallmark, as though now she was no longer a being of spun glass, but was made of something more flexible and infinitely more human. The small facial scars were not noticeable. They had faded and she had covered them with fluid make-up.

'Are you going out?' I asked, trying not to show surprise.

'Yes. I'm seeing someone about music.'

She volunteered no further information and left the room. But, a little later, when the doorbell rang and Rachel answered it, I heard my mother's voice in the hall and then a man's deep laugh and then the door shut behind them.

James darted to the window. 'It's a man. He's got an E-Type Jag.'

I joined him and stared through the net curtain. I saw a man in his late thirties open the car door for my elegant parent and then drive her away in a vehicle which purred like a tiger.

'Wow!' James said. 'Did you see that, my old darlings?' He rushed to the kitchen stairs. 'Rachel, who is that man?'

Rachel's voice came from the basement loud and clear. 'What man?'

'If you apply your great brain to the question,' James said after a second's pause, in which he glanced at us and raised his eyes to heaven, 'you might, albeit dimly, glimpse the answer! I am referring to the male being who, just this moment, intruded his person upon these premises for the purpose of abducting my mother.'

'Watch your tongue, you little brat!' Rachel responded equably from below decks. 'His name is Mr Savin'-glee . . . or somethin'!'

James took a deep breath. 'Saving-glee? The woman is nuts!' he murmured. 'There is no such name, Rachel dear,' he called. 'Of your wisdom, will you try again?'

There was silence from below stairs. The sibyl evidently declined to comment further. But James never took no for an answer and he strode downstairs to the kitchen door.

'This is a formal request for an answer, O wise one,' he announced sententiously.

'For the love of God, Jamsie McPherson, will yez stop pesterin' me, or I'll get the stick to yeh!' came Rachel's tormented voice.

James grinned up at us, as we watched from the top of the kitchen stairs, angled his bottom provocatively in the direction of the kitchen door, and murmured, 'Ooh, la la . . .' He was playing to an audience and would not give up. 'Obey me, woman,' he said when he could get no further response, entering the kitchen. 'I am the master here!'

There was a sudden yowl and James fled from the kitchen.

'I'll give yez "master",' Rachel roared, breathing heavily and emerging behind him with a wooden spoon in her hand. She looked up, saw Kieran and me at the top of the stairs, sighed loudly and announced in a suddenly patient and pragmatic voice, 'Sacred Heart o' God, and they say women are inquisitive! I never yet in me life met a man who wasn't either a nosy parker or a poor creature full o' tantrums!' She paused, pursed her lips and then said, enunciating each word as though she were addressing three lunatics, 'The man's a Frenchie . . . she's gone out with a Frenchie. He was here the other day about her music.'

'What would he know about her music?' I asked.

'Didn't he hear it outside in the street? Hasn't he ears? Isn't it a free country?' She went back into the kitchen and slammed the door.

James, finally defeated, looked at us and made a face. 'She's been bloody picked up,' he said, coming back up the stairs to the hall. 'Our mother!'

The three of us went into the West End that evening, ending up in my old haunt, the Café des Artistes. I hoped to see Chantal, the sultry French girl with whom I had fallen in love two years earlier, but she was not there. So we sat in one of the 'caves' and drank wine and talked. The walls were bare cement and the seats were British Rail surplus and a waiter took our order for spaghetti Bolognese. The songs of Buddy Holly, Elvis, came pounding in at us and the dance floor swirled with rock and roll.

'Don't you want to dance?' I asked Kieran when we had finished eating.

He was lounging back on the opposite side of the table. He had been telling a joke and James had howled with laughter at the punch line. Kieran never laughed at his own jokes, although he was always gratified by the mirth of others. He smiled now and said he was too full to dance, but for me to try my luck.

'Sure there's a welter o' grand colleens out there,' he announced in the thick brogue he sometimes affected, as though he would mock the stereotype so hated by the Irish. And then he started to tell another anecdote about a bloke who, at his first hop, wanted to ask a girl to dance, but was unsure as to the approved formula . . .

'I dare you,' James cried when Kieran had finished, tears of laughter in his eyes, 'I dare you to go out there and ask someone the same question!'

Kieran's eyes assumed a mischievous glint. He shrugged, got up lazily, went out to the dance floor and we followed him.

A bored-looking girl, the kind I always found intimidating, was leaning against the wall with a cigarette in a long black holder. She had the bouffant hair style, stiffly lacquered, so popular at the time. Earrings and bracelets dangled. A sneer of contempt for the race of men was nailed to her mouth.

'This tart will do as well as any!' James murmured.

Kieran stood in front of her and inspected her with leisurely detachment, as though she were a heifer at a mart. He seemed impervious to her gathering outrage and, when he had completed his inspection, enquired genially in the thickest brogue I had ever heard him use, indicating the dance floor with a sudden inclination of the head: 'Hey, worm, are yiz comin' for a wriggle?'

A mélange of emotions, not the least of them disbelief, raced across the girl's face. But this was no shrinking violet. She narrowed her eyes, stared at Kieran as though she were viewing something particularly unpleasant through the wrong end of a telescope, and said, 'Piss off, Paddy.'

Kieran stood his ground. 'Begorrah,' he said, giving her his most innocent and wounded gaze, 'what's the matter with yiz at all?'

James and I melted back to the safety of our cave where we could laugh in peace.

Kieran, who had foolishly stayed behind to offer further blandishments, looked a trifle woebegone when he joined us. 'You do your best,' he announced lugubriously, 'and what do you get?' He hung his head in mock self-pity.

James began to think of other dares he might dish out and I realized with dread that Kieran was perfectly capable of undertaking them all. So I discovered that I had better things to do and left them. I vetted the place in case Chantal had arrived in the meantime, but when it was clear that she had not, I found myself a partner and rocked and rolled for thirty minutes or so, half afraid that Kieran would materialize with some more buffoonery. But he didn't appear and when I went back to the cave I found him still there with James, wrapped in smiling conversation, urbanity restored.

'I'm going home!' I said. 'Are you coming?'

'We're too lazy to move,' James said. 'But you toddle off!' He look a cigarette out of his pocket and Kieran leant forward and lit it for him. Then they both looked at me as though I had become surplus to requirements.

''Bye' I said, feeling suddenly abandoned. 'See you later!'

I passed the laconic girl with the stiff hair who was still holding up the wall. She blew cigarette smoke down her nose and looked at me suspiciously from under her false eyelashes. I saw for the first time that her nails were bitten to the quick and was suddenly smitten by a sense of her fragility, standing there blowing defiant smoke, secretly uncertain after the addresses of the mad Irishman, which, in retrospect, I found I resented. For some reason the thought of the rain streaming down the valley at Lough Corrloch came to me, and Helen, also fragile and half defiant, laughing as she ran, hair a-tumble, nails well bitten, for the shelter of the house.

My mother arrived home at midnight and brought her escort in for a nightcap. I was on my way upstairs to bed when they came into the hall.

'This is Monsieur Sauvingler,' she said to me. She turned to him: 'This is my son, Dan.'

We shook hands. He was six feet tall, with the kind of mobile face peculiar to Frenchmen, in which sensitivity and humour play with each other.

'You have a brilliant mother,' he said. 'We have been having a chat about her future!'

For a moment, because I was piqued in any case by my dismissal by James and Kieran, and because I was tender on the subject of my mother and did not see what her future had to do with a perfect stranger like him, I wanted to box his nose. I realized, however, that he was perfectly serious and had intended nothing presumptuous.

'Where did you meet her? Is it true that you heard her playing from the street and knocked at the door?' I demanded, directing a covert glance of reproach at my parent who was pouring a brandy for this monsieur. He seemed a bit taken aback.

'What on earth gave you that idea?' my mother asked with a laugh. 'I met Charles two years ago at the Spicers!'

'Rachel said he had heard you playing while he was passing!' I muttered sheepishly, glancing at him apologetically, and she went off into a peal of laughter.

Charles, a little embarrassed, went to the piano and asked her in French if she would sing.

'No, my voice is not good,' she replied. She glanced at me, but I remembered the lullabies, the sweet, haunting songs of my childhood.

'She can sing very well,' I said. 'She has one of the sweetest voices you ever heard.'

My mother blushed like a girl and I saw in her eyes, as she glanced at me, surprise mixed with sudden tender speculation. I said good night then, but heard, about fifteen minutes later, the sound of the piano and the soft clear notes of her voice singing one of Schubert's compositions: 'Oh music come and light my heart's dark places . . .' For some reason it touched me to the heart.

I did not hear James and Kieran come home. I fell asleep and dreamt I stood on the hillside and saw a nude girl, a composite of Helen and Chantal – Helen's madonna face and Chantal's precociously ripe body – emerge out of Lough Corrloch, like Venus from the sea.

Next day I cornered my old friend and asked him to get me an invitation. 'I just have a yen to stay there again,' I said. 'I would like to see Helen too. It would be nice if we could all be there, like four years ago. It's a smashing place!'

He grinned. 'Are you suffering from nostalgia, old fellow?' He made a *moue*. 'Leave it to little *moi*!' He asked James later if he would like to come to the lake the following year and James shuddered a little and said he couldn't possibly manage without running water. This made Kieran laugh.

'There's water running everywhere, the trouble is to stop it.'

'You don't understand how lovely it is!' I exclaimed in irritation, and my brother turned laconic eyes on me and said his holidays were precious and he wasn't in the business of running risks with them.

'But you buzz off and see the little paragon Helen. Prepare however to be disappointed. The angelic face of the child is often the chocolate-boxy face of the woman. Beauty requires more than symmetry, more than mere robust health, more than adolescent confusion.'

I was sick to death of James's exuberance at other people's expense. And he didn't even know what he was talking about.

Kieran watched the exchange and when I left the room I heard him say *sotto voce*: 'You shouldn't tease him so much.'

'He's my brother,' James said. 'If I can't tease my own brother, whom can I tease?'

Kieran laughed and made some reply which was too low for me to hear.

It was a couple of months later, at the end of September, that my mother announced at breakfast one morning as she opened her post: 'I'm cutting a record, my darlings. Charles has got me a contract!'

Both James and I stared at her stupefied. She had been dropping hints for some time, but these we had ignored as parental rambling. Parents did not cut records. In fact there were lots of things that parents did not do which my parents were doing anyway.

'What kind of record?'

'I'm singing a few of Charles's songs to my own accompaniment.'

'Oh,' James said, 'does the bold Charlie write songs? I thought all he did was ogle you with those soulful French eyes! Does he write the music or just the lyrics?'

'I've written the music. Charles just does the lyrics.' She looked at James severely. 'And don't refer to him as Charlie!'

James sniffed. 'What is his stuff like? Maudlin, I suppose – unrequited ardour and so forth.' He glanced at her. 'Well, it is unrequited . . . isn't it? I mean you wouldn't . . . would you?'

My mother gave a sigh of exasperation, met my eyes and half closed her own as though searching for patience.

'Jamsie, me boyo,' Rachel said from her position by the cooker, 'yer too smart for yer own good. Sometimes I do have an awful lot of sympathy for those poor unfortunates, your patients.'

'Never mind my patients, you old bat,' James said with a grin. He rose, kissed my mother on the cheek, bade us goodbye and left for St Bartholomew's Hospital where he was a houseman.

Later, I sat in the drawing room and listened to my mother singing part of the repertoire which was to become familiar to anyone who listened to popular music. She looked very much in control of her life as her fingers caressed the keys and the sweet low sounds came from her throat. She leant back her head and smiled at me.

'Well, darling, what do you think?'

'Very haunting; very catching . . . And you look wonderful!'

She tinkled the piano, watching me. 'I never told you, Dan, but you made me change things. That lecture you read me – it came at a critical time.'

'No one can *make* anyone do anything,' I murmured, embarrassed. 'Maybe I jolted you, and I'm sorry if I lectured you, Mummy, but I couldn't bear to see you sinking.'

She shook her head as though the subject were dropped.

'You are a bit withdrawn yourself these times,' she said after a moment. 'Is anything bothering you?'

'Nothing,' I said.

'For goodness' sake, Dan,' she murmured, frowning, 'go back to Lough Corrloch if you need to; find Helen if you want to see her. Take your own advice and do not let your life escape you.'

I raised noncommittal eyebrows: 'I'm going back next summer. It's not a big deal! Nothing is escaping me!'

'Good!' she said. 'You were always sensible,' and went back to her playing, and I saw the small pearl drops in her ears and how her strong fingers made the keys ripple.

I went upstairs to pack my bags for Cambridge.

Chapter Six

Cambridge, its mellow stone and brick, its antique grace, seemed over-civilized that winter and spring. I began to sense in it a distillate – of sagacity cornered by the establishment and nursed in privilege. I knew that, despite the front I cultivated, Cambridge and I were not really a snug fit. Something untamed in me, something almost savage, cried out for expression; but St John's College was not the place for it.

The days passed, the biting Fenland wind softened, the gentle river became a place of pleasure once more and with the seasonal improvement my own turmoil lessened. The quintessential English peace of the place crept into me, seducing me with its perfection, as though it knew that the struggle for expression of my untamed self and its radical hungers, was a battle I was fated to lose. England, old England, its charmed circle to which I was affiliated, swamped rebellion without even confronting it.

And something else had happened to preoccupy me. I had met Marion.

I met her just before the end of Michaelmas term; there was a sherry reception in someone's rooms to launch a new student magazine. I saw the girl in the dark blue tailored dress. I caught her eye; she regarded me with amused curiosity. I was wearing a black evening cape lined with red satin, which Rachel had found in an old chest of my father's clothes.

'You remind me of something,' the girl said in her slightly affected voice, in which I detected half-concealed Liverpudlian vowels. 'I suppose you look a bit like a vampire!'

I bowed. 'Madame is all kindness!'

She laughed. She leant back while she spoke, and I saw that she had a lovely figure, curved, slim, pneumatic chest. She examined me over spectacles which were pushed halfway down her nose. 'My name is Marion Chatterton. Will you come to the party?'

'Which party?'

'The one my cousin is giving. She's has a flat on Jesus Green. She works for Pye,' she added, seeing my expression. Women students, like the rest of us, lived in college.

Marion was a Newnham girl, a scholarship student from Great Crashaw, near Liverpool. The ambitious product of a grammar school, she was clever and pretty, but also, privately and surprisingly, acerbic and resentful. Cambridge, for her, was to have been the door into the world of preferment, where her abilities were to have led to great things, but despite her academic prowess she had found that she was still only an outsider, almost an interloper. She told me all of this at a later stage, but I felt it probably had more to do with her own attitude than with anyone else's. She had a funny accent, which she was perpetually adjusting, honing away at its edges, but it rolled in here and there despite all her efforts. I understood, although it irritated me, her fear of the highly tuned English ear, which is able to place birth, breeding, social standing as soon as someone opens his/her mouth. But she would have done better to blast them with her authentic, native sounds than try, unsuccessfully, to erase them.

I went to the party in the house on Jesus Green. Some other Newnham women were there, a sprinkling of men, Marion's cousin Prue and some of the latter's colleagues from Pye. I chatted up some pretty girls, but every time I looked up I found Marion eyes on me. Eventually, with the deliberate courage I tried to cultivate where the opposite sex were concerned, I cornered her in the kitchen when it was momentarily deserted, held her against the wall and kissed her.

I knew from experience that this approach might work. It required no consent from the girl, so her honour, in her own eyes, was not compromised; at the same time it gave her a chance to sample the sensual delights I had to offer. There was only an instant's resistance. Marion's mouth was soft. I felt the thrust of her breasts against me. Her long fair hair came adrift. I pulled out the hairpins and put them on the table, letting the coils spill around her shoulders. I took off her glasses.

'You look beautiful,' I said.

She did look beautiful, with her grey eyes staring at me diffidently and her sudden myopic vulnerability making her seem very young. I was always astonished at how women reacted. This ice maiden was already melting, and only because I had taken a liberty with her for which she might have slapped my face. In those days, I saw girls as belonging to two categories: the ones on the pedestal and the ones who were fair game. We, my male peers and I, did not know who women were. We alternately distanced ourselves or patronized them, worshipped those who were beautiful and unattainable, believed whatever would enable us to despise them as a class, whatever would elevate us to relative invulnerability. And all the time flattering them if they played the game we had invented for them, while we looked over our shoulders at how much we had impressed each other by our prowess.

I asked Marion to dinner, took her to the Corner House in King Street, watched the candlelight dance in her eyes. My credo at this time was see, court, conquer (if possible). I was unconvinced of my attractiveness, craved sexual success as much for validation as for ecstasy. I had burnt my fingers in the early stages of earnest adolescent courtships: had been treated dismissively by girls who knew callowness when they saw it. So I had learnt how to act, to project a confidence which was false.

My *modus operandi* was to act decisively, kiss the girl, ask her out, wine and dine her and, if she was willing, which was rarely, bed her. Few girls sensed my self-doubt, because it was the one thing I disguised with the whole force of my will. I kept a barrier between my few conquests and myself. I followed the model set by James. He always spoke dismissively of women as though they were an endearing joke. He occasionally hinted at carnal encounters, but he seemed untouched by the corrosive passion of unrequited yearning. I wanted to emulate this cool progress in sexual success.

In the event, my mantle of self-sufficient charm may have made me more attractive to some women, may have constituted a challenge; few women I asked out could resist the temptation to puncture it.

'You're a cold fish,' I was told more than once.

'You have engaged in emotional self-refrigeration,' one girl said, while telling me to get lost. 'Kissing a robot gives me a toothache.'

Marion, contrary to my first impression, was basically easy prey. I had managed to capture her imagination in some way, initially with my affected flamboyance, and latterly because she discovered that I was not as simple as she had thought. The child of a broken home, she still carried with her the scars of her childhood's disruption. She was vulnerable to romance, to an emotional haven which she could call her own. She had sought this once or twice already, been singed in the process. She also identified me as someone who represented the milieu into which she so craved admittance.

She was not a virgin and at the time I found this both reprehensible and exciting. I was too obsessed with the prospect of sexual licence to acknowledge her entitlement to care, to responsible treatment. Her early coyness gave way, revealing a hopeless romantic. I would really have preferred the ice; it would have prolonged the challenge and might even, in the end, have punctured the thick membrane of my self-protection. But I sensed in her romanticism a core of desperation, tiresome to someone dedicated to opportunism.

She was, when relaxed, often interesting, her observations sharp, particularly when she was not trying to make an impression.

'This university,' she said one day as we were having coffee in the Copper Kettle, 'is predicated on presumption!'

I glanced at King's College which loomed on the other side of the street, at its fretted stone magnificence, and then back to her.

'Why do you say that?'

'Oh, I know it's beautiful, but don't you see, it's all a balancing act between learning and pantomime?'

'I find Cambridge full of grace.' I said, unwilling to follow her into these perspectives, which too closely echoed my own short foray into private rebellion.

'You make it sound like the Hail Mary! The grace you're talking about is sustained by place . . . by the worship of place. Have you asked the bedders what they think of the grace of Cambridge?' She was referring to the maids who cleaned the students' rooms. She looked at my expression and laughed. 'Never mind – my left-wing sentiments are purely provocative.'

This was untrue; but she had an ability to suppress her opinions, and with them the power of her own vision, leaving her very identity a commodity to be decided by extraneous circumstances, something to be bartered for position and love. In this way she was self destructive.

* * *

A letter eventually came from Kieran's Aunt Dru inviting me to Lough Corrloch in August when the family and Helen's French friend would be there. The open, friendly words addressed a different Dan to the one I was beginning to dislike. My relationship with Marion was now fully blown sexually and moribund emotionally. But I enjoyed her sexual availability too much to end it. I replied to Aunt Dru's letter and said I would be delighted to accept her invitation. I longed for the valley, the pure vistas, the simplicity of being. I wanted to enclose a note for Helen with my reply, but realized how silly it might seem. After all, I had last seen her when she still a little girl.

'What are you doing in the long vacation?' Marion asked me one evening a little wistfully. We were lying on the sofa in her cousin Prue's living room overlooking Jesus Green; Prue was away for the weekend and had given Marion the key to her flat. We had used the respite to good advantage, making vigorous love. From our first lovemaking, when she had guided me – 'Oh yes, darling, oh yes . . . that's wonderful . . .' we had progressed to a physical intimacy which indulged itself at every opportunity. But for all her expressed sensual delight, she seldom had an orgasm, although she frequently faked it; now I was irritated because I was certain that she had just done so again. Her desire to please me was in fact displeasing, although it licensed me in presumption. I was also secretly censorious because one of my peers, who had escorted her during her first weeks in Cambridge, referred to her as a slag. How she could be a slag and we, her lovers, untarnished, was something which did not even occur to me.

'I'm going to Ireland,' I said. 'I have friends there.'

'Oh . . . that's lovely. What part?'

'A place in the Wicklow mountains. It's very beautiful.'

'You've been there before?'

'Once.'

She sat up, began to put on her stockings. 'I suppose there wouldn't be a pretty girl there or anything like that?' she asked archly as she fastened the suspenders.

She kept her voice cheerful; but I felt the pain in her and, because I was the cause of it, I experienced it as a trespass.

'No, it's very cut off from the world.'

I thought of Helen, the child, sitting by the lake, diving half-naked into the pool, running down the hillside, laughing as the rain came in great rolling clouds down the valley. 'Will you be my friend?' she had whispered. The quality of her friendship, child as she had been, bore no relationship to any other camaraderie I had ever experienced. Helen had seen me, had found me, effortlessly, almost casually. I still found this discovery of my private, my secret self, one of the most extraordinary experiences of my life.

'Will you send me a card?' Marion asked then in a light tone.

'There are no cards. It's not a tourist trap. It's a private valley. The nearest postbox is in a village eight miles away. But when the postman calls, who knows . . . I may give him a note for you!'

She looked at me reproachfully. 'Don't strain yourself,' she said with some acerbity.

I reached for her and kissed the back of her neck. 'Don't get truculent, darling. It doesn't suit you!'

She pulled away. 'What you really mean, Dan, is that it doesn't suit you!'

She spoke the truth; in it was a recognition of the balance of power between us. In every relationship, except the rare ones possessing perfect charity, one of the parties is always more vulnerable than the other.

Marion finished dressing; I buttoned up my trousers.

'Are you hungry?' she asked. 'Would you like a bite? There are a few steaks in the fridge.'

Despite her invitation, I knew that she expected me to take her to dinner; but I was longing for some time alone. This longing always suffused me after lovemaking with her; I did not want to engage her in conversation, dine with her, doze with her, hear her breathing, have her snuggle close to me. Such intimacy, after satisfied lust, disgusted me. It was as though she laid claim to my essential self, as though my self were a commodity for which she had paid. Now, and not for the first time, I wanted to end our relationship; sex without love was debauchery. And I could not love her; I did not hear in her the echo of any depth worth exploring; I sensed her insecurity, her desire to hold me. Her personal centre was too unfixed, too ready to accommodate me. She was clever, but prepared to compromise her intellectual integrity for no other reason than to please. I could not respect her, and I sensed, even then, that love is absolutely predicated upon some essential esteem.

'I'm going to evensong' I said. 'Do you want to come?'

Her surprise was evident. 'I didn't think you had a religious bone in you!'

'I haven't,' I said blithely. 'But the music is sublime and I can't help reaching for transcendence!'

She studied me. I felt the pressure of her wounded eyes. 'You mean after lovemaking? Anyone would think you were a Catholic, running to be shriven! Do you know what I think?' she added slowly, with gathering ire. 'I think you are a fraud. I think you are a delayed adolescent. When you have sorted yourself out you might make a fine man. If you do – make a fine man that is – you can try to find me, if I'm still available. But for now, I've had enough!'

I turned to stare at her and saw the tears brimming in her eyes. She left the room, but turned back at the door. 'You can let yourself out.'

I crept away, the young man carbuncular, ashamed of his relief. The wind along the river at the Quayside was very cold. A few sweet papers floated desultorily by the bank and the overhanging willows were stark and skeletal.

I accepted Mrs Fitzgerald's invitation to stay at the lake. Kieran wrote to me when his exams were over in June to suggest dates and to say that he would meet me in Dun Laoghaire.

My own second year exams, part of the Law Tripos, ended at last. I hoped I had done well, although I had not been happy with my performance in Roman Law.

But the arrival of May Week put everything out of my head. I asked a first year Law student called Sarah Jessop-Porter to the May Ball. She wore a pink silk dress and giggled a great deal; we dined and danced and drank oodles of wine in the warm night. At about four o'clock the music stopped; two kilted pipers took up position outside the gates of New Court and piped in the dawn. Then we took to the punts and floated down the river to the Orchard Tea Gardens in Grantchester for a champagne breakfast, Sarah trailing her hand in the water and crooning softly from Elvis's *A Date With Elvis*, while I kept the punt moving, and preserved my balance with the pole. I hardly gave Marion a thought, and kissed a sleepy Sarah when I saw her to her door.

I went home to London. My mother was busy with her new career, and the house echoed with her music and buzzed with her friends. Charles was still on the mat, still writing the haunting lyrics which she set to haunting music and the relationship between them was, to my more adult eyes, definitely not Platonic.

'It's disgusting,' James confided. 'He stayed the other night. I had told her I'd be sleeping at the hospital, but I had a very bad throat and Dick Lowes took over my shift. When I came back that impertinent car of Charles's was in the street and he was at the breakfast table in the morning. Rachel didn't turn a hair, but Mummy was embarrassed.'

'She's pushing fifty,' I said in the tone of one certain that at fifty life has come to its natural denouement and it is time to get off the stage. 'What does she think she is playing at?'

'She's not playing. I think he wants to get married!'

'But he must be ten years her junior!'

James sighed and said with some acerbity: 'There's no law against it!' He directed an amused stare at me. 'The great white hope of the legal profession should know that!'

I ignored the provocation. An unprovoking James would have been worrisome.

'Have you seen Dad?' I asked.

My brother's face clouded. He had never forgiven my father, blaming him entirely for the rupture of our parents' marriage.

'Yes and no. I didn't contact him, but I saw him with that woman in Harrods recently and I was certain that she was pregnant. She was wearing a loose coat, so I couldn't be absolutely sure, but they were looking at baby things and she had that silly, maudlin expression women wear when they are in the family way!'

I digested this. 'I'll phone him,' I said. 'I'd like to see him and I have something I need to say to her too!'

'Like what, for God's sake?'

'Like an apology!' I answered. 'I owe her one.'

My next interview with my father took place at a restaurant near his office in Grosvenor Square. I entered the place feeling oddly nervous and for a moment I thought he had not come. But then I saw him, sitting alone at a corner table. He was wearing a grey pinstripe suit, and was perusing a folded copy of the *Financial Times*. He had become quite grizzled; the wiry brown hair had been flecked with grey before he had left home, but now there were silver swatches at his temples. I felt a lump in my throat, some kind of subliminal reminder of mortality. This was my father; I knew every lineament of his face, the small mole on his chin, the crinkling of his grey eyebrows. I realized how much I loved him, how nothing would ever alter that.

He looked up, saw me approach, and his face brightened.

'Hello, Dad.'

'Hello, Dan.'

I stood uneasily. 'For heaven's sake, sit down,' he said. 'You look like a stork when you shift your feet about like that!'

I put my bottom on the chair which the waiter held for me.

'Is Kelly with you?' I asked stupidly.

'What does it look like?' And then he added mildly, but with the steel in his tone that I knew from long ago, 'Most people avoid occasions of insult, you know!'

'Yes.' I leant forward. 'I'm sorry, Dad. I wanted to apologize to her. I was completely out of order that day.'

'You were in pain,' he said flatly, after a moment. 'And because you were in pain you were unmanly enough to lash out. She understood that, you know; she pointed it out to me. She forgave you quicker than I did! She said you were very young. I wanted to kick your butt. I should have kicked it!'

I looked suitably contrite. 'Yes, you should!' Then I asked, 'Is it true that she's pregnant?'

He started. 'Who told you that?'

'James saw you both together and thought she might be expecting.'

My father became very quiet, his voice very low. 'She lost it,' he said. 'She lost the baby! She is still not over it.'

'I'm sorry.'

He changed the subject, perused the menu, asked me what I would have, gave the order and relaxed against his seat.

'Well, my son, and how is Cambridge treating you?'

'OK.'

'Still on for the Bar?'

'Why not?'

'What about pupillage? Have you applied to chambers?'

'Not yet.'

He gave me a name – Sir William Ryce – who practised in Lyle Court in the Temple. 'Go and see Billy. He'll look after you. I've already spoken to him about you. First-class chambers . . .' He wrote the name and address on a piece of paper. Then he asked me about James and, finally, broached the question I was certain was at the forefront of his mind. 'How is your mother?'

'Mummy is very well now. She's busy with her new career. You must have heard her songs on the radio? She was on television recently.'

He smiled, nodded. 'Yes, she's becoming quite famous. If she had not married me she might have had the whole world at her feet.' Then he added tentatively, 'We are getting a divorce, you know.'

I knew this, but to hear it in his mouth filled me with pain. It was as though nothing in life could be relied on; that everything was flawed, everything contained within it the seeds of its own destruction.

'Is she very fond of this Charles Sauvingler?' he asked suddenly.

'I think she probably is. They have a lot in common . . . and he writes the lyrics for her songs!'

'I know that. I wanted to know if he makes her happy.'

'I think so,' I said. 'She has chosen happiness, or at least contentment. She was in a bad way for a while after you left, but then she learnt to put herself at the centre of her life . . . instead of putting you . . . and after that . . .'

He winced, was silent, ate his soup.

'I do love her, you know, Dan,' he said with sudden tension, 'but not in the way that would enable me to live with her. Kelly and I will be married as soon as the divorce is through. I called on your mother recently to tell her, to have a talk, but she refused to see me, although I'm sure she was in. Rachel was apologetic, but what can I expect?' He looked at me carefully. 'But I can expect you at my wedding and . . . James?'

'Yes,' I said. 'I will come. I can't answer for James. He's as black as they come.'

'I know,' my father said. 'He's your mother's son!'

'What are you doing this summer?' he asked after a moment. 'Have you a job?'

'Yes, I'll be working in the Midland Bank. But I'm going to Ireland in August.'

'To Lough Corrloch?'

'Where else?'

'What is Kieran up to these days?'

'He's reading Science.'

'I suppose he's as charming as always?'

'After a fashion. In a way he's like a fly in amber. I don't think he has really grown up! He's still very proper, very amusing, and, I think, religious. He always goes to church when he comes to London. He reminds me of something out of Dickens – a kind of caricature – Mr Proper Young Gentleman.'

My father laughed.

'I'm serious. I think it's because I have never seen him angry. I don't believe in people until I've seen them stung, with anger, or joy or excitement . . . or grief,' I added, thinking of Helen long ago by the lake. 'Especially grief.'

My father was watching me quizzically. 'Have you,' he asked with some amusement, 'grown up yourself?'

'Probably not!'

He laughed. 'Don't worry. Growing up is an inexorable process, slow, inescapable, like death. And, like death, it generally takes a lifetime to accomplish!' He sighed. 'I would like to go back to Ireland myself. I will bring Kelly. We might go there on honeymoon . . . But enjoy yourself at the lake.'

'I will.'

The day came at last. I was up at first light, hovered for a moment outside my mother's door, wondering if I should knock to say goodbye. I heard her moving inside and then the door opened and she came on to the landing in a pale blue silk kimono.

'Oh . . . you startled me. Are you off already? Have a good journey, darling. Give my regards to Kieran.' She regarded me questioningly, pushing back her hair. 'You should invite Helen to stay with us . . . if you would like her to.'

'Thanks, Mummy.'

I hovered for a moment, as though one of us should say something more to the other. Then I pecked her cheek, humped my bag to Euston, caught the train to Holyhead.

The crossing was calm; my fellow passengers were playing cards, drinking Guinness, talking and laughing; some of them had such broad brogues that I could barely understand what they were saying but, even though I knew perfectly well that the Irish exaggerate their accents for the sheer love of the sound effects, their voices seemed a harbinger of everything that was, like the valley, spontaneous and untamed.

Kieran was there to meet me. I came through the ferry terminal at Dun Laoghaire and saw him standing at the barrier, leaning back a little to look over the heads of the crowd. He was wearing a tweed jacket, an open-necked shirt, and an expression of candid expectancy. I already felt the change of tempo in the air, the different perceptions, the falling away of the usual constraints, as I progressed towards the exit and my oldest friend.

He grasped my hand with genuine delight. 'Dan, old fellow, great to see you!'

'You've got even taller,' I said. 'There has to be a limit on how big you're going to grow!'

He laughed, picked up my bag. 'My poor mother is on her knees doing novenae about the size of me. There are dark mutterings about clothes bills. But the car is waiting. There's someone in it who's been looking forward to seeing you!'

'Not Helen?'

'The very same,' Kieran said. 'You talk to her while I nip up to the newsagents in George's Street. I won't be a minute.'

She had changed in all kinds of ways; she was the same; she was different; she was a young woman and she was still a child. I saw her through the window, the long hair on her shoulders, a little darker than it used to be, saw the soft angle of her chin. She turned, saw me, widened her eyes in recognition, opened the door of the old black car and got out, a shy girl with a gravely beautiful face. She looked at me for a moment, gave me her old quirky smile, put out her hand and said I had grown up.

I could hardly speak. 'So have you!' I answered after what seemed an interminable moment. 'You're quite the young lady!'

This provoked a laugh. 'You sound very prim, Dan.' Her recognition of my sudden diffidence seemed to make her relax. 'If I said you're quite the young gentleman,' she teased, 'would it please you?'

'No!'

'Where's Kieran?'

'Popped off to the shops.'

Helen nodded. 'Probably buying one of his magazines.' She opened the boot. I stowed my bag in its musty depths and she shut it with a flourish.

I examined her covertly. She was wearing a summer dress with a collar and belt, and the sleeves were down to the wrist, where they were caught by white cuffs. Her figure was slender; her waist was small. Her face was animated, the lashes thick and darker than her hair and a few freckles clustered like daisies on either side of her straight nose. She wore neither lipstick, nor scent, but I knew she had recently washed her thick hair because I could smell the shampoo. Her young womanhood was lush, in the spring of her hair, in the sheen of her skin, in the hidden promise of her body. Her maidenliness, her half-present, half-departed childhood, made her seem as unattainable as the stars.

'Would you like to walk down the pier a bit while we're waiting?'

'Why not?'

We went as far as the old bandstand and looked over the wall at the breakwater. The sea was calm; the great granite cubes, connected by heavy iron bars, seemed an unnecessary reminder of winter turmoil. A number of strollers moved along the pier and further up we could see one or two fishermen with their rods angled over the sea wall. I felt the stone bench beside my knee.

'This is where I last spoke to you!'

Helen gave me a swift unfathomable look and for an instant I felt known, visible, as I had felt with her before. 'You have a good memory!' She turned her head, gestured. 'We should go back. There's Kieran looking for us!'

Kieran had a folded magazine under his arm. He saw us approaching, waved and strolled back ahead of us to the car. When we joined him he was reading the *Scientific American*, resting it against the steering wheel. He closed the magazine and put it in the glove compartment.

'Get into the car, let ye,' he said in his thickest brogue, the one he reserved for mockery. 'And let us be off to the mountain fastness in the name of God!'

I wondered how Kieran felt about Helen now. But when we were in the car and Helen was seated beside him I did not notice that he paid her any particular attention. He seldom glanced at her. She's like a sister to him, I thought. That's how he sees her, and I remembered how he had impatiently referred to 'little Helen, always tagging around after one!'

No, it was safe enough for me to watch her, to feel the strange pull at the middle of my chest as though she had touched my heart with her white fingers. She was in the passenger seat, but turned to chat to me, her right elbow positioned over the seat back. She was so close to me, leaning near to talk, that I could see the down on her face and the clear unblemished whites of her green eyes.

'Tell me about London. I want to know all about your life!'

'That's a tall order,' I said. 'I'm at Cambridge now, so I don't live in London all the time. But I come back at weekends sometimes.'

I wondered did I sound banal? But she listened eagerly and plied me with further questions and when I caught Kieran's eye in the rear-view mirror he winked.

'She's such a chatterbox, this girl,' he said severely, and she turned to look at him and there was something in her expression which was pleased to have his approval, although she said, 'The cheek of you, Kieran Fitzgerald!'

Dun Laoghaire and its spires disappeared behind us and the mountains approached. We headed for Rathfarnham, turned right at the landmark pub called The Yellow House, and were soon making our way up by Kilakee and to the wilderness beyond. The car rattled and gave strange growls at corners.

I was in an old Rolls-Royce. The leather on the seats squeaked a bit. There was a hump where the big end divided the leg room at the back. The car and its exhaust shuddered, assaulting every pothole. The only thing which had struck me at the ferry terminal was that the vehicle was prewar, but now I saw the winged lady on the bonnet.

'When did you get the Rolls?'

Kieran smiled at me in the rear-view mirror. 'I was wondering when you'd notice. It's a 1934 model. I had to beg, borrow and steal for it, spent my shirt on it – fifty quid – couldn't resist it! It's basically sound, guzzles petrol and could do with a – small modicum of work!' This was the year's understatement.

'It can only increase in value – if you spend about half a million on it. You should hold on to it.'

He grinned.

The heather was in bloom, great sweeps of purple and new green. The morning light played over the vale of Glencree. The road went ever upwards, the precipitous drop falling away on the left-hand side. There were more potholes and acute bends and I saw that Kieran, for all his easy badinage, drove his growling vehicle with intent concentration. Within the hour we had arrived at the gate to the long winding driveway down to the house and the lake. The sign said, 'PRIVATE PROPERTY: TRESPASSERS WILL BE PROSECUTED.'

Kieran roared up to the gates, changed down gear and nosed the car through the stone gateposts.

It was all below us now; the valley was spread out between the mountains. There was a haze over it and it seemed to sleep.

Helen turned to me and smiled. 'Is it as you remember it?'

I looked down into the valley, saw the steep rise of the hills around it, the blue-grey of the haze, the shimmer of the lake bedded down in the furthest end and turned back to her lovely, grave eyes.

'More beautiful!'

'It seems to have made quite an impression! You would have been welcome to have come back whenever you wanted, you know; you should have said. When Kieran told us how you were longing to see the place again we felt quite guilty. The house is empty most of the time and you could have come over and stayed for whatever time you wanted . . .'

She paused, glanced at Kieran, who was moving the Rolls slowly down the steepest path that car had ever traversed. 'Personally, I think the valley is the most beautiful place on earth,' she added in very low voice, 'so I can understand how you feel.'

She turned back to staring out of her window and Kieran brought the car down to the sharp left-hand turn which led to the house.

'I hope your brakes are OK,' I murmured.

Kieran grinned. 'O ye of little faith,' he intoned, leaning mockingly towards Helen and whispering, 'now, me little darlin', yeh would never give voice to a negative suggestion the like o' that!'

Helen chuckled and looked at him fondly.

The road levelled out and we crunched over the stones, negotiated the U-bend and then rolled the few hundred yards to the turn into the avenue. A businesslike terrier came tearing out to meet us, barking wildly.

'That's bossy old Ivan,' Helen said, 'named for Ivan the Terrible. He's as cross as two sticks, so watch your ankles!'

Kieran drove the car into the yard, the back door opened and Helen's mother came out to greet us. Mrs Fitzgerald had put on weight, was noticeably grey, but she was welcoming, wreathed in smiles and extending both hands.

Helen jumped out of the car and grabbed the unpleasant Ivan by his collar. 'This is Dan,' she said to the dog. 'You're to be nice to him!'

Ivan rolled over when she released him and presented his tummy. I got out of the car and shook hands with Aunt Dru.

'You've become quite grown up!' she cried. 'I must be getting old!'

'Nonsense!' Kieran said. 'You're the youngest Aunty Dru in the valley!' He caught my eye and winked.

Lunch was on the table – tomatoes, crisp lettuce and rolls of lean pink ham. The bread was homemade, as I remembered; the kitchen was full of its freshly baked scents.

The tea tasted wonderful, something I had forgotten. When I alluded to it I was told it was the water, 'Spring water – so clean and full of lime – but it leaves a terrible fur in the kettle. I suppose you have soft water in London?'

I said I supposed we had. It was not something I had ever adverted to.

I had my old room back; the walls were still painted pale blue and the bed was the same, iron with brass knobs and a white bedspread. If you lifted the fringe you could see the chamber pot – for emergencies – which still resided discreetly beneath the coiled steel springs. Mod cons had evidently not yet arrived in Lough Corrloch. But I remembered that the lease forbade any improvements without the landlord's consent and the Malcolms, I knew from Kieran, were no longer contactable. I saw them in my mind's eye – an ageing childless couple who had fled Ireland at the advent of independence, living out their declining days in what they would regard as the 'mainland', and the Irish would look on as a foreign country.

The bathroom was unchanged. There was the huge enamel bath, the marble-topped toilet table, the sandlewood shaving box with its Victorian tackle, the cutthroat razor lying in its bed in the open box, the pale green bar of Palmolive soap.

Kieran came up the stairs. 'Well,' he said, 'are you glad to be back?'

I moved to look out the landing window, watched Helen tickling the fawning Ivan in the yard. Beyond her was the avenue with its trees and its dog roses, and beyond that the half-glimpsed sweep of the valley.

'This place is wonderful! I missed it, you know.'

'Did you?' He raised his eyebrows. 'In Cambridge . . . where you must have had so much to think about . . . and so many female distractions too?'

This last was said slyly and he looked at me with an interrogative man-to-man twinkle.

I sensed his curiosity, and unable to resist starring for a moment as some kind of Don Juan, muttered with foolish bravado that I 'couldn't complain'. Kieran kept his eyebrows raised. 'You needn't think you'll get a kiss-by-kiss account,' I said, 'so you can take that look off your face.'

Kieran said that I was a lucky dog and preceded me down the stairs.

The haze lifted in the early afternoon and the three of us, Kieran, Helen and I, went for a walk as far as the lake. En route we detoured to view the pool, which was unchanged, and I recalled again the child stripped to her knickers, joining us in the cold brackish water. I glanced at Helen, but she seemed so dignified and graceful in her young womanhood, so self-contained, that it was difficult to imagine her as the little hoyden of my recollection, just as it was difficult to imagine her abandoned to any tyranny of the emotions, be it love or grief.

I was filled with a sense of happiness and peace as we walked along the spongy boreen to Lough Corrloch, between the heavy granite walls. 'Famine walls', Kieran called them – work farmed out to the starving in exchange for a pittance with which they could buy food during the Great Hunger of 1845 to 1849, when the potato crops had failed.

When we reached the lake I mused a little on its depth and Kieran indicated the height of the surrounding mountains. 'The lake is as deep again,' he said, 'as the height of the mountains. These tarns are always bottomless!'

Helen snorted. 'There is no such thing as a bottomless lake!'

Kieran turned indulgent eyes on her. 'Is my liggle dear waxing knowledgeable?'

Helen evinced pleasure at being teased, but I felt a kind of resentment that he would attempt to put her down in any way, however jocosely. But he radiated such centrality, such certainty that the world was as he perceived it, that it was almost hypnotic.

He wandered along the shore, picked up a handful of brown-white froth, inspected it and threw it away from him, wiping his hands on his trousers. Helen sat on the remains of the wall, which at this point was a jumble of stones.

'Why didn't you keep writing to me?' I demanded, when I saw that Kieran was out of earshot.

'You didn't answer,' she said. 'I don't blame you . . . you must have had much better things to do! Anyway, I was such a kid!'

'But, Helen, I did answer you! I answered all your letters – I sent mine to your home because I didn't want them confiscated by that awful headmistress of yours!'

She raised her curved eyebrows, shrugged and muttered darkly, 'Probably my overprotective mother again!'

'Tell me about your school,' I asked, trying to disguise my angry dismay at the thought of her mother intercepting my missives. 'It sounded bloody in your letters, if you don't mind me saying so!'

She turned to stare at me, laughter in her eyes. 'Oh Dan, it's not so bad. I'm so used to it now and I'm not a junior anymore and I'll be out of the dump in a year, and the food has improved and they have a reasonably decent library. You should visit me!' There was trace of archness in this suggestion.

'Could I?' I demanded. 'I thought you were held in some kind of durance vile, some kind of purdah, where no male visitors, other than kin, need darken the door!'

Helen seemed vastly amused. 'I suppose that's true; but what's to stop you being "kin"? You could always be my cousin.'

'OK, you're on! Maybe next term. I'll come over for the weekend . . .'

But, perhaps because I was serious, this suggestion did not meet with any great enthusiasm, and the subject was dropped.

We talked then of what she wanted to be 'when she obtained her freedom' and she said she wanted to study Arts – English and French – and maybe become a teacher. 'I thought I would try for a teaching job in Kenya!'

'Why there?'

'It seems romantic . . . far away . . . good pay, safaris and all that kind of thing. I'd like the adventure!'

Kieran made his way slowly back to us and Helen stood up as he approached, as though he were someone of note, like visiting royalty. But he seemed insensible to her gesture, and indeed of her, treating her with cheery condescension.

'How do you fit six elephants in a Mini?' he asked her in his grave talking-to-the-child voice.

Helen groaned in laughter. 'Oh Kieran, everyone knows that – three in the front, and three in the back!'

'Very good,' Kieran said and then, almost abruptly, addressed himself to me, changing his tone, walking along beside me and asking about my mother and Walton Street and finally about James. Helen walked beside us and listened to the conversation in which I tried to include her by looking at her while I spoke.

'Is James off to Paris this summer?' Kieran asked. 'I was thinking what fun it would be to take the Rolls over . . . go for a bit of a spin.'

I heard Helen catch her breath, felt her disappointment at being excluded.

'I don't know,' I said shortly. 'No one is privy to James's schemes. He doesn't have much holiday time now.'

'Hmmn,' Kieran said and we walked on in silence.

The evening turned into a long chess game with Helen who did not beat me this time and who did not play Kieran. The latter was sunk into the *Scientific American* with a thorough dedication. There was no turf fire in the drawing-room grate on this occasion, because the night was close and very humid, but the lamps were lit, burnishing the mahogany of the old upright piano with its brass sconces, the black marble of the mantelpiece, the veneer of the radio, sitting up huge and ugly in the corner beside the car battery which served as its power supply. We got the half-ten news and then had cocoa and went off to bed like good people – or like children, as I thought, half amused by my docility before the managing Aunt Dru. I was so glad to be back in Lough Corrloch that I would have obeyed much more intense strictures to be allowed my sojourn.

I suspected that evening that Helen was in love, or in fascination, with Kieran and that, to her, I was only her acquaintance, or at best, her friend. This, although I did not want to admit it, constituted a powerful challenge. She looked utterly inaccessible, reading in the lamplight with her hair spread on her shoulders.

I took my candle from her hand and found my way up the dark staircase to my room.

It was a very warm night. The curtains had not been drawn; the sky was bright with moonlight; the window was open, but the air was heavy and still and without any hint of a breeze. I threw off the bedspread and blanket and lay naked beneath the sheet, ran my hand along my chest, feeling the matted hair, the latest acquisition of manhood, aware of the scent of my sweat, the life in my body. I tried to sleep, but my thoughts kept returning to the conversation at supper, to my walk with Helen, to her voice and her laugh, to the sweet imperious quality she had, the arrogant innocence. I felt indulgent about innocence, subsumed as I was in the rush towards manhood and autonomy, towards the shedding of vulnerability.

I was erect. I would have released these tensions once, ploughing some favourite fantasy; but tonight I felt that this was something fit for adolescents, but unfit for a man. I was a man. I desired a woman. I desired Helen, young as she was, but with more yearning than the stuff of fantasy had ever permitted me. My dreams of sexual prowess had had to do with conquest, where I was king, master, admired and worshipped, recognized. My dream of Helen had its own ferocity, but there was definite homage in it.

In spite of what I had again felt with her on the pier at Dun Laoghaire, in spite of her friendliness on the drive home, I suspected that Helen did not really want to know me; she had been distant after our walk, had hardly glanced at me at supper. Piqued, I told myself it did not matter, that my experience of women, to date, had never lived up to the promise. Sex was a shadow of some hunger in the soul, which could be neither realized nor assuaged. This girl was just a girl. They were all the same when the lights were out.

I thought of reading. There were several books on the mantelpiece beside the absurd statue of Our Lady of Fatima, blue cloth-bound volumes of Dickens and George Eliot and *Fabiola* by Cardinal Wiseman. But I would have to strike a match, light the lamp, adjust the flame. The moths would come through the window to dance in the hot draught and die in the mini inferno. The spell of the darkness, which was not darkness, would be broken. I lay, torpid, watching the moon through the open window, imagining what its craters were like, forcing myself to perceive them as pits and quarries and, finally, allowing the first predominant perception which had stayed with me from childhood, a bright night-time face watching the world. And then I heard a sound, very faint, the squeak of a door, followed by the creak of the top step of the stairs.

Someone was up. I wondered who it could be. Was it Mrs Fitzgerald? Was it Helen? Could it be Kieran? His room was near the top of the stairs across the landing from hers. For a moment I wondered if it were remotely possible that he would attempt to enter her room. The thought was breathtaking, as was the attendant jealousy. But the unlikelihood of maidenly Helen and Kieran the burgeoning scientist coming together in clandestine passion was such that I threw out the notion. It was nonsensical, I told myself, especially with Mrs Fitzgerald, just two doors away, perfectly capable of raising the roof.

I heard one further creak on the stairs and then there was silence. I waited but there was no hint of returning footsteps; whoever had gone downstairs did not return. I strained unsuccessfully to hear the sound of the back door bolt. The silence wrapped the house once more.

Sleep was now entirely out of the question. In fact even stillness was impossible. I needed movement, to go out, walk in the night, meet Kieran and talk. I tried to pretend there was no possibility of Helen having been the source of the sounds. For a brief instant I imagined myself walking with her in the warm darkness.

I got out of bed, pulled on trousers and a shirt, picked up my tennis shoes and gently opened the bedroom door. The landing was in darkness, except for the moonlight through the window, and I padded on tiptoe down the worn carpet of the stairs, letting the banister take most of my weight, so that no creak would alert anyone listening. This was only partially successful, but I made it to the hall without any intimation that I had wakened the household, and crept to the kitchen door.

The kitchen too was in darkness, but when I approached the back door I found that the bolt was already drawn. Someone had indeed gone out. I stepped into the yard, looked up at Helen's window and saw there was a light burning. I imagined her propped up with pillows, hair loose on her shoulders, reading. At least I was now sure that it must have been Kieran who had left the house and in a rush of comradely spirit I thought I would track him down, roam through the moonlight with him and luxuriate in one of our old conversations, our old friendship.

I set off down the short avenue, but saw no sign of him. At the boreen I looked in each direction, again without success. So I decided to retrace the route which we had traversed earlier.

It was when I reached the pool that I saw her. She was bathing and her naked body looked silver in the light of the moon. Her hair was dripping around her. She swam from one end of the pool to the other, a breaststroke, followed by a sudden change to a crawl. She emerged, stood with her back to me, raised her arms and dived in again. She radiated the joy of life, of being female and without fear, of something utterly primeval, a private universe where the feminine reigned. I hid behind a rock and watched, aware that I was a voyeur, but fearful of betraying my position lest she think I had followed to spy on her. I felt like someone in a dream. The night was warm and violet; the moon threw its silver over the still land; a medley of scents came from the earth and the vegetation. And in the midst of this a beautiful young woman was bathing naked before my eyes.

I did not want to lose a glimpse of her, of her soft curved body, of her naked grace. She turned at the far end of the pool, clambered out on to the flat rock, and wrung out her hair, twisting it over her shoulder. Then she turned, staring down at her body, running a hand slowly and tenderly over her beautiful breasts, in a gesture of autoeroticism which was private and full of pleasure. I almost felt the soft silken pressure of them, the stiff nipples erect from the cool water. She looked down at them, down at the length of her body, in solitary virgin appreciation. And I watched. I watched the slow movement of her hand down her belly, the tentative gentleness of her self-caress, which stopped shyly at her pubic hair, the grace of her self-regard. I did not know it then, but I was lost forever.

Suddenly she raised her head and looked straight in my direction, as people do instinctively when they are being watched. I repressed the impulse to move; I was sure she could not see me and she did not evince any realization of my presence, although she seemed to stiffen for a moment and then she lifted her head and walked away from the pool into the shadows behind the two stones; I saw the momentary flutter of a shaken towel.

I crept away. I walked away from the pool, down to the lake, hardly aware of the shimmer of the moonlight across the mirror surface, the pungent scents of gorse and the perfume from the honeysuckle twisting around the wooden fencing which marked the end of the boreen. I felt the coarse sand of the shore under my shoes. I took them off, took off my clothes and slid into the water, submerging quickly. I brought fire into its coolness, and confusion and a passion which burnt like white phosphorous.

The wind of dawn was shivering in the reeds when I returned to bed.

After my swim I had walked around the northern shore of the lake, as far as the old stone boathouse. The door had yielded to my shoulder, with a sound of cracking wood and a whine of rusty hinges. I glanced back at the violet lake and the light night sky, at the contours of the sloping land, and knew that this was indeed one of the most private places on earth. In the mountains on the far side of the lake no lights burnt. No one lived there. The whole valley might have been an enchanted other world; it was so secret and private, full of unearthly peace, that it seemed lost to the tides of time and strife. I sought for the white gazebo on the southern shore, which was near the hunting lodge itself, and saw it standing there, its classic lines cold in the moonlight. I remembered the dead son, whose ghost was said to haunt the lake, and thought there could be no more lovely spot in which to spend eternity.

I half hoped, in that enchanted night, to meet his spectre. I was aware by now that almost everywhere in Ireland was said to be haunted, everywhere had its own story of loss or sorrow which reverberated down generations, creating a kind of echo. This lingered, something in the air, something melancholy in lonely places, something waiting just below the ordinary levels of perception. Kieran had told me often that the Grehans, who had the grazing of the valley, swore that if anyone used the boathouse, the spirit of the dead son would come and knock on the door. But then the country people would swear to hearing the banshee, and some of them to having seen leprechauns – and some of them, it is said, for the pure pleasure of the articulation, would swear to anything.

But the night was too bright for fear and I was not afraid. If I had met a spirit it would only have capped the magic of the hour. So I pushed the door and found myself in a small room where cobwebs festooned the one small window, cutting out most of the moonlight with the corpses of dead flies and daddy-longlegs. I could hardly make out the contents of the place, but as my eyes adjusted I saw the outline of a table and in the corner a decaying bamboo chair and, leaning against the wall, what looked like old fishing rods covered in cobwebs.

I moved back outside and sat on the step. I waited, but all I heard was the lapping of the water. I wondered about the dead boy, about his life and times, about the Ireland of the last century when he had lived. I tried to imagine the poverty, the incredible wretchedness of the mass of the people, the plunder of the nation, the resultant reaching of the Irish psyche for God.

I waited by that stone boathouse, beside the silver lake, under the pale sky of high summer, but no phantom came to call. I could not pull myself away from the extraordinary combination of silver lake, blue and dark blue light and, our custodians, the lonely violet mountains. I heard the remonstrance of one or two sheep, momentarily disturbed in their slumbers, and saw a few bats winging out of the darkness. And as I sat listening and watching my mind abandoned the prospect of spectral visitation and the problems of the past. Instead it returned with a sense of sinking sensuality to Helen, dwelling on her with a half-torpid ecstasy.

When I went back to bed I slept until noon. I rose to find the place humming with activity; Kieran was chopping wood in the yard: Mrs Fitzgerald was baking in the kitchen; Helen was trying a few bars on the piano which was more than a little out of tune.

'Good morning,' Mrs Fitzgerald said. 'Did you sleep well?'

'I went out,' I said in explanation. 'It was so hot I couldn't sleep. I swam in the lake and then went for a walk as far as the boathouse.'

She frowned. 'I hope you were careful. It's not a good idea to swim alone in that lake; the currents are treacherous. Why didn't you swim in the pool? It's safe in the pool!'

Helen came into the kitchen. I glanced at her and felt the unexpected rising embarrassment. I shrugged in answer to my hostess's question, said I was a strong swimmer, and turned to sit at the table, while she moved the kettle on to the hotplate of the range to boil it up for tea. I did not know what to say to Helen, so I murmured, 'Good morning . . .'

'What was that?' she asked with a tight smile. 'Were you swimming in the lake last night?'

'Yes. It was too hot to sleep.'

'I was asking why he didn't bathe in the pool; it's nearer and it's safe,' Mrs Fitzgerald said. 'The lake is dangerous!'

Helen looked at me sharply, a shocked interrogative glance, then blushed scarlet, a sudden, sweeping tide that spread to the roots of her hair. She left the room. Her mother looked after her and then back at me, drawing her brows together in perplexity, but she said nothing.

At lunch Helen was taciturn; she did not look at me and when I spoke to her she answered monosyllabically. Kieran was on good form, but he disconcerted me by turning and suddenly enquiring, 'Were you up last night, old fellow? I thought I heard the stairs creaking.'

'It was too hot to sleep!' I stammered, conscious of Helen's eyes. 'I went for a swim in the lake!'

'Where exactly?'

'You know where the boreen wall edges to the shore . . . ?'

'There's a superstition about swimming there,' Kieran said with the hint of a smile. 'Has to do with the drowning of poor old Jasper!'

'Jasper?'

'Jasper Malcolm. You remember the gazebo?'

'Of course . . .'

'Oh for God's sake,' Aunt Dru said, 'don't be bothering him with such nonsense.' She put some hot toast in front of me. 'Now!'

'Thank you,' I said. 'But what's the superstition?'

'Well, you know the boy was drowned?' Kieran said affably.

'Some say he was murdered!' Helen interjected suddenly. 'Some say the poor kid was done to death, dragged out of his boat and drowned by starving, disaffected tenantry who had been evicted because they couldn't pay their rents! They were really looking for his father!'

'Why would they do a thing like that?' I asked.

'Why do you think?' Kieran asked gently. 'If you take people's means of life away from them, you must guard against the possibility of their taking yours!' I stared at them, aware that they spoke of this event as though it had happened yesterday.

'Don't look like that,' Aunt Dru said laughing. 'It's only an old story!'

'That's right!' Helen said. 'It's an old story. And this old story says that the spirit of the dead boy is out there waiting, seeking revenge!'

I was surprised at the brittle tone to her voice and looked at her, but she refused to meet my eyes. When our eyes accidentally did meet, towards the end of the meal, there was such reproach in them that I wanted to blurt out there and then that I had not followed her the night before, that I had seen her bathing purely by accident. But I was dumb, searching for the elusive right words which would clear me without making an issue of the thing.

Helen avoided me for the rest of the day. I saw her after lunch setting off towards the lake and thought to follow her. But when I turned the corner of the boreen she had disappeared and throughout all the two miles to the lake shore there was no sign of her. I wandered around by the reeds and listened to the quiet slapping of the wavelets and looked back and around me, from time to time, at the waiting mountains. I had a sensation of being watched, which was uncomfortable, so I found a nook behind a heather-covered boulder and sat there in sombre contemplation of the day and the sky, and the water which shivered with every tiny breeze across its surface. I had my diary in my breast pocket, so I opened it, wrote: 'I'm here . . . amid the heather, the bracken, and confusion.'

I heard Kieran's voice calling at one point, a bellow which reverberated down the valley, and I thought, at first, that he was calling my name. But it was Helen he was seeking and the shout – 'Hel-len' echoed across the water as he approached the shore. I saw him from my nook and was about to stand up and go down the incline to meet him, when I heard Helen's voice replying from some point higher up, and turned my head to watch as she emerged from the heather and walked obediently down the slope to him, about five hundred yards away. I watched him greet her, saw the familiar hand he put on her shoulder, the priestlike gesture, as though she had earned this honour in some way. She bent her head and they talked for a moment and then walked back along the boreen. I emerged from my hiding place and followed, my wellingtons squelching in sudden muddy pockets where small streams from the mountain ran haphazardly, but covertly, among the tough grass and the bracken.

'Ah, there you are!' Kieran said, turning to greet me. 'I was wondering where you had got to!'

'I was communing with nature.'

I picked bits of heather from my jumper and said nothing to him about the sense of unease which had overtaken me at the sight of this young woman, rushing down the hillside to meet him, bowing her head as he spoke to her with condesending affability, as though he possessed some power over her. I glanced at Helen. Her face was pale, and without the winsome mischievousness I so loved. When I tried to meet her eyes she looked away.

'Helen won't talk to me,' I said to Kieran that evening, when the two of us went for a walk after supper, leaving Helen and her mother to tidy up. 'I'm in the doghouse.'

'Well, you see, Dan, old fellow, she thinks you were spying on her last night. She saw something move while she was in the pool; and as you were the only person out, it can only have been you.' He smiled at me with his boyish charm. 'I told her, of course, what a great man you are for the ladies. How you can't help yourself!'

I wanted to hit him. It was the first time in my life that I wanted to strike out and break his teeth.

'It might interest you to know,' I said coldly, 'that although I did go out last night, and although I did see Helen in the pool, I did so by the sheerest accident. I knew someone had gone out and thought it was you! I would not do anything to upset Helen and I certainly would not have spied on her!'

He glanced at me quizzically. 'Well, there's no harm done. It's not a big deal!' He looked at me with raised eyebrows. 'Pretty girl swimming nude by moonlight . . . why not have an eyeful if you can!'

'It wasn't like that!'

'No? I bet you didn't run away immediately all the same.'

Kieran bent down and picked something from the ground. 'Hmmn,' he said, showing me the piece of vegetation in his hand. 'This is an interesting example of an acrocarpous moss – the sporophyte is growing on the apex of the main axis of the gametophyte.' He glanced at me, as though certain of my shared enthusiasm. 'It only happens in mosses!' and then he started talking about London and when he would like to come this year. And all the time I could think only that Helen must believe me to be a Peeping Tom, and that Kieran was an insensitive clodhopper for all his charm.

That evening, instead of taking her usual place by the hearth, Helen went out into the twilight, leaving the rest of us to play cards. I saw her through the window, slipping across the small garden. When I could make my excuses I went outside and waited by the yard gate for her return. She came slowly back along the avenue, started when she saw me.

'Helen, I must talk to you!' She would have turned away, but I pressed on: 'I just want you to know that I did not follow you last night. I thought Kieran had gone out and because I couldn't sleep with the heat I had an idea that I'd keep him company. I wandered to the pool by chance, thinking I might take a dip. But you were there . . .' I glanced at her face which was turned sideways to me, and added to ease her patent embarrassment, 'It was so dark that I could hardly see you.'

She shook her head impatiently.

'In the moonlight you seemed a spirit, some kind of Nereid. I did not mean to spy on you; I'm not a voyeur. I generally avoid any kind of sneaking.'

When she did not answer, I added, 'If you like, I'll go home tomorrow and not spoil your holiday! I felt that this speech was clumsy, overearnest. But I was desperately in earnest. I looked at her, but her face was set and, even in the half-dark, I could see that she was flushed. I turned and walked away from her across the yard.

'Wait!' Her voice came behind me. She caught up with me. 'I believe you,' she went on. 'I should have known it was you, because Kieran would not have hidden. He would probably have come to the pool and talked to me.'

'Would you have minded?'

'Yes and no. Because he wouldn't see me, if you know what I mean. Irishmen are not good at seeing women. It's their way of coping!'

'Well, I didn't see you either, Helen. Not really. Anyway; I couldn't be sure it was really you. You might have been Diana bathing and have turned me into a hind!'

She gave a soft little snort. 'Some hind. You wouldn't suit the part . . . Besides I don't possess any magic power!'

'Don't you?'

Her laughter broke the tension and we moved together across the yard to the door.

'You asked me once to be your friend,' I said before we went in. 'I would be honoured if you would always so consider me.'

She turned to me and whispered half laughingly, 'My friend? Oh, but I do, Sir Galahad!'

'Will you write to me when I go home?'

'If you like. But don't you have a girlfriend? Kieran would have me believe that you are a terrible ladies' man!'

I cursed Kieran silently. 'No,' I said. 'Who'd have me?'

She laughed again. 'Go away with you. Is it fishing for compliments you are?'

She turned the door handle then and we came into the lamplit kitchen. Kieran was there and Aunt Dru.

'I was just going out to find you,' Kieran said, addressing Helen with a slightly proprietorial air.

'Did you think I'd be eaten by wolves?' she asked a little coolly.

Kieran just smiled, looked at me a little superciliously as though mentally vetting me for the part, then, as though dismissing anything so ludicrous, said he was going to bed.

Mrs Fitzgerald bustled around, asked if I would like some milk and biscuits, or cocoa, or tea, 'although it would keep you awake'.

I declined and as I turned away, saying good night, I heard Helen being asked by her mother whether Monique, the French girl who was coming in the next few days, would sleep in her room. 'The box room,' she said, 'is a bit cramped for a guest.'

'Give her my room, of course,' Helen said. 'I'll take the box room.'

The box room was at the top of the landing, next door to my own.

Chapter Seven

At breakfast next morning Kieran was a little taciturn. Helen had recovered her bounce and was obviously suing for his favour, as though she felt she had slighted him in some way the night before and was trying to make amends.

After the meal Mrs Fitzgerald mentioned that we would have to stock up on groceries in anticipation of Monique's arrival. She would have to pay a visit to Glendockery, she said, giving Kieran a look from the corner of her eye.

Kieran immediately volunteered to drive there and pick up whatever she wanted. 'No bother,' he insisted when she said that he was very good, but that it would be an imposition. 'The drive'll keep the battery charged. The car could do with a bit of a spin.'

'I'll come,' Helen said.

Her mother sniffed. 'What about the washing up, Helen?' she said in a tone which indicated that her daughter was in dereliction of duty.

Helen sighed. 'OK, I'll do it first, then we can go to Glendockery.'

I was already aware that Helen always did the washing up, that when I tried to help I was shooed away by her mother who clearly thought this was 'woman's work'. Now I stepped into the breach.

'I'll do the washing up; I'm a dab hand. I do it at home . . .' I glanced at my oldest friend. 'Ask Kieran!'

Kieran gave a sudden crow of laughter, but did not substantiate the claim.

'But wouldn't you like to come too, Dan?' Helen said.

I watched Kieran's face, but it did not register any great welcome, although he stopped grinning and said politely, 'Do come, old fellow. It might amuse you.'

I immediately suspected that I would be *de trop*, that Helen wanted to be with him and he with her.

'Not at all. I'd rather make myself useful for a change.'

'That's very nice of you, Dan,' Mrs Fitzgerald said.

I went to the sink, poured in hot water from the cauldron on the range and started to wash the dishes. Evidently something in the way I set about this gave away my amateur status, amused Helen. She caught my eye, looked quickly away, as though she were afraid she would laugh out loud.

Kieran turned to her, 'Well, my liggle dear, rush off and get your things.'

Helen obeyed. Kieran disappeared into the drawing room and Aunt Dru hurried over to supervise my efforts at the sink.

'No, no, Dan. You must stack them like this . . .' and she inverted a cup on the oilcloth of the back table and laid each of the washed plates against it. 'Now do you see?' She laughed when I reddened. 'Never mind, I'll take over.' She took the dishcloth from my hand and ousted me from the sink. 'Look, you can dry, if you like.'

I took a red check teatowel from the line before the range and set about drying the dishes. 'Where shall I put them? I asked.

Another chirp of mirth met this enquiry. 'Typical man . . . Oh, just leave them. I'll put them away.

I remembered Rachel's frequent admonitions about my laziness in matters domestic: 'Lord God Almighty, anyone would think yez were a prince of the blood!' I was aware, however, that in this house one person filled that particular role. Kieran never washed up. He might gingerly remove his dirty dishes to the table by the sink, but he never dirtied his hands in any household chore. He brought in the water from the well sometimes, but that did not require that he sully his fingers, and, of course, he enjoyed being chauffeur.

'Let me do something else. I'd like to be useful for a change!'

She looked at me sideways. 'Well, let me see . . . If you really want to be useful you could put a new hinge in the stable door. I hate to see it falling off. You'll find the tools in the box in the scullery.'

Helen came downstairs dressed in a simple starched blue cotton dress with a full skirt and a tie-belt hugging her small waist. She was wearing tan leather sandals with the hint of a heel. Her hair was freshly brushed and the waves of it rippled and sparked in the sunlight from the window. When Kieran arrived he looked at her, leant back on his heels for a moment, as though he were inspecting some interesting species he had found in the heather, before murmuring, 'You're looking nice. Are we ready then?'

I couldn't help the jealousy, even though I had detected no sign in him of the simple awe which her remote and untouched beauty inspired in me.

But even as I looked at Helen, surreptitiously traced the line of her body from top to toe, I became aware that her mother was watching me. I turned to find her with a closed expression tacked on to her face, an expression teetering between doubt and consternation.

Helen, as she left, raised her hand, gave me the sidelong ghost of a smile, and I felt it again, the sense of being read, of being known, of utter and complete complicity.

I went to the back door with Mrs Fitzgerald. I watched Helen get into the car and stood staring after them while Kieran turned the Rolls in the yard and nosed carefully out to the boreen and up to the U-bend, to climb the precipitous slope that joined the road to Glendockery. Then I murmured to my hostess that I would go and find the tool box.

Fixing the old stable door was the work of but a few minutes. The paint had peeled from it and the bottom of the door was rotten. I wondered why it had been left in such a sorry state. It occurred to me then that as the place was going to revert to the Malcolms in the 1990s, when the lease ran out, perhaps the Fitzgeralds felt it wasn't worth their while putting money and trouble maintaining a rapidly diminishing asset. The Irish, I knew, tended to value only property which was long term, fee simple, nailed down, with all the force of the law, to them and to their heirs for ever. Their history had taught them the folly of improving other people's property. The old unjust system of penalizing improvements by rent increases and evictions had sent deep roots into the Irish psyche.

With the hammer in my hand I looked around for something else to work on and found a variety of tasks to which I might bend my new-found skills. I repaired the manger in the old stable, replaced missing screws in hinges, hammered supportive pieces of wood at the back of shaky doors, and when I thought I had exhausted all the possibilities I found a tin of paint at the back of the coach house. I prised open the lid and found some of the contents still liquid. It was then only a matter of finding a still serviceable paintbrush.

I brought the tool box back to the house and entered a kitchen which was fragrant with the scent of freshly baked bread. Mrs Fitzgerald, in her wrapround apron, was cooking potato cakes on the griddle. We had lunch together by the open window, hot, strong tea with hard-boiled egg and salad, freshly buttered griddle cakes, while the beeches in the avenue roared and whispered by turns and the clock ticked on the mantelshelf over the range.

She asked me about London and my parents in a way she had never done. Her voice, which was usually pitched loudly enough for the far corners of the house to hear and obey, now assumed a quieter register, as though, now that she had me alone, it would not be indelicate to ply me with personal questions, providing she did so decorously. She evidently knew about the rupture of my parents' marriage and evidently disapproved. I could see that she viewed it in much the same light as my family contracting some dubious disease; she was sorry for me, but I was of their seed and breed, and however much, in good Christian charity, she might pity the circumstances, she could not but regard me as untainted by them.

She spoke of Helen with concern, said that she was too solitary, tended to read too much and that she would not have allowed her to spend the summer at Lough Corrloch were it not for the visiting French girl, Monique, whom Helen had told about the valley and who said she was longing to see it.

'It took her a long time to get over her stepfather's death, you know – years in fact, although she hid it. She was so angry with him for dying, so questioning as to why. I don't know whether you know she lost her best friend a few years before that? It's been hard for her, but when she finally accepted it, it was because she realized that God has plans for all of us and that we must all bend to His will . . .'

She looked at me for a moment as though weighing my soul, gave me a pious smile and added, 'Our own inclinations must always give way to what God wants from us! Our own inclinations count for nothing!'

I made some noise which could be interpreted one way or the other. I had long since decided that God, if He existed, had more to do than concern Himself with human foibles.

'In fact,' she went on, 'Helen told me once that she would become a nun and not bother with the world at all!'

Some instinct told me not to react, although privately the prospect of Helen entering a convent was too ludicrous to contemplate. I kept a poker face and when my hostess saw that I had nothing to say on this subject she continued: 'Well, I think she saw that she has duties elsewhere . . .'

There was silence, except for the song of the trees.

'It's so lovely here,' I said, ill at ease and unwilling to be drawn on the subject of Helen. I indicated the great outdoors. 'There's such peace!'

'Yes, I love the peace here too . . . and it's nice when Kieran comes. Helen is very fond of him, you know!' she added pointedly, looking straight into my eyes. 'And Kieran is very fond of her. It would be very suitable if . . . well, if they were to decide, someday, to get married . . .' She laughed then, said I must think her a dreadful matchmaker, that Helen was very young, of course, and that all these things took time.

I realized with sudden clarity that she was trying to tell me something, to warn me not to tread on Kieran's patch. My not being a Catholic meant, so far as she was concerned, that I need never consider myself a contender for Helen's hand, and indeed, this unspoken intelligence brought with it, for the first time, the thought of being married to her stunning daughter. I also knew, that provided I understood what she was telling me, provided I knew the terms, she enjoyed having me to stay at Lough Corrloch and found my company stimulating.

I affected as much innocence as was proper, and while I vetted the undertones of what she was really saying, I chatted about London and Cambridge with as much drollery as I could. She listened avidly to the edited extracts of my student life. She had a hearty laugh and the Irish love of the amusing anecdote. She asked me if I had a girlfriend and I said I had.

'Are you fond of her?'

I thought of Marion. But the word 'fond' was innocuous. One could be 'fond' of half the world.

'Of course!'

This seemed to satisfy her, as though I had already been bespoken and was therefore out of the running, and so she relaxed.

I like to think that it was in the course of this exchange that I first decided that I would marry Helen, woo her and win her, and to hell with the lot of them. She deserved better than what they had lined up for her – Kieran who, as she had said herself, did not see her, and a life spent as second fiddle to his self-centred agendas – his little presumptions, his certainty that his perspective was the only window on the world.

Beautiful Helen, the face that would launch a thousand ships, the unconscious grace that commanded homage, deserved more than Irish domesticity, in a setting that would condescend to pat her on the head for good behaviour (good liggle girl), poison her with religiosity, encumber her with too many pregnancies, while denying her the blossoming of her womanhood, the power of her femininity and the fulfilment of her life. It was arrogant, this thought process; but I was young and self-righteous, self-centred myself, insensitive, perhaps, in ways I hardly dreamt of.

The car returned from Glendockery at about four that afternoon. I saw its black thirties shape approaching slowly down the dreadful incline from the main road like an intruder from another era, and hoped, once again, that the brakes were nothing short of perfect. But it came to rest without mishap in the yard and Ivan the Terrible came barking and yapping from the turf shed. The groceries were unloaded; the returning messengers confirmed they had had a sandwich in the village and Helen, having glanced at me and said she was jaded, disappeared upstairs to her room. Kieran made his way lugubriously to the outdoor privy.

When Helen reappeared she was wearing old slacks and a cotton sweater and asked how I had amused myself during her absence. 'Were you sorry you didn't come?'

'He was simply great,' her mother enthused. 'He mended all the out office doors and painted two of them! Now!'

'I would have painted the rest of them,' I murmured, to show that I was not lacking in willingness, 'but the paint ran out!'

'You're very good,' Helen said in a slightly abstracted manner, smiling at me then with sudden affection. 'I'll view your handiwork!'

'By all means,' I said, 'no time like the present.'

Aunt Dru cleared her throat. 'Helen, *a grá*,' she said, 'you're looking a bit tired. Why don't you sit down and have a cup of tea?

There are times in a woman's life,' she added, 'when she needs to take things easy.'

Helen flushed. 'For God's sake, Mam...' She looked at her mother in open exasperation, and around the kitchen as though it were a cage. 'I just want to go outside for a bit and stretch my legs.'

I followed her from the kitchen and around to the stable, where the door was now shining with dark green paint.

'Be careful, it's still wet.'

She touched it with the tip of her finger and said it was tacky, and then turned to me half apologetically and said in a low voice that she hoped I wasn't being bored to death, stuck in the valley and painting stupid old doors, when I might have been in London or somewhere wonderful and enjoying myself.

Her eyes clouded as she said this, and she turned away, walking to the gap in the stone wall which separated the stable yard from the rough land of the hillside, crossed the wall without looking back.

'Where are you going?' I called after her. 'May I come with you?'

She looked back, said of course, if I wanted to. I followed her to the rise of heather-covered land behind the house and then up the side of this bluff along a sheep track, so that in a matter of minutes we were overlooking the house. I looked down and saw Kieran crossing the yard, but he did not raise his head. Helen continued on, disappearing in some dip in the land, and after a while, panting with exertion, I found her seated on a flat rock under an overhang in a dell hidden from all sides.

'This is my den,' she said as I approached. 'I sit up here and dream, or read, whenever I need to get away.' She moved to give me seating room on her boulder, and I sat down beside her.

'What do you like to read?'

'Everything I can get my hands on,' she said with a smile, as though the question were silly.

'For example?' I persisted, realizing that I sounded patronizing, like Kieran, but genuinely curious. If I knew what she read I would know something of who she really was.

She sighed: 'Well, I've gone through all of Dickens up here, and the poetry of people like Blake, Keats, Shelley, Tennyson, Yeats... I've read Kate O'Brien, de Maupassant, Flaubert, Tolstoy,

Dostoevsky, Turgenev, James Joyce – but I couldn't understand *Ulysses* – Canon Sheehan, Arthur Conan Doyle; oh and so many others; it's the great pleasure of my life!'

She gave a small deprecatory laugh. 'There are hundreds of books in this house; most of them are stacked in the dining room. I asked Mam not to get rid of them after Dad died. But I have to hide some of them because she wouldn't approve! She always wants to know what I'm reading. She's terrified I might find something unsuitable which would warp me for all eternity.' She laughed lightly. 'And now, Sir Galahad, what do you like to read?'

'I'm not much of a poetry man but I like good prose; in fact I like the Russians best.'

'So do I!'

'There . . . we do have something in common!'

She turned to look at me squarely, frowning. 'I think we have much more than that in common, only I'm not sure what it is! I felt it a long time ago, when I was little and you came here! Perhaps I knew you in another existence?' She said this musingly, then suddenly reddened as though afraid either that she had said too much or that her comment would be misconstrued.

'I have felt this too, Helen.' Then, as she did not respond, I added rather idiotically, 'Is it true that you thought of becoming a nun? Your mother was talking to me while you were in Glendockery!'

She glowered. 'Mam shouldn't tell you these things. She talks too much. I did toy with the notion once; I was trying to find acceptance in myself . . . for various things. I thought it was the route to God, but now I'm not so sure.'

I waited, hoping she would go on. 'You see,' she continued after a moment, 'I believe in absolutes . . . I think that without them life is meaningless. I want to do something worthwhile with my life.'

'Like what? Will you get married?'

'Of course.'

'And will that be an absolute?'

'Absolutely!' she said, bursting into laughter. 'You're quite an interrogator!'

'Sorry . . . Will you come to London sometime?'

She glanced at me with amused eyes. 'What's that got to do with absolutes?'

'Everything! London is absolutely wonderful!'

Helen narrowed her eyes, but her mouth smiled. 'If I hear the word again I'll thump you!' She raised her small fist threateningly.

'But *will* you come to London?'

'Why not? Maybe next year. Will your mother have me?'

'Oh yes,' I said with alacrity. 'I think you'll like her. She's absolute enough.'

Helen gurgled, but she did not administer the hoped-for thump. 'How dare you make fun of me, Daniel McPherson. But I suppose I asked for it.'

I lay back in the heather, looked at the clear sky, feeling a kind of triumph that I should be here in the heather with Helen O'Callaghan, that I should be her confidant.

'God's in a good mood today,' I said.

'Do you actually believe in God?' Helen asked suddenly. 'Mam says you probably don't.'

'I believe in life,' I said, leaning up on my elbow to look at her and feeling less than charitable towards Mrs Fitzgerald. 'I find it strange enough to be getting on with!' I paused, looking at her serious face. 'I also believe in love, Helen.'

I stopped. I had never before made this avowal to a woman.

She turned her face away. 'Yes,' she whispered. 'So do I! I believe in God and in love. They're the same thing!'

I sat up, put out my hand, pulled her to me and then, sliding my arm around her shoulders, I kissed her lips. It was a very gentle salute, but the sensual resonance of it was not gentle at all. The power of it thrilled from my head to my feet. I controlled myself rigidly, afraid that this beautiful creature would either take flight or turn on me. But she just drew back, wiped her mouth with the back of her hand, and bowed her head. I suspected, I hoped, that she too had been moved by the same force as had shivered through me, although I was not at all pleased that she should have wiped her lips.

'Don't be annoyed with me. It's just a gesture of friendship,' I whispered, half sick with desire, but frightened that I had either offended or shocked her.

She frowned, raised her eyes to look at me and I tried to read her response. 'Yes . . . I know . . . a gesture of friendship,' she said with an uncertain laugh, standing up suddenly and moving away.

I followed her down the hillside, around the bluff and back to the house. All the way I was in turmoil. Had I done wrong? If she was so damned religious how might she not dress up our brief encounter?

'Have I offended you, Helen?' I asked as we approached the avenue. 'I didn't mean to!'

'You didn't. You have different perspectives.' She sighed. 'You see, I have been brought up to believe in a very strict code. I have never kissed a boy. For example, I will never . . . you know . . . do things that are wrong . . .' She flushed. 'You know what I mean. Kieran says that you have already . . . made love . . . several times. Is that true?'

I was stumped at this directness. Her censure was patent as was her full-blooded disgust. I urgently wanted to break Kieran's head.

'No,' I lied. 'No, I too believe in high standards. I was brought up to a fair degree of self-discipline myself, you know!' I tried to sound miffed and succeeded, probably because I was so furious at Kieran and his busy mouth.

She touched my arm. 'I'm sorry. Kieran shouldn't say things like that!'

'You know why he says them?' I demanded. 'He says them to put you off me.'

She laughed. 'Don't be silly. He just thinks you're a bit of a pagan.' She smiled. 'So do I, for that matter. But we're old friends just the same, you and I!' But her laugh sounded relieved, as though the idea that I had made love with someone else was a spectre which she was glad to exorcize.

When we reached the house I went upstairs and flung myself on my bed. It was crazy. The most gorgeous girl in the world, a girl full of a latent sensuality she was completely unaware of, talking and thinking in a rationale that smelt of closed piety. Her talk of my having made love elsewhere forced the comparison between her and Marion. There could be no comparison. The latter craved the endorsement of the world; while Helen stood back and wondered if the world was even worth her noticing. Helen was centred, proud, even haughty in her idealism; while Marion had never paused to measure reality against her own worth.

But the red-haired Venus was very young. I tried to dish out mature self-counsel. Time would do so much. Play it slowly, I told myself; play it very gently. The girl will be a woman. Someday . . . oh, someday!

I was almost afraid to look at her at supper; her eyes averted whenever I did, just as they regarded Kieran with a new speculation. For his part, he was waxing voluble, taking off the shopkeeper and the butcher in Glendockery with a mimicry which convulsed us all.

'Ah now, Mrs O'Brien . . . that's a grand bit of steak. Sure you'd sin eatin' it.'

'If that was the worst thing the divil can get me for, Peader *a bhuachaill*, I'd better order the coffin while the goin's good.'

Helen said accusingly, 'You almost made me laugh in the shop. I was afraid to look at you.'

'Never mind,' Kieran said. 'Your little French friend will be here soon and you will have suitable female companionship of your own age.' He sounded like a Victorian duenna addressing a child. 'We will all have to sharpen our parleyvoo.'

'She's coming to learn English,' Helen responded with her chirp of a laugh, 'so you can save yourself the trouble!'

Kieran looked at me and winked. 'This fellow here,' he announced, 'speaks French fluently; he will put us all to shame.'

'If Monique is to learn English the best thing to do is not to speak French to her at all,' I murmured.

'Very proper!' Kieran said with mockery.

Mrs Fitzgerald looked at me as though Kieran's comment about my fluency had placed me among life's exotica. 'Is that true,' she asked, 'that you speak French fluently?'

'Well, yes,' I said. 'Fluently enough. My mother was a Québecoise and I went to school in the French Lycée in London.'

'Sure where would he leave it?' Kieran demanded in his affected brogue. 'With all that goin' for him wouldn't he be the half-eejit if he couldn't blather *en Français*.'

He went on in this vein, which provoked laughter in his hostess and a small apologetic smile from Helen. Sometimes I found Kieran's badinage wearying. Then he gave me the open candid grin which was so infectious, as though to say, 'Hey, don't take things so seriously, old fellow!'

The French girl, Monique, arrived on the following Saturday. Kieran, Helen and I went to meet her at the airport. I could sense

Helen's excited anticipation at the prospect of her arrival. En route to Collinstown she chattered about France, about the little town of Amboise in the Loire valley where Monique lived and where Helen had spent three weeks the year before.

'There's a huge old château there; it used to be one of the seats of François Premier – he was the king back in fifteen something – and it was supposed to have an underground passage to Le Clos Lucé – the house nearby owned by Leonardo da Vinci. I was there,' Helen said, turning to me. 'I was in the house where Leonardo da Vinci died!'

I digested this. 'Does Monique have brothers?' I asked.

Helen sighed in exasperation. 'What's that got to do with Leonardo da Vinci?'

Kieran chortled. 'He's trying to find out if you were importuned by Frenchies. He has a proper concern for your moral welfare.'

Helen made a small sound of exasperation. 'Monique has one sister . . . she's very small,' she said. 'There were no boys around, except one or two friends.'

'They're all pansies anyway,' Kieran opined; 'Frenchmen!'

'Don't be so ridiculous,' Helen said crossly. 'They certainly are not!'

Kieran glanced at her, grinning. 'I was joking, my dear.'

I heard the 'my' and I heard the 'dear'. I smiled at Helen through my jealousy when she turned to glance at me. She gave me a mischievous smile devoid of coyness. That first small kiss, that moment of eternity, was evidently safely forgotten.

Monique turned out to be blonde and blue-eyed. After initial introductions she eyed Kieran and me with a friendly curiosity and then looked at Helen as though wondering how she happened to have with her two young men, and only one of them even tenuously related. She was neither tall nor small, this young French girl, but put together with a certain Gallic fragility, as though bird-boned. She was not, despite her delicate colouring, a beauty, but she held herself with such assurance, moved her hips when she walked and, all in all, radiated such absolute confidence that the world was a good place in which to be a woman, that she exercised a definite seductiveness.

Helen was clearly overjoyed to have her friend with her and sat in the back of the car with her on the return journey, while I took the passenger seat. The girls were chattering; Kieran was concentrating on driving, putting in his oar from time to time, pointing out, as we came to the lights at Whitehall, the distant mountains and the city spread below.

For some reason I found myself speculating on what kind of man he really was, what made him tick. For all his bonhomie there was something inscrutable about him, something secret. He was always in the same mood – the playful mood which prodded others into pleasantry – and this, I now felt, in so far as it was indefinitely sustained, was unnatural. It was as though he always felt himself to be on the stage. The unconsidered spontaneous reactions of the ordinary person were not his. I had never, ever, seen him angry or depressed, at least not since childhood. Did this mean that he was profound, that he had depts which none of us could plumb? Did it indicate a lack; or did it mean that he was so careful of the impression he made that he watched himself, in company, every minute? For the first time it occurred to me that if any of this were true, it could, in fact, mean that something either powerful or lacking lay at the basis of Kieran's charm.

I had been cool with him since Helen had told me of how he had squealed on me. I realized I had made a mistake in divulging to him anything about my private life, realized that his discretion was not to be taken for granted. I wanted to tackle him and tell him what a skunk I thought he was, but decided against it. I needed his continued goodwill to come again to Lough Corrloch.

We drove back from the airport in increasingly buoyant mood, which was mostly due to Helen and Monique giggling in the back of the car. They chatted in a lingua franca composed of French and English, while Kieran looked at me from time to time, adverting to them with a sideways turn of the eyes and raising his eyebrows indulgently. He asked Monique questions about France and said he was thinking of bringing the car over the following spring 'for a bit of a holiday'.

'Zis car is very wonderful,' Monique said. 'But France is a very big country and you will have to make sure zat it is able . . .'

Kieran assured her that he would make sure it would be able, adding a little lugubriously that he thought it was able already.

This provoked a laugh. 'Don't mind Monique, Kieran,' Helen said. 'She's teasing.'

I glanced back and saw that this was true. Monique had her head hunched into her shoulders, and her lips compressed with the attitude of a girl trying to restrain her mirth. I became aware that they were a catalyst, the pair in the back, each to the other, and that the two young men in the front of the car were fair game for successive fits of the giggles. I thought this was in proper order where Kieran's pomposity was concerned, but was not too sure where I fitted in to the peals of mirth behind me. I found it unsettling until I decided that Kieran and I were probably screamingly funny and didn't know it.

As we went into the mountains the sun came out and the whole wonderful vista was there in all its glory, mile upon mile of moor and mountain and valley. Monique ceased her chatter to gaze spellbound out of the window.

'*Mais c'est vraiment merveilleuse*,' she breathed.

'Of course it is,' Helen said. '*C'est ma patrie!*'

Mrs Fitzgerald made a big fuss of Monique. At supper she opened one of the bottles of Sancerre which Monique had brought as a gift. Monique and Helen refused a glass, but Kieran and I accepted. The wine was tepid, although it had been left in a bucket of water, but nonetheless the supper table was very mirthful. I had never seen Helen so joyous. I was spellbound by the change from grave young woman to gleeful schoolgirl who lost herself in gales of giggles over apparent trifles.

Monique responded to Kieran's amusing blandishments with arch indifference and I wondered if this piqued him. She answered questions freely, unconcerned if she made mistakes, and used charming idioms which were translated directly from French.

While I watched the two girls it occurred to me that one of them was already something of a woman of the world; her giggles were never as full of surprise, nor of innocence as the other's. There never waited behind Monique's laughter the gravity that lingered in attendance on all of Helen's utterances, as though she was perpetually challenged by standards that were not entirely human.

To show I was not, after all, a pagan, I accompanied them to Mass the next day. This was in the limestone church at Glendockery where the congregation was still segregated, as though men and women did not belong to each other, but to the antiseptic perceptions of a religious police. Men had the pews to the right of the aisle while the women had those on the left. Our entrance caused a few whispers. We found ourselves appropriate pews and I watched my companions. On the other side of the aisle I saw Mrs Fitzgerald incline in fervent prayer. I saw Monique assume the bearing of the pious ingénue, although she eyed the men's side of the church more than I would have thought was strictly necessary. I saw Helen in her white gloves, lost in her own world, stand and kneel, close her eyes and bend her head. I watched her, drinking in the sight of her, the grace, the innocence, the other-world quality she had, before I realized that Monique, who was in the pew behind her, was watching me.

I saw that Helen was immersed in prayer and would even have gone for Communion, to impress her, if it had not occurred to me that she would think it odd – for an unbeliever.

Kieran was involved in the collection during the Mass, and I put two bob into the plate, tried to catch his eye and failed. He was wearing an expression of pious abstraction.

The sermon was extraordinary; it was given by the curate who was fired with what would now be regarded as fundamentalist zeal. It revolved around sex and the carryings-on in the boreens roundabout when the weekly dance in the local parish hall was ended. The sermon had to be a little oblique, because of the presence of children, but hellfire was mentioned. I watched Helen from the corner of my eye, but she seemed intent on what the priest was saying. Monique, on the other hand, was covertly examining the men's side of the church as though trying to suss out the principal culprits.

When Mass was over people gathered in knots outside to talk. Mrs Fitzgerald latched on to someone from the village and launched herself into a conversation which bore all the hallmarks of something which would go on for the day. The priest joined us young people, where we stood apart reading the tombstones in the adjoining graveyard, Monique driving us into sudden snorts of laughter with her accent and her irreverent mournful rendition of '*la poésie*' offered here and there to the dead.

'Who's this now?' the priest demanded of Helen, and she immediately introduced Monique and me.

'Father, this is Dan McPherson from London and Monique Bouthemy from France. This is Father Rafferty, the new curate!'

The priest spoke jovially, asked Monique which part of France she came from, but he reserved most of his attention for me. Sensing this, the others drifted away a few feet into the cemetery proper and left me to his mercy.

'You're not a Catholic!' he said almost conspiratorially, dropping his voice, as though this were something to be discussed in low tones behind closed doors.

'No.'

'I saw you at Mass. You seemed unfamiliar with the ritual!'

'I'm a Protestant – well, sort of . . . I'm really an agnostic.'

'Ah . . .' He looked at me with compassion. 'Are you interested in the Church?'

'No, Father.'

He sighed. 'Well, you're welcome in any case. What do you think of Lough Corrloch?'

'I love it!'

'It's a great beauty spot – and of course there's a grand young beauty living there,' he added, with a barely perceptible inclination of his head in Helen's direction.

I did not move my head, unwilling to alert Helen to the fact that she was topical.

'She's the best,' the priest went on in even tones, 'the flower of the flock, the purest girl you'll ever meet, high-minded and idealistic.'

I was silent, wondering why he was talking to me like this. Did he think me a potential marauder on Helen's virtue?

'But she's also innocent,' he added, looking at me with an inscrutable expression, 'and the innocent are impressionable, especially by the more worldly-wise.'

As I looked into the eyes of the priest I knew with sudden crystal clarity why he was saying all this. Helen had been to confession; she had told him about the kiss in the heather. What else had she told this little man in black? That I had watched her while she had bathed naked in the pool? Was that a sin too?

A shadow moved across the sun. The spectre of sin darkened the landscape, oppressed the sunlit churchyard, and again I felt the defamation of sexuality, the wedge driven by religion between people and their own power. I excused myself and left the priest, joining the others.

'Look at zis,' Monique was saying, 'a whole family who died in ze same year.'

Over her shoulder, I saw the weathered Celtic cross, made out the inscription through the lichen, saw the date: 1848.

'It was the Famine,' Helen said quietly, as though the Famine had been yesterday.

On the way home Aunty Dru was waxing voluble about the new curate and the sermon, which Kieran had commented on because it had an unusual topic for a Sunday.

'He was right. There's shocking carryings-on after these dances. I remember in the old days . . . the parish priest would be out, and woe betide anyone courting in the bushes ... Sometimes I think the country was better off without these dance halls; they've been the cause of more girls getting into trouble . . .'

'For God's sake, Mam,' Helen burst out later in the pantry when she evidently thought she was not overhead, 'don't be going on about immorality and things.'

'I will go on about it, Helen. It's a good thing that it's brought out and people are warned about the danger to their souls, especially young people. Oh you can purse your lip, miss, but I can tell you one thing: if there was a choice between seeing you pregnant out of wedlock and seeing you dead, I'd rather see you dead!'

I crept away, back to the yard where Monique was making friends with Ivan the Terrible and Kieran was looking on phlegmatically.

After supper that evening Monique roused herself from her corner of the sofa and began looking through the rows of cloth-bound volumes on the shelves near the fireplace. She found a book, brought it back to the sofa. It was still bright outside, and I leant, from my chair by the window, to pull back fully the heavy old curtain and maximize the last of the light. Helen and I were playing cards; Aunt Dru and Kieran were in the kitchen; their voices could be heard, his low and slightly teasing, hers louder and ready with sudden forays of laughter at things he said.

When they came into the room Aunt Dru asked Monique what she was reading.

'Eet ees a book by Oscar Wilde.' She made two syllables out of Wilde, which might have pleased him. Mrs Fitzgerald took the book from her, saw that it was *The Picture of Dorian Gray*.

'Oh him,' she said, dropping her voice. 'You could find something better than this to read. Wilde was . . . you know . . .' she gesticulated with her hands, 'one of those perverts.' Her voice minced, as though the words had been picked up with tongs.

'Pardon?' Monique asked. 'A what you say?'

'A pervert . . . you know a dirty creature.'

'She means a homosexual,' Helen said.

'*Ah oui*,' Monique said, as though this was a matter of no moment. '*Je comprends*.'

Mrs Fitzgerald shook her head. Kieran shook his too, his expression even more severe than hers.

'Filthy faggot,' he muttered with a disgust more heated than I thought necessary.

'Really, Kieran!' Mrs Fitzgerald expostulated.

Monique directed a curious, lingering gaze on Kieran, then allowed her hostess to select another book for her, one of Beatrix Potter's.

I left Lough Corrloch at the end of the following week. I extracted a promise from Helen that she would write to me and I said I would reply. She also, jokingly, half promised to visit me in London.

'If your mother will ask me and if Kieran is going, Mam will probably let me go,' she said, as though hearing my doubts. 'I'd love to see London.'

On the eve of my departure I went halfway up the steep hillside at the back of the house. I had been looking for Helen, hoping to say goodbye to her on our own, hoping to find her in her dell. But I heard a voice behind me and saw Monique, in slacks and wellies, scramble up the incline behind me. 'You are going for a walk?' she called. 'I too will come! Maybe we will find where ees Helen.'

There was nothing for it but to wait for her. I was pleased to see that she puffed and panted even more than I did. When she came within a couple of feet of me she said, 'Zis is a very hard climb! When you go back to London you will be glad to walk on ze flat ground!'

I said that this was indeed true and would have changed my course, so that Helen would not think I had intruded on her privacy with someone in tow, when Monique indicated that she was *au fait* with Helen's arrangements: 'If we go zis way we may find Helen. Zere is a place she likes . . .'

I followed her, but as we came in sight of Helen's dell, Monique put a hand up to stop me. Then I heard Helen's voice, low and upset, 'Please leave me alone!' She could neither see us nor know we were close by; she was either talking to herself or to some other person whose presence was irksome. Monique indicated by a finger to her lips that I should make no sound and that we should retrace our steps.

'Eet ees not wise to come when a person wishes to be alone.'

We stood uncertainly for a moment and then I saw the movement further down the slope. It was Kieran, coming from the direction of Helen's hideaway. He was making his way back to the house.

Monique watched him with narrowed eyes. I heard the words she muttered under her breath: '*Mon Dieu, il y a quelque chose là-bas qui me donne des frissons dans le dos!*' She glanced at me, as though suddenly suspecting that I had understood, but I pretended ignorance.

'Did you say something?'

'No . . . He is a good friend of yours – Kieran?'

'Yes. My oldest friend!'

'*Ah, bon*,' she said politely. Then she added: 'You zink that Helen, she loves him?'

'Does she?'

She raised her hands, palms upward. '*Mais oui*. He is important to her.'

'I see.'

'You have not the jealousy?'

'Why should I be jealous?'

She shrugged, looked at me with cool matter-of-fact eyes. 'Oh, if I love someone . . . like you love her . . . I would have the jealousy. But,' and here she regarded me musingly as though wondering what my reaction would be, 'I zink that he is very bad for her!'

'Why do you think that?'

She shrugged. 'I zink people try to . . . create other people; maybe she try to make Kieran be . . . someone else! But it is a waste. He cannot be what he is not!'

I stumbled back down the hillside without another word. But my regard for the small, slight French girl had blossomed into respect.

That night and many a night after, I thought of Monique's words, the words she had whispered in French while watching Kieran appear near Helen's dell and disappear towards the house, 'There is something down there which gives me the shivers.'

When I said goodbye to her next day I found a moment, mindful that she would be in the valley for the next month, to whisper to her: 'Mind Helen for me.' She looked at me without speaking, widened her eyes in a Gallic gesture, as though I were being absurd.

Helen came along, extended her hand. 'Goodbye, Sir Galahad.'

Monique looked from one of us to the other, gave a private knowing smile as though she knew something we did not suspect ourselves.

Kieran drove me to Dun Laoghaire to catch the boat, chatted with relaxed bonhomie. The girls had stayed behind in the valley; Aunt Dru was taking them in her Mini to see the monastic ruins of Glendalough.

As there were only the two of us in the car Kieran, for once, answered questions about himself and his plans for the future. He wanted to do postgraduate studies in Trinity College. But he kept returning to the question of London and James and mentioned again about his proposed motoring trip to France.

I told him I would pass on his message and then I mentioned, as casually as I could, the subject which had been burning me.

'Helen would like to visit London. When you are coming next, why not ask her to come with you?'

He considered this for a moment as though it were a novel idea. 'I suppose it would do the poor kid good. What would your mother say?'

'Oh, she'd welcome her with open arms! You know Mummy! She even told me to invite her.'

'Your mother is hospitality itself. But we'll have to clear it with Aunt Dru. She's very protective of her only kid, you know!'

'I know. The woman is a religious nut!' I glanced at Kieran to see how he took this comment, but he just smiled. 'She told me the other day that we were all part of the Mystical Body of Christ!'

Kieran shrugged. 'She has strong beliefs.'

'But if you moot it to her, Kieran, if you tell her we're a good solid God-fearing family, she'll surely agree. You seem to be the white-haired boy. She listens to you. To tell you the truth,' I added carefully, 'I think she has you all set up as the prospective bridegroom.'

Kieran started. 'The prospective what? You mean . . . with Helen?'

'Of course.'

He laughed as though I had said something too ridiculous for reply. 'You can't be serious?' He changed gear, grunted. 'Christ, Dan, what an imagination you have. Me married to Helen! Have you lost your marbles?'

I made some light response, but I was greatly cheered.

'No, you'd be more suitable yourself – if you weren't a pagan, of course,' he smiled, 'and if you weren't already . . .' he raised his eyebrows, '. . . carnally bespoken, as it were.'

I felt as though the wind had been knocked out of me. 'I'm not "carnally bespoken"!'

Kieran glanced at me. 'Sorry,' he said with a half-laugh. 'What I meant was you're involved with someone else, an adult. Helen is a child!'

The car shuddered over a pothole.

'Dru thinks of me as a sort of son,' he said in a pragmatic voice. 'That's all. Uncle Tim left Lough Corrloch to her, but only for her life. I'm to have the leasehold reversion – if there is one – when she kicks the bucket! It creates, at least in her mind, a sort of nexus with me, if I can use that word to describe her thought processes.'

'But you'll be ancient when you inherit!'

'It won't happen. The lease is due to run out in the nineties. Unless she dies prematurely, it will expire before she does; but she makes a thing of it!' He glanced at me. 'You know what she's like!'

'Well,' I said, bringing the conversation back to Helen, 'do ask her if Helen can come with you. I think she could do with some cheering up!'

He seemed surprised at this, frowned and asked why. I thought of the words which Monique and I had heard on the hillside and remembered how we had seen him shortly afterwards negotiate the incline towards the house.

'I just got the impression when she came in yesterday evening that she was upset!'

'Oh that!' he said vaguely. 'She gets a bit upset sometimes; she's emotional – gets involved with the characters in those novels of hers. I've often found her weepy over some silly little tragedy, some bloody awful dead heroine. You know, she sits up there on the hillside, stuck in those books. I've known her to stay there for days on end when the weather is good, only appearing for her dinner. She's out of her mother's clutches there; Dru hates the climb. But I've often told Helen it's not healthy to live through fiction.' He sighed. 'But when I try to interest her in reality, in the flora and fauna around her, in the minerals, the rocks . . .' He shrugged, sighed again. 'She used to be interested once, but now she more or less tells me to get lost. I must be losing my touch.'

I searched him unsuccessfully for any sign of disingenuousness.

'By the way, I hope I didn't bore you, old fellow, with my waffle?' he said genially when he saw me off. 'You were a bit subdued part of the time. Sometimes I need to be told when to shut up!' He smiled at me a little mournfully. 'I like the valley, but it can be quite a strain, you know, being the prop for poor old Dru and little Helen. Sometimes I feel like the male lead in a piece of crazy theatre. You probably found me a pain in the arse.'

I was taken aback. I demurred, shook hands with real friendship, feeling suddenly ashamed.

Chapter Eight

James looked at me closely on the evening of my return home. He had come in just as Rachel had zestfully walloped the old brass gong outside the kitchen door. We trooped downstairs to eat.

'How's the bold Kieran? And, dare I ask, did you find the fair maid lived up to expectations?'

Rachel dished out lamb chops which she had prepared with her own delicious tomato and garlic marinade; Charles Sauvingler, who had joined us, opened the wine and poured my mother a glass. I watched him with new awareness, saw how he bent towards her, saw his tenderness. My mother was blooming. Initially I had feared for her vulnerability with this Charles Sauvingler, but I had come to sense in her a new toughness; it was as though having concealed some essential part of herself out of the reach or the ken of any man, she was now prepared to make merry with the rest in a way which was new to her.

I turned to James who had one eyebrow raised and was about to repeat his question.

'Will you listen for a minute?' I said. 'Kieran wants to go to France next Easter. He has bought an old Rolls, 1934 model – it looks like something from a war film – and he has some notion about taking it to Paris. He wants to know if you would be interested, but said he would write.'

James, to my surprise, evinced instant pleasure at this prospect.

'What a lark!' he said. 'Driving a Rolls to Paris! Sounds ever so decadent! You mean, of course,' he added hurriedly, 'that he would bring the car to London and we would drive from here?'

'Something like that! But be warned! The car is a rattletrap and may never reach London, never mind Paris!'

'Mmn,' he said with a kind of purr. 'Don't be such a killjoy. I must apply my great brain to the burning question of whether I can get the time off!'

'What if the car breaks down halfway?' my mother enquired with her maternal frown.

'Fiddlesticks,' James retorted.

After the ensuing silence my mother leant towards me and asked gently, 'And how were Helen and Mrs Fitzgerald? You haven't said a word about them.'

'Mrs Fitzgerald lives through her daughter,' I said in a sudden burst of bitter candour, taking a gulp of the vintage burgundy Charles had brought with him, and letting its velvet smoothness slide down to soothe the soul. 'She is an overprotective mother who realizes she has a daughter of rare quality and wants to capitalize on her.' I glanced at my mother's suddenly attentive face. 'Never mind, it's just a feeling. I think it would do Helen good to get out of the place for a while.'

'My, my,' James murmured with a sententious growl. 'I thought this Lough Corrloch was the gateway to paradise. It now seems that there is a worm in the apple!'

'Did you invite her to London?' my mother asked, ignoring her elder son.

'She would like to come.'

'Well then . . . ?'

'She might come with Kieran, but you will have to write to her mother to invite her.'

'And you would like that?'

There was a loud sigh from James. 'For God's sake, Mummy, can't you see he's just panting for the fairy damsel to cross the threshold?' He shook his head at his food, intoned softly: '"Oh, what can ail thee, Knight at arms Alone and palely loitering . . ." He wants to palely loiter,' he added, 'with intent, if at all possible. Ha-ha . . .'

'Oh shut up, James,' my mother said. 'I shall write immediately,' she continued to me. 'You can enclose my note with your bread-and-butter letter.'

I met Charles's kind, shrewd eyes. He was attending very closely on every nuance of what I said. He smiled, made a gesture with his hands which was entirely French, as much as to say that he divined my problem, but that love would find out a way. 'Thanks, Mummy,' I murmured, giving Charles the kind of look which I hoped would show me as a man of the world.

'But you still haven't told us,' James persisted, 'what the fair Helen is like. I mean, it was aeons since you had last laid eyes on her – she was just a little kid! What's she like? Is she the cure for glandular fever?'

'Shove off, James. If and when she comes you will see what she is like!'

'She's too young for him, Mummy,' he keened. 'My brother is a cradle snatcher. The girl is but sixteen.' This reminded him of another verse and he was off again: ' "When I was but sixteen or so I went into a golden land . . ." '

Charles sighed, said something *sotto voce* in French, at which my mother laughed.

'Oh for goodness' sake, James,' she said fondly, 'will you leave your brother alone?'

'But I can't leave him alone,' he said reasonably. 'I'm dying of curiosity!'

Rachel came to the rescue. She had been whisking something in the pantry and now reappeared under full throttle. 'In the name of God,' she said, 'will yez let dacent people eat their dinner in peace?'

James grimaced and applied himself to his lamb chops. Rachel, who had words at will, was the only one who was able to deal with him.

I saw that Charles was trying to suppress his laughter.

Later that evening there was a knock on my door and James came into my room. I was unpacking, hanging up my tweed jacket in the wardrobe and throwing dirty clothes into a heap for the wash. He sank into the armchair in the corner, legs thrown over one arm, and looked at me with a smile.

'Well, old thing, spill the beans. Tell old Doctor James everything. Is she absolutely gorgeous?'

I looked at the languid person of my brother with a great deal of affection. 'In a word – yes!'

'Did you roger her?'

I started. 'Roger her – Helen? Are you out of your mind? If you knew what she was like, if you knew anything, you wouldn't ask such a question.'

'Sor-ree,' he murmured smoothly. 'I was just being nosy. Not even a teensy-weensy little kissikins?'

I thought of the touch of her lips, the electricity of the contact, the way she had withdrawn and stared at her hands. 'No,' I said, 'and mind your own bloody business!'

'Mmn,' my brother said, watching me with a grin as though he would read my soul. He suddenly seemed to me, there in the evening light, very young, almost childish. It was as though he were really trying to evaluate not just my own mores, but those of the wider society; sometimes he surprised me by his apparent ignorance, as though the ways of the world were something he could not easily read, something of which, despite his age and his profession, he was still unsure. In seeing him, in his naïvety, it was as though I had sloughed off some old skin, some old mode of evaluating reality and I felt again the certainty that so much of perceived truth is nothing more than our own invention, concocted by us to put a shape on experience.

'So tell me about the bold Kieran,' he asked gently then, and I sensed a sudden diffidence in the question. 'Did he get his degree? What does he want to do next?'

'He's waiting for his results, wants to do postgraduate something or other – probably a thesis on small bug-eyed monsters or weird flora. Ask him when you see him. Why don't you write to him? You don't have to wait for his letter!'

'I might.'

Then I asked him if he had seen Dad.

'No.' His tone had changed to one of abrupt decision. The light went out of his eyes.

'Oh James,' I said, 'isn't it time to heal the old wounds? He's still your father and he loves you. He's getting married to Kelly, you know, when the divorce is through!'

'I know. He needn't expect me at his wedding!'

'You're being unreasonable!'

'You would really expect me to attend that wedding and leave Mummy on her own – on a day like that?'

'She won't be on her own. She has Charles, and you can be quite sure that she has come to terms with everything. She has come out of this much stronger than any of us thought she would.'

'Maybe. But remember the price. She still won't see him and I'll never forgive him!'

His face, which shortly before had been bright with mockery and curiosity, had darkened.

'I used to worship him,' he muttered. 'I used to think he stood against everything that was low and treacherous.'

'But he does.'

James shook his head.

'You are a funny mixture,' I said after a moment. 'Anyone would think you were all froth, all bubble. But you run as deep and dark as they come!'

He smiled a little grimly. 'Everyone does, old thing. That's what you don't seem to realize! Everyone does . . . run deep and dark as they come . . .'

I went to see my father the following week. Kelly answered the door. She did not look well, much thinner than when I had last seen her. She greeted me kindly, her face brightening as I handed her the bouquet I had selected with some care: roses. She smelled them, breathing in deeply.

'Kelly,' I said, 'I want to apologize for my behaviour the last time I saw you. I behaved like a pig.'

She shook her head and drew me into the sitting room. 'Never mind all that. I did understand and I don't want you to say another word about it. Children always try to own their parents!'

This made me uncomfortable. It put a complexion on the thing which dragged me down several rows of pegs.

'Where's Dad?'

'He popped out a moment ago. He'll be back in a jiffy. I'll make some coffee – or would you prefer tea?' I said I would die for a cup of tea and followed her into the kitchen.

It was a compact little room, overlooking the courtyard, with a trailing plant hanging in the window. She put on the kettle and stood uncertainly, as though still fearful that I might still be judging her. She seemed vulnerable, uncertain. Her strong black hair had been cut in a bob, and framed a face that was newly pinched and hollow.

She prepared a tray with cups, saucers, plates, spoons, cake forks, moving in a semi-automated kind of way, the china clinking.

'There are some napkins in that drawer behind you,' she said.

I opened the drawer, found the napkins, and as I extracted them something fell out. I stared at the small blue woollen bootees on the floor, picked them up uncertainly. 'I'm sorry,' I said, seeing her stricken face. For a moment I thought she would cry, but she just took the two tiny baby boots, rubbed the palm of her hand over them in a fleeting caress, and put them back in the drawer.

'I can't bear to throw them out. I crocheted them myself,' she said, turning away. She hunched up her shoulders, as though they would yield the strength she needed and, acting on impulse, I reached out and put my arms around her.

'Dad told me. I'm so sorry, Kelly.'

We heard the key in the hall door and she pulled away from me, wiping her eyes. She put a finger to her lips.

'Not a word,' she whispered, shaking her head furiously. 'Not a word!'

I made the tea and carried the tray into the sitting room as my father emerged from the hall.

'Dan!' he exclaimed with delight. 'My dear boy . . .' and I could see how pleased he was that I was helping Kelly, that we were on familiar terms. He looked into the kitchen, but she was arranging the flowers I had given her. She brought them out in a big glass vase and put them on a table in the sitting room, saying how lovely they were.

We had the tea with a chocolate walnut cake.

'I made it myself in honour of your visit. An old recipe from back home.'

Kelly told me about her home in Tennessee, glossed over her short first marriage. 'He was unfaithful and I divorced him,' she said simply. Then she described the job in the American Diplomatic Service which had taken her to London.

I wanted her to go on, to hear everything about her life, but she suddenly changed the subject and asked me what I had been doing with the summer. 'Your father tells me you've been to Ireland?'

I described Lough Corrloch, the valley, the lake, the inhabitants, Glendockery and its population of eager conversationalists, Kieran, whom my father remembered well, Mrs Fitzgerald, and Helen, whom he had never met.

'Are you . . . a bit sweet on Helen?' Kelly asked with a smile. 'Or maybe I shouldn't be asking personal questions.'

For an instant I wondered whether I should deflect this question with a reply which would dismiss it. But I looked at her open face and told the truth.

'Yes. But Helen is terribly young, only sixteen!'

My father seemed amused. 'Well, well,' he said. 'It's a strange feeling – seeing one's son romantically involved! Yesterday's baby, yesterday's piggyback rider, yesterday's midnight wailer, confronted by passion!'

'Thanks, Dad! It may have escaped you but I've moved on a bit since,' I said as drily as I could. 'Anyway, I think Helen's mother has her all lined up for Kieran! So there may not be much chance for me!'

'She's a child!' he expostulated. 'Give her a few years. She's much too young to know her mind. Goes for you too, you know! In the meantime meet lots of other girls.'

I glanced at Kelly, who had narrowed her eyes. I realized that she knew my father had not understood. But I felt that she did, that she understood intuitively that Helen was my dream.

'Sometimes, you know, darling,' she said softly to my father, 'it happens like that. Sometimes when people are very young . . . love is an imprint, almost a matter of identity. That kind of love cannot be overridden, cannot be forgotten. It's as though someone is allowed in while the door is still open . . . and so becomes part of who one is!'

He leant across and took her hand. 'You're a romantic, Kelly. Does it matter that we didn't know each other as youngsters?'

'But I did,' she said with sudden sparkle. 'I knew you. I just hadn't met you.'

He laughed and squeezed her hand, glanced at me as though remembering certain etiquette, and then held it tighter.

He came with me as far as the tube. I had agreed to make an appointment to see Sir William Ryce in his chambers in the Temple; my father had spoken to him about me. I knew that this was the next chapter in my life and wondered if I would succeed in impressing the eminent QC with my potential. I experienced the energy like a burn, the wish to succeed, to drag forth the possibility within me, or at least the potential I prayed was in me. I was a believer in the future, the future I wanted to make fit for Helen if I could ever, by any means within my power, persuade her to have me.

I received a letter from Helen a few days later.

Dear Dan,

Here's the promised correspondence! I hope you got home safely. Mam has just received your letter and the enclosed letter one from your mother (it was terribly nice of her to write and is mulling over the invitation. Thank you for that. She will let me go, I think, provided Kieran accompanies me. (When do you think I will manage to convince her that I'm grown up?)

I'm looking forward very much to next Easter and have got out the atlas and traced the route from Holyhead. It will be a very long drive to London, but I'm dying for it.

Kieran is going back to Dublin tomorrow. He is really very good to us, looking after us and giving us so much of his time. Monique teases him; sometimes I wonder if she even likes him. She whistled at his socks this morning (the red and green check ones – I don't know if you noticed them and he looked at them, raising his eyebrows in the way he does, and said they were a present from an enemy! Isn't he funny?

It was very nice to see you again. You're all grown up, of course, but still the same kind Dan. It was very sweet of you to remember that I asked you all those years ago to be my friend. I was such a forward brat, but I do treasure your friendship and I will write to you more often. You can write to me at school next year as the sixth years' letters are not opened (this is a recent big concession!).

Kieran got a double first. We are all very proud of him. He will be starting a Master's in Trinity in October. I wouldn't be surprised if he won the Nobel Prize some day, he's so clever!

So between clever you and clever him I know two brilliant men! I'll have to pull up my own socks now and try to emulate all this prowess.

Must dash! My presence is required below decks. Kieran is

driving Monique and me to Glendockery and I'll post this letter there.

Love, Helen.

I held this missive to my lips, breathed it in, hoping for some scent which would be quintessentially her, but it smelt only of paper. I held it to the light and saw the watermark, 'Basildon Bond'. The writing was carefully formed, a good convent hand. The tone of the letter, I thought, showed good convent restraint. And there was far too much in it about Kieran. I wished I were there and going to Glendockery in the battered Rolls; I wished I could be anywhere where I could watch Helen, see her throw back her hair, hear her laugh.

I remembered the injunction I had heard on the hillside and Kieran's explanation. I did not think Helen was overly emotional, although given the strictures under which she lived, it would not be surprising if she occasionally erupted.

Monique had put it well: '*Il y a quelque chose là-bas qui me donne des frissons dans le dos!*' But, for me, the *frissons*, despite my protestations to the contrary, had been pure jealousy.

And I remembered with a wave of desire and longing how I had seen her bathing in the pool that first moonlit night; the magic of it, the beauty of it there in the silence. She had not alluded to that in her letter, and I knew she would never refer to it again. She had probably consigned it to the ragbag marked 'Embarrassing moments'.

I remembered our talk in her dell in the heather, her tentative interest, her acknowledgement of our strange kinship, her withdrawal, her talk of God, her reaction after I had kissed her.

I felt despair, unreasoning fear that there was a malign momentum which would part us for ever.

Oh Helen, I prayed, I hope God – if there is a God – is on our side. Grow up, my darling girl, and see what is happening! Whatever is between us, if it can have shaken me, half drowned me, it must, at least, have touched you. Even if we believe ourselves to be islands, the same tide breaks on all our shores.

Chapter Nine

The walk from the tube – down the Embankment to the Inns of Court, along an impressive section of the Thames, bounded on both sides by imperial London – was short. My head was full of anticipation, what Sir William Ryce would look like, whether I would impress him, the best way of presenting my curriculum vitae. Deep in the pit of my stomach various demons struggled, the demons of pride, hope, fear.

I ventured down the cobbled precincts of Middle Temple Lane, walking slowly, aware that these august precincts would probably be the ambience of my future life. There was a spectral dimension to the thought that the cobbles would be worn by my more mature feet, by my middle-aged feet, even by my old feet before it was time for me to pack up and finally shuffle off. I passed the Middle Temple Library, looked to the right to Elm Court of the Inner Temple, paused outside Middle Temple Hall. Its wrought-iron gateway, bearing the Pascal Lamb symbol, was locked. I gazed around Fountain Court where the trees would shed their leaves God knew how many times while I would be there to see it. I was like a postulant presenting himself at a monastery, knowing that the stones around him would be his companions for the rest of his life.

There was a collegiate atmosphere here, if not a monastic one, a sense of order, purpose and dedication which was at odds with the noise and rumble of the city which surrounded it. It smelt of incisive efficiency, arcane lore, courteous power. It was an atmosphere qualitatively different from the one in Cambridge; there was little room here for undergraduate whimsy; it was a calm place for the pursuit of what I then regarded as the loftiest of the professions.

I was early. I walked around, into the Inner Temple, saw its symbol of Pegasus over various doorways advertising lists of tenants – 'First

Floor, Sir Roderick and Lady Staunton' – proceeding through all the floors of each chambers, with the names of the legal sages who tenanted the same.

Self-consciously I sauntered as far as King's Bench Walk. I looked around curiously at the tall Georgian windows, at the stacks of briefs which, tied in pink ribbon, could be seen on desks within, at the rows of books cladding the walls of all those chambers, at the good lined curtains tied back, and the occasional leather armchair. I was the neophyte, the eager voyeur.

Sir William Ryce was not ready to meet me and I had to wait in the antechamber next to the clerks' office for about fifteen minutes, until invited to make my way up the stone staircase to my prospective mentor's rooms on the first floor. His office was similar to those I had peered into from without, book-lined, with a huge mahogany desk, and a table by the window stacked with neatly bound documents. He was balding, tall, with a prodigious tummy, shook my hand with avuncular affability. But his eyes were measuring me and were not avuncular at all.

'Well, well,' he said. 'Good to meet you, Dan. Your father tells me that you have a burning ambition to join the ranks of the profession!'

I said that I hoped to do so and perched, when invited, on a Victorian spoon-backed chair. Sir William asked me a few questions, gave me a spiel of information about the profession (most of which I already knew), the course which would have to be attended at the Middle Temple's Law School, the dinners in Hall I would have to attend, and demanded what kind of practice I saw myself aiming for. I had my answers ready. I wanted to be a common lawyer, with the emphasis on Criminal Law.

'You'll have to do tort and divorce as well . . . you know that!' Sir William said. 'The criminal stuff is all very well, but a good common lawyer cuts his teeth on a wide spectrum.'

Acquiescing was easy. Sir William was voluble, and if you did not watch his eyes you might have thought his geniality unadulterated. But his eyes were steel, slightly bloodshot.

'As a QC I don't take pupils myself, of course.' He added that he had arranged for me to meet Matthew Hartley, a junior tenant, who would be willing to take me on. He picked up the phone, spoke to someone, said Matt would see me when I was leaving. He exchanged a few pleasantries, asked after my father, wished me the very best, told me not to hesitate to contact him if I had any further queries, and got rid of me.

Matthew Hartley was on the third floor. His room was smaller than Sir William's; his wig had been thrown on the mantelpiece of the cast-iron fireplace. He was thin, balding, thirtyish, wore bifocals and had a fruity voice. Small piles of briefs bound in pink ribbon were stacked on the floor. One wall sported four humorous cartoons of judges, all of them looking as though they came out of the same stable as Judge Jeffreys.

Mr Hartley seemed to have more time than the great man on the first floor, asked me some questions about court jurisdiction, repeated what I had already been told about terms and dinners, tossed at me sudden questions on the Law of Evidence, the McNaughten Rules, proposed a hypothetical case where a murder was committed under the influence of drugs, listened lazily as I responded, my heart quickening, my wits sharpening under my private injunction, 'Think, don't panic.' Then he suddenly smiled, said he would be glad to take me on when I had my 'good honours degree' and had sat my Bar exams, and concluded the interview. I went home feeling like Mercury. Wings had sprouted on my ankles; my feet barely touched the earth.

Now it was a question of encouraging Kieran to follow up his planned jaunt to Paris. I wrote to him appropriately, a letter in which I said we all looked forward to seeing him and Helen.

His reply was in his usual pragmatic style with a soupçon of wit, but the gist of it was that he would arrive on Easter Monday, complete with Rolls which he was having serviced, and that Mrs Fitzgerald had agreed that Helen could come with him, and was writing to my mother to so confirm and to thank her for the invitation. It would be a birthday present for Helen, he said; she would be seventeen in April. She would be able to stay for the week and return with him when he got back from Paris.

'I saw her last weekend,' he wrote, 'when she and Aunt Dru were in Dublin. You should have seen Helen. The poor kid was as excited at the prospect as if she were making an expedition to the moon!'

I knew that James had already been in contact with Kieran about the Paris trip, but I went to his room, where he was studying, and jubilantly confirmed that Kieran would be bringing Helen to London. His head was bent over his desk, but he got up when I came in, rubbed his eyebrows and stretched like a cat.

'Good,' he said, grinning, reading the letter. 'I can see that we are overjoyed the little wench is visiting at last! I suppose there's no use in inviting you to accompany us to Paris?' he added slyly. 'After all, Mummy can look after Helen!'

'I'll pass this time, James. Besides, Kieran hasn't extended the invitation to me . . . and it is his car!'

'Very true,' he said musingly. 'He probably assumed you wouldn't be on for it – that you would be far too sensible!'

'James, stop trying to make me sound like a prig. I'd take off for Paris or anywhere else in the morning, but I'm not passing up the chance to entertain Helen when she's here!'

'I'm joking, you miserable half-wit,' James said, handing me back the missive. 'Do you think I don't recognize the symptoms of that infamous, that potentially terminal complaint, Besottums Desperandums?'

'Very amusing. You should go on the stage!'

'But all the world's a stage and all the poor, demented, infatuated little brothers merely players.'

'And you're not?'

'Me? God, no. I never play,' he said with a wide smile, lighting up a cigarette. 'I'm always deadly serious, but no one believes I am.'

I watched him blow smoke for a moment before articulating the true reason for my visit. 'I have something to ask you . . .'

He turned, raising his eyebrows with sudden, sharp curiosity. 'What?'

'Will you promise me that, while you are with Kieran, you won't tell him . . . you won't say anything . . . about . . . my being interested in Helen?'

James threw back his head and laughed. 'Goodness gracious, we are very earnest. We must be exceedingly smitten!'

'Never mind all that. Will you promise me? It's important, James!'

'But Kieran already knows!'

'How would he know? Have you said something? I hope you didn't put anything in that letter you wrote him.'

'Take it easy! I'm just assuming he knows. It shines out of your ears! What harm if he does?'

'He may say things, tell her things about me which will put paid to any chance I might have!'

James sat back and looked at me curiously. 'Have you been taking drugs or something? You sound quite nutty! Why would he tell her "things" about you?'

I sighed. 'Because, brother dear, I am afraid that despite all his protestations he may want her for himself.'

'You've put the matter to him then?' James asked levelly.

'Sort of. He protested indifference. But you never know with these things. Her mother is clearly all for it; and Helen cares for him, I think, and she's so gorgeous that if he looks at her at all, if he stops thinking of her as a child, he's bound to fall head over heels!'

James turned away and became absorbed in something out the window. 'Well,' he muttered after a moment, his voice very flat, 'maybe they have good taste! Why mess it up if that's what he wants? He is your friend!'

'Because she is too good to be thrown away on either the cold or the bloodless! Now will you give me your promise? Yes or no?'

He laughed drily. 'I won't mention the two of you in the same breath! Is that enough for you?'

'Thanks, James. You're a brick!'

I tried to see his face, but he did not turn from the window and was silent. I left his room curiously uneasy, almost certain that I had offended him in some way that I could not fathom, without knowing the how or the why.

I went back to my room and mulled over the photographs I had taken at the lake, of Kieran and Helen, of Helen and me, of Mrs Fitzgerald with two bemused German hikers who had stumbled into the valley one afternoon and whom she had pounced on with great delight, treating them to tea and scones and a barrage of nonstop conversation until the poor things had looked around for polite means of escape.

But I lingered on any photo containing Helen. There was about her face in repose a gravity, almost a melancholy, and her eyes had a way of looking far away, as though she focused on something just beyond one's ken. Smiling, she looked positively mischievous, an impulsive schoolgirl, and there were many photographs of this sort with Monique. But there was a sad little turn-down to a corner of her mouth in one of the photographs, and an earnestness in her eyes which was close enough to pain. I remembered taking the photo, tried to remember if she had been looking at Kieran, who was not in the picture, but had been nearby rubbing Ivan the Terrible's tummy. He had paid more attention to that dog than he had to his beautiful cousin. It was almost as though he deliberately ignored her or tried to diminish her. But then, I reminded myself, Kieran would never be deliberately cruel; insensitive yes, but cruel no. Kieran, for all his ostensible coldness, could not bear the sound of a rabbit in a snare, or the sight of a cat playing with some punch-drunk little mouse.

But one thing was clear. Kieran did not, could not, love Helen. You could not love someone and treat her as he did. Thinking thus, I again gave myself *carte blanche* to attempt the winning of her. In fantasy I thought how I would build a splendid future for her, surround her with the comforts due to her beauty, and with the passion which was her birthright. I saw our life together as a long unchequered happiness.

For a moment I wondered how I struck the female of the species. The mirror told me that I was neither handsome nor ugly and when I looked for character I found only a middling chin with five o'clock shadow. But my eyes were expressive, I told myself. Yes, with expressive eyes like those, deployed to advantage, she would surely fall for me. And then, I thought, if she hasn't fallen for your manly charms by now, she never will. But this exercise in self-admonition was short-lived.

My weekends at home always made me glad enough to take the early train back to Cambridge on Monday mornings. Sometimes I went back on Sunday evenings. I kept my bicycle at the station and would cycle the relatively short distance to St John's.

On one such dark November night, bitterly cold, I came cycling along King's Parade, my head down against the wind.

I saw Marion on the pavement ahead of me. I had not spoken to her since our rupture the preceding spring. I remembered her caustic comments, and acknowledged in my heart that she was perfectly correct in what she had said. I had, in retrospect, behaved like a cad. I even knew why, because I had had plenty of time to ponder it while lost in the heather at Lough Corrloch, with only the chewing of the sheep around to distract me. I had used Marion because I was horny as hell. If I had allowed the sense of her humanity and intellect to intrude on the fantasies I was so busy satisfying, my joy ride would have had to either cease altogether or assume a different rationale. I would have either fallen in love or not have been able to function at all. Not that poor Marion had been necessarily easy. She had simply been ready for, had expected, something more than I could offer.

I slowed, caught up with her. She quickened her pace. She did not glance back and I called out, 'Hello, Marion. You're certainly in a hurry!'

She turned then, said, 'Hello, Dan,' coolly enough and slowed her progress, wrapping her muffler around the lower part of her face. I put one foot on the ground and walked the bike.

'God, it's cold,' she said.

'How are you?' I asked. 'I hadn't seen you for ages!' I could hardly see her face.

'Oh, I've seen you,' she said. 'In the distance . . . scurrying.' She gave a small, brittle laugh while I inwardly flinched from the momentary image of myself as some kind of rodent. Then she glanced at me and said I looked well. I sensed in her a false bonhomie, a resentment which surprised me because it indicated that she was, despite herself, still involved with me at some level, however tangential. I tried to be humorous, talking about one of my tutors who was acknowledged as the college oddity and steered the subject around to her own work.

'So what's it to be when you graduate?' I demanded. 'Have you decided on your career?'

'I'll probably bloody teach or something,' she said. 'I can't see myself getting anything better than a third.'

'Why not?'

I turned to look at her when she didn't answer, but she did not face me and I could only see her profile and that her eyes were watching the pavement.

'Did you do anything exciting in the summer?' I asked then, reaching for safe ground and she said, after a lengthy pause, as though she were vetting the events of the summer vacation with something less than ecstatic recollection, that she hadn't, actually. Then she asked me if I had been to Ireland, to the wonderful place I had mentioned, and I said I had.

When we reached St John's I said goodbye, extending my hand awkwardly, as though I would, by this friendly gesture, make amends for whatever I had done to pain her. But she did not take my hand. Perhaps she did not see it. She was gone, turned into Bridge Street, without another word. I went through the college gate into First Court, wondering if I should have invited her out, but then decided that as there was no future in the relationship it was better left as it was.

I was aware that now, if I was to fulfil my own life plan, there was nothing left to me for the next seven months but work. I was high with it; the adrenaline flowed as evening after evening, night after night, I researched the legal precedents, absorbed the substantive law in one subject after another. I found I enjoyed the Law of Evidence and its careful precision as to admissibility, as much as the Law of Real Property, although the latter had seemed so weird to me at the outset that I had wondered if I should ever be able to master it. But its very weirdness, its ancient terminology, had eventually bewitched me. But my first love remained Criminal Law, although I did not have it in my final year. Criminal Law was easy, stimulating, fascinating and someday, or so I promised myself, I would, in all the regalia of wig and gown, shine in it. Someday.

Kieran invited both James and me to Dublin for the New Year. As it was clear that Helen would be in Dundalk, I declined, but for some reason James, who had always said he had no desire to revisit Dublin, accepted. He left on Boxing Day and we did not see him again until 2 January. He returned looking cheerful and said he had enjoyed himself no end. 'There was no sign of the paragon Helen,' he said to forestall the expected question.

He had been to two parties, one of them on New Year's Eve in a Georgian country house at the foothills of the Dublin mountains, a full-dress affair with a live band. 'If Lough Corrloch is like that you've certainly been keeping things from me!' I assured him it was not like that, nor anything so civilized.

'I wanted to see the place, seeing you're so fond of it – even suggested it to Kieran, but he said the mountain roads were snow-clogged and that we would never make it. He was thinking of his precious car, of course,' he added sardonically. 'I don't think he was half so worried at the prospect of yours truly being trapped in the wilderness, or himself for that matter!'

'Why should he?' I asked. 'If you were a rare moss with a sporo-something growing on your doings, he'd cherish you. But as a mere human you're expendable.'

James looked at me, cocking an eyebrow. 'My my, we have gone hard and bitter!'

'No I'm not . . . just more aware than I used to be.' This remark provoked a sudden questioning glance from my brother, an interrogative narrowing of the eyes as though he were trying to penetrate my thought. Then he smiled.

Thinking of survival made me think of the valley. I mentally traced the road across the mountains from Rathfarnham, as it rose higher and higher to the exposed plateau which seemed like the roof of the world. I heard the wind whistle, driving powdery snow across the open moorland and saw the valley shrouded in stark white loneliness, with the shuttered house. I imagined the snow falling in the shelter of the valley; great soft flakes, a gentle blizzard of them, blanketing everything in a profound silence. Someday, I thought, I will spend Christmas in the valley. Then I wondered how one would get out of the valley should the snow continue for any length of time; walk through the drifts and all of the eight miles to Glendockery? But even there, it being the highest village in the country, there was no guarantee of any transport being available. So I knew that if I wanted to realize this particular dream I would have to come prepared for a siege. I imagined a siege with Helen beside me; turf fires, lamplight, candlelight, chess games, Scrabble, big double bed, kisses – oh yes, everywhere, teaching her, the unwittingly sensuous, the innocently sensuous Helen, to make sensuous love . . . It was possible, I told myself. Why should it not be possible? If I could win Helen we could be snowed in every winter until we died of exhaustion. Years later, when I saw *Doctor Zhivago*, and the scene where Yuri and Lara are marooned together in the snowbound dacha, I felt that Boris Pasternak must have read my mind.

But for the moment I had to content myself with the delicious knowledge that she would be coming at Easter. Meanwhile, I more or less immured myself from the activities of college life. I divided the work into sections and subsections, researched the cases most salient for each particular area on the course, scrutinized the legal argument, memorized the principles. I no longer went home for weekends and took to attending evensong on Sunday evenings on a regular basis as my one break from the work. My friends, the people who last summer had been clowning on the river, were busy with their own studies and in fact the mood was contagious, as though at some subliminal level we spurred each other on.

One Sunday in early March I bumped into Marion coming out of evensong. It was cold in the vaulted chapel and she was shivering even before she encountered the east wind outside. She hung back, pretending for a moment that she hadn't seen me, but I waited for her outside and offered to walk her home. She nodded in silence and we took the short cut over the Kitchen Bridge beside the pretty Bridge of Sighs and then through the Backs to the Queen's Road. The river seemed glacial; the daffs were up; the day was still alive, although the light was fading. I asked her how her work was going.

'As well as I can expect.'

'Ah, come on, Marion; you're a brilliant student; you know you'll do well.'

She turned to look at me, eyes hooded. 'Will I? What makes you so sure? You don't know that much about me!'

I regarded her pale face in the gloom. 'I know enough about you to think you highly intelligent.'

She sighed. 'Typical man,' she muttered after a moment, 'patronizing, consciousness on one level . . .'

'Sorry?'

'I just said that you're a typical male.'

'There's no such animal!' She didn't respond and I ventured coldly after a moment, 'In what way am I a typical male? I take it the term is pejorative!' I was irritated, but wondering what I had done to provoke her.

'Men skate over the surface of things!' she said. 'They live life unsuspectingly, even cruelly. Everything to them is a thing – life, love . . . slaves to their gonads, slaves to their ambitions . . .'

'Untrue!'

She did not glance at me. 'It depends on your perspective. You are not in a position to know, in ultimate terms, what is and is not true. You can only vet things as far as your own horizon, for that is the limit of your sight!'

I put a hand on her arm. She turned to look at me and I saw that her face was tense with unshed tears.

'Marion,' I said, aware that she was in genuine pain and that I was the cause of it, 'I am truly sorry if I have hurt you. I did not mean to and I hope you will forgive me!'

'Ye gods!' she exclaimed, while the tears released themselves and rolled down her cheeks. 'It's so easy, so pat, for you: "I'm sorry, Marion. Please forgive me," and off you go, self-absolved; the whole thing may as well have been done with mirrors!'

'What are you talking about? I know we were lovers; we had a good time; that doesn't make either of us into a villain. It didn't work out; you told me to get lost – that was your prerogative. I got lost and now you're weeping and talking about male shallowness!' I freeze-dried my voice; 'I'm afraid I have no time for hysterics!'

Marion dried her eyes. She stared at me and her face gathered itself into lines of contempt. 'What else can you expect from something with only one and half chromosomes?' she demanded with a snort of derision, addressing the gelid trees along Queen's Road, as she turned with a gesture of dismissal and walked quickly away.

Astonished, I debated whether I should run after her, get her to tell me what was making her so angry. But then I thought, how dare she come spitting venom for no reason! It was much easier to let her go, to chalk the whole episode down to female irrationality. It was much easier to feel relief that I no longer had any relationship with her, that I even had cause to nurse a righteous grievance.

The taste of our encounter, however, lingered for several days, filling me with a self-doubt I detested, as though the mirror Marion had spoken of had begun to reflect a self I neither liked nor recognized. The only way out of this was to assure myself that the girl had always been a bit loopy. So, little by little, I managed to rationalize the encounter, making sure that if I saw her again in the distance we did not meet. I gave up going to evensong. I lived now for the new world which would open to me when I graduated, and most of all I lived for Easter and the sight of Helen arriving at our door.

Chapter Ten

Rachel got the flu coming up to Easter and my mother engaged a young part-time help called Sandra to look after her and run the house. She was herself so taken up in her new career and in Charles Sauvingler that she had little time for matters domestic. The household was very quiet when I got back from Cambridge for the Easter break; the background noise – radio, kitchen clatter, occasional tuneless song – associated with Rachel, was missing; she was confined to bed. I delayed my visit to her room for a while, knowing how she would plumb me for news. I was tired from weeks of study; I just wanted to talk to my mother and James and bask in the curious comfort that family affords, when you need family.

On the evening of my arrival my father phoned and asked to speak to my mother.

'Mummy, Dad is on the phone!'

We were in the drawing room after supper. Charles was there; he had arrived for supper and consequently I had not had the intimate family interchange which I had expected. I liked Charles – so did James – but there was always the sense that he was an outsider.

Now my mother registered nothing at the intelligence that my father was on the phone, not pleasure, not displeasure.

'Tell him I'm not in, darling,' she said smoothly. 'I'm sure if he has something to say he can put it in a letter!'

I saw James's face darken.

'He knows you're in,' I said, keeping the palm of my hand across the mouthpiece. 'I can't tell him a lie! It's not as though he's just anyone!'

James left his armchair and reached for the receiver. 'Hello, Father,' he said in a voice devoid of any intonation: 'I'm sorry, Mummy is not in. Is there a message?'

He was silent for a moment and then said, 'I'm quite well, thank you.' His voice had a 'Will-that-be-all?' tone to it, which I found intolerable. I tried to grab the receiver back from him, but when I had it in my hand again the phone was dead.

'You shouldn't treat your father like that!' I hissed at James. 'You shouldn't speak to him in that tone! He's still your dad.'

He looked at my mother. 'Well, he needn't presume too much on that,' he said softly.

'For God's sake, James!'

'There's no point in for-God's-saking me. He was the one who buggered off. I didn't. Mummy didn't. You didn't! So why are we not a family any more? Because Dad had an itchy prick; he sold us out to it . . . he even got her pregnant!'

'She lost it!' I cried. 'She lost the baby. It's been terrible for her. How can you be so callous?'

'I'm not callous,' he said in a very low voice; 'I'm betrayed!'

He turned and walked out of the room, head high, with the rather ponderous dignity he had at his command when offended.

I was afraid to look at either my mother or Charles, but the former made some comment about the evening being quite cold and told me to go downstairs and see if Rachel had everything she wanted.

Rachel was sitting up in bed in her pink bed jacket, her two cats curled into the eiderdown beside her: she was reading a woman's magazine; there was a heap of them beside her on the bedside table. She adored love stories. Once we used to tease her about them, but she no longer seemed to care if we caught her reading them.

'Ah, there yez are!' she announced with delight, patting the eiderdown, and putting down her journal. 'Sit down here and tell the oul' bird in the bed what ye've been up to!'

I looked into her eyes, now rheumy with influenza. 'Is Sandra looking after you properly?'

'She's grand, the poor little creature; she does her best. But tell me the news. It's shockin' borin' being stuck here in the bloody bed!'

I entertained her for a few minutes with the bones of some criminal cases; she was particularly partial to murders.

'Well, thanks be to the Sacret Heart that one o' yez is studyin' something halfway interestin!' she announced when I had finished. 'The other fellow is into kidneys and bits o' blubber and the Lord knows what!'

'Is there anything you'd like, Rachel? Mummy said to ask.'

'Nothin' in the world ... tell her thanks.' And then she leant towards me in old camaraderie, lowering her voice. 'But to tell yez nothin' but the naked truth, I do have a terrible yen on me for a drop of Jameson!'

I laughed. James had suspected for some time that Rachel took the odd medicinal drop at night – 'to aid restful sleep' was how he put it, keeping his face straight.

'Leave it to me, Rachel!'

'Don't tell herself!' she warned.

I went quietly into the dining room to fetch the whiskey and when I was coming out I glanced through the crack in the dividing door into the drawing room. Charles Sauvingler was on his knees beside my mother's armchair and he was cradling her head in his hands. I don't know if she was weeping, for I couldn't see her face. All I know is that the moment was tense with intimacy. It made me feel like one who had awakened from sleep and found himself in a strange land. My mother, in that instant, was no longer a parent, but a woman loved by a man with whom I had no connection, and a willingly loved one, it would seem, for her hands touched Charles's face with the same fierce delicacy with which they touched the piano.

For some reason I experienced this moment between these two people as a personal rejection. It made me aware of how I stood at the periphery of the new life my mother had forged for herself, how I was excluded from the heart of it. I knew my feelings were unreasonable; I remembered my own exhortations; but the child in me, the son, ached for something lost for ever. In that moment I understood James's anger and his anguish.

Before I could vacate the room I heard my name mentioned. I paused by the partition door, and heard Charles say: 'Dan seems very practical. Of the two of them, James is the one taking it badly; have you talked to him at all?'

Her response was whispered: 'Not really; he doesn't want to talk.'

Then she added, 'But Dan is another kettle of fish; he read me the riot act, you know, told me to pull myself together. He was perceptive, but he's a cold fish. Funny combination – ice and sensitivity . . .'

I took the whiskey down to Rachel and poured until she shrieked at me to stop. 'Put that back. I only want a nip. D'yez want the smell of spirits rising out o' me room like a bloody distillery?'

I returned the bottle to the dining room. The connecting door to the drawing room was now closed, but I could hear the piano, which was being very softly played – some new melody perhaps, if the exploratory tinkling of the keys was anything to go by. Feeling defeated of the familial intimacy to which I had so looked forward, feeling deflated because of what I had overheard, I went upstairs and examined myself in the mirror. I sought in my features the ice which my mother had found in me. 'A cold fish', she had said. My eyes stared back at me, dark blue, darker if anything from the internal turbulence which her comment had caused. I'm not cold, Mummy, I insisted privately; I'm not cold at all . . .

Helen swam into consciousness the way she did a hundred times a day, floated out of the wings of emotion, where she lived within me. One of the blessings I imagined in a life with Helen was the prospect of understanding, of not having to act a part invented for me.

I took out my photographs of Lough Corrloch, saw her smiling, laughing, looking grave. I brought the snaps in to James, who was lying on his bed with one of his endless medical textbooks, but it was apparent at a glance that he was not really studying. He had that slightly haunted look to him which always overtook him when my father was mentioned or when he spoke to him on the phone.

'Only another week!' he reminded me with an obvious effort, glancing at the photographs with scant interest, 'and the fair Helen will lighten the door!' Then he laughed, pointing to one of the snapshots. 'Christ, what is Fitzgerald up to? He looks like he's just cleaned the chimney!' It was a photograph of Kieran covered in black earth from the bog.

'He fell in a bit of old worked bog near the top of a hill; Helen had the camera with her!'

'What an ass!' James continued, enjoying the sight of the laconic Kieran with filth to the eyes.

'James,' I asked, 'what did Dad want? Did he say?'

'He wanted to get Mummy to meet him to discuss the settlement. He should know by now that it's no good trying to contact her. Nothing will persuade her to talk to him again! He can do all that through his solicitor!'

'Yes, but I think he wants to talk to her. I think he's looking for her absolution!'

James shrugged and gave a bleak little smile. 'Tough!' he said.

'Will you come out?' I asked, suddenly unable to face the exchange which would logically follow this remark. As far as I was concerned what had happened between my parents could not be undone and the best must be made of it. But James saw the whole affair in terms of personal betrayal. He never adverted to damage limitation; he was childish enough to want revenge.

'We could go to the cinema or something,' I offered. 'I don't feel like studying tonight!'

He glanced at me; for a moment I thought he was going to make some excuse, but in silent brotherly solidarity he put his book down, reached for his jacket and we left the house together, calling out to my mother that we would be back at midnight.

We spent the evening in a pub, drowning our mutual sense of void and emptiness and strange, stubborn sorrow.

'Everyone needs someone to share this plot of dust and soul,' my brother announced later that night, paraphrasing Omar Khayyám in a slightly slurred voice and a moment of rare confidence. 'What the bloody hell is it all about if you dare never be yourself?'

'Find yourself a nice girl,' I enjoined him and he looked at me from alcohol-pink eyes. For a moment I felt the desire in him to unburden some confidence, for he frowned, leant stolidly forward and parted his lips as though to speak seriously, something rare enough for him. But he seemed to think better of it, laughed a little harshly and ordered another drink.

James was twenty-six and I was not far off twenty-two, but we came home that evening feeling like orphans. Mummy and Charles had gone out. She had left a message that she would be back in the morning, something she now did with increasing frequency. We knew that when she was not at home she stayed with Charles in his flat.

Reckless with the gins and tonics earlier consumed, I tiptoed down to Rachel's room, but she was asleep. I closed the door, but the scent of John Jameson wafted gently into the lower hall after me. I went to bed, but as I drifted into sleep the world seemed to spin and whorls of darkness waited to carry me away, threatening certainty and continuance, threatening my understanding of reality, as though there were no absolutes, but only perception.

At last it came, the Easter Monday of 1962. Helen and Kieran arrived in the evening. They were late and I had begun to get a bit anxious, aware that Kieran was unused to the volume of traffic which he would encounter on the road to London. I wondered if the ancient Rolls had let him down, or if they had got lost, or if they could possibly have had an accident.

I saw them arrive, but James, who had spotted them from his window, rushed down the stairs and beat me to the front door, opening it with a flourish. The car had pulled in to the kerb and Kieran and Helen were getting out; she was smoothing down her skirt. I saw that she was wearing a jacket loosely over her shoulders and that underneath it was a grey woollen dress with a white collar, straight skirt and a belt of the same material with a buckle. She stood by the open passenger door, was a little taller and seemed remote and almost sophisticated. I devoured her with my eyes, but when I saw the jerky way she put her hand to her hair I realized that she was nervous, that her new patina was a deliberate projection to hide the fact that she was ill at ease. Her hair was intended to have been contained by two tortoiseshell combs, but its unruliness had evidently reasserted itself in the course of the journey and the combs were loose and ineffective. Her eyes were unusually diffident, a little startled, as though shyness had suddenly overwhelmed her despite her best intentions, and she did not know how to cope with it. She patted her hair as though to tame it fit to be seen, looked up and saw me. Her face changed, lit up with laughter, reminding me, for a moment, of the scruffy eleven-year-old mocking me in the avenue on our first encounter.

I called a greeting to Kieran, who was groaning as he stretched himself after the journey and then I took her proffered hand. 'You're very welcome, Helen.'

'So this is where you live!' she exclaimed, looking around. 'I often tried to imagine it!'

James, who had greeted Kieran and exclaimed over the car, 'God, what a smashing oddity!' now approached Helen, smiling with his customary lordly address, but unable to keep the curiosity out of his eyes. 'This is my brother, James. James, this is Helen!'

'How do you do,' James said in his lofty-but-friendly voice, directing an all-encompassing gaze at hers 'You must be simply prostrate after that journey!'

'No,' Helen said nervously, unused to such close scrutiny and clearly embarrassed by it, 'Kieran is a very good driver and we had a few stops . . . but it was a long drive. England is . . . quite big!'

I knew at once that Helen felt this to be a weak speech, for she suddenly blushed furiously and I could almost feel her self-directed rage. For someone as generally articulate as she was the pronouncement that England was quite big was not calculated to advance her self-confidence.

'Stop annoying that child,' my mother's voice said behind us and she came out of the house to rescue Helen from her elder son's unflagging scrutiny. 'Helen, my dear, I'm Dan's mother and I'm delighted to meet you. Come in at once and let these great rude fellows get on with the luggage.'

Helen, taken in charge by my formidable mother, glanced at me with a kind of mute desperation and in her diffidence, in her fresh and unconsidered uncertainty, she looked younger than her years and more beautiful than I had ever seen her.

My mother shook hands then with Kieran and said he was looking horrendously handsome, which made the latter hang his head a little in mock self-deprecation.

'I can't help it!' he said lugubriously. 'I try to be ugly, but no matter what I do . . . !'

My mother chuckled. Helen followed her into the house.

''Tis the fairy Lady of Shalott,' James's voice said in my ear as the two women disappeared indoors. 'Perhaps a little gauche, but becomingly so. She gives the fleeting impression that butter wouldn't melt; but don't bank on it! Anyone who can blush like that is almost certainly sitting on a furnace!'

'For God's sake, James,' I hissed, 'keep your curiosity decent. You embarrassed her!'

He grinned. 'I know,' he said *sotto voce*. 'I'm a louse, but I do have a passion for testing human mettle. And seeing that you're so besotted I want to be sure that you're not throwing yourself away!'

Kieran, having taken out the suitcases from the boot, came and clapped me on the back. 'How are you, old fellow? You look a bit spare and hungry. Are you working too hard ... or thinking too hard?'

'It amounts to the same thing,' I said, returning the friendly thump, 'as you should know! No rest for the wicked!'

'That may indeed be so,' Kieran responded mournfully, 'but even when I'm being very, very good ...' He shook his head and James laughed a light, happy laugh.

I studied the luggage. 'Which is Helen's case?'

'That one is, of course,' James announced, indicating the smarter of the two suitcases, but Kieran, with an inscrutable glance at James, handed me the other one, an old leather affair with a worn handle.

I brought it into the house, leaving Kieran to follow with James. In the hall I thought, hearing the feminine voices above me in the landing: She is here; Helen is here, in my home. Tonight she will sleep here; tomorrow I will show her London ...

I wanted to leap up and swing on the chandelier. But I carried her case up the stairs and put it into the guest room, now her room. Helen had disappeared into the bathroom. On the landing, my mother took my arm briefly as though touched by a sudden maternal nostalgia, and whispered, 'A lovely girl, and nice!'

I smiled at her gratefully.

From the kitchen Kieran and James could be heard in shared laughter. Rachel, now recovered from the 'flu, was giving them the benefit of her considered opinion on some topic, but it was too garbled for me to decipher. I waited in the return of the stairs, where there was a small chintz-covered armchair, and stared into the darkening garden until Helen emerged from the bathroom. She did not see me as she crossed the landing and I called up to her that I would wait for her.

She jumped, gave a startled laugh, said, 'Hang on a sec; I just want to fix my hair,' and having spent a minute or two in her room, she joined me.

I took her hand and kissed it ceremoniously. 'Welcome to London!'

She giggled, hunching her shoulder a little uncomfortably, in the old gesture of her childhood. I saw that the two combs had been sternly replaced in her stubborn curly locks.

'Thanks, Dan.' She withdrew her hand, looked into the garden and down along the row of neighbouring gardens with open curiosity. 'It feels different – London, I mean. It has an atmosphere completely unlike anything in Ireland. It's impersonal . . . or something, which is such a relief in a funny kind of way! I'm terribly excited to be here, you know; I feel so grown up!'

'Well, you even look grown up!'

'Do I?' she asked with delight. Then she added diffidently when I made no attempt to move, as though she sensed the tension in me, 'Do you think we'd better go down to the others?'

I was too busy soaking up the touch of her shoulder against mine as she had turned to look out the window, the subtle hint of her scent, the scent of a young woman mixed with soap. I wanted to take her hand, to put my arm around her waist, to feel her hair against my face. *Festina lente*, I told myself sternly; don't ruin this. I gestured to the stairs. 'After you, mam'selle!'

In the kitchen Rachel had the table laid for supper and was in the process of ordering James and Kieran to pull it out from the wall as there would be six this evening instead of four. She studied Helen with open interest as she walked through the door.

'Helen,' James said, 'this is the intrepid Rachel O'Mahony who looks after us and puts up with us, although, it must be said, not always without complaint!' He turned to Rachel, 'This is the lovely Miss Helen O'Callaghan of whom you have heard much in despatches!'

'How are yez?' Rachel said. 'Don't mind that fella; he'd talk the leg off a jennet!'

Kieran regarded the proceedings with sardonic amusement and narrowed his eyes at Helen who was laughing.

'I've heard loads about you, Miss O'Mahony,' Helen said extending her hand. 'I'm delighted to meet you!'

'Are yez! Well, yeh can start by calling me Rachel!' She looked at me. 'Will yeh let yer mother know the supper is ready?'

I went to the brass gong outside the kitchen door, rapped on it twice and its loud, mellow boom echoed through the house.

My mother's voice came faintly from the drawing room above, 'Coming . . .'

I went back to the kitchen, seated Helen, sat beside her, spoke to Kieran, feeling the happiness of the moment, the full house now that she was here, the full life in my heart and soul. I watched Helen from the corner of my eye and did not miss the small, intimate smile she gave to Kieran and his tiny inclination of approval as though she had acquitted her self well and made him proud.

My mother came in then, apologizing for keeping us, and deputizing Kieran to open the wine.

'Where's Charles?' James demanded.

'He's in Paris,' she said. 'He'll be back in a few days.'

'We'll see him when we're there in that case!' James said to Kieran. 'He's letting us use his flat, you know!'

Kieran glowed. 'Hey, that's very decent of him; it'll make the money stretch much further! Where is it – what part of the city? I mean – is it central?'

'Oh, some seedy little dump in the sixteenth *arrondissement*!'

Kieran looked taken aback and my mother clicked her tongue and gave James one of her reproving looks.

'The Avenue Foch is not exactly a seedy little dump, James. In fact, it's probably the best address in Paris.' She added with a sigh. 'I don't know why you have to be so eternally provocative!'

'The badness has to come out somehow!' Kieran returned in an innocent tone, making everyone, particularly Rachel, laugh.

James and Kieran excitedly discussed their itinerary while Rachel served the soup. My mother then engaged Helen in conversation, talking of her favourite places in Ireland and I sat there and listened in a great peace. Rachel winked at me as she went about her business and looked as though she was ready to deliver some caustic comment – I could even imagine it – something to the effect that I was looking constipated and whey-faced, but she evidently thought better of it and was a model of decorum for the rest of the meal.

'Where are you taking Helen tomorrow after Kieran and James have left?' my mother asked eventually. 'Is there somewhere you particularly want to see, Helen?'

'Oh, I don't mind,' Helen said. 'It's all new. I'll leave it up to Dan! I want to see Westminster before I go home, though, Big Ben and the Houses of Parliament and Westminster Abbey.'

'She's a culture vulture!' Kieran said, breaking off his conversation with James and glancing from me to my mother. 'She'd like to see the art galleries,' he bent towards her, 'wouldn't you, my liggle one?'

Helen blushed. I saw suddenly that Kieran was keeping the strings of his influence taut, and thinking that he regarded me a challenge I felt a mélange of emotions, sudden adrenaline, sudden uncertainty in the face of our old friendship. James sat looking on at this exchange, his face inscrutable, but his mouth had tightened and the smile had died in his eyes.

'Well,' my mother said to her young guest, 'play it by ear. There's so much to see and no point in wearing yourself out. You can always come again – whenever you want!'

Helen glowed. 'Thank you very much, Mrs McPherson.'

'There's no reason why you shouldn't just hop on the boat and take the train from Holyhead whenever the humour takes you,' my mother went on without glancing at Kieran. 'You'd be with us in no time.' There was a moment's silence after Helen murmured her thanks yet again. I looked at my mother gratefully.

'She'd get lost!' Kieran announced on a note of levity. 'The big bad boat and the train, all on her own!'

Helen turned to him, sudden sparks flying. 'I'm not an imbecile, you know; and I'm grown up now!'

'Good girl yerself!' Rachel muttered behind her as she collected the plates. 'That's the way to talk to them!'

Kieran seemed taken aback at his cousin's riposte; James raised his eyebrows and my mother laughed. 'Yes,' she said, 'there comes a point when one reaches for one's freedom! It happens in every life . . . sooner or later!' She looked mischievously at Kieran. 'Cheer up. The worst that can happen is that you'll have some competition. It's very healthy, in love as in business!'

Kieran gave a polite laugh. 'But I'm not competing,' he said sorrowfully. 'I'd have to bestir myself and I'm much too young and selfish!'

'A man after my own heart!' James interjected. 'Youth and selfishness are qualities dear to my soul!'

'Yeh don't have to tell us that!' Rachel sniffed.

'Oh shut up, you batty bird,' James murmured amiably, adding, 'Rachel thinks that if brute force fails she can civilize by innuendo.'

Helen was laughing. 'Do you think selfishness is sanctified by youth?' she demanded, turning her eyes from James to Kieran. 'I think you two make a good pair – you think you can convince just by sounding plausible!'

James laughed. 'Well, if politicians can do it . . .'

'Anyway,' Kieran said, widening his eyes mischievously, 'the matter is academic. It all really boils down to action versus laziness, because if, and when, I compete, I win!'

He smiled at me when he said this and I smiled back and said he was all modesty, hoping that what I felt was not written on my face.

I caught my mother's eye a moment later and saw that it was bright with speculation.

When the meal was over my mother acceded to Kieran's request and played for us in the drawing room.

'When is your record coming out?' Kieran asked when she had finished and we had applauded, and she said in time for Christmas.

'What will it be called?' Helen asked.

My mother hesitated. '*Pathways of the Heart*,' she murmured, staring at James as though daring him to utter one word of sarcasm.

'Well, I'm taking this heart out for a walk,' he said after a moment, rising to his feet. 'Anyone coming?'

Kieran said he would and Helen said she would, and we all trooped out into night-time Knightsbridge.

'What about a nightclub?' James suggested. He looked at Helen. 'Are you game?'

I saw the excitement in her face. 'I've never been to one! I've read about them, though!'

There was a hurried muted exchange between Kieran and James and I heard the former say that Helen's mother wouldn't approve.

'Well, some other time maybe . . .'

I saw Helen's face fall. 'I'll take Helen home,' I said. 'You two go off and do whatever you want!'

When they were out of earshot I reached for her hand. 'Helen,' I said, 'there is nothing like a bit of autonomy. I know just the nightclub you would enjoy,' and I hailed a taxi to take us to Zarathustra's in the West End. I was in heaven.

Chapter Eleven

The awakening next morning was blessed. There was the sense that something wonderful was afoot without actually knowing what, a feeling I had not had since childhood. My somnolent horizons were searched; the reason materialized.

I remembered Zarathustra's the evening before. Helen had asked for an orange, which I had duly purchased at the bar, and I had bought a gin and orange for myself. She finished her drink quickly and then, laughing and saying she was still thirsty, grabbed my drink and downed it. I stared at her in astonishment.

'Yuck,' she said, putting the glass aside; 'I think that orange was off!'

Nervous of telling her the truth I escorted her to the dance floor, only to find she moved like a dervish.

'Where did you learn to dance like that?' I asked when we had returned to our table. The needle of jealousy was there, absurd and acid. Did she dance with other boys, other men?

'At school,' Helen said between gasps as she regained her breath. 'We partner one another during rec – when it's raining and we can't play netball or hockey.'

The sudden vision of umpteen girls in gymslips, swirling to rock and roll, navy knickers on view, suspenders peeping below them, was not displeasing. It did not, however, square with my image of convent life.

'Mother Aidan usually supervises us. She doesn't care about the dancing so long as the music is proper!'

'What's proper music?'

'Oh, anything with lyrics she can't understand. You know the song about "kissin' and huggin' with Fred"? Well, we convinced her that Fred was a dog!'

Helen laughed so heartily that I began to mentally revise my idea of her. This was no tremulous snowdrop. This young woman had a history!

'It sounds quite improper!' I said with my most grown-up voice.

'What is?'

'Kissing Fred, when they could be kissing me.'

'But Fred wouldn't stand a chance if you were around.'

She was flirting with me. I took her hand and drew her to the floor for a slow dance, held her close to the strains of Elvis's 'Love Me Tender'. I felt her cheek, soft and hot, against my own; I felt her body, her breasts crushed against me; there was something in her posture which yielded to me. I wanted the slow dance to go on for ever.

'Helen?'

'Hmmn?'

'I'm crazy about you!'

She drew back a little, searched my face, and a melancholy seemed to come over her. 'No you're not! Don't say things like that!'

'Why not?'

'Because I'm behaving very badly. I don't know what was in the orange, but it's made my knees all wobbly!'

'It was gin!'

She stopped, stared at me. 'But I'm not supposed to drink! I have the Pioneer Pin and now I've broken my pledge!'

'No you haven't; you didn't know! And it was only a tiny little soupçon . . . and I'll mind you!'

She looked up at me, eyes fathomless, slightly glazed, slightly pink, and then she touched my face. 'I know . . .'

'I'll take you home whenever you like.'

We finished the dance. I was on fire. I wished I had my own car and thought of Kieran's Rolls, locked and parked uselessly outside our front door.

'I think we'd better go home,' Helen said, when I tried to get her another drink. 'Your mother will be wondering . . . and I'm jaded!'

In the taxi I said to her, 'Helen, this is a special night for me!' I said it into her hair. She laid her head back against the seat in a gesture almost of surrender, or maybe it was just weariness, but I drew her face towards me and kissed her, slowly, the slowest burning kiss of my life. I felt her quiver; she drew away.

'It's just a little gesture of friendship,' I murmured, repeating the old formula, trying to find her lips again, but she drew back from me, her eyes dilated, her face uncertain.

'Please . . . Dan . . .'

I acquiesced, but I held her hand, feeling it warm and small within my own.

My mother had been still up when I got home and disapproving, although she hid it from Helen.

'That girl is very young!' she said to me reproachfully on the landing after Helen had gone to bed. 'And I smelt drink on her!'

'Just one little gin and orange, Mummy. It won't do her any harm!'

'Maybe not. But I'm responsible for her while she is here and I take that responsibility seriously! And it won't do your suit any good, you know! She won't be so starry-eyed in the morning. She'll probably think you were out to take advantage of her!'

'Well, I wasn't. I think too much of her for that!'

'I hope you think too much of every woman for that,' she returned a little stiffly.

'She drank it before I could stop her!' I said, annoyed. 'It was my drink, not hers! She was thirsty and lowered it in one gulp!'

My mother's eyes widened. She laughed in spite of herself.

'Yes,' I went on, 'it had the most extraordinary effect; she danced like something out of the Crazy Horse and asked me why her knees were wobbly!'

'Oh dear,' my mother said, 'these over-sheltered convent girls! The nuns do them no favours; they should prepare them a bit for life. That kind of innocence leaves one very vulnerable!'

'I solemnly promise,' I continued, putting my hand on my heart, 'that I will behave towards Helen with every possible decorum. Do you need me to swear it on the Bible?'

'Good heavens, Dan, I wasn't implying that you're a rake! I didn't imagine for one moment that you'd do anything cheap!'

'She trusts me!' I said indignantly, realizing the truth of it as though for the first time. It had a good sound, the word 'trust'. It brought with it the image of a Dan I approved of, one I knew. I was glad now that I had brought Helen home, that I had not insisted on a second kiss, that nothing had transpired to mar the *entente* between us. But I knew that this was due more to Helen than to me. I did not dare to trespass on Helen's forbearance: her opinion of me was more important to me than almost anything else I could think of. It was central to what I hoped of life.

And then, as I stood there, the thought of Marion intruded without warning and the haze of happiness evaporated. I bade my mother good night and went to bed, and after a while sleep came and with it strange, troubled dreams.

The breakfast table is a good place for philosophy. Rachel had been quizzing me about my evening and, to shut her up, I asked her what she thought of the Austinian theory of Law. This did not have the desired effect, but it did bring about a change of topic. 'Will yeh stop coddin' me!'

'Oh, I see what you mean, Rachel. That analytic positivism and John Austin, the father of English Jurisprudence, are all a cod? I've suspected as much for some time . . .'

Rachel looked at me suspiciously. My mother was still in bed. James and Kieran had gone; they had left earlier than intended. I had heard the noise and got up to see them off. Kieran said to convey his goodbyes to Helen: 'Give her my love and tell her I'll be back in no time with all the news!' They had driven away without a backward glance, heading for Dover and the ferry.

'What do I know about yer oul' waffle?' Rachel said indignantly. 'Why don't yeh tell us a good murder and be some use?'

Helen slept late. She came into the kitchen almost shyly, glancing at me from half-lowered lids, a more demure Helen than the one I had known at Zarathustra's.

'Sit down there like a good girl,' Rachel said, indicating the place set for her.

'Is Kieran gone?' she asked.

'Yes,' I said. 'He and James set off at seven thirty. He said to say goodbye for him!'

'Oh . . . I should have got up earlier.' She seemed crestfallen. She shook out her napkin and in answer to Rachel's query said she would just have tea and toast.

'Yeh won't get far on that!' Rachel opined. 'A growing girl needs a good breakfast; now what about some bacon and eggs?'

I turned to our housekeeper. 'You heard what she said!'

'Of course I heard what she said. Do yeh think I'm deaf?' She turned back to Helen, assumed a coaxing voice. 'Now youse young ones are always thinkin' about yer figure. But if yez don't eat properly . . .' she shook her head at the dire possibilities.

Helen smiled and said that tea and toast was fine and that she had stopped growing.

'That's what yeh think!' Rachel said compressing her lips putting a pot of tea on the table. 'But no one takes any heed o' me', no heed in this life . . . and if they fall sick, oh it's a different kettle of fish then, I can tell you . . .'

When Rachel vacated the kitchen for a few minutes Helen turned to me. 'Is she always like this?'

'Oh yes. Living with Rachel is an art unto itself! Mummy adores her and I suppose we do too – or would if she would only shut up sometimes! But when she was sick recently the house seemed horribly silent.'

Helen ate her toast and sipped her tea and glanced at me sideways. 'Do you think badly of me?' she demanded in a low voice.

'Helen! What a question!'

'Drinking gin! Dancing like that . . . and kissing you! It sounds like something out of a risqué nineteenth-century novel!'

'It sounds to me like something out of life!' I leant across to her. 'I loved kissing you. I love you!'

She shrank back. 'You shouldn't say things that aren't true.'

'But they are true.'

Helen gave me a strange look. I was about to elaborate, to tell her how she featured in all my thoughts, in my dreams, but Rachel returned with a, 'What's true? What are yez talkin' about?'

I sighed and said, 'Nothing Rachel,' and we finished our breakfast in silence.

When Helen went upstairs to get ready for our foray into the city, I swore a mental oath that I would not say another word that day about how I felt about her. She's young, she needs space, I told myself. And space she shall have. Oh Helen . . .

* * *

When I look back on it I know I thought that day would be the template of all our days. We wandered wherever the fancy led us: to the Tower, down the river, to St Paul's, had lunch in a pub, laughed a good deal. I kept my self-made promise. I did not crowd Helen and as the day wore on she became increasingly relaxed and more full of anecdotes, silly, funny little stories at which she laughed a good deal. At such times she was a child. Then she would be serious, delighting in landmarks she had come across in some history book or other, or in Pepys' *Diary*. Evidently well read, versed in history, literature, poetry, she already knew quite a bit about every place of note that we visited. Was this the result of all that reading in her mountain fastness, or did she have a vast school curriculum? When I asked her she smiled and gave the stock answer, 'I read it!'

'You give the impression of someone who has never done anything except read!'

'There's nothing else to do where I come from! If you didn't read you'd die of boredom. No nightclubs there, you know,' she added a little wickedly, 'never mind gin. I've never even been to a hop!'

'Well, you were well able to hop last night!'

This was a mistake. Helen gave me a careful look and clammed up.

'I'm sorry. Don't get cross. Do you want to go to one again tonight?'

'No!'

'That's categorical!'

'It is. Maybe you were trying to get me drunk. Kieran did try to warn me . . .' She pursed her lips and looked at me slyly from half-closed eyes.

'Oh Helen, that's not fair. And what was a filthy thing for him to say! Did you believe him?'

'Of course not. He was joking and probably being territorial . . .'

'But now?' I prompted.

'Now . . . I don't believe it either!' she said with a faint grin. Then she added apologetically, leaning towards me as though to make amends for the fancied slight, 'Don't mind me! I'm teasing!'

The days flew. We went down the river, saw the old bricked-up entrance to Traitors' Gate, the oldest pub in London where the condemned men were brought for a last pint, the dilapidated Dickensian warehouses, which would have been Fagin's hideout in *Oliver Twist*. We went as far as Greenwich and then back, coming up the river in the twilight, the lights of London surrounding us. I drew Helen towards me and she put her head on my shoulder, watching the city assume its night-time aspect, its sparkle. I wanted to hold her closer, turn her face up for my kiss, but I honoured my resolution. I would give her space. She was tired; her head was still between my chin and my shoulder and for a while I thought she might be asleep.

'Helen?'

'What?'

'I thought you were asleep!'

'No . . . but I'm a bit dopey!'

I chuckled. 'Now that I do not believe! What were you thinking of?'

'Kieran!'

God! The injustice of it. She had just spent the day with me, and she was thinking of Kieran!

'What about him?'

'Oh I was just wondering what he was doing – what he was seeing in Paris!'

'He's having a great time and he isn't giving you a thought!'

She straightened. 'You sound jealous when you say things like that!'

'I am jealous!'

'But Kieran is my oldest friend – even older than you!'

'Helen, can't you feel that there is something between us . . . between you and me – something important? Something that has nothing to do with Kieran?'

'I do feel it,' she said gravely after a moment. 'I've told you so already. We're very good friends, and you're a good dancer.' I saw the mischief in her face. 'Do I sound flippant? Don't be deceived. I'm really an idealist!'

'I'm an idealist too! Did you think I wasn't?' I went on. 'What sort of nonsense has Kieran been telling you?'

She shrugged and made no reply. When I repeated the question she said diffidently, 'Well, he says you're a born hedonist and a terrible man for the women! He was warning me against you so that I wouldn't fall captive to your fatal charm, add to the list of your conquests, or something like that!'

'What conquests?' I said lightly, swearing that I would wring Fitzgerald's neck when I saw him. 'I'm a non-practising heterosexual.'

She smiled. I cradled her face and kissed her. I felt the answer between her lips, the soft, moist tremor of her mouth, the melting of her against me before she pulled away. I saw the pulse in her throat, the lowered sweep of her lashes, her breathlessness and uncertainty.

'We shouldn't do things like that!'

'Of course we should! Helen, I'm not messing around with you. I know you're very young . . . and maybe I shouldn't ask you this – but will you wait for me?' I hadn't meant to say it, but there it was, spilt into the air beyond recall.

She looked into my eyes, a speculative gaze, as though she would read my heart. For all her silent questioning she understood very well what I was asking her.

'Will you?' I repeated hoarsely.

She sighed and lowered her eyes. 'I have to finish school. How can I answer a question like that? My mother wouldn't approve of us . . . There'd be no end of problems! And I want to go to college, get a degree . . . And what would Kieran think?'

'It always comes back to Kieran! Why does he need you? Of all the people I ever met I think he needs no one whomsoever!'

'I don't know why he needs me, but he does . . .'

'Rubbish! I was just hoping you wouldn't forget what we mean to each other.'

She was silent. Her hair was like a cloud around her pensive face. She bit her thumbnail and looked at me unhappily, then turned her head away.

'All right,' I muttered. 'All right! You don't think we mean anything to each other! Fine, I'll just bugger off.' And I withdrew my arm from around her shoulders and drew away to stare moodily out at the Thames.

Helen did not offer any emotional salve. She went to stand a few feet away, looking out at the river. I saw how the other men on the boat eyed her. I saw how she stood, erect, almost stern. I began to wonder if I knew her at all, she seemed so strange and withdrawn. She had an ability to surround herself suddenly with walls and ramparts, so that she no longer seemed the young girl, the ingénue, but someone burdened with wisdom and sadness.

Other than the exchange of small pleasantries, we did not speak for the rest of journey. I found this frightening, this sudden gulf between us, the terrible ease with which she had drawn away from me.

We got the tube back to Knightsbridge to find my mother waiting dinner for us. Charles was there. He had returned from Paris where he had met James and Kieran, who were now, he said, installed in his apartment and given over to the discovery of the city. My mother introduced him to Helen and I saw his guarded appraisal of her.

'Do you play the piano?' he asked at one point, and Helen said she did, but badly. 'I only got as far as grade three.'

I was quiet during dinner but Helen chatted as though she hadn't a care in the world, more brightly than usual in fact, as though the sinking of my emotional mercury had given her additional strength. I knew, without any overt intelligence from him on that score, that Charles thought she was lovely. She told him about Monique and her sojourn in Amboise and he asked her if she had seen the châteaux of Chenonceaux and Chambord; she had and described them. The former she said was exquisite, spanning the river Cher, 'with the grace of a fairy tale . . . once owned by Catherine de Medici . . . and to think that her daughter-in-law, Mary Queen of Scots, had to leave places like that for dour, freezing Scotland and the invective of John Knox!' Chambord, she said was 'a great pile, with a roof like a riot . . . turrets and more turrets and chimneys and places to hide away among the sparrows and be lost. It reminded me of a book called *Gormenghast*.' The enthusiasm of her recollection warmed her face. She glanced at me in the course of this exercise, as though to ascertain whether she were being too voluble, but her face did not register any discomfiture with the blank she must have found in mine. She had rebuffed me earlier; I had nothing to give her now.

It was clear that both my mother and Charles were riveted by her enthusiasm as much as by her powers of description. I also knew that she was aware of entertaining them and that it pleased her. And so supper went on, Rachel telling me that I hadn't 'a word to throw to a dog. What are yez sulking about?'

'Oh shut up, Rachel. I'm not in the mood!' Rachel made a *moue* and looked at Helen as though she would be able to explain, but the latter affected innocence.

'I think you've tired yourself out, dear,' my mother said to me when dessert appeared. 'It's not like you to be so taciturn.'

I could sense her curiosity. I knew she thought it had to do with Helen. But I felt as though I was fragmented, as I tried to deal with the horrible vista of a future where Helen and I would have a sea between us and the years would drip away into pointless tedium.

When my mother and Helen had left the table to go upstairs to the drawing room and Charles was following them, he turned to me and said in my ear: '*C'est formidable!*' and raised his eyebrows. He was referring to Helen, and his admiration only fed the hot ache within me, the sense that she didn't need me and didn't care and that love was an entrapment, designed for my personal torture.

An old friend from school, David Garnier, called after dinner and joined us for coffee in the drawing room. I introduced him to Helen. He stayed for about half an hour, then said he had to meet someone and had better toddle off.

'Delighted to have met you, Helen,' he said as he left. 'I hope you enjoy your stay in London. If you get bored just give me a call.'

She laughed. I saw David out. When the drawing room door had shut behind us he murmured, 'Christ, where did you find that stunning creature?'

'Oh, she's an old friend from my Irish days.'

He sighed. 'Pity I have to go away tomorrow.'

'She's already spoken for, David.'

He looked at me, grinned ruefully. 'The gorgeous ones always are.'

I put my head into the drawing room, said I was going to bed, bade them good night. The prospect of making bright conversation was intolerable when I felt sure that Helen had no more feelings for me than she had for Ivan the dog. I heard their voices as I mounted the stairs, the sudden laughter at some joke, and then the piano starting up.

I knew immediately that it was not my mother's hand that touched the keys, nor Charles's either. Helen was playing 'Drink To Me Only'. It was the careful rendition of someone who is still at the stage of hoping she won't miss the keys.

I did not go to bed. I turned off the landing light, sat in the return of the stairs, staring out at the dim garden, at the lights in other houses, and listened to the music from below. When the music stopped I was half asleep, and I was not visible to Helen, when she came up the darkened staircase to bed, until she was almost upon me. She jumped when she saw me. But she did not speak. She stood for a moment uncertainly and then continued on her way.

'Good night,' she said in passing. 'Thank you for a wonderful day!'

'Good night, Helen.'

I stayed in my seat by the window for a long time. The music started again downstairs; I heard the muted voices of my mother and her lover; I thought of my father and decided that I would bring Helen to meet him before she went home. Then I went up to my room.

There was no light under Helen's door. She was evidently already asleep. I thought of her curled up in bed, hair spread across the pillow; I thought of her breast rising and falling with her breathing. I longed for a glimpse of her asleep. I wanted to stand beside her bed and look down at her, see her breathing deeply, try to trace the movement of her eyes beneath her dreaming lids.

Sick with desire and love I softly tried the door knob. It turned in my hand and the door opened. I stood at the jamb, listening to her even breathing, barely able to make out her shape in the bed. I moved forward and stared down at her. There was a warm scent of sleeping womanhood. I stood still, burning. To lift those bedclothes and get in beside her! I knelt, put my head near hers on the pillow, felt her hair brush my face. She stirred, seemed to stop breathing. She was awake. She said nothing, but reached for my hand and laid it, slowly and tenderly, against her cheek. I felt the firm soft flesh, the contour of her lips. The very air in the room was electric, a kind of shimmer, a tension similar to that generated by a naked power cable. I moved convulsively to embrace her, felt the melting of her body for one brief second, her bare upper arms – heard the step on the stairs. Helen jumped away.

'Go,' she whispered urgently. 'Go now!'

I obeyed, closing the door behind me as gently as I had opened it, finding my own room.

A moment later my mother knocked and put her head around the door.

'Oh you're still up. I thought you'd gone to bed. Is everything all right, darling?'

'Fine,' I said, pretending to look for a tome in my bookcase. 'Absolutely fine.'

'You look a bit flushed! You're not sickening for something?'

'I'm fine, Mummy,' I repeated peremptorily.

'All right,' she said, on a note of pique. 'There's no need to be sharp about it!'

Chapter Twelve

On her last day I took Helen to the Temple. I wanted to show her where my future would be spent, listen to her observations. In this way, I thought, she might absorb enough of me, of my projected life, that the thought of me would have to stick. I wanted to be the one who excited her curiosity, the one she thought of if she ever looked at her beauty in the mirror and wondered at its effect on men.

The days had flown. Except for that silent impasse on the return trip from Greenwich, the relationship between Helen and me had prospered. We had laughed, talked nonstop, shared easy, companionable silences, and charged interludes which, for me at least, were full of desire. The memory of that moment in her room when she had taken my hand and put it against her face haunted me, particularly the thought of what might have happened if my mother's step had not been heard on the stairs.

I had even essayed once more to discuss the future with Helen; she had listened gravely; although nothing definite had been said, nothing undertaken, there was between us a growing understanding which required few words. Sometimes we both articulated the same comment at the same time; sometimes we emerged from silence voicing the same thought. 'Snap,' Helen would say. 'We've done it again! Are you telepathic or what?'

I liked who I was with Helen. With her my innocence was restored; with her I felt imbued with clarity of vision; with her everything seemed possible. She had the gift of making one wish to be well thought of by her, as though she possessed some strange private authority. This encouraged an idealism I thought I had left behind me. The approval, the affection of this seventeen-year-old girl, touched even the coverts of my most secret garden. The tension between desire and control; the mastery of the latter in homage of the former, was new.

We sauntered down Middle Temple Lane in the spring sunshine, examined the precincts of 6 Lyle Court and the lists of tenants therein, beginning with the name of Sir William Ryce.

'Someday I will be on that list of names!' I said loftily.

Helen glanced at me. 'You sound very certain!'

'I'm not a bit certain,' I said laughing. 'But I thought you might have the decency to be impressed!'

'But I am! And I'll be twice as impressed when it actually happens!'

We came to the door of Middle Temple Hall. 'This is where I shall eat my dinners!'

Helen giggled.

'What's so funny?'

'Oh nothing. You sound so bloody pompous, make it seem portentous, like some ritual – eating dinners!'

'But it is. Dining in Hall is an important part of the education of a barrister! It's a way of learning the traditions and etiquette of the Bar.'

She glanced at me and stood back to examine the gothic windows. 'Is it very old?'

'About 1570.'

'Elizabethan! Do you know that glass was then as expensive as salt? And salt was very expensive!'

'How do you know that?'

'Read it somewhere.'

I pushed the door. It yielded. We found ourselves in a hallway. We were asked our business by officialdom. I said I was soon to attend the Bar School and would like to see the Hall. Officialdom took a look at Helen and deigned to be helpful.

A richly carved wooden screen separated us from the dining hall itself. We peeped into those august precincts, saw the panelled walls with their coats of arms, the magnificent hammer beam roof, the rows of trestle tables, the portraits and the high table on a dais.

'The high table is made of a single oak tree from Windsor Park. A gift from Elizabeth, it was floated down the Thames to Temple Pier!'

I was glad I had remembered this titbit. Helen's eyes lit up.

'And you'll be munching here! I can almost hear your molars!'

'That is not a graceful comment!'

There was a chirp of a laugh. She craned her head to look above at the gallery and the beams of the Elizabethan roof.

'You see how clever the craftsmen were? They were able to make the roof to span this space before they had girders or anything like that!' I offered.

Helen studied the black oaken beams. 'You can smell history here,' she said, 'almost see the ghosts.' Then she added with a small, wistful voice, 'I envy you.'

'Why? Would you like to study law?'

'No, but I envy your freedom, your kinship with a rich, unquestioning tradition. I am jealous of certainty.'

I turned, but she had already moved back to the door.

We sat for a while in Fountain Court where the trees nodded in the little breeze, strolled to King's Bench Walk and then to Temple Church. All around us were buildings hundreds of years old, where the Law had been matured carefully, methodically, like good wine. I waited for her comments, hoped she would expand on her envy of certitude, something I had never even considered.

'It's different!'

'That's profound anyway!'

'Stop mocking. I mean that it feels like a separate system, like a state within a state!'

'It is, you know, in its way. The Bar serves the state, but is independent from it. It is an old and honourable profession . . .'

I would have gone on, but she forestalled me, smiling. 'I'm sure it is. I'm sure it has nothing at all to do with anything self-serving.'

'What do you mean?'

'I'm kidding. But I sometimes feel about institutions that they are really a game, that people belong in order to win, to achieve status, security, rather than to serve something noble. Do you think I'm wrong?'

'Does that go for the Church too?'

'Leave the Church out of it,' she said. 'It's in a separate category.'

'Is it?'

'Of course it is. You know that!'

'I'll know it much better,' I said boldly, 'if you give me a kiss!'

She gave a startled gasp, but her colour rose. I drew her to one side, and beside the grave of Oliver Goldsmith, her compatriot of two hundred years earlier, now lying near the railings of Temple Church, I took her face in my hands, looked into the green eyes, found her lips. For the first time she put her arms around my neck.

'Helen . . .'

'Mmmn?'

'Tell me you love me.'

She drew back, wiped her mouth, and said crossly, as though my persistence were invasive, 'I might and I mightn't.'

'That is not a declaration of passion! And I wish you wouldn't wipe your mouth!'

'It's the only declaration of passion I can give you. I feel about two years old when I'm with you! And I had to wipe my mouth. It was wet!'

'Will you come and visit us in June, when your exams are over?'

She looked at me doubtfully, then took my hand. 'If your mother doesn't mind!'

'You know her well enough by now to know she'd be delighted! She thinks highly of you, you know!'

I glanced around. Above us, peering from the window of one of the chambers of the Inner Temple, I saw a bespectacled male figure, middle-aged, pinstriped, slightly stooped, greying. His specs sat halfway down his nose and he was regarding us with an expression of whimsical curiosity.

'Let's go and have some lunch,' I said. 'There's an old restaurant around the corner in Fleet Street I'd like to show you.'

I drew her back to Middle Temple Lane, looking over my shoulder at the whimsical face still regarding us from the window. 'Old busybody,' I muttered.

'But he isn't old! He's as young as you are,' Helen said following my gaze. 'It's something I've been thinking about. The human life span isn't long enough for people to grow old! You'll be young too when you're fifty, always assuming, of course,' she added gravely, 'that you don't die of pomposity in the meantime!'

'Pompous? Me? Helen! Take it back at once!'

She was laughing silently, watching me out of the corner of her eye.

'Well, maybe not pompous, perhaps "enthusiastic" would be a better description, and, of course, you're also sweet and nice and all that sort of thing.'

'Damned with faint praise!' I said. 'I'll remember that when I'm a judge terrorizing the punters!'

'You see what I mean about pomposity!'

I glanced back once more at the tall Georgian window, but the voyeur had disappeared and I imagined him at his desk and his mountains of papers. I felt sorry for him, stuck there, picking nits, while we were outside in the laughing sunshine.

In Ye Olde Cock Taverne we lunched upstairs on soup and roast beef. Helen was hungry. 'Yum,' she said, eating with unabashed relish. 'Isn't it lovely to be hungry?'

I held her hand between courses. 'Would you like to go to Zarathustra's again tonight?' I asked her. 'Your last night!'

'OK,' she said, surprising me by her ready compliance, 'but this time I'll make a superhuman effort and lay off the gin!' She said this a sly look at me, adding, 'After all, we can't have you in a perpetual state of consternation!' She laughed, made a face at me. 'I never said I was nice!'

I looked into her lovely eyes, into her open face, into the sensuousness she did not yet know she possessed, into the years ahead of us.

'Do you think you could shock me, Helen?'

'Easiest thing in the world! Except that I'm such a good liggle girl!'

'Don't ape Kieran!'

'Why not?'

'Do you like being called "a good liggle girl"? Isn't he terribly patronizing?'

'But he doesn't mean to be. He's known me since I was a baby! He loves me in his own way.'

'Do you love him?'

'Sort of.' She smiled at me from under her lashes, then said, 'Where I come from people are terrified of feelings. You probably remember that yourself. If someone loves someone the country people say they have a "great notion" of each other. And if it's an earth-shattering passion it's called being "astray in the head!"' She laughed heartily at this, shoulders hunched up to contain the sudden mirth. Then, watching my face, she added, 'But I'm not "astray in the head" about Kieran. And as to whether I have a "great notion" of him or not – well, you'll just have to wait and see.'

I did not reply, suspecting that she was deliberately playing me off against Kieran, suspecting too that her slightly brittle demeanour that day was geared towards testing me, towards finding the point at which I would no longer yield.

'That night when I went into your room and—' I began, but she shook her head, murmured swiftly, 'I was half asleep . . .'

I saw with startled pleasure that a blush mantled her face and neck, down into the white collar of her blouse.

'You do love me, Helen!' I whispered. I took her arm, looked into her face. 'Say it! I want to hear you say it.'

She looked at me in silence, then she smiled shyly and bent her head until it rested on my shoulder.

Later I pulled her to the window of a jeweller's shop.

'What kind of rings do you like?'

'Oh Dan . . .'

'I'm only asking!'

She pointed to a double string of pearls. 'I'm horribly expensive. You can buy me that when you're rich and famous and have your name on the door of Chambers!' Later that afternoon we went to Hyde Park, strolled by Rotten Row. The Household Cavalry were obliging and came clattering proudly by, jingling in full canonicals, burnished helmets, burnished horses, scarlet and gold, plumes cascading.

'Well? What did you think of that?'

'Power, wealth and beauty,' Helen murmured, watching them ride through the gate at Hyde Park Corner. 'Isn't that what London is all about anyway – power and wealth? The whole atmosphere shouts it.'

'Do you find that reprehensible?'

She twinkled at me. 'Power and wealth reprehensible? Depends on whether it's mine or other people's. If it's mine it's proper order. If it's other people's, it's bloody goddamned abuse!' She laughed as though surprised by her own wit. 'Well, at least I'm not a hypocrite!'

She looked around, pointed to the tower of the Hilton. 'When I'm rich and famous I'll stay there and spend the day at the window! Just think of the view.'

She moved back, tripped suddenly, turning her ankle, but I caught her as she fell, sat on the grass verge, removed the shoe and massaged the small foot, size five I estimated, until she pronounced it better. I took my time in this tender ministration, ran my fingers over the delicate bones of her feet, over the ankle, longing to venture higher, to the knee, to the thigh.

'It's fine,' she said after a moment, pulling back and frowning. 'Anyone would think you were making love to my foot!' She gave me an arch look, half coy, half interrogative, as though trying to plumb the realities of manhood, what it was like to live inside a male skin and hold a woman's foot in your hand; as though trying to provoke a reaction which would disclose both the extent of her power and the extent of my self-mastery.

As she moved her skirt rode up and I had a brief tantalizing glimpse of suspenders and vulnerable white flesh. She made a gesture of annoyance, as though this had not been part of the experiment, and pushed it down.

We went to the pictures – *Madame X*, an intolerable old tear-jerker. Helen put her head on my shoulder, let me hold her hand, and she sat there for most of the film, suddenly relaxed, like someone who had made a decision and was happy to be home. I began to congratulate myself. Helen was not the kind of girl to say things she did not mean. She was not the kind of girl to put a man's hand against her face unless she felt something important. All I had to do now was not to rush her, to let it grow.

'You're wonderful,' she whispered halfway through the film in a sleepy voice, warmed by the companionable darkness, and I hoped, by the patient, superhuman control of her escort. We drew closer together, me cradling her head, she yielding and weepy, in spite of herself, with the saccharine sentimentality on screen, pretending when I looked at her that she had to blow her nose. I realized that the emotional life in Helen was very near the surface, and that her fear of it dictated its constant suppression. I blessed Madame X and all her troubles.

At some relatively uncharged sequence in the drama on screen, Helen turned up her face to me. 'I knew the first day I saw you – you remember that morning in the avenue – that you were . . . not cut of common cloth!'

Here was an accolade to lift the heart! 'In what way, Helen?'

'In every way. I knew you were Kieran's friend, but I wanted you to be mine! You were the first friend he brought to the valley. There were others later, but you were the only one I could ever stand. And I don't believe the things he said about you.'

My small euphoria evaporated. I experienced a stab of pain and disbelief. 'Does he make me out to be so awful?'

'No, no, it's not what he says . . . it's a kind of joking innuendo – as though he enjoys what you do, in a male kind of way; but he makes you seem amoral and I know you're not, and it makes me furious with him when I think about it! Sometimes I feel he's nothing but a stuffed shirt!'

I wanted, unkindly, to cheer. Look to your complacency, old fellow, I thought. We're having a little volte-face here.

'What about Monique?' I asked, suddenly remembering the slight French girl and her strange observation that day on the hillside: '. . . *Il y a quelque chose là-bas qui me donne des frissons dans le dos.*' 'You never mention her.'

'We keep in touch. She's studying for her baccalaureate. Her letters in English are terribly funny because she uses French syntax . . .'

Someone behind us, who actually wanted to watch the awful film, prodded me on the shoulder and asked me with chilling English politeness if we would mind shutting up. Helen gave a snort, as though the small tensions of the day had distilled themselves into this moment which was too comical to bear. We took the wiser course and left the cinema, half smothered by suppressed laughter, venting it, once outside with shouts of mirth.

I phoned my father's flat from a call box, Helen squeezing in beside me very pleasantly. There was no answer.

'They may be away for Easter,' I said.

'Never mind,' Helen said, 'I can see them some other time!'

'You will,' I said. 'That much is certain!'

I saw her by my side in a white dress and veil and my father leaning down to kiss the bride.

That evening at Zarathustra's I offered Helen a gin and orange. 'It's breaking the law, of course,' I said airily, 'but a serious gin drinker shouldn't let that bother her.'

She laughed. 'I'll make a superhuman effort. Just orange this time!' She sipped her mineral primly and I sipped my drink and we smiled at each other and rose for a slow dance, moving together in a curious kind of mutual comfort, like old loves. It was only when I looked up from my absorbed pleasure in the feel of her body against mine that I realized I was being watched. The eyes, anguished, slightly glazed, belonged to Marion Chatterton. She was sitting at the other side of the room and she raised her glass to me in a cynical and slightly woozy gesture.

The foreboding struck at once. I felt with sudden horrible clarity that she was the worm in the apple, the canker at my life's core. I was instinctively afraid and I whispered to Helen that we should leave. Helen looked at me in some surprise.

'OK, if you want. I thought you were enjoying yourself!'

'I am, but as you're leaving tomorrow I think you should get a reasonably early night!'

Helen seemed startled, but was submissive. We went to the cloakroom, proffered the tickets, and as we took our coats Marion suddenly stood before us, smiling unsteadily.

'Hello, Dan, old thing. How are you?'

She was dressed in a black sequinned affair, showing lots of breast and arms and she smiled at Helen who, modestly attired in a skirt and blouse, looked at her curiously, as though she was drawing a mental picture of what it meant to be sophisticated.

'Hello, Marion. This is Helen . . . Helen, this is Marion!'

Marion's smile widened. 'I'm his ex, my dear; we had a big pash . . .' Then she lowered her voice. 'I hope you make sure you don't get caught . . . not like poor little me . . .'

Helen said, looking affronted, 'What do you mean "don't get caught"?'

Marion widened her eyes. 'Don't let him put you in the club, of course,' she said slowly, as though talking to an idiot. She studied Helen's uncomprehending face. 'You know . . . don't get pregnant, for God's sake!'

'Pregnant?' Helen echoed, looking at me.

'What are you talking about, Marion?' I hissed. 'You're drunk!'

'So sorry . . .' she smiled sweetly. 'Shouldn't be drunk. Not the thing . . . especially in front of your new sweetheart. But the point is, darling,' she continued, fixing Helen with her blue eyes, 'I had to have an abortion and it's mucked me up rather. I keep dreaming of the poor little bugger ... hawked out, you know ... in a pool of blood.'

Helen froze; an expression of horrified uncertainty moved across her face, like someone caught in an earthquake, and knowing that the trust of the years had been betrayed. She did not even look at me, but her eyes filled. 'I'm sorry,' she quavered.

'So am I, sweetie,' Marion said, and then, raising her eyebrows at me, she turned away, leaving me staring after her. I knew, just as Helen knew, that she had spoken the truth. I moved to follow her, but she turned unsteadily and hissed, 'You've done enough damage! Just bugger off.' She tossed her head towards Helen. 'Save it for your next victim.'

For a moment I was unable to think; the shock of what she had said could neither be assimilated nor overcome; the image of myself which rode on her words and her gestures was one I could not bear, would not recognize. The only thing I could do was to close my mind to it. I moved back to Helen, automatically helped her with her coat, but she flinched away from me, gave me a look of open horror and almost ran for the door.

Life watches you. It finds your weaknesses, indulges them and lies in wait. Sooner or later it all comes home to roost. You get away with little in this life, unless you are a seasoned knave and know the labyrinths of deception.

I did not know the labyrinths of deception. I had been foolish, selfish, insensitive, careless. But I had never wished death on anything, much less my unborn child. I was confronted with myself. I was confronted with the results of my careless presumption; I was faced with the harvest of my wild oats. There was no point in blaming Marion, although I tried to.

And I had lost Helen; that much was certain. I had lost her just as I felt I had won her. I knew neither how to remedy my loss nor how to endure it.

Helen went home with Kieran the next day. She hardly spoke to me, did not shake hands on parting and she adverted to Kieran as though he were her safe haven, the port in all her storms and tribulations.

'Goodbye, old fellow,' Kieran said. 'Thank you for everything, for looking after Helen.'

They drove away, but Helen did not wave as Kieran did, nor did she look back.

'Sulky kid!' James opined, turning to examine me. 'Did you have a little tiff?' He seemed, personally, very chuffed with his sojourn in Paris, full of small, secret smiles.

When our visitors had gone my mother took me to one side a little anxiously. 'Was everything all right between you and Helen? I thought you were hitting it off so well, but she seemed very quiet when she was leaving! She hardly looked at you! Did you have a fight?'

I muttered something I didn't understand myself and went to my room. I stared out at the spring sky, at the clouds, listened to the impersonal sounds of traffic from the street. Then I took out a pad and wrote to Helen.

Darling Helen,

I did not know! Please believe me. It never entered my head that such a thing could happen. This is to my shame, because I am acquainted with the facts of life. The best thing you can do is forget me. If you can forgive me sometime, so much the better.

My undying love, Dan.

James knocked and let himself in. I closed the writing pad. He looked at me speculatively, and seemed on the point of giving me the benefit of some piece of jocularity, but sensing that the timing was inappropriate, he talked instead of his time in Paris, of the apartment in the 'Avenue Posh', what he and Kieran had done, people they had met.

Finding me taciturn, he became quiet, hovered around for a few moments as though he hoped I would volunteer some titbit of information, would disclose the reason for my tense reticence, would set the tone for mutual confidences; but when the silence deepened he left and quietly closed the door.

And so it began, the period of adjustment. Life changed, was transmuted into an automatic process of existing and working, a process of trying to shift the focus of my expectations.

I went back to Cambridge and worked for my degree, but without the passionate impetus that had fuelled my work earlier that year, although I found that the events chronicled in some of the cases I perused moved me terribly. My emotions were raw and susceptible. My eyes would fill as I read about the father who died to save his small son, leaping on to the railway track to dislodge his infant from the path of an oncoming vehicle; I wept when I read of the two soldiers who had murdered a teenage girl for fun, tying her heels to her neck with piano wire so that the poor little thing piteously strangled, and they watched, the unspeakable monsters, without mercy.

I saw Marion once or twice in the distance, but she always disappeared into some doorway. I kept hearing her voice, the pain in it: '. . . hawked out, you know . . . in a pool of blood.'

How could she have done it? I asked myself, ready with the censure of someone who was involved without personal cost. Then I tried to put myself in her shoes, tried to imagine being trapped in a thickening body, plagued by nausea, horrified at being turned into a vehicle willy-nilly, staring at the terrible, inescapable prospect of childbirth, like a beast at the shambles, all without emotional or financial support; and the problems thereafter, the burden of a responsibility unwanted and eternal, the rifling of one's emotional capital; I imagined the defiance, the proud female anger against nature itself.

Would I, I asked myself, faced with poverty, with the actual dilemma being enacted in my own body, being filled with the same anger and defiance, have done any differently? I ducked the answer.

I sat my final exams, the second part of the Law Tripos, regurgitated the knowledge I had ingested. I did not get a first, but I managed an upper second. And, then I turned my attention to the prospect of Bar School.

This prospect, however, was scotched by an excitement I had not anticipated. My letter to Helen had been found by her mother and was returned to mine, with an angry note. 'I cannot get any sense from Helen,' Mrs Fitzgerald wrote, 'and I feel my confidence has been betrayed by Dan. How could he abuse my trust, and Helen's, by forcing his attentions on her, a young girl? She denies it, of course, but the letter speaks for itself.'

My mother handed me the missive and I tore my returned letter into pieces.

'I didn't force myself on her. That woman is a cow!'

My mother looked at me in perplexity. 'So what is she talking about? Your letter is a bit strange. What does it mean?'

'It's a private letter,' I said, 'about a private matter. It has nothing to do with Helen, because I have never done more than kiss her; and yet it has everything to do with her, because she will never speak to me again!'

'Is she . . . so important to you?'

'She is the only woman I will ever truly want. I wanted to marry her. I even asked her . . . after a fashion. But she will never marry me now!'

My mother frowned, and regarded me anxiously. 'Well,' she said after a moment, touching my hand with rare sympathy, 'it's not like you to speak in riddles; but if I can help – if Charles can help – will you tell us?' She sighed and said slowly, 'I can assure you of one thing, though – life is full of tides . . . and "never", however passionately feared, however sure it may seem, is a very long time!'

PART II

Chapter Thirteen

Grim Jim woke up when I mentioned the child's injuries.

'These are serious injuries, Mr McPherson. That a child of such tender years should have undergone such a calamity is very sad . . . very sad indeed!' He spoke ponderously and looked over his bifocals at the court. 'Very said indeed!'

'Indeed, my lord!'

Mr Justic James Shore, otherwise known as Grim Jim, was getting on and becoming a bit dozy. But underneath that nodding exterior, underneath that lugubrious expression, his heart was pure obsidian. He would sift the evidence with a fine-tooth comb, and not all the terrible injuries in Christendom would nudge him towards the easy solution.

The case before the court concerned a four-year-old girl, Dora Jennings. She had wandered, rather like Goldilocks, into a derelict house, into the kitchen and then up the stairs. But, instead of the three bears, she had encountered a shattered bedroom window. Through this she had climbed. She had stood on the windowsill for a few moments, observing the world below, before panicking and falling to the pavement, sustaining head and limb injuries. The point at issue was whether the local council, who had possession of the house under a compulsory purchase, were liable to the child in damages. They claimed she was a trespasser and, as such, someone to whom they had no duty. They claimed there was no enticement. They denied liability.

It was July and, even within the precincts of the court, it was humid. I felt the sweat trickle under my wig. A headache was threatening; in summer the wig was heavy, particularly across the temples where it reposed stiffly, an absurd irritant in the heat. The gown too felt oppressive, although I was so used to it by now that its enveloping folds were like a second skin. Indeed, without it and the wig, I would have felt like a Muslim woman out of purdah, strangely naked.

I watched Grim Jim carefully, honing my submissions to his susceptibilities, all my antennae alert to sense which way the wind was blowing. My leader in this case had been suddenly taken ill and the conduct of the latter part of the case had fallen to me. Grim Jim was now listening carefully, although his hooded eyes were expressionless.

I quoted the authorities, particularly Hetherington's classic case where a trespassing child had been electrocuted on a railway. The thrust of my submission, as supported by this precedent, was that the council knew the house was derelict; they knew the door was gone; they knew there were children in the locality; they could reasonably have foreseen that children would trespass, and yet they had done nothing whatsoever to prevent this occurrence, nor to lessen the likelihood of injury by boarding up the upstairs windows. They could not, therefore, exculpate themselves from liability.

When I was finished the judge turned to Dicky Whiston, who was representing the local council, and I sat down. Dicky got to his feet. I listened to what he was saying, knowing he was really blustering, although he could bluster with such calm aplomb that only the initiated could recognize the small signs of his uncertainty, the inadvertent fidget of his feet, the way he worked his thumb against his index finger.

I wanted to take my wig off and wipe my head, now balding in the same pattern as my father, a thinning space on the crown, like a tonsure. Instead I put a hand to my wig and pressed it down firmly.

I glanced behind at my client, the father of the 'infant plaintiff', and the girl's mother, both sitting with grim expressions in the public benches. I knew the case was painful for them; it had forced them to relive the trauma of the day when their little daughter had been taken to hospital in a coma. She had recovered from coma, but there was brain damage and the prognosis was not overly hopeful. So they sat and waited, with fury and indignation at the council's efforts to avoid culpability, knowing they were going home, through the hot London traffic, to a fractious child who would need specialized nursing care for the rest of her life.

I glanced at my instructing solicitor – an assistant with Wells Crother & Co. He was taking notes and had his young head bent over his papers. For a moment he reminded me of myself ten years earlier, setting out on the road to legal preferment with a sore heart and a belief in the anodyne of hard labour, personal immolation on the altar of rectitude. In those days I had thought that the law and justice were automatic bedfellows. Only the years had taught me that justice, like every other ideal, was the product of the human heart, and that systems designed to serve it were as fallible as their creators.

And did I still think of Helen? Yes, I still thought of her, though I had never returned to Lough Corrloch. And as for my dreams of a winter honeymoon, I had had one of sorts, but not with Helen. Life had overtaken us both; whatever had been plastic and idealistic in us had yielded to a concatenation of circumstances, to the demands of others, to our own projections, to the blindness of youth which cannot recognize the portent of what stares it in the face; all of which, lumped together, people generally confuse as Fate.

Strangely enough the final rift had come through Charles.

In July of 1962, some time after my final return from Cambridge, Charles went to Paris. He asked my mother to accompany him, but she demurred and James went instead, on the basis that he would only stay for the weekend. I knew that my mother felt her position to be ambiguous; she was not married to this man, although she shared his life; he was considerably younger than she was; the control of her emotions, which she had always served, was not something she had actually jettisoned; instead she gave them limited rein, while holding fast, all the while, to the end of the rope. I think she was afraid that if she lived with Charles on his territory, if she married him she would lose the sovereignty she had so carefully cultivated. She had her own career now and was, perhaps, wary of putting herself in the power of any man again.

But when Charles was gone to Paris my mother became edgy, as though suddenly afraid that she had driven her lover away. I could see the warring tensions, which she tried to conceal under a front of motherly concern for me on the basis that I had recently finished exams and needed cosseting. But she would prick up her ears when the phone rang and would move with unusual alacrity to pick it up.

Charles did phone twice while he was away, but this, I think, was not often enough for reassurance.

I sensed in her a two-pronged resentment: one, that she should be forced into a vulnerable position by becoming Charles's wife; and two, that she should be vulnerable anyway if she did not take up this option. I think she saw that if he were to withdraw from her life the vista would be bleak indeed.

Charles had returned a week later, leaving James, who had extended his stay, in the Paris apartment. My mother greeted her lover with an arch gaiety, like a young girl. He brought the news that Kieran had joined them in the Paris flat and was now there with James; that both would stay until the end of the week.

My mother frowned. The disquiet was an instant's shadow. I wondered at it. Did she dislike Kieran? She had always seemed to get along with him so well; he had been a favourite. There had been no sign of any change in this favoured status when he had visited us at Easter, although after James had returned with him from Paris I occasionally saw my mother's eyes rest on her elder son with something like concern. But there was no reason why she should object to Kieran staying with James in Paris again.

She glanced at me and then back to Charles.

'Was this arranged in advance . . . Kieran's arrival?'

'I've no idea,' Charles said with a shrug. 'I suppose James phoned him. Kieran has friends in Paris anyway.'

'Well,' my mother said slowly, 'I suppose both he and James could do with the break!'

Charles threw her a bemused look, put his arm around her. 'You could do with a break. What do you say to the Cotswolds next weekend?'

'Darling, what a wonderful idea!'

A letter from Helen arrived a few days later, giving the address as Lough Corrloch.

Dear Dan,

I've just found out that Mam wrote to your mother. I'm simply mortified and had words with her. Don't heed whatever it was she said. She gets a bee in her bonnet very easily these times. I told her you were a perfect gentleman and that she has a mind like a Borgia. I thought she wouldn't know who they were, but she hasn't spoken to me since!

Kieran has gone to Paris again (without the car this time). He has got his Masters and will be lecturing in UCD in the autumn. As soon as he comes back he'll visit us in the valley. It's lovely here at the moment; the gorse is still yellow in patches, but the heather is bright new purple. I saw a hawk this morning, at least I think it was a hawk; it was certainly a raptor. It hung in the sky the way they do and then suddenly dropped, like a stone, as though it had been shot. A few moments later it emerged from the heather and winged away slowly above the ground, carrying something in its beak! Poor little Tittlemouse, or whoever.'

We have had a surprise visit from a Mr Jocelyn Malcolm (Joss to his friends, he says). He is the heir to the lodge and the valley, and indeed to this house when the lease is up. He's an American, the nephew of the present owners, who are living in London (or somewhere in England). He's very big and pleasant, and a bit astonished to find the place so lovely (at least that's what he said). He thought it would be bleak and stony! I walked with him to the lake and we had a good chat. He is a doctor and lives in New York. He's about forty. He says that if he inherits the place before he gets too old he'll do up the lodge and come here on holiday!

Dan, forgive me if I seemed judgemental when I left London. The whole thing is none of my business and I've no right to interfere. Please don't be upset by my mentioning it; I had a dream about you recently and in it there was some kind of accident and you were sinking in the bog, the same one that Kieran fell into all those years ago, except that it had become a quicksand and I couldn't get you out, although I kept screaming for help. I woke up and my face was wet with tears.

I hope it will be all right if I still write to you sometimes? Will you send me your news?

Your loving friend (always . . . always),
Helen.

I read and re-read this letter in the privacy of my room and then I thumped my hand into the wall. The plaster impacted and then a few tears surfaced even as I wiped them away.

Helen, just forget me. I don't want you with your mind full of my misdeeds; I don't want your censure or your forgiveness!

Charles and my mother returned from the Cotswolds. He seemed a little dour, which for him was unusual; she had about her a certain brittle gaiety as though there were things she refused to address and thought she could circumvent by a distracting jollity.

James returned from Paris with Kieran in tow. My mother greeted her guest cordially enough, although there seemed a reserve, almost a questioning, in her demeanour towards him, which had not been there before. She had used to flirt with him after a humorous fashion; now this had disappeared in favour of a friendly reserve. If Kieran noticed any change in her attitude he gave no sign. James, who was in high spirits after his holiday, did not seem to notice it either.

Kieran was unchanged. He was still witty, charming, exerting himself laconically.

'How are you, old fellow?' he asked me. 'Worn out by the exigencies of the law?'

Suddenly the law seemed a dubious discipline for the disingenuous.

'Hardly worn out,' I said. 'I still have all my own teeth and hair!'

'Have you?' He raised his eyebrows, smiling quizzically. 'All? I'm losing mine . . . well, some of the hair anyway.'

And it was true. His hairline had begun to recede. He sighed and added with a note of the absurd, gazing out at me from behind his specs: 'No hair, knobbly knees . . . I'm hardly the answer to a maiden's prayer.'

I felt that this speech was unnecessarily modest, saw James look at him, suppressing a tight smile, as he muttered, 'It would have to be some maiden!'

I thought of Helen, thought of her frequent intimations that Kieran had tried to turn her against me. But it was no use blaming him for anything in that quarter any more; I had attended to its destruction quite thoroughly myself. I wondered if I should take him aside, break all my resolutions and disclose my heart to him. But I did not. The resentment which still smouldered at the bottom of my mind would not permit me. He had said things to Helen, wittingly or unwittingly, which were to my detriment.

Kieran stayed for the weekend. Before he left, something happened which changed the potential for all our futures. The cataclysm had come, after all, sneaked up on all of us one Sunday. It happened very simply.

Kieran dropped a packet of matches. It was an ordinary little fold-over packet, such as are given gratis by nightclubs. I picked it up and looked at the legend printed in black on gold: '*La Vie Sauvage*'. It reminded me of something Kieran had once said to me, when speaking of Lough Corrloch; now it was, evidently, the name of a Paris nightclub. I thought this a small coincidence and reminded Kieran, but he shrugged and said with a laugh: 'Did I really call the valley that? Great minds evidently think alike ... It's a nightclub James and I visited in Paris.'

'Any good?' I asked, wondering if there had been a floor show. The name conjured up visions semi-orgiastic.

'Yeah. Interesting!'

We were in the drawing room. My mother was perched on the piano stool studying a piece of draft music, to which she was making additions, fingering a few keys as she went along. James and Charles were both coming up the stairs from the kitchen where they had been the last to breakfast, and when they entered the room I said, 'Charles, do you know a nightclub in Paris called *La Vie Sauvage*?'

'I've heard of it,' he said. 'It's a notorious haunt for homosexuals!'

I remember the moment that followed principally for the quality of the silence. My mother's fingers fell away from the piano. I heard the tiny ticking of the clock on the mantelpiece, and was aware of the frozen stance of James, Kieran's clenched fist, and Charles looking from one of us to the other, aware of a faux pas, but momentarily bewildered.

I handed the packet of matches back to Kieran.

Charles followed this small movement. His face cleared, understanding dawned. He glanced at my mother, looked at the two of them, shrugged with Gallic tact and mutter, '*Pooh, ce n'est pas grand-chose* ...' Then he went to my mother, asked her, with his usual affectionate touch on her shoulder, some question about the music she was perusing.

But my mother ignored him. The anguish in her as she regarded her elder son was almost tangible. The expression on her face showed terror that her worst fears were realized. She shrugged aside Charles's pleasantry and croaked after a moment: 'Tell me it's not true!'

Nobody spoke. The seconds ticked by. 'Tell me it's not true!' she repeated, looking from her son to Kieran and back.

Neither responded for a moment and then Kieran said in a calm, smooth voice: 'Do I understand you to mean, Mrs McPherson, that you think that either James, or myself, is . . . ?' He didn't finish the sentence, adding with a deprecating half-laugh, 'You couldn't possibly?'

My mother hardly glanced at Kieran before returning her eyes to James's white face. 'Tell me it's not true,' she repeated.

But James turned aside and left the room. Kieran stood his ground, his demeanour changing from calm dissuasion to angry remonstrance as my mother's cold, accusing eyes reverted to him.

'How can you even imagine such a thing, Mrs McPherson?'

My mother's eyes were fixed on him with almost savage intensity. She repeated the question: 'Is it true, Kieran?'

'I am not a bum-boy!' Kieran shouted, squirming under her gaze and suddenly bereft of sang-froid. 'And I have never been so insulted in my life! The damn place was a curiosity; that's all!'

He turned on his heel and left the room, climbing the stairs two steps at a time. He collected his bag and left the house at once, although it was still more than two hours before his train was due to leave Euston. I went upstairs to James and stood with him by the window as he watched Kieran's departure. I saw the tall form in the tweed jacket hail a cruising taxi without a backward glance. But when the taxi turned at the end of our road I saw that its fare had his head in his hands.

James, who had already turned away, muttered, 'He said it was an insult! You heard him . . . Everything that I gave him . . . an insult!'

I did not see my mother again that day. By the time James had come downstairs to tell her his story, she had already gone out with Charles. When they came back that evening the earlier momentum was lost. James took her aside and told her that everything she had heard was just an unfortunate coincidence. They had gone to that nightclub out of curiosity. They thought it would be a bit of fun.

She seemed to accept this, expressed sorrow for any embarrassment, but I felt she was simply postponing the issue until she could bear to examine it.

James went back to the grind of hospital life. I started studying for my Bar exams, came home one evening and heard the voices in my mother's bedroom, she saying she was older than Charles, he saying that he didn't give a damn.

'Don't you realize, you stupid woman, that it's you – the heart and soul in you, the passion in you – that I want? Do you think any youth, however glowing, makes up for shallowness and incompatibility?' Charles paused, adding with a husky voice, 'Take a chance on me, Anne; marry me. This is the last time. I'm not going to ask you again!'

I went into my room, feeling that another rent was pending in the fabric of all that was home. I changed into a fresh shirt almost angrily and went downstairs to talk to Rachel.

Rachel was no longer young. I had known this for years; she had been plump and middle-aged for as long as I could remember, but now she had begun to look like a pumpkin which had started to collapse. The weight of her midriff was no longer an important statement before the world, but something that sagged. Her double chin had also lost its buoyancy, and she tended to wheeze a little. She was less garrulous than had been her wont, as though her reserves of energy had become too precious to dissipate. She was sitting at the kitchen table hulling strawberries when I entered the kitchen. She smiled up at me, and I sat beside her and helped, and then she said, 'Yer a good boy!'

When the chore was done she brought the strawberries to the sink to wash them and then demanded, 'D'yez want a cup o' tea?' adding with something of her old conspiracy, 'There's a gorgeous little chocolate cake in it!'

My heart rose a little, not so much at the prospect of the chocolate cake, but because the invitation was so typical of Rachel, and curiously reassuring. She had always assumed that some small culinary treat was the panacea for life's vicissitudes; indeed, her certainty of this was contagious, for the little ceremony which accompanied the opening of the cake tin, the putting of the cake on the plate, the admiration for it, the careful cutting of each slice, lent it a quasi-religious importance. One felt welcomed into a select mind-set, where an arcane mystery was about to be shared.

'Well, how are yez, anyways?' she demanded as she put a slice on my plate. 'Ye've been keeping yerself to yerself lately.' She looked at me as she said this with narrowed eyes and an expression which indicated her suspicions as to the cause for my taciturnity. 'If it's a woman,' she continued softly, savouring a morsel of the confection with a sigh of pleasure, 'always remember there does be plenty more fish in the sea! She was pretty, that little thing . . . but cute enough for all that!'

I started, wondering if she knew everything, if she could read minds.

'No, Rachel, I'm just a bit tired.'

'Hmmn . . . well, maybe. But, all the same, I think yez could be a bit anxious because yer life is changing.'

'How do you mean, Rachel?'

She sighed. 'Life is full of little lives, small chapters; and every time one of them ends we die a little. Now your life is changing; yeh can never be a child again with other people to do yer worrying for yez! And yer probably anxious about losin' the things yeh knew, because whenever there's change there's loss!'

I was silent, thinking she had wisdom and that I never knew it.

'Oh come on,' she added; 'don't look so gob-smacked!'

I laughed. 'But I don't want to be a child, thank you! I'm perfectly happy to be an adult!'

'That's better,' she added half apologetically. 'I do be philosophying while I'm here in the kitchen.' She drank some tea, holding the teacup daintily, little finger cocked in perfect propriety. 'Ah 'tis grand stuff, this cake!'

She looked at the window, indicating her two fat cats, sunning themselves on the sill.

'What'll happen to poor oul' Minky and Jinky when I'm not here any more!'

I turned to her, feeling suddenly bereft. 'What do you mean, Rachel? Are you going away?'

'Eventually, not yet . . . we all go away eventually. There'll be changes here before long; I can feel it in me bones.'

She glanced at me, lowered her voice and leant towards me

confidentially. 'Your mother has to make up her mind, because that man o' hers is fed up hangin' on to the end o' the string she has him tied to. Oh, I can see it. She outta marry him and be done with it!'

I was silent for a moment, thinking of the exchange I had overheard upstairs. 'Do you think she will?'

'If she doesn't she needs her head looked at! I think she will; and then all the pieces on the board will have found new places; and it will be Rachel's time to do the same.'

I took her hand, the first time I had done so since my childhood. 'Mummy needs you, Rachel; why would you go?'

'I'm old, Danny,' she said with a sad smile, returning the pressure of my hand. 'Once I thought time only affected other people, that I was just a looker-on. But it's a mill and we're all caught in it, whether we like it or not.'

The autumn came. My mother married Charles in November and moved into his apartment, but she still came back to be with us in Walton Street one or two days a week, as though fearful of cutting the apron strings too precipitously. Rachel, who was now seventy, said she wanted to go 'home'. She had an old friend in Dublin who had recently become an inmate of a new retirement home, and had advised Rachel to book her place there while places were still available.

'London is a grand place,' she said, 'but when yeh get old yeh need to go home! And now's me chance!'

She went away in early December. My mother spent some time alone with her in the kitchen that morning, and emerged looking tearful.

James hugged Rachel in the hall. 'Mind yerself,' she said to him admonishingly. 'That oul' tongue of yers . . . that black streak in yeh . . . is the divil's own business.' But she suddenly kissed him as though he were still the child he had been.

I escorted her to Euston. I had already told my father and he came to see her off, gave her a fat cheque. She had a pension and was well taken care of, but she cried as she left. I had tears in my own eyes and my father had the half-sad, half-lugubrious expression of one who sees the end of an era.

'I'll come and see you in Dublin,' I promised.

'Ye'd better,' she said grimly, through her tears, getting into the train. I saw her to her seat, kissed her tired wet cheek.

'Thank you, Rachel ... for everything. It won't be the same without you! We'll miss you dreadfully! I'll write ...'

She nodded, tried to smile, squeezed my fingers with her leathery ones. 'Look after them two cats!' was the last thing she said before I had to leave her. I went out and stood on the platform, watching her as the train pulled away, until all I could see was the blue of her best felt hat and then the back of the train as it snaked out of Euston.

I had not replied to Helen's letter. Mortified to the quick that she should know so much about my past, I told myself that if she couldn't see how unfair it was that my casual relationship with Marion should have precipitated the misfortune that it had, I was better off without her. I began to cloak my memory of her with small disparagements; she was narrow, I told myself, a typical product of the closed, religious educational system in Ireland; she could keep her piety and inflict it elsewhere. How dare she presume to advise me?

But, then again, I would think of the plaintive note in that last letter, her dream of my being stuck in the bog, she screaming for help to get me out, while I drowned in the black peaty water. Oh Helen, if you care, if you love me, write and say you do ... There is hope for us yet.

I was still tossing the ifs and buts around in my head when I got a Christmas card from Kieran. It was his usual kind of thing, a snow scene, a witty comment, as though he had never left our house in angry circumstances, and down at the bottom, by way of a postscript the small note, 'Helen and I are getting engaged at Christmas!'

Her own card which followed within a couple of days, confirmed this. She administered the *coup de grâce* with a certain pragmatism.

> Kieran and I are getting engaged, but we probably won't get married for a year or so. I suppose this will come as a surprise to you; but, Dan, it seems the best thing; Mam is poorly since she had a fall and needs a lot of care. She has become very forgetful

> and strange in herself. This means I have to stay with her nearly all the time; but Kieran kindly offered to have her live with us. He has, as I think I told you, a lectureship in UCD.

I should have seen it years ago, I told myself bitterly. Of course Fitzgerald had it all worked out. Helen was his ticket to respectability. She was innocent and had always loved him. She was trapped with a sick mother and without the means to effect any kind of escape. She was to be the proof that his sexual tastes were orthodox. Now she was going to enter into a marriage which could contain nothing for her, nothing, nothing, nothing!

'You don't know that!' James assured me, white-faced, when I poured out my heart to him that evening. 'He could be Greek in his tastes.'

'He could be double Dutch in everything, for all I care. I hate him. Did he ever write to you or phone after he was here that last time?'

James regarded me coldly. 'No!' he said. 'And hating him will change nothing! Both of us must confront our own stupidity. We allowed our own projections to steal away our souls!'

'What about her?' I said.

'What about her? She has chosen him; let her have him!'

'She hasn't chosen him freely,' I said. 'I'm sure of that!'

'Oh for God's sake, when will you get sense?'

James had changed since summer, become taciturn, lost the provocative sallies which were his hallmark. He came to see me one day, shortly after Christmas, and said he had made plans to go to America. There was a practice in California where he had friends.

I did not send Kieran a Christmas card; I do not know if James did. But I sent Helen a note:

> You know how I feel about you; you know I cannot congratulate you on your news. I would like to see you as there are things I think you should know before you embark on this course. I will meet you anywhere you like. I want to go to Dublin anyway to see Rachel, who left us before Christmas.
>
> I am sorry to hear about your mother. Please write, Helen, please phone. My relationship with Marion is over. What

happened happened, and I can't undo it, although I would if I could. But I do want to talk to you; it's important.

God bless you, Dan.

I waited. About two weeks later, when I had just about given up hope, a letter arrived for me with an Irish stamp.

Dear Dan,

Thanks for your letter; you sound very mysterious. But the die is cast. Kieran and I will be married in June, sooner than expected, as Mam continues to deteriorate. Kieran points out that if we leave it much longer she may not be able to understand what is taking place.

There is very little point in our meeting now. I have new obligations; I care for Kieran a great deal. But I will never forget you and that wonderful week in London. I hope with all my heart that things work out for you. None of us is free to indulge our own wills; we must all do the right thing, and I'm sure that you will too.

Don't forget me.

Helen.

I threw this letter on the fire. Very well, I thought, let her marry him. Let her throw her life away. What was it to me? Why should I care? And why the hell did she have to bloody preach?

But despite myself, despite my anger and pique and sense of rejection, I found myself a week later, almost without thinking about it, on a plane to Dublin.

Chapter Fourteen

The Belfast train left Dublin's Amiens Street station on time, slid through the redbrick rooftops to the coast. It was a disappointingly modern affair, diesel, not the splendid sooty business I remembered from my Dublin childhood.

I knew I was breaking all the rules, but was stubborn in perfidy. Kieran, friend of my childhood, was engaged to Helen; my journey's purpose was to end that engagement. The ties of the past were not enough to deter me, even though he regarded me still, if his Christmas card was anything to go by, as his friend. It was true that he had broken no relational canon with me; but he had hurt my brother in ways I could only surmise. And every instinct in me insisted that his forthcoming marriage was founded on expediency. Of course it suited me to think this; it was the rationale to which I clung for justification. But if it were true, I owed Helen more than scruples. And I was sure it was true: I had never glimpsed in him a moment's passion, never detected in him an instant's vulnerability, except on that Sunday morning when he had stalked, in high dudgeon, out of our house in Walton Street. Quite apart from my own self-interest, the prospect of Helen being married at eighteen to someone who saw her as sister, as a good liggle girl, who had nothing to offer her emotionally, seemed to me an obscenity.

The railway ran, for much of the journey, by the sea. I tried to rehearse what my approach should be, my lines to Helen, my argument, my succinct reasoning to persuade her, open her eyes. I watched the cold green breakers. They caressed the rocks, dark summits of besieged outcrops which could be seen above the waves. The white foam surged over them, penetrated every crevice, retreated again, only to return. Persistence, I thought, and even the rocks will yield.

At Balbriggan the railway ran beside Loreto Convent, a girls' boarding school. Teenagers in green divided skirts played hockey on two adjoining pitches, and I imagined Helen as a schoolgirl, remembered her comical stories about the learning of rock and roll.

But my mind kept visualizing the moment of meeting. Helen would answer the door; after the initial surprise she would invite me in. It would be up to me then to try charm, cajolery, or whatever would make her receptive, until I could tell her what I believed to be the truth. She was no fool; she would not throw her life away; she would at least take time to pause and consider. And whatever feelings she had ever had for me, whatever goodwill she still possessed, would rise and vindicate me.

If she broke her engagement the future was still possible; if she broke her engagement no door was slammed on possibility; if she even postponed her marriage no die was cast, certainty was only a word and the future still a real dynamic.

Of course, I considered the possibility that Helen would not see me, or would not be at home, or the dread prospect of her mother answering the door. But at least I would have tried. I would not have to live with the knowledge that I had done nothing, that I had stood by and failed her, and us, and the unforgiving future. I dreaded the accusing march of the years.

It was mid-afternoon when I got to Dundalk. The bright, deceptive January light was already fading into the brackish grey of winter sundown and a thin drizzle had started. At my request the taxi dropped me at the end of Dunmore Park, and I walked, my collar up, to number 12, the redbrick semi with the white Venetian blinds, and with a nervousness which I could not suppress, opened the squeaking gate.

I went up the narrow path between the small lawn and the herbaceous border, rang the bell. I could hear a hoover inside and I rang again.

Helen opened the door. She was wearing an apron and her hair was pulled back in a ponytail. There was a smudge on her nose. Her demeanour was brusque; she seemed tired and distracted.

'Yes?' she said, almost crossly, but the exasperated sibilance was cut off immediately, died. She gave a gasp, a small intake of breath. 'Dan!'

'I had to see you!'

She reddened, touched her hair awkwardly, a nervous gesture I remembered from the evening of her arrival at Walton Street and still found touching.

'Come in.'

She admitted me to a red carpeted hall and closed the door softly. From a room on the left came a querulous voice, 'Who's that? Helen ... who's that?'

Helen put a finger to her lips, put her head around the sitting-room door. 'Just someone collecting for the parish.'

'Oh, always looking for money . . . always money. Gimme, gimme, gimme, all they're good for,' the voice said.

'I'll shut the door, Mam,' Helen said, 'so you won't be in a draught.'

I caught a glimpse of a coal fire and a woman's profile, a woman sitting in a fireside chair, Aunt Dru, but, judging from the feeble tilt to her head, not Aunt Dru as I remembered her.

Helen gave me an apologetic smile, motioned me to silence again, and led the way into the kitchen, closed the door, turned to me.

'I'm sorry about this. Mam is not herself these days. She had a fall in October and has not been the same since.' She stood uneasily. Her face was quite red, her eyes uncertain. She seemed embarrassed to the point of paralysis.

'Would you like some tea?'

'Thank you.'

I looked around at the suburban kitchen, the packets of sultanas and raisins on the table, the mixing bowl and electric whisk, the eggs and yellow packet of Stork margarine; Odlums flour and the red tin of Royal baking powder. She reached nervously for the kettle, followed my eyes. 'I was going to make a cake when I had finished the housework! It's one of the few things Mam is still partial to.'

'I didn't know you could cook!' I said, trying to square this little housewife, this wielder of hoovers and electric whisks, with the wild, free Helen of the valley.

'If you can read you can cook!' Helen said tartly, recovering her powers of articulation, and giving the small chuckle she always did when she delivered herself of some witticism. Our eyes met. 'I know what's wrong with you – you have never known me in any milieu except Lough Corrloch. You think I'm a maid of the mountains, like something out of Sir Walter Scott. But I do belong to this century, you know.'

'Yes.'

'Take off your coat and sit down, Dan,' she said, with something like her old authority. 'You gave me a shock . . . arriving like that!' Then she added, deliberately disingenuous, 'What brings you to Dundalk?'

'The scenery.'

She laughed in spite of herself. I felt the old camaraderie, took off my overcoat, pulled out a kitchen chair and straddled it happily, watching her fill the kettle, get out cups and saucers, search for biscuits she knew she had somewhere. There was a small, square mirror hanging near the sink, and she glanced at herself almost surreptitiously, wiped the smudge from her nose in a sudden irritated movement with the tip of her finger. When she turned around the colour in her face had deepened; her eyes when she glanced at me were vulnerable, the pupils wide; her mouth curved in the old sensitive quirk of the child. I was aware of everything, the flush at her throat, the suppressed sense of excitement, the tight waist of her apron, the grace of her shoulders, the thrust of her small breasts. Above all, I was aware of my own strange sense of arrival, as though peace had ambushed me.

I took the plate of biscuits, nibbled a custard cream. The rain had intensified outside and the garden was melancholy in its winter darkening, but the warmth from the Raeburn cooker made the kitchen cosy. We could have been in a capsule remote from the world. The world had withdrawn, but had precipitated all its magic and power into this suburban kitchen in the winter dusk.

I examined the room covertly, saw the row of porcelain coffee cups hanging from hooks on the dresser, the few old blue plates with the willow pattern and a couple of inverted sherry glasses, saw the books piled in two untidy stacks, jostling for space with some ornamental crockery, and a number of letters, which could have been bills, and which were wedged upright between a small blue jug and the edge of the dresser.

'You're still reading as much as ever?'

'Yes, I'm trying to work my way through the local library.'

'You mean to say you haven't done that yet?'

She raised her eyebrows, said primly: 'Well, there are one or two books I haven't yet got around to . . . Seriously, because of the way Mam is I haven't been able to go to college so I really do have to educate myself. The money my stepfather had earmarked for my education has to be conserved now because of Mam. She'll need specialized nursing at some point. But I can't endure the prospect of being some kind of God-help-us, without an idea in my head.'

I wanted to tell her what I thought of all that, the waste, the plunder of it! A first-class mind, sharp, open, inquisitive, confined at eighteen to the kitchen! She sat down opposite me across the table, poured the tea. It was very strong.

'What do you do except read? Do you go out much . . . the cinema . . . dances?'

'Kieran takes me sometimes, although I don't think he likes dancing much. Sometimes I try to write. I've started a few short stories, but they're indescribably awful!'

'Helen . . .'

She looked into my face, looked away, said abruptly, in an urgent whisper as though she were in pain: 'Why have you come? What good can it do?'

'Helen, you can't go through with this marriage; you can't sacrifice your life.'

This was not the speech to make to Helen. It was too direct, too challenging of her judgement and autonomy. She turned, looking affronted, pushed back a tendril of hair from her forehead.

'What makes you think I'm sacrificing my life?' Her voice was resentful; the whimsy of a moment before was gone.

In the ensuing silence I heard the wheeze of fuel settling in the Raeburn. I felt the tension in Helen, in the way that I was always able to sense her mood, sometimes even her thought. I knew with instant clarity that she was secretly deeply angry, and that she was stretched and unhappy. Any indignation I felt at her ready resentment was suppressed by instinctive fear. If I muffed it now the door would slam and the last chance would be over.

'I'm sorry, Helen. I put it very badly. I cannot bear to lose you, but that is only one of the reasons why I've come! I genuinely do not believe that marriage to Kieran will make you happy! You're too young,' I went on, encouraged by her listening face, 'you need time to get your bearings, get to know the world a bit before you settle down.'

There was an uncomfortable silence in which I knew I was ridiculous. Helen retained her speculative expression, glanced at me, chewed her lip, turned to regard the dim wet garden, but all that could now be seen in the window was our reflection.

'You come here to tell me this! But I have responsibilities,' she said in a low voice, meeting my eyes and then dropping her gaze. 'I'd rather not have them; but I can't just run away and forget them.'

I leant across the table, took her hand. 'Why don't you rebel, Helen? They expect too much of you, your mother, Kieran . . . Revolt! You're clever, beautiful; you have a right to your own life.'

She straightened and leant back, withdrew her hand, gave a short laugh.

'Oh, but I do rebel, Sir Galahad!' she said, tapping her forehead. 'I am a compendium of warring factions. But my rebellion is where it cannot be seen. Anything else would be nothing but selfishness, no matter how many fine names you dressed it up in!' She stopped, sighed, slumped a bit in the chair. 'But it's nice of you to concern yourself.'

'It's not "nice" of me! You are everything to me,' I burst out desperately. 'I love you. I want to marry you. I'm not perfect, Helen. I've made mistakes; but if you will marry me, I will make you happy. I promise it! Please think about it, Helen. Please say you will!'

Helen closed her eyes for a moment, then said: 'I don't suppose you want my mother for ever, and that's what you would be getting. She's had a stroke and is not . . . what she was; she's not the full shilling any more. That's the truth of it! She will never be right again! Am I to abandon her for some righteous rebellion? Kieran, at least, will help me look after her!'

'Are you marrying him for that?'

Helen regarded me balefully. 'Oh, I could listen to you,' she said, her eyes suddenly angry and reproachful, 'but I am a bit afraid of you. You come here behind Kieran's back, and he is your friend! You say you love me. Did you also tell Marion that you loved her? Was that how you got her into that terrible mess? Is that something you say to women?'

It was later, when the anger and hurt had faded a little and I was going over and over what she had said, that I realized how the episode to do with Marion had preyed on Helen, how it had eaten away at everything I thought we had built. To Helen, steeped in idealism, subscribing to an idealized perfection, my sexual history and its aftermath had been an obstacle too great to contend with. But at the time, there in the suburban kitchen, I heard mostly a pique, a wounded pride, and I felt her bitter query like a slap in the face. I rose to my feet.

'Is that what Kieran has been telling you? It's not true. I never told any woman I loved her – except you!'

'Did she, or did she not, have an . . . abortion?' Helen demanded in an even voice.

I could not meet her eyes. 'I have only her word for it. If she was pregnant, I didn't know.'

'You didn't even know! And all the time I was with you at Lough Corrloch, all the time we walked through the heather and sat in my dell, and when you watched me bathing in the pool, when you kissed me, when you came into my room in London and . . . Even then this other girl was pregnant by you! And I was imagining you as fine and honourable!' Helen's breathing had quickened and her eyes had filled. Her mouth took on the bitterness of grief. 'You know what you should really do, don't you? You should forget all about me and make amends to that girl!'

Suddenly the tears came in good earnest. 'I told Father Duggan in confession about you and he said that's what you should do. He said I should avoid you, that you were a danger to my soul!'

I watched her sob. For a moment I hated her. I had come this distance and she had answered me with the moral high ground. To hell with her, I thought. Let her stew in her own piety, along with Father Duggan, Kieran and the rest of them. Let her see how it would answer life.

She turned, wiping her face. 'Why don't you just go away and leave me alone?' She raised her voice. 'Can't you see how things are? Just leave me alone!'

I stood back, immobile, searching for the wisdom which had failed me, at war with reason and blind with loss. Now I knew that she had neither forgotten nor dismissed as the trivia of the moment my seeing her in the pool, our first tentative kiss in the heather, the charged moment in her room in Walton Street.

Now I knew that Helen forgot nothing, but had woven everything between us into the weft of her lonely life. And I also knew that she was vulnerable, but proud and stubborn, romantically pious, and that I had affronted her beyond pardoning. I hated the sexual opportunist I saw reflected in her accusing eyes; I squirmed at this new persona of the heartless bounder. This was not me; and yet the hat fitted and was mine to wear.

How do you protect yourself from the harvest of your own folly? I quelled my anger, my pride, searched for words to elicit understanding. But, tongue-tied with fury and frustration I found nothing.

The kitchen door opened and a faded vestige of Mrs Fitzgerald, evidently attracted by Helen's raised voice, shuffled into the room.

Even in the midst of my turmoil, I was astonished by the change in Aunt Dru. She seemed diminished, as though all the managing life she had possessed had deserted her, leaving her only motor reflexes. Her hair was grey and thin. She shuffled in her pink carpet slippers, looked at me without immediate recognition, turning her head a little on one side to examine me, like a bird. Beside her, Helen was the glowing epitome of youth, hope, life.

'Who's this?'

'Dan,' I croaked, reaching for even vestigial urbanity. 'Dan McPherson. How are you, Mrs Fitzgerald?'

She stood with head bent, her eye cocked at me like one of the Grehans' hens. Helen had already taken her arm as though to bring her back to the sitting room, when the travesty that had once been Aunt Dru turned, shouting something at me in a reedy voice, full of rage. It was the anger of someone who knew she had a just cause, but couldn't remember the whole story. It took me a moment to decipher the tirade, but it seemed that I was the 'pup' who had 'raped' her daughter.

Helen, now pale and quiet, her face streaked with tears, seemed deflated. She gave me a gloomy look halfway between sorrow and apology.

'You'd better go,' she whispered. 'When she gets like this . . .'

I put on my coat and she came with me as far as the front door.

'Don't mind her! She would have hated it if she could have seen what she would become. It's so unfair for her. And Dan, I shouldn't have said those things to you. What do I know about it, after all? What can I know? I'm sorry,' she added in a whisper. 'I'm very upset. Don't mind me . . .'

I looked at her, at her eyes blurred from her tears, at her beautiful body in the wrapround apron, at the burden on her slim shoulders, at the coils of her hair, at its Romanesque ponytail, at the half-obliterated smudge on her nose.

'Helen, whatever you think about me . . . you shouldn't marry Kieran. That's what I really came to tell you.'

She started back. 'Why not?' Her voice had lost it softness. 'Give me one good reason.'

'He's . . . almost certainly homosexual.'

She drew back from me as though she had been struck. 'How can you say such a thing?' Her face closed; she held the door open for me with a gesture of contempt.

'I did not come to offend you, Helen,' I said in the pompous, toneless dignity of defeat. 'Perhaps I was wrong, but I thought you cared for me. I see I was mistaken, that you think badly of me. But you are quite right! I deserve it, I shouldn't have come.'

She did not answer, but bent her head so that I could not see her eyes.

'I won't trouble you again,' I added. 'If you want to see me you know where to find me.'

I walked to the gate in the rain. She called out, 'Wait!' came out after me, handed me an umbrella, ran back. 'Keep it,' she called when I said something about returning it.

She lingered as though reluctant to close the door. Her eyes as they locked with mine were uncertain, questioning, miserable. The rain fell between us. I turned, closed the gate, heard her whisper, 'Dan . . .' looked back to see that she had put a hand out as though to detain me. But the querulous voice of her mother, 'Helen, shut that bloody door. There's an awful draught . . .' came behind her. She shook her head at me, gave me a half-smile, raised both hands a fraction as though in acknowledgement of life's perversity. Then the door was shut and I retraced my steps down the suburban roadway in the sleet.

I went back to Dublin, stayed overnight in a private hotel in

Landsdowne Road, sought out Rachel the following day. I needed to talk to her.

St Sebastian's Retirement Home had formerly been a Georgian mansion. I arrived at eleven and was shown across an elegant tiled hall into a room full of seated elderly people. The room itself was pleasant. It had several windows on to a formal garden, was warm and carpeted. But the incumbents were silent, except for occasional monosyllabic bursts of noise, directed at no one in particular. Some were staring out of the window; others examined their hands.

There was an unmistakable smell of urine. I walked down the length of the room, a room which felt empty although it was full of people, and tried to find the face of our former housekeeper among the living dead. At the end of this chamber, seated in an armchair behind a huge rubber plant, I found Rachel. She was wearing the blue woollen dress she used to reserve for state occasions, with a new cardigan over it, had a copy of *Woman's Way* on her lap and was staring into the garden.

It took me a moment to recognize her. Her grey hair was white now, caught back in some kind of bun, and her eyes were glassy. For a dreadful moment I thought she too had joined the ranks of the starers around her, the voyeurs of the grave.

But then I saw her reach into her pocket and pull out a baby Power, uncap the bottle, take a slug, dump it back into her pocket with a smooth, practised, movement. The French expression came to me on a sudden surge of levity: *Plus ça change; plus ça reste la même chose.*

'Rachel!'

She started, staring up at me guiltily, like a schoolgirl caught in a prank. 'Jaysus!' she said then, reaching up her gnarled hand to me as I bent and kissed her cheek. 'Is it yerself that's in it! I thought it was one o' them Nazis.'

'Nazis?'

'The gang o' lousers that does be in charge o' this hellhole.'

I pulled up a chair and sat beside her. 'How are you, Rachel?'

She straightened a little; her eyes brightened, lost their glazed appearance and assumed something of their old combativeness. 'What are yeh doin' in this neck of the woods? Yez didn't come to Dublin just to see this oul' bird.'

'Of course I did, Rachel.'

She examined me doubtfully. 'Yeh were always a bad liar!' But, liar or not, she held my hand and wouldn't let it go.

I looked around. 'How do you like it here?'

She grimaced. 'It was all right while me friend was alive. But nothin' would do her but to fall down the bloody stairs; and that was the end o' her.' She gestured at the rest of the company, sitting compliantly, staring across the carpet at each other. 'She's well out of it, of course, but yez needn't imagine there's any *craic* to be had,' and here she indicated her fellow residents with an inclination of her head, 'from that lot of oul' stuffed vultures. I think they do all be drugged.' She dropped her voice, drew me down until my head almost touched hers and confided in a whisper, 'They do give us pills, mornin' and evenin', but they never do tell us what does be in them.' She grinned at me, gave a conspiratorial cackle. 'But I bury mine in the rubber plant.'

I looked at the rubber plant. It seemed to be bearing up well enough considering.

'Who gives you the whiskey?'

'What whiskey?'

'The noggin you just slipped into your pocket, Rachel!'

She almost jumped in the chair, patted at the pocket of her cardigan. 'There's a cleaner . . . a kind soul,' she whispered, looking behind me as though some Guardian of Retired Morals would materialize. 'I give her the money. Sure the odd drop keeps me sane!'

The conversation then veered to a hungry demand for news and I told her all there was to know, including that my father had been recalled to Ottawa.

'What happened to that girl, the one you were always moonin' over? The pretty redhead? Are you still keen on her?'

'Yes, but she's engaged to someone else!'

'Who?'

'Kieran, as a matter of fact!'

'What! But sure that fella isn't interested in her! Sure unless it had bug eyes and forty-five legs he wouldn't give it a second glance!'

I shrugged, turned to stare into the winter garden. 'Actually, I went to see her yesterday, to try to get her to change her mind. But she won't . . . change her mind.'

Rachel sighed, stroked my hand. 'So that's what yez came over for!

But it's her loss,' she opined, after a moment, shaking her head. 'Her loss – and there's more fish in the sea than ever was caught. Remember that!'

'There may be, Rachel, but how many of them are sharks or simple herring, and how many are opah?'

'Opah? What's that?'

'A rare fish of exquisite colour!'

She glanced at me, sighed again. 'Oh Danny boy, I'm sorry. But the little strap will be sorry yet . . . to turn my Danny boy down!'

'It will be too late then, Rachel, if she's ever sorry – and she's not a "strap"!'

'Well, she's a fool, which is worse. Mark my words, she'll live to regret it.'

After a moment I asked with feigned jocosity, desperate for any salve at all: 'Have you any advice for me?'

'Advice is useless,' she said in a serious voice. 'Yeh wouldn't take it anyway.'

I looked at her, at her mottled cheeks, at her tired eyes, at her spirit in the midst of senescence. She had never grown old; it was a matter of choice and she had chosen the road of defiance.

'All right!' she said. 'You'll never get over her. Yeh want the truth and it's better to face it. Always face pain; if you go right through it you'll come out the other side! But there are years and years ahead of you, and her, and she may yet find that the great Kieran is only her own invention. Oh, he's real enough all right,' she said, by way of brooding addendum, 'only she's a child and his reality is not the one she thinks!'

I had always suspected that Rachel missed very little, and now I was sure of it.

When did Marion come back? Was it by accident, or design? I know she was at a party in Dicky Whiston's at which I became idiotically drunk. I had had a bad day; one of my more ambitious attempts at advocacy had fallen flat; a client who had not told me the truth had divulged facts in cross-examination which he had seen fit to keep from me. This ensured that I had both lost the case and looked like a fool into the bargain. None of this was, I felt, in keeping with my stature as the latest pupil in chambers.

'You won't win them all!' Matt Hartley, my pupil master, said, but this was scant comfort.

Marion emerged from the party haze of cigarette smoke. She was dressed in a pale blue mini-skirt and clinging blouse, and looked seductive, although the whites of her eyes were bleary. She was pleasantly tipsy, looked somehow soft and gentle, not at all like the bitter young woman I had last seen at Zarathustra's.

'Hello, Dan,' she said, parking herself beside me on the sofa, as though she had never met me in anything but the most pleasant of circumstances. 'Long time and so forth! What have you been up to?'

It took me a moment to register that it was her. She was the last person I wanted to meet, but I was drunk and couldn't have cared less if the sky fell.

'Everything and nothing; a deed without a name!' When she didn't respond, but looked at me pityingly, I added, 'There's no use giving me the evil eye! I am what I am, a bumbler, a bumbling barrister . . . as the Lord made me . . .'

'God didn't make you a bumbling anything. You managed that all by yourself!'

'Believe in God now, do you, Marion?'

'When it suits.'

'I'm terribly sorry, you know, about . . .' and I was suddenly unmanned by the well of feeling, a composite of everything that had refused to go right with my life. Judgement and control deserted me; I felt the tears fill my eyes . . . 'about the baby. Why didn't you tell me?'

'Oh that! Well, I've put all that behind me!' She leant towards me and whispered in my ear, 'Pull yourself together, for Christ's sake; I don't want you blabbing my personal history to the whole room!'

'Sorry.'

'What happened to that girl you were with? Is she here?'

'What girl?'

'The one with the brogue – in Zarathustra's.'

'Oh, Helen. No, she's not here. She's married my best friend!' I looked at Marion's pink eyes and thought how well they went with her skirt . . . pink and blue. 'She buggered off and married a bugger!' I guffawed at my wondrous wit. Marion said drily, 'You haven't improved! You should supply nitrous oxide with your pleasantries!'

'I'm serious. He's a bugger and she married him!'

Marion frowned and pursed her lips. 'Are you still living at home?'

'No, home is gone; my mother is remarried; I'm all abandoned, all grown up now, sharing a flat in South Ken.'

'Are you any good as a barrister?'

'No, but I'm an ace sycophant. I grovel for a living: "Yes my lord; No, my lord!" Sometimes, when I'm feeling particularly frolicsome, I even retreat into eighteenth-century affectation and use "M' lud"! Can anyone execute a better grovel than that?'

In a way I was trying to impress. The rituals of advocacy were still novel to me then, and I knew that others, lay people, associated the Bar and all its dramatic trappings with secret and arcane power.

However, Marion merely narrowed her eyes as though trying to envisage the sozzled spectacle before her as a warrior in the lists of Justice. She did not seem particularly impressed.

'Well, if you want the truth . . . I'm useless; not sufficiently cynical; too ready to believe what clients tell me. But, on other fronts, I do know a few interesting little tricks.'

'Like what?'

I squeezed her breast. 'Don't you remember?'

Marion removed my hand and said conversationally through her teeth, 'If you weren't so drunk I'd slap your face!'

'If I weren't so drunk I'd roll you in the hay!'

Her face filled with anger. 'That's one thing, duckie, you'll never do with me again!' She clicked her tongue. 'You've become coarse, you know! I'm not surprised your little Irish bird ran away . . .'

My eyes filled again. 'She was lovely, you know, my little Irish bird.'

'She was pretty,' Marion conceded, 'if you like red hair! When did she get married?'

'Six months ago. Her husband sent a card to me from their honeymoon retreat. Do you know what he said?'

'How the hell would I know what he said?'

'He said . . .' and here I tried to think, to remember the card that had stood on the mantelpiece since the day it had arrived, but whatever it was that Kieran had put on the card from Italy eluded me. Marion looked at me and stood up, pulled at my hand.

'I'm off. Come on, I'll give you a lift home. You look like you need one!'

I went with her almost gratefully. When we got back to the flat she declined the offer of a nightcap and I let myself in and collapsed on my bed, welcoming oblivion.

Marion came by the next morning.

'I just thought I'd pop in to see how you were. You were pretty mouldy last night.'

I was still mouldy. My head felt like an overripe melon. The melon had now split and the contents were inconveniently oozing through the cracks.

'I'm fine!'

'You don't look fine. You look like death warmed up!'

'Do you want some coffee?'

While I made the coffee I watched her from the corner of my eye. She sat on the sofa and idly leafed through the pages of a magazine. Then she got up and examined my record collection, selected Handel and put it on the turntable. The stylus clicked into position and the strains of 'Where'er you walk . . .' filled the room. I wondered if she were psychic. It was the very piece I tended to play when I was alone and thinking of Helen, evoking the tenderness, the divine passion, of the great god Jupiter for the mortal Semele.

Playing it, lying back and staring at the ceiling, while the sounds of London were muted and the record whirled on the turntable, I would think of Helen at Lough Corrloch, think of the breezes that came down the valley and Helen walking to meet me along the avenue; Helen making tea in her Dundalk kitchen while the day darkened and her anger spilled over into angry tears. And all the while her ailing mother had oppressed the house from the sitting room.

Now I turned to Marion. 'Why did you select that?'

'It was lying on the top. Are you fond of Handel?'

'Yes.' I poured coffee into two red mugs. 'So what are you doing with yourself, Marion?'

'I have a job in the Patent Office.'

'Oh, in Chancery Lane? You're quite near the Temple!'

'Yes.'

There was silence. We had little to say to each other; the politeness was stiff, embarrassing. The alcoholic *entente* of the night had no currency for the morning. Marion sipped her coffee, looked around, expressed admiration for the flat, the oriental rugs, the couple of impressionist paintings.

'I like your taste.'

'It isn't my taste. The rugs are Freddy's; he brought them from home; and the paintings are Gerry's. I have a few things from home in my room, but otherwise just some books and an electric razor!'

Marion gave a small half-laugh as though I had said something witty. She was being deliberately agreeable, despite my trespass of the night before, despite the past, despite everything. But it seemed, in the cold light of morning, too vast a history to bridge so easily. I could think of nothing to say and in the ensuing silence she reached for her handbag, rose to leave. 'I'd better go; I have to meet someone.'

'A boyfriend?' I enquired tentatively, curious in spite of myself.

'No actually; a girl friend. We're going shopping.'

As she was leaving she picked up a slightly dog-eared postcard lying on the mantelpiece. It was Kieran's card, sent while on honeymoon.

Marion, as though she wanted an excuse to delay her exit, examined the Emerald Grotto and the blue of the Mediterranean and then turned the card over.

'All things wax exceeding well!' the message said, in the neat, square handwriting that was Kieran's.

'Well, someone's enjoying himself anyway,' she said, replacing it, 'although it sounds more like a successful business trip than a holiday!'

'That's from the bloke who married Helen! I mentioned him to you last night! He was on honeymoon!'

Marion picked the card up again. 'Christ!' she muttered after a moment. 'Talk about coy triumph . . . He's really saying he screwed her! He's sharing the good news!'

'Yes,' I said, 'he was all delicacy!'

'I knew she'd dump you,' Marion said, 'but I feel sorry for her all the same . . . married to someone who wanted to share his nuptial embraces with his male friends!' When Marion's tongue sliced into truth it ignored charity.

'Why did you know she'd dump me?' I demanded, stung to the quick.

She smiled at me almost fondly. 'Because you were too old for her, of course! And much too eager!' She paused; 'Eagerness is almost always a mistake . . . as I know to my cost! If you are eager the other person thinks you are either easy or a waste of time. You could be neither, but the other person wouldn't know.'

At the front door she turned, her face grave, bereft of sociability. 'Dan, I'm sorry I was such a bitch to you in Zarathustra's. I know you knew nothing about the pregnancy and it was unfair of me to blame you! But that's all in the past now. Can't we have a new beginning?'

She stood there at the open door, holding herself still to summon her courage. Only the slight quiver at the edge of her mouth betrayed how great was her effort. I was touched. This new Marion had learnt simplicity, even dignity.

'Give me your phone number,' I said and I wrote it down on the back of an envelope lying on the hall table.

That was the new beginning for Marion and me. I remembered Helen's voice when I thought of her one night: 'You should make amends to that girl!'

Marion told me herself, much later, what it had been like, the pain, the despair, the loss and relief, the aftermath, the hatred for herself and the man responsible, the man who was me.

But the telling me of the horror of the abortion was a mistake; the pity and compassion it aroused in me was the death knell of any hope of resurrected passion. I could love Marion, this troubled being, as a fellow traveller along the road of life, but I could not give her the burning hunger of my heart. Familiarity, on some levels, may breed compassion but it destroys desire.

Marion and I were married the following year. We had a June wedding and went away on honeymoon to Minorca. We slept together in a huge bed and ate pasta and drank wine and laughed and made love. But underneath the gaiety there lurked a shadowy spectre. We were not right for each other and at some subliminal level each of us knew it. We worked, at least for the moment, at constructing the marriage into something which would accord with our internal picture of what a marriage should be, at private dissembling. It was easy to enjoy lovemaking; it was easy to laugh tipsily as we wandered on to the beach at night; but sex and laughter were in some way a deliberate wallpapering, an exercise in energy and optimism. Because we had decided it would work, because we were prepared to make it work, we reasoned unconsciously that it had to work. But the true alchemy of love and successful marriage runs deeper than the human will. It has more to do with vision and kinship of soul than with sexual athletics or deliberate, consciously worked out kindnesses.

Marion reckoned she loved me. But in her love was a soupçon of desperation which gave it the lie. I loved Marion, because I had willed it so; but in my love was guilt and the desire for redemption. Neither love had anything to do with the unbridled and unbidden rush of the spirit into mutual recognition, into ecstasy, into the flowering of everything it means to live.

Marion longed for a child. Two years went by; she occasionally suspected she was pregnant and, each time, was disappointed. She went to see a specialist and was eventually informed that because of her abortion she could never again carry a child. To her it felt like a death sentence, like the wrath of heaven.

She reacted savagely. She had crying jags. I tried to comfort her, to suggest adoption, troubled and guilty myself. But nothing could comfort her. She began to drink. The careful relational diplomacy she had observed with me fractured and gave place to brittle and artificial mood swings between alcohol-induced euphoria – they could be wrong; she had read something in a women's magazine – and depression.

I buried myself in work, began to make a reputation. Chances came my way, briefs were thrown at me which no one else wanted; they gave place to briefs which everyone wanted; my fees escalated. I worked late, at weekends, almost lived in the Temple. Marion began a relationship with someone she met at a garden party. I found out by accident, by returning home earlier than anticipated. She had a blazing row with me; I was useless, a cold fish, she said. Why shouldn't she have some happiness, some pleasure?

By now I had learnt enough of humanity to know that women needed as much life as men had traditionally arrogated to themselves. I knew I was not much of a husband; I was considerate, remembered birthdays; anniversaries, but I could not halt the process of alienation which marched beside us, under its own apparent momentum, down the years.

I did not pretend too much chagrin at my wife's infidelity. In some quiet recess of my own soul I felt I was owed nothing better. I winked at being cuckolded; it was a flagellation I almost welcomed. The thought of my wife's body naked in another man's arms filled me only with a perverse masochism. He was, as I once had been, out for a quickie.

The affair ended. I comforted Marion when she wept.

'Men are all bastards,' she moaned.

'No,' I said. 'They are dealt a certain hand and they play it to win; that is what all of us, women included, do with life.'

'Are you saying the whole human race is nothing but little ambient bags of chemicals?'

'Thou hast said it!'

She looked at me dubiously from tear-stained eyes. 'Since when have you gone in for Shakespeare?'

Work was the anodyne, the ultimate pleasure, the place where brain met challenge, where intellect and cunning sliced into problems. Love, sex were meaningless, a mirage, a shimmering in the desert through a trick of the light. I knew all this. I congratulated myself; I no longer ached for Helen; I had found surcease in effort. Marion and I could not fulfil each other, physically or otherwise, and although we slept together there was no spark, no flash of carnal or emotional ferocity. If things got desperate I could go to King's Cross, or Piccadilly and vent the urgency of the flesh in the female flesh so ubiquitously for sale. But the mind was another matter, and in the exquisite honing of its capacity was a pleasure beyond all pleasures. My room in Chambers became my castle; my hold, my keep. Even to sit there, eyes closed, held mastery and certain rest.

And then, when I felt that little would happen to upset the tenor of my days; when I assumed that I had worked everything out, the projections, the traps, the lies, I walked into Kieran on Fleet Street one Saturday morning. I wondered afterwards if he had been on the other side of the street would I have bestirred myself; if he had had his back to me while looking in a window, would I have bothered? But there was no escaping each other and the delight which each of us had in the sight of the other was genuine and unbidden; it rose up from our roots as something older than anything which had taken place in our adult histories.

He could have been a country squire. He was dressed in tweeds, had a slightly donnish look to him. We first started and then laughed as we were confronted with each other.

'Well, well,' he said. 'Nice to see you, old fellow.' He clapped my back with a gesture too spontaneous to be feigned. 'You haven't changed a bit – except for the patina of authority. I was half thinking of dropping in to see you!'

I felt as though I were a child again and the slightly superior Kieran, my friend, was teasing me. I asked him if he had time, and we went into Twinings for some tea.

Of course we swopped our intervening histories; he told me his father had died, berated me for losing touch – 'I wrote last,' he reminded me – and said that he and Helen had a son, Jonathan, and that Aunt Dru was, as he put it, 'in a home for the bewildered'.

I said I was sorry.

'Premature senility or something,' he added. 'Terrible, of course, but even Helen is used to it now. We go to see her at weekends. Can't get much sense from the poor woman. Sometimes she thinks she's back in the valley and wants to make us tea!'

I thought of Rachel, to whom I wrote periodically, although I hadn't seen her for two years, but who was no more senile than I.

'How is James?' Kieran asked then, in a tone which indicated that there was no reason why he should remember James with anything more than simple friendship and civility.

I told him that James was living and practising in California and that we seldom saw him.

'Oh,' he said. 'Probably making a packet. It has to pay better than the groves of academe, at any rate.'

Then he proceeded to tell me about his thesis for his PhD, and I tried to evince interest.

'Remember me to Helen,' I said, when we were parting, and he said that of course he would, and that we should not lose touch again.

When Kieran wrote to me afterwards his note was addressed to the Temple. It was a short missive which touched something forgotten; the freshness of its address harkened back to a time before cynicism.

My dear Dan,

It was wonderful to have met you again, albeit by chance. Helen and I were saying the other day that if you would like to visit us in the valley we'd be delighted to have you. We'll be there this summer (just ourselves and Jonathan). Why not visit and bring your wife? Why not come for a week in August or September and we'll say a prayer for the weather?

With very best wishes,

Kieran and Helen.

Helen, I saw, had signed her own name. I touched the signature, ran the tip of my index finger along it, held the missive in my hand for a long time, ignoring the load of paperwork waiting on my desk. I went to the window, thinking of the young couple, the red-haired teenager, the ardent youth, who had looked up from the cobbles by Temple Church and laughed at their elder. I almost saw their ghosts, as they kissed and went away hand in hand.

Should I accept this invitation and everything that it possibly entailed – the reopened wounds, the heartache, or, worse, the threat of disillusionment, just when I had managed to put all illusions behind me? Or should I play it safe?

It was years ago and it didn't matter any more, I told myself eventually. There was no point in being childish. Life did not last for ever. Why play hard to get with a generous-minded invitation? Why cling to any pique because of my last interview with a confused and angry girl? The years had gone. The girl was a woman. The perspectives of teenager belonged to almost another era! I would love to see Lough Corrloch. I would like to re-establish my friendship with Kieran; it would be so very nice to see Helen. Everything that I had felt for her had been predicated on my personal presumption. So long as I knew that, so long as I chalked it all up to adolescent projection, I was safe.

Knowing that they had a child, I wondered if perhaps Kieran's sexual orientation had been experimental; perhaps he and Helen were happy. I could have been wrong about what I had sensed in her. I could have been wrong, come to think of it, about absolutely everything. I had agonized often enough at my presumption in going to Dundalk that long ago day, in saying to Helen what I had, in making assumptions which I did not know for certain to be true. After all, what had I to go on? A packet of matches from a Paris nightclub and a few oblique mutterings from James, which could, in retrospect, have meant almost anything. I wondered if Helen had told Kieran of my Dundalk visit, where she had routed me so thoroughly. But I felt in my bones that she had not. His welcome for me that morning in Fleet Street had been too ingenuous for that.

That evening I said to Marion over dinner: 'We've been invited to Ireland, to stay at Lough Corrloch – the place I told you about!'

'By your old flame Helen?'

'By her and her husband!'

I took the letter out of my pocket and handed it to her. She perused it indifferently. 'Hold on. Isn't this the guy who wrote to tell you of his successful honeymoon?'

'Well, he sent me a card. Its interpretation is another matter!'

Marion clicked her tongue. 'You men always stick together!'

'Would you like to go?'

'No!'

'Why not? It would be some place different.'

'Because it will only rake up a chapter of your life which should stay closed. But that's only my opinion.' She studied me with raised eyebrows. 'But you go by all means! I can see you're straining at the leash. I suppose you're dying to see that girl again!'

'No—'

'Oh come on, Dan. You've never got over her!'

I sighed. 'Look, Marion, if you don't want to go, fine. Leave it at that. I won't go either!'

'Oh, but I think you should,' Marion said sweetly. 'I think it might help you get her out of your system!'

'Don't talk nonsense. What on earth makes you think she's in my system?'

'You keep her letters in that old box of yours! You know, the old Black Magic casket you have in your wardrobe!'

I kept my temper. 'How do you know what I keep in that box?'

'I wasn't prying!' she said defensively, without meeting my eye. 'It fell down one day when I was tidying!'

That box contained Helen's letters, a stone from the lake shore, a small ring made of dried grass, some photographs. Marion had gone through it, scanned every page, picked up the fragile desiccated grass ring.

I was silent. It was the way I had learnt to cope with anger, until I could school it to deadly purpose. It was useful professionally, this supercharged energy, when properly focused. But on the domestic front I felt it too dangerous to express it at all. In the opening of those floodgates what might not be swept away?

'I know you're furious; your mouth is white . . . it always is when you're mad. And that old box is so silly. It's like hanging on to your old teddy bear. A man of your age should have more sense!'

'That's enough, thank you, Marion!'

I rose and went to my study. Marion's dismayed reaction was genuine; she feared my remove, my coldness. I knew that her small forays into spitefulness were cries for love. But how could I give her what I did not feel? And she was right about Helen, and I had lied. I had lived this lie so well that I hardly knew where it ended and I began. Marion did not know the extent of it. She did not know that more than once, while ostensibly visiting Rachel in Dublin, I had hired a car and driven to Helen and Kieran's home in Clonskeagh, had parked it there in the darkness of the suburban road and watched the house. I had seen Helen, coming to a window to pull the curtains, had seen Kieran greeting visitors at the door. The exercise had only heightened the pain, the knowledge that Helen was a few yards away and that I could not see her, speak to her, ring that doorbell. Besides, it was absurd behaviour, teetering on obsession, and I had seen enough obsession in my professional life to fear it. So I had refused it, this encroaching possession, but I had, privately, to acknowledge the truth, now that it had surfaced again. My carefully constructed front was false. I was not over Helen. I would never be over her.

It was the next day that I decided, sweating in the airless London of July, as little Dora's case ended satisfactorily, as Grim Jim rose and the usher gave the age-old cry, 'Be upstanding in court,' that I would take up Kieran's invitation. The break would be welcome; there would be fresh air at least and perhaps, in this return to the enchanted valley, I might find disappointment, or at least acceptance. And in it I might, finally, find peace.

Chapter Fifteen

It was a pleasant rain-washed morning. I had a window seat on the plane and waited eagerly for the coast of Ireland to appear in the distance. I saw the greater Sugar Loaf first, that extinct volcano, exotic in the green land. Then came the whole panorama of the coastline, from Drogheda to Greystones. As the plane swooped over the bay I made out the twin piers of Dun Laoghaire, where I had said my goodbyes on more than one occasion. I had the heart-stopping feeling I always experienced when returning to Ireland; I felt as though I was vindicated – that a place really existed which, in all its esoteric strangeness, I sometimes suspected was a figment of my imagination.

But there it was, real enough, sea-washed Ireland's Eye, Malahide beach, and suddenly the fields came up to meet us and we were roaring down the runway at Collinstown.

Kieran was there to greet me. He was alone. I saw him first, with a curious wrench of feeling. He still represented my childhood in ways I had almost forgotten. He was standing with his hands clasped behind his back, looking slightly abstracted. He had a grey tweed jacket and shirt and tie. As I had noticed on our surprise encounter in Fleet Street, he had become adult; responsibility sat upon him, invisible but patent. This was yesteryear's infant, who had wailed at the loss of his 'whee' in the garden wall. This was yesteryear's youth, walking roughshod over my family with emotional hobnails, untouched by, and unaware of, his depredations. This was the friend who, running, I had once suspected, from his sexual orientation, had married Helen.

It is given only to old friends to know, and to forgive, so much.

His face lit up with genuine delight when he saw me and he crushed forward to grasp my hand and I took his proffered hand and shook it.

I noted again how his hairline had receded, how his youthful whip-like slenderness had left him and how he had put on weight around his tummy. But he was very pleased to see me and I was touched.

'Is Helen with you?'

'No. She's busy preparing for your advent. And Jonathan, our son, is not very well, so they stayed behind. But she's really looking forward to seeing you!' He led me to his car and I was absurdly disappointed to find it was a new Renault Four.

'What happened to the Rolls?'

He laughed. 'I still have it. But I don't drive it any more! It's too costly now to run and to insure, and we're mortgaged to the hilt with our new house!'

I was aware of all the 'ours' and I steeled myself towards acceptance. After all, why should it be any different? They were a married pair, Kieran and Helen, and whatever foibles had touched their early lives, they were established now – Mr and Mrs Fitzgerald, responsible parents, striving for the good things in life, pillars of society, doing their best.

I spoke of Marion as though she had failed to come because of some pressing engagement, as though we too were a real couple, with mutual agendas. Kieran asked me a few questions about her and expressed what seemed to be real regret that she had not been able to make the journey. Then, as we left Rathfarnham behind and moved into the mountains he began to point out old landmarks. 'You remember Glencree?'

He stopped the car. The vale below us was breathtaking in its crystal visibility; the greater Sugar Loaf looking down on it, and, peeping beyond it, the blue haze of the sea.

Kieran nosed the car down into the valley with the same care as I remembered, laughing a little as he recalled the first evening I had visited.

I thought of yesterday's grown-ups, his parents, one of them now dead; Aunt Dru suffering now from Alzheimer's disease. When I mentioned her he said that she always recognized him although she did not always know her daughter. 'Isn't that odd?' he asked. I muttered something in reply. I wasn't really listening; I was waiting for the sight of Helen.

We turned into the avenue and stopped in the yard. I saw at once that nothing had changed. Perhaps a fresh coat of paint had been put on the door, but otherwise Time might have stopped still. The whole ambience of the place was unchanged; the light pattern from the trees in the avenue, the sound of the branches sighing in the breeze. The kitchen door was open, as always, and in a moment it was filled by the person I most longed to see.

Helen came towards me, extending her hand, smiling.

'How are you, Dan? It's so lovely to see you after all this time!'

I took her proffered hand, trying not to examine her too openly, almost surprised at the easy welcome, drinking her in. Her thick titian hair lay burnished on her shoulders. She was poised, as though we had never parted in bitterness ten years ago in the Dundalk rain. She was slim as ever; she wore jeans which hugged her, showing her small waist. Her feet were encased in rope-soled sandals. She was wearing lipstick, a concession, perhaps, to my arrival. But she had changed; the girlish expression of open wonderment was gone; the face of the young matron had replaced it. A few vertical lines had scored her forehead as though from frowning. She had moved into adult awareness; there was a tinge of gravity, even melancholy, around her eyes. But the smile was sudden mischievous dynamism, Helen of old, and in this respect she was little different, except that she wasn't a girl any more; except that she had lived and I had lived and we had not done so together.

'Beautiful as ever!' I said as lightly as I could, although my throat was dry. 'How dare you not change when the rest of us have receding hairlines and worse!'

'Ah, go on with you,' she said. 'Would you have me balding?'

Kieran put a proprietorial arm around her shoulders, smiling at her with pride.

'No,' he said, 'but it wouldn't matter if you did! Any little bald spots would be tended until they sprouted again!'

Helen made a *moue* of exasperation and feigned, jocosely, to swat him, like a troublesome fly. Then she asked after Marion and said she was sorry she hadn't come.

Kieran showed me to Helen's old room. 'You don't mind, I hope, but Johnny, our son, has your old room.'

I said that I didn't care in the least. I looked out at the familiar vista of the valley and the eastern face of the mountains.

'It's wonderful to find everything so exactly the same,' I said.

'The valley was much the same for thousands of years before we came to it,' he replied. 'Why should ten years make any difference?'

I looked around the room, at the iron bed with brass knobs, the white bedspread, the small deal wardrobe, the statue on the mantelpiece, the blue china lamp on the bedside table, the selection of cloth-bound books. 'I've often thought of this place, you know,' I went on, 'especially when work seemed interminable and the problems unyielding. It was a place of mental retreat!'

'Well,' Kieran said: 'It's just the valley. But there's no excuse for you. You should have come to visit us sooner, old fellow. You would have been welcome, you know that!'

He spoke with jocular sincerity, concealing perhaps a genuine query as to where our relationship was now, whether it was truly reparable, and I murmured some response about never having a spare second and Marion liking to go to the sun for our summer break. But I was very aware of him; he stood there briefly with his hands in his pockets, smiling at me. For a second I thought he was going to say something about that fateful Sunday when he had walked out of our house in Chelsea, leaving us in disarray, and James, who infrequently contacted us now, in a seething anguish. But he evinced no such overt attempt; his demeanour was one of urbane jollity as perhaps he thought became a host, as though he had forgotten everything uncomfortable; as though it had never happened. He said he would let me get my bearings, and to come down for lunch when I was ready.

I took my things out of my bag and hung them in the wardrobe. I examined my face cursorily in the mirror above the chest of drawers; it was certainly different from the youth's who had gazed into the speculum in the nearby room so many years before. Compared with that raw visage it was adult, and beginning to bear the marks of the rigorous mental discipline which was now my life; there were stern lines around the mouth, incipient weariness around the eyes, vertical frown lines had already ploughed my forehead. But it was still a young man's face. I brushed my hair and walked downstairs to my hosts, noting en route how the hole in the carpet had been mended with another piece which almost matched. Other small improvements had been made, new landing curtains, a new pink lampshade.

As I slowly descended I felt the sense of peace begin to subsume me, and knew it welled, in all its welcome strangeness, not so much from this place where I had been so happy, but because Helen was waiting for me in the kitchen.

Helen had lunch laid out on the kitchen table. There was soup and homemade brown bread, cold roast beef and salad.

'Sit down,' she said, as she prepared a tray. 'I'll be back in a sec. And then I want to hear all the news!'

I suddenly knew that she was making a particular effort at normality; the poise was a fraction too careful, the cheerfulness too even. I had been in her house for the better part of twenty minutes and I already knew that she was covering up for the oddness of our estrangement over those past years. You cannot hide from me, Helen; you never could. And I cannot hide from you.

I sat as instructed and watched her don an apron, with an appliquéd blood-red pocket in the shape of a heart.

'Is this for your son?' I asked, indicating the tray, on which she had placed a bowl of soup, a slice of buttered bread and a glass of milk.

'Yes. Johnny has tonsillitis; he's plagued with it!' She glanced at me. 'He's very delicate, you know!'

'What age is he now?'

'He's nine.'

Nine, I thought. Nine! So he would have been born the year following their marriage; Helen had done her duty immediately and produced the son and heir. And there had evidently been no other children.

'Do you have any children?' she asked after a moment. The question was gently put, and I answered it quietly.

'No, unfortunately. I would have liked them – and so would Marion!'

I did not meet Helen's eyes as I said this. I wondered if she remembered her meeting with Marion in Zarathustra's, and then knew that of course she did. Had she not even written to me of her shock? Had she not turned on me that afternoon in Dundalk because of it? Had it not placed a wedge between us that nothing had bridged?

But Helen did not betray recollection.

'Never mind,' she said. 'They may present themselves yet!'

Kieran, who was tuning a transistor radio with a view to the 1.30

news, looked up and said, 'Kids are a mixed blessing anyway. You're never done with the ailments and the anxiety! When they're babies they're dribbling from both ends! And when they're older your heart is in your mouth if they're late home, or fall off their bikes, or whatever.'

'Don't mind him,' Helen said. 'He makes paternity out to be a chore.'

'I was referring to maternity, Honey-bun. It's the little mother who always imagines the worst.'

'I don't respond to "Honey bun",' Helen said lightly.

As though the child knew he was the subject of adult discussion he appeared at the door, pyjama-clad, slightly flushed. He had dark red hair, like his mother, but, unlike her, his face was sprinkled with fine, light freckles. His eyes were blue and sleepy.

'Hello, darling,' Helen said. 'This is Mr McPherson – an old friend.'

The boy looked at me. 'Will you be staying long?' he asked a bit huskily.

'Just a few days.'

'If you like fishing I'll show you the best places!' I expressed my thanks.

'How's your throat?' his mother asked and he said with a gesture of impatience that it hurt when he swallowed. She beckoned and he moved to her; she laid a hand on his forehead. 'Still feverish,' she murmured, glancing at Kieran. 'I think we'd better get the doctor!'

Kieran sighed. 'All he needs is a spot of penicillin. I wish they'd let us have it without prescription.'

'Or we could take him to Dr Mahon's surgery in Glendockery. It's from two to four,' she went on as though she wasn't listening. 'Would you mind that, darling?' she asked, addressing the child. 'It would save the doctor having to come out all this way!'

The boy shrugged. 'Can I have ice cream?'

Kieran laughed. 'You can!'

'OK!'

'Well,' Helen said, looking at the tray she had prepared, 'seeing as you're here you may as well join us for lunch. Go and get your dressing gown so you won't be cold.'

The boy obeyed, joined us again, toyed with his soup and declined anything else. He asked me about London, and whether I fished in the Thames, of which, he said, he had heard. 'I suppose there's roach there,' he said expectantly, but I was not much help, except to say that in the higher reaches of the river there probably was, but that the portion which flowed through London was not likely to have much in the way of a fish population.

The boy looked unimpressed. 'You don't fish!' he exclaimed, as though he pitied me.

While I talked to this child I marvelled at life. This relatively new being, who knew nothing of his parents' history, would inherit their world. The parameters for our generation had changed largely because of his; our gilded irresponsible youth, which had looked to the future with the wild freedom of the artist at his canvas, was weighted down with his existence, his generation's existence, and the tending of it. His being constrained Helen's; his life would be paramount for as long as he needed her, her freedom a memory. And for all of this he evinced only impatience.

'Do you want to come with us to Glendockery?' Kieran asked me as he ate his soup. 'You might like to see it again. It hasn't changed a bit.'

'No, he wouldn't,' Helen said. 'Dan would be bored stiff. He can stay here and keep me company!'

Kieran grinned at me, pursed his mouth and said, lowering his voice and leaning towards me in a kind of comradeship, 'The woman is a terrible boss!'

Helen smiled. 'No I'm not!'

'Yes you are, Mummy!' the boy said and Helen looked momentarily taken aback. 'You're the one who's always making me do everything I don't want.' His voice, which had a triumphant pipe to it, resounded with male solidarity. 'Daddy is the only one who lets me do what I like!'

'Pooh,' Kieran said. 'Strictly within reason, young man!'

Helen was silent. I felt rather than heard her sigh, felt her moment of concealed hurt.

'I make you eat and go to bed and do your homework,' she said in a suddenly flat voice. 'Perhaps you would prefer not to do these things?'

'Yes,' the boy said categorically. 'I would!'

He looked at his father for endorsement and Kieran smiled at him as though he were being endearing.

'And I don't want this soup!' Jonathan said, as though he would cash in on his small victory, pushing the plate away from him. 'I hate soup!'

'It's easy to swallow,' Helen said reasonably. 'Well, if you don't want soup what will you eat? Will you have meat and some salad?'

'Yuk!' the feverish little monster exclaimed. 'I want ice cream.'

'We haven't got any ice cream!'

'What's for dessert?'

'There's just cheese and biscuits,' Helen said.

'Yuk!'

'I'll get you ice cream in Glendockery!' Kieran said hurriedly before his son could give us the benefit of his opinion on cheese. 'Why don't you go back to bed now? I'll bring you to the doctor as soon as lunch is finished and I'll buy you the biggest ice cream you ever saw!'

The boy looked triumphantly at his mother and then back to his father. 'All right,' he muttered with a bad grace, slipped from his chair, and made his way back upstairs.

Helen looked at me apologetically. 'I'm sorry, he's very fractious when he has a temperature . . .' She rubbed a finger along her eyebrows in fatigue.

When lunch was over, Kieran rose from the table and said he would go up and tell Johnny to get ready. He smiled at me in apology and said it was grand to have me back in the valley.

'You should go for a walk to the lake while it's still fine!' he said. 'Do you good to get the circulation going, shake off all that London dust!'

Helen began to tidy things away, stacking the plates beside the sink for washing. She put some hot water from the old cauldron at the back of the range into a plastic basin, squirted in washing up liquid, and began the chore, saying, 'Go on, Dan; go out while the weather holds. I'm sure you're dying to revisit your old haunts. I'll get these done in a jiffy.'

'I'd rather help, if I'm not in the way?'

She turned and looked at me, said in a strange, low voice; 'You, in the way!'

I dried the dishes, answering her questions about my career.

'I'm probably too busy at the moment; you start your practice pathetically grateful for any crumbs that fall to you and after a while it's rattling along under its own steam! One doesn't realize the pressures until one gets away from it all.'

'You should take more time off.'

'It's not leisure that's important,' I said, thinking of several boring sun holidays I had endured, while poor Marion drank too much Sangria, conversed volubly with every English person she met (of the right sort) and tried to mould me into the kind of husband who would set the social scene on fire. 'Leisure can be worse than work.'

'What's important then?'

I looked at the back of her head, at the way she had tucked her hair into a clip, at how a few tendrils were curling from the steam, at the calm curve of her cheek, at the strange hush which surrounded her like an aura, as though she needed nothing from outside to make her complete.

'You are!' I wanted to say. 'You're what's important!'

But I simply shrugged and muttered, 'Whatever actually punctures the tedium and doesn't just try to escape it!'

She laughed with her old joyful chuckle. 'God, Dan, you're a tonic! I suppose it boils down to that all right!'

'What are you two so mirthful about?' Kieran demanded as he came into the room. Jonathan was with him, dressed for the road in jeans and shirt.

'He needs a sweater!' Helen said, without answering the question.

'No I don't. It's too warm.'

'He has tonsillitis,' Helen said patiently to her husband, ignoring her son. 'He has a temperature. He wears a sweater!'

She went to the line above the range, took down a grey pullover and put it on her son without a word. Her pregnant silence seemed to quell his incipient rebellion, for he submitted, albeit with a bad grace.

'Well, we'll be off,' Kieran said. 'We'll get back as soon as we can.' He grimaced at me apologetically and turned back to his son. 'Well, come on, young man . . .' I followed them into the yard to wave them off. Kieran turned the car and started slowly down the avenue, turned into the boreen. I watched them climbing to the hairpin bend, turning the red Renault through more than ninety degrees to tackle the steep climb to the main road.

And then Helen and I were alone in the valley.

We stacked away the last of the dishes. Helen took off her apron, put it in a drawer, looked at herself in the kitchen mirror, smoothed her hair. She gave me a funny nervous smile, one teetering between diffidence and laughter, and went into the yard. I followed her.

'Come on,' she said, suddenly, as though she had made a decision, 'I'll race you! Last one to the stile is an imbecile!'

And before I could react she was gone, out of the yard, running down the avenue. Her laughter came back to me on the warm August breeze.

I ran after her, uncomfortably aware that my leather-soled shoes had little purchase on the stony ground. But I caught up with her a few yards down the boreen from the avenue gate.

She stopped, looked at me laughing, pushed back her hair.

'Well, you're still able to move. You're not that decrepit!'

'I never said I was decrepit!'

'No need to protest! We'll have the roses back in your cheeks before you leave us!'

'But I don't want any roses in my cheeks!' I protested, imagining Mr Justice Shore: 'What's that I see in your bonny mien, Mr McPherson? Roses, my lord . . .'

She looked at me consideringly as we walked along together. 'No, I suppose it would spoil the image! But, all is not lost . . . if your cheeks don't suit you can have them anywhere you like!'

'Can I?' I demanded wickedly.

She glanced at me again, eyes mirthful. 'Oh Dan, don't give me that old come-on voice. You are strictly responsible for your own rose gathering. You needn't be looking at me!'

In the lower part of the valley the boreen became soft and grassy, yielding to marshiness. We mounted the bank at one point to circumvent puddles. I looked around, at the sheep, at the heather in bloom, at the spangles of bog cotton clustered here and there, at the surrounding mountains, at the busy sky. The lake came into view, unchanged, full of ancient calm. There was not another living creature to be seen, except the white sheep moving slowly in the distance.

'Ten years,' I said, 'and nothing has altered!'

'Did you expect it to?' Helen was grave now, adding with sudden diffidence, 'Do you find me changed?'

'No.'

'The truth, Dan.'

'It is the truth. You haven't changed, and in a way you have. Your beauty has changed; it has acquired an edge, like something that has been sharpened. Your mind, I think, has had time to permeate it, and this makes it utterly formidable!'

'You really think I'm beautiful?' she asked in a small voice.

'Yes. You must know it?' Even as I spoke I realized that she did not, that she had been undermined in some way and was unconscious of her power.

'You think I have a good mind?' she asked with the same note of surprised diffidence.

'Absolutely first class! You always had.' She glanced at me, as though to ascertain if I were joking.

'I didn't get to college, you know! I got married instead. Kieran thinks I'm a bit of a dodo!'

'Does he indeed!'

'Well, he's makes jokes . . .'

'He knows what you're worth, Helen. It may suit him to pretend otherwise. But I wonder – do you know your worth?'

It was out. I had no right to say it; I had not meant to say it, but the sight of her at lunch, in her beauty and her patience, unappreciated, dragged down by domestic tyranny, had thinned all resolve.

'I'm sorry,' I added. 'I had no right to say that!'

After a moment of silence she said in a low voice, 'You know perfectly well that you have the right to say anything you mean to me. We have an old friendship, and I was very sorry that you didn't write to me any more . . . after . . . everything! And I'm very sorry – no let me say it – about the things I said to you the last time we met!'

I thought of Dundalk, the kitchen, her livid face, the rain. 'It's all right . . . We were children.'

'I often wondered how you were. I often thought about you!'

'Does that mean you missed me?'

'I missed you!'

'How much did you miss me?'

'More than you could imagine!'

'I have a very good imagination!'

She smiled. 'I know, but I missed you more rather than less as the years rolled around. Kieran often said it was a shame the way you had lost touch and he muttered something about a disagreement. I didn't know that he had a quarrel with you!'

'It wasn't exactly a quarrel. James was involved . . . it's a long story! Anyway you could have written whenever you wanted. You knew the Temple would find me.'

She gave me an arch smile. 'I was too ashamed. That's the truth of it!'

We had reached the edge of the lake and were making our way in the direction of the old boathouse. I hardly knew where I was putting my feet, I was listening so intently, listening with more than my ears, listening to more than her voice.

'You see,' she said, as we sat down on a boulder to look at the lake, 'there is a kinship between the two of us that nothing will take away! I said it to you before, but it takes years to realize that it the rarest thing between people in the world! I shouldn't be saying this to you with such a rush, but you're only here for a few days and I don't know when you will come back, or when I'll get another minute to talk to you alone!'

'Is that all? A kinship?'

She looked at me. I half expected the quick dismissal she had given me in Dundalk all those years before. But her gravity was unaltered.

'Isn't that everything? Don't look at me as though you expected knowledge of the world from me,' she added with a quiet dignity. 'I grant I am not a child any more, but outside of what goes on in my head, I am experienced in almost nothing!'

I took her hand. 'Helen!'

She squeezed my hand. 'It's enough that you're here. Don't ask me questions . . .'

'Are you happy?'

'I have chosen it. I work at it. It's not important!'

'Why not?'

'Because what is important is that I keep the show on the road, the family as a family, my son alive and well.' She glanced at me. 'He's always been delicate, you know . . . one illness after another: double pneumonia twice, complications from measles, skin rashes . . .'

'And Kieran?'

'Kieran is Kieran.' She shrugged. 'He means well.'

I was silent, thinking that this was not the accolade I would have expected from the old Helen.

She glanced at me swiftly as though afraid she had disclosed herself. 'And what of you? You have a successful career, you have done something with your life. You'll probably end up as a judge. You look distinguished and wonderful. Are you content?'

'Right now,' I said, 'I am surrounded in peace.'

She smiled, as though accepting this as a deflection of her question, which it was not. She rose. 'Shall we go on a bit further, or would you prefer to go back?'

'When is your family due to return?'

'The round trip, visiting the doctor and the chemist and the toy shop, will take about two and a half-hours!'

'Do they have a toy shop now in Glendockery?'

'No, but Cafferty's have a good selection, and Kieran is a very doting father. He spoils Jonathan rotten!'

'Yes,' I said. 'I noticed. Shall we walk further around the lake? I used to read up there,' and I pointed to a rock on a slope further on.

We were silent for a while as we ploughed on through the heather and the bracken. We heard the swish-ripple of the lake, the whisper of the wind, the panting of our breaths as we moved higher up towards my old seat in the heather. I slipped once or twice, but refused Helen's suggestion of going back for our wellies. 'It's not much further now.' We reached it at last, my old reading place, the spot from which I had once descended to the lake while a young girl called to me to be careful, a girl who asked me to be her friend.

'Whew,' Helen said breathlessly, plopping down gratefully, 'I'm not as young as I was!'

'No,' I said. 'You've turned twenty-eight!'

She laughed and I sat beside her in the shelter of the grey rock. We were alone, invisible to everything except the mountains and the sky. The clear susurration of the lake followed us up the side of the hill and a few larks sang piercingly not far away. I lay back in the heather, closed my eyes and reached for her hand.

After a moment she lay back too. I pulled her head into the hollow below my shoulder, as though we had been together yesterday, as though this was the most natural thing in the world. She did not demur, but settled against me and made a small sound, like the sigh of tired child.

'Dan,' she whispered.

'Yes?'

'This is—'

'Don't move,' I said. 'Don't even think. Just listen to the silence!'

And so the great cynic and the young matron lay there together, silently, in the heather.

Chapter Sixteen

I spent three days in the valley. Kieran had acquired a shotgun and, on my second day, took me on a walk to the high bogs where we brought down a few snipe. We had them for supper, Jonathan complaining that they were poison and leaving the table with everyone's blessing to play with his new toy – a red lorry and trailer. His tonsillitis had improved, courtesy of the penicillin prescribed by the doctor. I helped Helen with the chores and Kieran disappeared to his books, or his thesis, which he was writing for his doctorate.

Kieran never adverted to his unhappy departure from Walton Street and I had not the stomach to mention it; I began to feel it was a figment of my imagination, that I had simply imagined James's suffering after Kieran's departure, which had continued for a long time, especially as no letter had arrived from Kieran. I puzzled it over, stayed awake late, lying in Helen's old bed, savouring the sense of her girlhood hidden in the room.

Kieran was not the kind of person to enjoy inflicting pain. He had always detested brutality. He was a besotted and patient father. He was a charming and considerate friend, devising plans for my entertainment, shelving his thesis to do so. But he simply did not recognize the depth and profundity of other people's emotions, or so I reasoned. He did not know what he did.

Was Helen happy with him? I could not make up my mind. She told me little of their relationship, and tended to change the subject if I skirted too near the issue. I tried to tell myself to mind my own business. But, after our strange tryst in the heather, where we had lain motionless for what seemed a long time, as though communicating on a level beyond speech, I knew I was more desperately in love with her than I had ever been. The years had given her a sharper definition; the unconscious force she carried around with her was more patent and more mysterious. I was also certain that she was far more interested in me than she would have liked to pretend. You cannot lie beside the woman you love, even in the heather, without knowing something of her feelings. Helen had lain curved against me, limp, eyes closed, as though communing with a peace which surpassed understanding. And I had lain beside her, drunk with desire and, at the same time, floating in serenity. I wanted to embrace her until she cried out; I wanted to penetrate her, possess her, harshly, tenderly, there by the lake, under the lonely August sky. But it was I who had broken the spell, sat up and said we'd better be going back; it was I who thought of the returning husband and what he might think if his wife was missing in my company when he got home. In this I had exercised a rigid control. And Helen had readily complied with my suggestion that we return, giving me an apologetic smile, ruefully commenting on the dishevelled state of my new tweed jacket on which both of us had lain.

'Am I very badly behaved?' she asked suddenly on the way back.

Instantly I thought of the morning after our first foray into Zarathustra's when she had articulated some similar question. I thought she was joking and would have made a glib response, but a glance at her showed she was perfectly serious.

'Don't be absurd, Helen. We didn't do anything!'

She gave me sideways look. 'Didn't we? Perhaps we don't have to do anything to do everything!' she added with a low laugh. 'Don't mind me, I'm skittish. Heather has that effect on me!'

'What do you like to do in your spare time?' I asked her after supper that first evening.

'She's a great reader!' Kieran said, 'and she has her little sewing operation to keep her busy.'

Helen flushed. 'He means the bit of dressmaking I do for myself.'

'Bit of dressmaking!' Kieran expostulated. 'She makes things she'll never wear – all sorts of things. If you look in the dining room you'll see her plant – machine and dressmaker's model and a veritable mound of patterns.'

'You shouldn't make fun of me,' Helen said in a quiet voice.

Kieran was instantly contrite and indulgent. 'I'm not making fun of you, sweetheart. I think you're very clever to be able to do these things.'

She turned to me. 'It's just that I like to be creative.'

'Yes,' Kieran said. 'Helen has a thing about creativity!'

'I just feel,' Helen said mildly, 'that it is the central force in all humanity.' She caught my eye. 'If creativity is blocked in one direction it will find another!'

I thought of my criminal clients, of their ingenuity, of the force which propelled them. 'That's very true,' I said. 'I see it all the time!'

Kieran was still wearing his indulgent smile. 'She writes as well, you know.'

'Just short stories,' Helen said hurriedly, although her eyes flashed fire for a moment. 'Little things . . .'

'Have any of them been published?'

She nodded. 'Women's magazines.'

'Romance,' Kieran intoned, 'with a bite to it!' I saw that Helen's face was now tight.

'Do you still play chess?' I asked, to change the subject.

'No,' Helen said, relaxing and raising her eyebrows sardonically. 'Kieran lost interest after I beat him three times in a row!'

'I didn't lose interest in the chess,' Kieran muttered equably, glancing at me with a conspiratorial smile, 'only in the length of time between each of Helen's moves.'

'Fibber!' Helen cried. 'You were simply hopping mad because you didn't win!'

Kieran smiled again, a private smile which contained its own comment on the foibles of women.

Helen put Jonathan to bed and joined Kieran and me by the fire in the drawing room. She was very vivacious, and Kieran was very witty and we laughed a good deal, helped by the wine I had brought from London, one bottle of which we had consumed at supper and another as we sat around the fire.

I began to feel certain, despite all my earlier reservations, that here was a marriage which worked; there was too much humour, too much gaiety in the conversation for it to be anything else; it was as though they sparked each other off. It was the kind of evening where the bright young couple would find their way to bed and consummate the teasing tensions of the evening by making passionate love. It was either a happy marriage, or a deliberate display, a virtuoso performance. I looked at the old gramophone with its trumpet-like speaker resembling a great brass lily, and asked; 'Does that thing still work?'

'Of course it does,' Helen said.

She wound it up, put one of John McCormack's records on the turntable. The needle scratched its way over the old 78; 'Lord for tomorrow and its needs I do not pray . . .'

She turned to me, laughing. 'The scratching is nearly as nice as the music; it seems so old and echoy.' It did indeed seem echoy, of the past when I was sixteen and Helen a child, of the first time the ancient thing was played in my hearing.

'It's an antique,' I said. 'Is it safe left here in the valley?'

She shrugged. 'Sure who'd break in? The house is shuttered when we are not here.'

There were other things; a stuffed otter in a Victorian display case on the mantelpiece, a heavy brass fender with claw feet. I loved the old things, loved the sense of the many lives that had sat around this fireplace. I made some comment about the Lodge, wondering what antiques were hidden behind its shutters.

'There are a few old massive pieces of furniture. I think the Malcolms sold off most of the moveable stuff!'

'How do you know?'

'I was in the Lodge last summer,' she said. 'Joss Malcolm, the new owner, came to view his inheritance. He called here and stayed to supper and the next day he showed me the Lodge!'

'Helen loves these old places,' Kieran said indulgently.

'What's he like?'

'A charming man – you know how open the Americans are! He's divorced and has a grown-up son somewhere in the States. But he loves the valley, keeps saying it's "primitive".'

She laughed. 'I was a bit taken aback initially. I always associated the word "primitive" with cannibals and woad-stained natives!'

'You'll just have to learn American!'

I said good night at eleven. Neither of my hosts showed any sign of leaving the fire. Helen said good night as she gave me the candle, which she had lit with a paper taper from the embers in the grate. Her hand brushed mine for an instant, and her eyes, very bright, pupils wide, flickered into mine and withdrew.

I thought of Jonathan and went upstairs carefully, waiting for the creak on the second last step, afraid of waking him.

When I got to my room I lit the lamp, and noticed as I got into bed that the bolster and the pillows had fine linen covers with edging. They smelt of camphor. I got into the bed where Helen had slept, while I had dreamt of her in the room on the far side of the landing. I listened and heard a light step on the stairs; that would be her, I thought, coming to her matrimonial chamber, the room formerly occupied by her mother. I heard her proceed down the landing, open a door on the other side, my former room, heard Jonathan's sleepy voice, 'I wanna drink . . .' heard her whisper and retrace her steps downstairs, heard her return. There was another exchange, her voice coaxing, Jonathan's peevish, before she went across the landing and the door of her room shut.

But although I lay in the dim yellow lamplight for a long time after that, I did not hear Kieran's step following her.

I dozed and woke after an hour or so, but found I couldn't go back to sleep again. The lamp was still lit. I got up, went to the bookshelf and glanced at the tomes on offer. *Little Women*, *Good Wives*, *Jo's Boys*, *Twenty Thousand Leagues Under the Sea*. I had read the latter many years before, and had no interest in the thoughts of Miss Alcott or the doings of her Little Women, so I directed my eyes elsewhere in the hopes of turning up something more appetizing. I knew Helen read widely and was rather disappointed with the selection on the shelf, until I remembered that this was no longer her room and that she would have taken with her the books that mattered to her.

Still searching, I opened the wardrobe, saw a couple of books on the top shelf. One of them turned out to be *A Hundred Things for a Girl to Do*, but the other was *King Solomon's Mines*. I took it down and brought it back to bed.

It was an old paperback version. I had not read any of Rider Haggard's work and began to leaf through the pages, to get a flavour before commencing the novel. And as I moved to position the book better against my raised knees, some sheets of folded paper fell out onto the bed. I read them before I knew what I was doing, or before I realized that what I had before me was private to Helen. It was some kind of journal. She had evidently written it shortly after her marriage and by the time I realized that I had her report on her honeymoon I was too immersed to heed the voice of self-reproach.

Monday

A honeymoon in Positano! So wonderfully romantic, with the sea outside the window, and Capri to be visited as soon as I get better. We'll be able to visit Axel Munthe's house there. Can't wait . . .

I have a sore throat, the same kind I used to get sometimes during exams; Mam used to say it was psychosomatic. It's quite bad and I have a temperature which makes me feel rotten, so I have to stay in bed.

K. is out, down at the beach, talking to some people. If I go to the window and look out through the slats of the shutters I can see him at their table. I don't know who they are; they're in the shade of the umbrella. He's been talking with them all day, and seems to be enjoying himself; I can hear the laughter. He came back at midday and brought me some fruit and was funny. I wished he would stay and keep me company for a bit, because it is so lonely here on my own, with only silly stuff to read. But he didn't wait long, gave me a kiss on the top of my head (it's always on the top of my head) and went back to his friends. I suppose it's nice that I'm able to see him if I look out through the shutters, and I don't want to appear demanding.

Tuesday

In bed again today. God, what a bloody bore! Kieran is still somewhere with his new friends; he visits me twice a day for about ten minutes as though I were his maiden aunt! I'm supposed to be his wife! Maybe I shouldn't feel so cross. Am I unreasonable? He even stays out until all hours, and I have my little supper alone here in this great bed.

But the throat is getting better; I can swallow more easily and the temperature is almost gone.

I've been reading *King Solomon's Mines* which is OK, but as I've already seen the film there are few surprises. So I'm fed up. I sleep a lot from sheer boredom.

Wednesday

Up and about, bright-eyed and bushy-tailed. K. came to bed very late last night.

When I woke up, feeling so much better, he was fast asleep. I tickled him, to make him wake, but he opened his eyes and was horribly grumpy, so I left him to his slumbers and went down to breakfast. The dining room was half full; plenty of Italians in this hotel, which is nice; it makes it feel foreign and exotic.

There's an English couple at the next table and I overheard her say to her husband, 'Look at the little bride . . . all on her ownio.'

She leant over and asked me if I was better, saying that my husband had told them I was poorly. I said I was fine now, but she had a sort of knowing tone to her voice as though she put my indisposition down to the stresses of being on honeymoon! Prurience with a capital P! Yuck! Yuck! Yuck!

Saturday

We've been to Capri, seen Axel Munthe's house; I remember how he said in *The Story of San Michele* that he wanted 'Light, light, light everywhere!' He certainly got it! It's fairytale, breathtaking! We had a look at the Emerald Grotto too, and kept our heads down as we went in so that we wouldn't be brained by the rock!

Sunday

K. just doesn't want to. He won't. It must be my fault. I wore that semi-transparent thing and he didn't like it. Maybe he thinks it's improper.

It makes me feel very strange . . . sort of invisible, that he has no time for me, no interest in me, and doesn't want to touch me. That's what it feels like, at any rate. Am I imagining all this?

I want to talk and . . . everything . . . I thought he would love me.

No use in tears. I sigh inside and think of dear D., whom they all told me I should forget. I remember his kisses. They turned my bones to water.

K.'s gone out again without me, telling me that I need an early night!

Tuesday

Into our second week. I suppose I could say, 'Mission accomplished!'

K. and I had dinner on the terrace last night and he drank quite a bit. Then back to our room and he told me to get into bed. He turned off all the lights and got in.

It hurt like hell. I don't know why they say it's nice; he kept saying, 'Relax, relax . . .' But I didn't feel as though he was really addressing me. It felt as though he had someone else in his head.

He went to sleep then.

Wednesday

I'm looking forward to Saturday when we go home.

I was crying today and K. was awful and I asked him to forgive me and said that I was very mixed up.

He looked a bit scornful. I suppose he thinks I'm childish, or something.

We haven't made L. since. I think he didn't like it the last time. I hated it; it felt mechanical. It must be my fault. But what am I supposed to do? After all, he's the one with the bits and pieces. Oh God, I try to make myself laugh! But I just KNOW there's more to love than this!

I folded the pages and put them back in the book, and replaced it in the wardrobe. I got back into bed, blew out the lamp and watched through the window the clouds scudding in the moonlit sky. My mind was in turmoil.

Madness . . . madness . . . Why did she do it – marry him? She was in a desert, a veritable desert . . . 'dear D.' she had written . . .

'Oh Helen . . .

I got up early the next morning. Helen was in the yard. She was sitting on a kitchen chair in the sunlight, writing on a pad on her knee.

'Ah, good morrow,' she said lightly, closing the jotter. 'Did you sleep well?'

'Like a top,' I lied.

She rose to go into the kitchen. I forestalled her. 'I'm perfectly capable of making some tea. Stay where you are and I'll bring it out. Finish your letter.'

'It's not a letter. It's one of my short stories. Kieran says they keep me out of the pubs!'

'How many have you had published?'

'A dozen or so.'

I moved a small table from the corner of the kitchen into the yard and brought some brown bread, butter, marmalade, cups and plates. The kettle only needed to be moved to the hotplate to boil up and I made the tea and brought it out. Then I fetched a second chair and poured the tea.

'This is the life!' Helen exclaimed. 'I'm not used to being waited on!'

I thought of the life I had once dreamt of giving her; she would have had a housekeeper, a nanny for the children. I would have given her freedom. We would have travelled; we would have laughed. I would have dressed her in couture, loved her, lived with her, slept with her, listened to her sharp, original perspective on the world. But, most of all, we would have dwelt together in that private dimension where parameters dissolve.

'Do you remember the day we first met?' I said. 'I watched you from over there . . . you were running down the avenue, leaping up at the branches.'

Helen followed my gaze. 'Yes, of course. You were the year's exotica – Kieran's friend from London. I had a strange experience when I turned and saw you!'

'What was that?'

'I felt that I knew you already! What do you make of that? You approached me and I felt you were known to me, and that you saw me – I mean the real me, not just the snotty-nosed kid!'

'You weren't snotty-nosed!'

She chuckled.

'Where's Kieran?'

'Still in bed. He works late . . . at his thesis. He postponed his doctorate when Jonathan was a baby and perpetually sick, and crying. He's making up for it now! He needs it,' she added, 'if he is to progress to a professorship some day!'

I thought of what I had read the night before.

'Can we go for a walk?'

'Why not? Where would you like to go?'

'Down to the pool.'

The pool was the same, cold brackish water; the two sentinel rocks stood as they had when Helen had disappeared behind them with her white towel in the moonlight.

I sat on a rock near the edge and she sat beside me. I knew that we were out of sight of the house, or the boreen and I turned, looked into her eyes, held her face in my hands and slowly kissed her mouth.

'I love you!' I whispered when I was able to. 'I told you that a hundred years ago! I'm telling you now. I'll tell you the same in forty years' time!'

She started, but did not otherwise move, and she studied the ground.

'But it's too late!' she said, her voice very low and grave.

'Why is it too late, Helen?'

'You know why. We're married. We both have responsibilities!'

'Where have I heard that before? We have responsibilities ... Perhaps one of them is to ourselves.'

'Are you advocating immorality?' she said with an attempt at a laugh.

'Isn't our happiness a moral good – at least some happiness, sometime, somewhere?'

'What are you saying?'

'I don't know. Come to me. I'll give you my phone numbers; or you can write to me at the Temple! Find an excuse and get away. Anywhere you like, Helen.'

'I can't!'

I sighed, turned away. 'You can! You must!'

She was silent, stood up. I stood with her, kissed her, kissed her neck, found the sensitive spot below the ear, ran my hands over her breasts, felt the nipples strain against my fingers. She stood perfectly still, as though trying to evaluate what was happening, as though listening to the crescendo of something powerful hidden in the recesses of her being. I closed my eyes and heard my own sound, a muted groan.

'You can,' I repeated into her ear, while her hair brushed my face and my body felt as though it would explode.

'What about . . . our commitments?' she whispered shakily. 'What about my son? It would make his mother an adulteress.'

I pulled away. 'Oh Christ, Helen, that's only a word! It has nothing to do with your son; it has everything to do with you, with your life, your fulfilment! And our "commitments" need not be upset!'

As though he knew the psychological moment the piping voice of Jonathan could be heard from the avenue. The little monster had evidently woken and found the slave missing. 'Mummee, mummee . . .'

She called out, 'Coming, darling!'

She pulled herself from me and walked away. 'I can't,' she repeated over her shoulder, with finality.

I followed in silence. You can, I said to myself. You can. And, what is more, you will.

I picked up a piece of flint and, with another small stone, carved in the flint a small heart pierced by an arrow. It was badly done; the heart was a skinny affair, lacking in the lush passion I wanted to portray, but I caught up with Helen and handed it to her. She looked surprised, glanced at the shard of flint as though I were sharing something of geological interest, assumed the patient listening mien I had seen her use with Kieran, and then, with a perceptible start, saw the small carving. With a smile, and a full glance at me, she put the piece of flint into her pocket.

'Can I see it?' Jonathan cried. 'Is it a fossil?'

'No,' Helen said. 'It's not a fossil; and you can't!'

I was a model guest for the rest of that brief holiday. I wanted to take my hosts to dinner in Dublin, but Jonathan was the ever-present menace. There was no babysitter and he proclaimed that food in restaurants was 'bad', so there was no point in trying to take him and we stayed put, drinking more wine than was good for us after the small, white hope of the future had been put to bed. Kieran told me something about his thesis, but I have forgotten it. He stayed up late working each night I was there, which gave me a little time with Helen each morning.

They were precious those mornings; we had breakfast together, while Jonathan played in the yard. I did not press her again to come to me. I was happy for the moment to watch her, to follow the grace of her movements, the sweep of her hair, the sudden light of her laughter. I was haunted by what I had read in her memoranda, hidden in the pages of *King Solomon's Mines*. Was this a true window on her marriage, I wondered; or had it changed and healed? Perhaps I shouldn't have come; I was making a fool of myself, like some sort of delayed adolescent, like the time I had gone to Dundalk. After all, for the second time, she had said no.

It was raining on my last morning. We sat over the full breakfast of bacon, eggs, sausage and tomato that Helen had insisted on preparing. We could hear Kieran moving about upstairs and knew he would join us shortly. Jonathan was distributing his time between the hall and the kitchen. He had set up a flotilla of trucks, led by the red lorry, his latest acquisition.

As Kieran's step was heard on the stairs, as he spoke to his son in the hall, Helen said evenly, in a very low voice, as though afraid of being overheard: 'I was thinking of going away for a short holiday myself sometime soon. On my own, just for the break.'

'Where were you thinking of going?'

She blushed. 'I don't know yet. Anywhere . . .'

'London, Paris, Rome?' I asked softly. 'Big cities all. Or Connemara, or Kerry? Would I be permitted to join you for breakfast?'

Helen bowed her head as though she were abstracting herself from possibilities she hardly dared to consider, and Kieran walked through the door.

'Ah, good morning!' he said jovially. 'Such a pity that we have rain on your last day!'

'I've no complaints,' I said. 'I've had a lovely weekend.'

They drove me to the airport that afternoon, shook hands and saw me off.

'Come again any time, old fellow,' Kieran said. I waited to hear if he had a message for James, his good wishes or something of that order.

'Will I tell James you were asking for him?' I said. 'I write to him from time to time.'

'Of course. I hope he's doing great things. California you said . . . Nice climate.'

I glanced at him, and thought for a moment that I detected a moment's vulnerability, for his face softened and his mouth became sensitive. Then he changed the subject, made a joke and the moment passed.

Helen had been anecdotal and funny on the drive to the airport; but her eyes were tired and a little sad when she said goodbye.

'Will you be alone at home this evening?' she asked in a whisper when Kieran moved away for a moment in pursuit of the escaping Jonathan.

I thought of Marion, of the evening, of the empty house whether she was there or not.

'It's likely,' I said. 'Will you phone?'

Her eyes followed Kieran for a moment. She didn't answer, but she smiled at me slowly, which was answer enough.

London seemed vast and impersonal on my return. Marion was in the drawing room with a couple of her charity committee friends.

'Well, the wanderer returns! Did you have a nice time?'

'It was enjoyable. Weather all right until today.'

'And how was she . . . Helen?'

I was aware of the significant glances of the other two in the room.

'Helen is fine. She and Kieran have a son, and he was a bit under the weather with tonsillitis.'

'Oh,' Marion said, 'poor kid!' She turned to her guests in explanation. 'Helen is a little Irish girl Dan fell in love with when he was just a boy.' She took a sip from her gin and lime. 'But what about the father, Helen's husband,' she continued, 'the bloke who wrote to crow about his sexual athletics with his bride? I do hope the poor fellow has got used to it by now!'

I glanced at her two friends who were listening with the avid disbelief of people who are terrified that they are about to witness a scene.

'Don't be so foolish, Marion,' I said.

The visitors stood up, almost simultaneously, saying they had to be off and they left with forced, smiling thank yous and with alacrity.

When they were gone Marion turned to me.

'I'm sorry if I'm "foolish". I suppose it is unreasonable for a wife to feel unhappy when her husband runs off to see another woman! You see, Dan,' she said, dropping the confrontational tone and reaching for woozy gravity, 'I know it was her you wanted to see. Women know these things! That damn place wouldn't mean a straw to you unless she was there! Deny it if you can!' She waited, hoping for my denial, longing for my embrace and reassurance, hungering for the romantic interchange which would have filled her insecurity, which would have fulfilled her need for recognition.

But I was unable to give it. My flesh crawled at the prospect of her forgiveness, her ownership, the size of the space she would permit me to inhabit, her gratified victory. And I was tired of the lie which was my life.

'I'll be in the study,' I said, moving away.

'He'll be in the study!' I heard her announcing to the walls when I had gone. 'Isn't that nice. Is he ever anywhere else?'

I heard her glass, one of a crystal set which had been a wedding present, shatter as she flung it at the wall. I thought of Helen and Kieran and the pest Jonathan. At least the pest was real, and the relationship there between mother and child was real, whereas I inhabited a house echoing with emptiness. No small footfall broke the emotional tensions; no childhood tears or laughter created reasons for going on.

And I knew that Marion had, unwittingly perhaps, spoken the truth. It wasn't the valley, it was Helen herself. She was more than just a person to me. Helen was a place; our relationship was a fifth dimension, almost a religion in its promise of concord and peace.

In my study I took up the brief I had been working on before I left, and soon I was immersed, making notes, then drafting the defence. I was immediately at home in the milieu of legal problems; its complexity was a haven. Its intellectual rigour allowed me to distance myself from the malaise of my homecoming and my strange homesickness.

A few minutes later Marion opened the study door and said that as I hadn't a word to throw to a dog, she was going out. 'I'll be home late!' she announced then, and waited for moment to see if this would provoke a response, a question as to where she was going, an instant's reassurance.

But all I could feel was the accumulated pressure of irritation, and my own utter failure as a husband.

'If you're hungry, there's chicken and salad in the fridge,' she added then, as though trying to show reasonableness after all.

I glanced at her, at her wounded air, at the disappointment which was beginning to corrode her.

'Thank you, Marion,' I said.

She withdrew, shut the door. 'Thank you, Marion!' I heard her repeat in a thin exercise at mimicry. 'Thank you, Marion!'

It occurred to me that she had cause for complaint. I had just returned and I had immured myself at once. Spurred by guilt I got up and came into the hall. I hated all this angst on her part. It was tantamount to a perpetual accusation.

'I'm sorry, Marion, I'm a bit tired this evening! Did you want us to go out?'

The phone rang as she was searching for a response. She was beside it and picked it up.

'Hello . . .' She replaced the receiver.

'Who was it?'

'No one, darling. The caller hung up!' She looked at me accusingly, opened the front door and was gone.

I took out my pocket diary. I knew there was no phone in the valley, but I rang a Dublin number which Helen had given me, the number of her home in Clonskeagh, in the faint hope that my caller might be there. But the phone just rang and rang to no purpose.

Chapter Seventeen

The months passed. Autumn came, the Long Vacation ended and the new law year began. Matt Hartley, pressed with a case which was taking all his time, passed a brief my way. It was a homicide.

A young man, twenty-eight years old, had killed his young wife. She had left him but had agreed to see him one last time, to visit the matrimonial home one Saturday morning. She had arrived, but had refused to consider a reconciliation, saying that she had met someone else. He had hit her in the face, strangled her with the flex of the iron, cut her wrists.

'Do you want it?' Matt asked. 'Not an easy station; no defence worth a damn.'

'Well, we'll have to see, won't we?'

'Good luck!'

James Michael Cladwick had been remanded in custody and I saw him in prison. A perfectly ordinary young man who had, he said, lost his rag when the wife he loved had refused to consider a reconciliation, refused to explain why she had left him.

'I hated her so much that morning. I had gone to trouble to make the place nice; got some flowers . . . you know the stuff women like.' He wept then. 'I loved her . . . I'm ashamed.'

The trial was held in Court 18 of the Central Criminal Court. The ambience was typical, pale walls, fluorescent lights, the lion and the unicorn holding aloft the coat of arms, *Dieu et mon droit* staring from the wall; dock facing the bench, public gallery above it, weeping relatives, reporters, stacks of legal tomes and papers. It took two days. The Crown was represented by Bob Tensworth, from the Inner Temple, at his precise and courteous best. Whatever chance I had of succeeding with either of the pleas in mitigation, namely that the accused had been provoked by his wife and was suffering from diminished responsibility, was scotched by two pieces of crucial evidence. The first was the evidence of James Cladwick himself that he was not 'beside himself' when he killed his wife, 'angry yes, but not out of control,' he said, foolishly clinging to face; the second was the evidence of the psychiatrist on behalf of the Crown. The latter said that Cladwick was essentially 'an ordinary bloke' suffering from no disease of the mind.

I watched the jury. They wore grim faces as the evidence was trotted out; as the pieces of blood-stained clothing were produced; as the photographs of the dead girl's body were handed around. Bob was persuasive without belligerence; he never bullied a witness. His horn-rimmed glasses, his pin-stripe suit, might have been replicas of my own; but his command of language was entirely unique; Bob possessed rhythm, pockets of surprise, never let the jury sleep. Even his habit of turning coins over in his pocket with his left hand might have been specially designed to focus attention, if not on the direct issue, at least on him, on how normal he was, albeit the prosecutor, how unlikely that such as he would seek to send someone down for life unless it was truly warranted.

'Never mind, old boy,' he said when the jury brought in a verdict of guilty. 'Nothing else was possible!'

But I did mind. Not so much that I had not succeeded in convincing the twelve honest brokers that my client had been a man possessed, sick in mind, provoked to the point where a reasonable person would have acted as he had done. No, clearly the man, for all his repentance, was a brute, a fanatic, a would-be possessor of his wife's body and soul, whose actions had insisted that if he could not have her no one else would. But what exercised me most about him, and others like him, was why! Why were some people capable of perpetrating evil? Why were some driven to acts the very idea of which would make most people run away in horror? Why were some compelled in ways they did not themselves understand and often tried unsuccessfully to circumvent? People with open faces, who looked normal?

It was as though there was no such thing as normality; as though the face of humanity was the face of Janus, the Roman god who looked two ways at once. I could not see, in this thought process, how soon, in my own way, I too would wear the face of Janus, how circumstances and expediency would dictate duality, even duplicity.

Mr Bushwell, the chief clerk in Chambers, was a small man, balding, with the remnants of his hair carefully plastered across his pate. His demeanour was quiet, but the gentleness of his expression belied the steel at his heart. He came into my room on my first morning back in the New Year, moved obsequiously, as soundless as though he were in slippers.

'This one here,' he said, handing me a brief tied in pink tape, and raising his eyebrows as though to impart the bizarre nature of the contents, 'is an interesting one, Mr McPherson, sir, a very interesting one! Another murder!'

Mr Bushwell tended to the servile, although his power in Chambers was almost total. He probably earned as much as I did, but his demeanour belied it.

I looked at the brief, saw the name Wells Crother & Co., Solicitors.

'Mr Crother asked for you specifically, sir,' Bushwell said, to forestall my question as to why the brief had not been sent to Matt Hartley, who was, when it came to homicide, still the powerhouse in Chambers.

'He was very impressed, sir, at the way you conducted that case, where the little girl was injured – the Jennings case.'

'What's this one?'

'I gather it's to do with a djinn, sir.'

He enjoyed my stupefaction. 'What are we talking about here, Mr Bushwell; gin or evil spirits?'

'Evil spirits, Mr McPherson. The accused – a lady of Pakistani origin – killed her cousin by jumping on her to exorcize the djinn! She thought she was possessed, you see.'

He left the brief gently on the desk as though the spirits might rise up to follow him.

'You're welcome to it,' Matt said when I had lunch with him and told him about the new brief. 'Should be interesting; mind you, it's the backlash of Empire, isn't it, all these people with their weird bloody religions swarming into the country? Still don't know what the government thought it was about in '68 to have allowed it. Country's gone to hell. The Common Law of England knotting itself over demons! What will we have next, I ask myself!'

'Matt, what would you do if you really believed that I was

possessed and I believed it too and begged you to help me shift the nuisance, implored you to hop up and down on my guts?'

'*Volenti non fit iniuria*, and all that, you mean? Still, I wouldn't have jumped up and down on your guts, dear boy; unless one is C3 one simply knows what that does to the insides; I mean . . . even in the East they must have heard of internal bleeding!'

He finished his wine. 'Must go. I'm in the Court of Criminal Appeal tomorrow. Heaps to do!' He found his coat, turned with a brief gesture and was gone.

I sat back, poured another glass of wine, surveyed the clientele, listened to the buzz of conversation, the clink of glasses, the small clatter of cutlery and plates.

From somewhere behind me came the smell of hot whiskey with cloves and instantly I was back in the kitchen at Lough Corrloch with Kieran stirring sugar into my hot toddy and crushing a few cloves with the back of the spoon. For a moment my mind dwelt on the valley, on Helen, on the phone call I had placed again to her home in Clonskeagh when the summer was over and I knew they would have returned from the valley. This time she had answered.

'Hello, Helen.'

There was a fraction's hesitation. 'Dan! How nice to hear from you. Where are you phoning from?'

'London. Can you talk?'

'I thought I was!' she said with a laugh.

'I just wanted to hear your voice. I miss you!' Her answer came back, suddenly soft and very low: 'Yes, I miss you too.'

'Did you ever have that holiday you spoke of?'

'No.'

'Why don't you take one in London? Helen, it's really nice here in autumn.'

Her laugh was so low it was like a whisper. 'I'd need an excuse.'

'Try. I'll show you the city . . . again.'

'It seems a long time ago, doesn't it? You were a wonderful guide.'

'I would like to be more than that!'

'Oh Dan . . .'

'Helen . . .'

'I hear the car, Dan. I have to go. God bless you.'

The line went dead.

My reverie was broken. I was joined by our new pupil, Catherine Wilson, five foot three of acerbic dynamism.

'Hi there!' she said. 'Mind if I join you?'

Catherine was Scottish, a dark, pretty girl, with a first-class honours degree, an irreverent tongue and an incisive mind which she treated with the same covert disrespect as she did everything else. She was Jeremy Witherspoon's pupil, a harbinger of the new order, the first woman to have been admitted to our Chambers.

'Hello, Catherine. How are you getting on?'

'Fine,' she said with a twinkle. 'I'm working hard, giving satisfaction like a good girl, addling my poor little brains . . . and hoping like hell to be kept on at the end of pupillage.'

Catherine had no awe of the profession and less of its practitioners. But she was a genuinely interested lawyer; she was fascinated by the precision of legal precepts, by the teasing out of the issues in complex cases, by the sense of control and objectivity central to a good practitioner. And behind her rather flippant demeanour lurked an iron ambition.

'Well, we don't know. It's a toss up between you and Nathan. We can only keep one of you on!' I teased. Nathan Timpson was our other pupil, a clever, gangly young man, with a shock of mousy hair and a concerned expression, as though forever sensible of the gravity of his calling. One of the two would be invited to become our newest tenant in a matter of months and I already knew which one would have my vote.

'I know . . . but Nathan is thinking of frying other fish. He has his eye on journalism, writes bits and pieces for some rag or other, you know. He would do well in that milieu. He's really good; would be waste in law.' Catherine looked sad for a moment. 'I hate waste!'

I listened, amused. Nothing gentlemanly about Catherine.

'What do you think of him as a lawyer?'

She puffed her mouth. 'Well, he's like a coconut tree – impressive at first. You know the kind of thing: tall with very big nuts, but destroyed by the first frost!'

I choked on my wine. 'And what about you, Catherine?'

'Oh I'm just small, hardy and deadly!' she said airily.

'Would you like to help me with a djinn case?'

Her brow furrowed. 'Are you taking the mickey?'

'I'm on the level; djinn as in evil spirits. I'll ask Jim if I can borrow you – make a change from accidents in the workplace?'

Catherine was enthusiastic. 'You bet!'

She came around that afternoon and I set up a table for her by the fireplace. She examined my wig which was on the mantelpiece, sighed and said: 'I can't wait for mine to be that awful, seedy colour.'

'Why? For the hallmarks of sweat and toil?'

'Christ, no. For stature.'

'Just wear high heels.'

She groaned and narrowed her eyes at me.

Catherine and I struck up a good working relationship. We sometimes worked late. Nathan, the coconut tree, would hang around, and would just happen to be leaving at the same time as Catherine.

'That young man is not just competing with you,' I said, when she complained that she couldn't move without falling over him. 'I think he's in love!'

She scrunched up her mouth. 'He's got nice eyes,' she conceded. 'If he wasn't a pupil here . . .' Then she turned limpid brown eyes on me and asked, 'What do men feel when they're in love?'

I looked at her with raised eyebrows.

'Never mind, I'm a nosy little cow! But I can't help wondering if they feel the way we do.'

'How do women feel?'

'Oh squiffy, weak at the knees – soul music, all the mushy stuff. I was wondering if men felt anything like that – or anything at all, come to think of it!'

'How can you be so cynical at your age?'

'I didn't come up the Clyde on a water biscuit,' she said darkly. 'I'm afraid of investing in a man. You know, have a grand passion and find out that, as far as he was concerned, it was all just another rush of testosterone from his busy little gonads!'

I glanced at her, but she didn't look up, although a private smile quirked the corner of her mouth.

'Well, you'll just have to live and learn, won't you, Catherine? Now, are you going to work or not?'

'Sorry!'

One day, early in the New Year, the phone rang while I was reading some precedents which my assiduous helper had researched. Catherine picked up the receiver.

'It's for you,' she said, putting her hand over the mouthpiece. 'A personal call.'

'Who is it?'

'It's someone called Helen Fitzgerald! Will I tell her you're busy?'

I took the receiver. Catherine returned to her work. I felt the sudden constriction at the base of my throat as though the air passage had blocked.

'Helen?'

'Am I being intrusive?' the uncharacteristically small voice said, and I heard the soft, flat, Irish sounds like the echo of a lost melody, one almost too personal to bear. The accent intruded on my working world, undermined the professional in me, touched some vital component, summoned my personal demon, the part of me which was secretly and deliciously untamed.

'Of course not. Where are you phoning from?'

'London!'

'Whereabouts?'

'I'm in the Regent Palace Hotel in Piccadilly. I got a special package – a long weekend. I'm going home on Sunday.'

'Are you on your own?'

'Yes!'

I glanced at Catherine. She was ostensibly absorbed in making notes from a heap of law reports open on her desk, but I could almost hear her ears flapping.

'I shouldn't have phoned you – I think you're very busy.' Helen's voice sounded suddenly proud and uncertain.

'No. Well, a bit at the moment. But I'll pick you up at six. Is that all right?'

'Yes . . . but—'

'See you then!'

Catherine looked at me speculatively when I replaced the receiver and, when I stared back at her, reapplied herself to her work. I glanced at my watch. Three o'clock. My mind feverishly scanned my weekend. Marion was in the Canaries, taking a winter break. I had a dinner engagement for the following evening with an old friend from school, which would be easily cancelled. Except for work, I was free. But work would have to take a back seat this weekend. Nothing would be allowed to come between me and the dizzying possibilities suddenly presenting themselves.

Helen was in London and on her own!

I went back to my work, forced total concentration, but my mind kept returning to the burning questions. Where would Helen like to go? I could take her out of London; or we could stay in London. And then, unbidden, came the recollection of her looking up at the Hilton in Park Lane when I had brought her to Hyde Park all those years ago.

'When I'm rich and famous I'll stay there,' she had said. 'I'll spend the day at the window!'

When Catherine was out of the room I phoned the Hilton and booked a double room overlooking Hyde Park: Mr and Mrs McPherson, for two nights. I was being presumptuous, but I was too old to care. Without audacity, without the courage of one's desires, there is only stagnation.

At five I said goodnight to Catherine.

'Do you want me to come in tomorrow?' she asked.

'No. You go off and have a nice weekend.'

'Thanks, Dan, you too,' she said sweetly, adding as I was halfway out the door, 'don't do anything I wouldn't do!'

I put my head back around the door, but she was looking innocent.

'It's only advice,' she said in a reasonable voice, without looking up. 'You don't have to take it.'

The drive from the Temple to Piccadilly, through rush hour traffic in the winter drizzle, was one of the sweetest of my life. I felt like a teenager heading for his first tryst.

Helen was waiting for me. I saw her at once. She was ostensibly immersed in a magazine, but glanced a little nervously now and again across the crowded expanse of the foyer.

I approached swiftly and circuitously, and was behind her before she realized I was there. I studied her, saw that she had had her hair cut in a new trendy style with a swing to it, was wearing a tailored black suit, with a white shirt, and looked stunning. Her overcoat was folded beside her on the seat. Her legs, clad in dark tights, were crossed. Her feet were encased in plain black court shoes. She had a tense, straight-backed demeanour to her, and perhaps it was this which gave her the classical aura.

I sat behind her, feeling a surge of joy, of pleasure in being so near when she did not realize I was there. I felt the peace in the midst of my private turmoil, as though all sounds were muted, the calm at journey's end. I leant over.

'That must be one hell of a good magazine!' I whispered into her ear.

She started, gave a relieved laugh. 'You're early! Oh Dan, it's so good to see you!'

'You look wonderful!'

'So do you!'

I took her hand. 'Come on,' I said, pulling her to her feet. 'I need to have you to myself!'

I steered her to the street, to the waiting car, to the lights of London.

Over dinner, I asked her why she had decided to come to London.

'I thought I might look in on the sales!'

'Helen . . . is that all?'

'No!' She glanced at me, smiled uncertainly.

'How is Kieran?'

'Fine.'

'And Jonathan?'

'Fine also, touch wood. He's pulling up now, beginning to make progress in school too. We're very relieved!'

'And you will be staying until Sunday!'

'Yes.'

'You should stay for ever!'

She looked at me levelly and her eyes suddenly filled with tears. 'I would if I could!'

'Helen, has something happened?'

She brushed the tears away angrily. 'No, nothing out of the ordinary. Except what is ordinary for my life would not be tolerated for two minutes by any woman worth her salt!'

'This has to do with Kieran?'

'Yes!'

'Why do you tolerate it?'

'Because I'm half-witted. I bought all that stuff, you know, about goodness and duty, and self-sacrifice. But it's really downright evil masquerading as something else. All it serves is power, Kieran's power over me! I've wasted some of the best years of my life . . . and I'm tired pretending.'

'Has this been precipitated by something in particular, Helen?'

'Yes. He more or less put me out, and Jonathan, told me to stay with his mother. He wanted to give a party; he didn't want me there!'

'Why not?'

She shrugged. 'The excuse he gave was that his friends would not appeal to me, that some of them were heavy drinkers. But what I can't stand is the assumption that I can be turfed out of my home to make room for his friends, for a party, while they can make merry in my house, among my things, whether I like it or not. Perhaps I'm being unreasonable, but there's something so intolerable about the assumption that I don't count, that I'm secondary!'

I watched her smoulder, but I could not allude to what I had once told her of Kieran. It was none of my business; and I might have been wrong.

'Why did you marry him, Helen?'

She dropped her eyes. 'He was held up as the good and pious prince. He made me laugh. My mother wanted it desperately. She made you out to be a pagan. She was immersed in religious orthodoxy, and Kieran filled all the criteria. Then she became ill and Kieran filled the vacuum. I was desperately insecure. I didn't know what I wanted; I wasn't able to judge things; I felt that you and I were impossible, especially because of Marion; I was very angry about that and most of it was pride. I was ripe for the noble gesture with Kieran . . . And I loved him, very much when I was a child, and later in an obligated kind of way.'

She raised her eyes to mine, smiled grimly. 'Shall I go on? You are the only friend I can talk to, the only one who would understand! The relief of being able to tell someone is sublime!'

'You sound bitter, which is terrible. You're young, Helen. If you're unhappy you can leave him!'

'Can I? And go where? What about my son? How can I support myself? I'm trapped.'

'There are always ways out of traps, if you are prepared to seize them!'

She sighed. 'Easily said.'

'Do you love him still?'

She considered this. 'I don't want to talk about him any more!'

'OK.' I looked at her empty coffee cup. 'More coffee? A brandy . . . a gin and tonic?'

She laughed. 'You remind me of Zarathustra's! But no, I'm finished!'

'Dear girl, you're only beginning. Shall we go and look at night-time London?'

She smiled slowly, nodded and I signalled the waiter for the bill.

We drove to the Temple, down Fleet Street. The drizzle had stopped and the streets were wet and shining. I turned down by the Old Bailey, pointed it out, glanced at my companion who sat there so avidly interested, who questioned me and was silent by turns.

I took her hand, feeling the wonder of it, small and cold but not as silken as formerly, feeling the short nails, the roughness along the edges of her thumbnail.

'I still gnaw them,' she said in answer to my unspoken question, 'when I'm furious!'

'I didn't say a word.'

'You don't need to.'

A little later she said suddenly: 'Do you remember the day you left, when you visited the valley last summer?'

'Of course!'

'I phoned your home that evening. A woman answered. Was it Marion?'

'It was. She's in the Canaries at present. I suspected it might be you and I did try to phone you back,' I added, 'but of course there was no answer from your Dublin number. Why did you phone me that night, Helen?'

'I wanted to hear your voice. Everything seemed lonely and intolerable in the valley after you had gone. I cycled into Glendockery and phoned you from a call box!'

'And then cycled the eight miles home?'

'Naturally. Mind you, Kieran hadn't even missed me. He was so busy with his thesis that he didn't realize I'd been gone for hours. Johnny was asleep. I sat in the kitchen, thought of the future, of how I would never be of any real moment to anyone. I was just something to be used. It was self-pitying . . . and terrifying. Eventually I made a pot of tea, but I didn't drink it. Instead I did a very foolish thing!'

'What was that?'

'I got out the bottle of whiskey Kieran keeps in case we have company, and I drank it. I wanted to die.'

'A whole bottle?'

'God, no. There was about half left. Kieran came into the kitchen and saw me, but he made no attempt to stop me, just ignored what I was doing, a contemptuous expression on his face, as much as if to say – "If she wants to kill herself, let her."'

I drew my breath sharply, and Helen added matter of factly, 'Well, he's very proud and some men will sacrifice everything for pride. It was only when I went outside that he followed. He was afraid that I would end up in a ditch and he'd have to answer embarrassing questions!'

'Were you very ill?'

She laughed. 'Not really. I puked into the bushes. But I had one hell of a sore head the next day!'

I sought her hand. 'Poor Helen.'

'Don't pity me, for God's sake! It was a stupid thing to have done. Crass . . .' She giggled suddenly. 'And it's put me off whiskey for life!'

I didn't laugh. Privately, I felt slightly sick.

'Are you shocked?' she asked in a low voice. 'You're looking very grim!

'No. Angry, but not with you!'

'Kieran told me weeks later that he hadn't known what to do; but I'm certain that, on a subliminal level, he was really establishing some kind of mastery.' She sighed. 'It's so wearying, his insistence on control . . . so unnecessary.'

'It should not be offered you! It's an affront.'

'Dear Dan, I must appoint you my champion. Will you enter into the lists for me and wear my favour? But, seriously, I'm sure Kieran didn't consciously mean it. I'm to blame too. It took ages for me to work out that there was something very wrong. Kieran and I had a child, a house, a car, the ability to converse, to crack jokes; but we did not have the ability to communicate. And we did not have the kind of core which underpins a marriage.'

I was silent. I held on to her hand, encouraged her to talk, sensed the relief it gave her. We cruised around Whitehall towards Trafalgar Square and the bronze lions forever guarding Nelson.

'The unauthentic life is not worth living – that's what you're saying!'

'That's true. Is my life unauthentic?'

'Only you can answer that!'

She was silent. Then she said, 'I wish tonight would never end.'

'It needn't.' I held her hand tightly. 'Will you . . . come with me, Helen? Will you be with me tonight?'

She did not reply, but glanced at me swiftly, shyly, looked away. I saw that she was blushing, a dark mottling over her face and forehead. Her silence gave me courage.

'Tell me I'm a presumptuous fool if you like. I won't take offence. But I have booked a double room for us. We can be together all night and all tomorrow and all tomorrow night and most of Sunday.'

When next I glanced at her I saw that she was looking down at her hand in mine. 'Please, Helen, we needn't do anything if you don't want, but just be with me . . . just lie beside me all night.'

In the silence I could sense the *frisson* of excitement, almost hear her mind racing.

'I will,' she said then, in a voice so low I could hardly hear her. 'Of course I will.'

I turned towards Hyde Park and the Hilton.

We were in our tower at last, looking down, our room in darkness, the curtains pulled back so we could see the city. There was a sofa by the window and we sat there for a while, in silence, holding hands, watching the traffic, the lights, the city we could not even hear, far below. I kissed her eyes and the hollows by the bridge of her nose and down her neck, very softly, feeling how she shivered, aware of the inclination of her body towards me. And then I drew her to the bed and she lay inert, like someone in a trance, while I slowly undressed her, until she was lying naked in her milk whiteness, her eyes closed.

I stood and looked down at her, a man who had found the shrine for which he has spent his life searching. Taking my clothes off I lay beside her, holding her, kissing her, stroking her satin skin, forcing restraint upon myself, waiting for her to respond. After a while, the tension left her, her arms encircled me; her lips and body answered mine, at first tentatively, then feverishly; I tasted tears.

'Are you unhappy?' I whispered, suddenly fearful.

'Oh no . . . oh no . . . I am just lost.'

I heard the rain start, pattering on the window. And that was the last I knew of where we were or who we were. Time and place and identity deserted us. But space unfolded, and in its warmth and darkness we found each other at last.

That was the beginning. It was not an affair; it was the *summum bonum* of my life. It is impossible for me to describe passion, its flights of unreasoning hunger, its terrifying vulnerability. Helen loved me! The initial thrill of it filled me with such happiness that I thought I would suffocate.

Our idyll in the Hilton, was mostly spent in bed. The DO NOT DISTURB sign stayed on the door for long periods. We did manage to stagger out for lunch next day, laughing like teenagers, and then, 'because London is so tiring,' Helen said gravely, we had to go back to bed. The sign went back on the door, and we slept, eventually, in each other's arms, waking at seven and wandering off for dinner.

Helen was shy in lovemaking, and I, because I was involved in her perceptions, was also shy, as though my body had been discovered by a woman for the first time. I was moved by her wandering over me, the gentle touch of her hands, her gathering instinctive certainty as to what would please. As our shared diffidence began to wear away, the true intensity of what we had to give each other became apparent. It was as though we had found a country known to both of us where we were entirely free, where we spoke the language, where, in the trust between us, nothing was forbidden.

If I had thought that in possessing Helen physically I would lay the passion which had smouldered in me for years, I was mistaken. The rapture, the ardour increased. In sexually possessing her I found the key to another dimension of hers, to a force which was not physical at all.

On the Sunday, Helen's last day in London, I woke in the dark and found the bed empty. I had put out my arm for her, but she was not there. I sat up, saw in the dim light from the city that the bathroom door was open. With a sense of horrible letdown I thought she was gone. But as my eyes accustomed themselves I saw her seated by the window on the small settee, wrapped in a white bathrobe, her legs tucked under her.

'Hello. I couldn't sleep and thought I'd have a look out at the city.'

'I thought you'd gone!'

'Dopey, in the middle of the night?'

'What time is it?'

'About five.'

'Come back to bed.'

She came back. We made love for an hour and fell asleep again. I woke at nine and saw that she was making up for lost slumber; she was almost comatose, her bare breast against my arm, her hair fluffed like a startled bird.

I let her sleep, watching the rise and fall of her breathing, the sweep of her lashes, the curve of her lip, the soft, warm caress of her breath.

When she woke I rang room service and ordered breakfast. She was hungry; her appetite had become as fierce as her sensuality. Everything about her was more vivid. Her hair shone; her eyes were dark green, the whites pure. She smiled at me impishly; the slightly nervous, slightly frightened Helen of Friday evening was gone. If I had worried that she might suffer from guilt, I was mistaken. She just looked radiant, and radiantly beautiful she was as she crossed the room to the bathroom, returning after her shower with damp hair, cocooned in white towels. I lay back watching her and she sat at the end of the bed, where, having breakfasted, I was lying like some kind of pasha. She stroked my feet.

'You have elegant ankles,' she said primly.

'Not as elegant as yours, my dear.'

'You have sensuous toes.'

'Not as sensuous as yours, my dear.'

She bent and bit my big toe.

'Ouch!'

'Lie still and behave!' She moved her hand up my bare leg. 'You have the biggest penis in London.'

'Not as—'

The response was smothered with a shriek of laughter and Helen was on top of me, her hand across my mouth. I was half suffocated with towels and damp hair and the whitest, most silken body on earth.

'Daniel McPherson, I will not tolerate gender confusion.'

But later, everything changed. We got dressed and Helen packed her small suitcase. Then she came to join me where I stood by the window, and looked down with me on the city and over the reaches of Hyde Park in silence.

'You remember the Serpentine,' I said, pointing to the lake, 'and Rotten Row?' A lone rider, a white horse, both minuscule, were moving between the bare trees.

'I know, where we saw the Household Cavalry, and I half twisted my ankle.' She chuckled. 'I didn't really twist it, you know. I was just curious to see what you would do.'

'I know. Helen . . .'

'Yes?'

'I love you!'

'I know. And I you.'

She leant against my shoulder. 'It's like a capsule up here,' she went on with a sigh. 'You could imagine you were in a flying saucer! If we were, I wouldn't have to budge. I could fly all the way home and spare Aer Lingus the bother!'

We were quiet then, oppressed by the realization of her imminent departure. I thought of her homecoming, of her home in the Dublin suburbs, of her child waiting for her, of her husband beside whom she would sleep that night. I wondered if Kieran had cleaned up after his party, or if this was something he expected of his wife.

'We don't make love, you know,' she said suddenly, as though she had heard my thoughts.

'You and Kieran?'

'No. Not since our honeymoon!' She glanced at me, as though weighing my reaction. 'You see, Kieran, despite appearances, is really in full flight from me!'

I thought of the journal I had found among the pages of *King*

Solomon's Mines. I sat on the sofa and put out a hand to her. 'Sit beside me!'

She complied. 'You don't seem very shocked!' she said after a moment. 'I had expected that you would be. It's normal for married people, isn't it – making love?'

'Of course.'

'And even when we did, it was not like . . . like us!'

'I should hope not,' I said, feigning collapse.

Imagining Helen's life was not a new exercise, but was one on which I now had a window. She had married young and was no sooner married than pregnant; she had acquired obligations; she had found out too late that her husband was not what she had expected; he did not want her, not the real Helen. She remained loyal, the loyalty of pride. She was financially dependent. She could not leave, not with a sick child and nowhere to go. She would not leave easily; the training of her life which exalted female duty, the duty to keep the family intact, had her secured. To have been capable of acting otherwise would have meant questioning the entire value system, to have stood back, envisaged an alternative. That kind of objectivity does not come to the very young. So she had gone on, nurturing, supporting, pretending, trying, and the sacrifice of her years was taken absolutely and entirely for granted; the wasted potential never so much as adverted to, while Kieran went blithely on his way and devoted himself to his own concerns, with the status she gave him safely nailed down.

Or so I imagined. I was hard on Kieran. I saw him blithe at Helen's expense. I could not even imagine his perspective.

I wondered if she was now convinced of his homosexuality, but it was not something at which I dared to hint.

'Darling,' I said, 'we have to decide now what we are going to do about us! I'll tell Marion I want a divorce; you can bring Jonathan with you and we'll live together.'

She regarded me in silence. Then she said, 'You make it sound so simple. I'd still be Kieran's wife; there's no divorce in Ireland!'

'I know. But if we live together, love each other, what does it matter?'

'Maybe not. But Jonathan is nine now and he'd go berserk. And you wouldn't want him. I could see you thought him the worst pest since the seven plagues of Egypt, which, in a way, he is. I love him but I know he's spoilt! Can you imagine him living in the same house with you, pining for his father, for his home?'

This idea did not fill me with any insupportable joy, but the prospect of having Helen more than made up for the prospect of the pest.

'After a few weeks we'd get on like a house on fire!' I said, with as much enthusiasm as I could muster.

'Unlikely,' Helen replied with a tight smile. 'But even if you did, do you think Kieran would let him go? He'd fight me all the way to the Supreme Court if necessary. And anyway, no court would give the wicked runaway mother custody of her child!' She paused, looked at me levelly, miserably. 'You must know that, Dan, better than I! You're the lawyer!'

'Is that an insurmountable obstacle?'

'Are you asking me if I would come to live with you without him . . . if I would leave my son behind?'

I did not answer. There was no point. I watched her stricken face and diverted the subject elsewhere.

'Well,' I said, 'children grow up. We have found each other now; we must not lose one another again, that's what's important! And when Jonathan is grown you will be free.'

She did not answer, but the tension left her face. 'Yes,' she said with a sigh: 'That's what's important!'

It was time to leave. I stood in the sudden winter sunshine and looked out the window once more, trying to impress it all on my memory, this view, this room, this veritable honeymoon. I took out my pocket diary and the gold-plated Sheaffer Marion had given me as a Christmas present, in order to ring the date, so that I would remember it. Helen had gone to the bathroom. She came out with her toothbrush, opened her case to put it in. She looked over at me with a strange expression.

'I'll remember you there, you know,' she said, 'standing by the window, the whole of London, like a great fairyland at your feet, while you frown at your diary, thinking of tomorrow's problems.'

'I was not thinking of tomorrow's problems, Helen.'

'Well, in that case,' she said, 'you may as well take the scarlet woman to the airport.'

I heard the uncertainty in her voice. I felt immediately that the bubble had burst for her; she was facing the reality of her life instead of the dream we had just lived. I crossed the room, held her as she turned away from me to hide her tears.

'I love you, Helen. I love you and love you and love you. There is nothing scarlet! There is nothing to be ashamed of. This is for ever . . . one way or the other!'

'Will you come back to the valley sometime?' she asked.

'Not only will I come back, but you will come to London as often as possible. I will buy a flat for us, where we can be together whenever you can get away!'

She looked at me doubtfully.

'I'll phone you, my darling,' I added. 'We'll work something out. Trust me!'

We drove to Heathrow like condemned persons. I watched her slim figure disappear beyond Departures. She turned and waved back to me and then was gone.

The envelope with the Irish stamp which came the following week was addressed to Chambers. There was no letter, just five typewritten lines:

> The rain hissed softly, and you slept,
> Soundlessly, almost breathlessly,
> And I listened in the dark
> Drowsy with all that we had said without words
> Knowing the impossible.

Chapter Eighteen

At the beginning I phoned her every day. For the first week there was diffidence in her voice, almost withdrawal, as though what had taken place between us in London must be consigned to the dungeons of the heart, where life's great mistakes are housed in darkness. It was as though she disbelieved what had taken place, and wanted to forget; her hesitancy, the small voice at the other end of the phone belonged to someone who had transgressed, who expected contempt. The system, the Victorian literature she had read so much of, the nuns, had no doubt told her that men despised the women who gave them sex. True as this may be, it was a maxim which did not apply here. Helen was not 'women' and she did not give me 'sex'. She gave me herself: and in this access, because the relationship was unconditional and uncontrived, because it was full and powerful, I found a liberty I had suspected existed somewhere, but had never hoped to find.

When I convinced her that she was utterly loved, that the relationship between us was a mutual flight into freedom, she began to bloom, to explore, to view passion in terms of her own truth.

Our meetings were carefully organized. It was always a weekend when Kieran was away, and he was away a great deal, it seemed – a seminar here, a conference there. Helen would leave Jonathan with her mother-in-law, who was besotted with him, and say she was going to visit an old school friend who lived in Cork.

Once we did even go to Cork. I met her there and we drove into the beautiful West Cork hinterland, as far as the Kingdom of Kerry.

But mostly it was either London, or Paris. I would arrange for her ticket to be available at Dublin airport and would meet her at the other end. I liked Paris; there was less possibility of meeting anyone we knew.

There was a feverish element to all these encounters. We devoured each other physically; when we weren't making love we talked and laughed a great deal, as though we never had enough time for all we had to say; the words tumbled over each other on every topic under the sun. But always the parting was gloomy and heavy with impending reality, on Helen's part more than mine.

I was increasingly resourced; she was increasingly spent, increasingly aware of her vulnerability, apprehensive. What if Kieran had found out she was not where she had said she would be? What if there had been an emergency at home while she was away? What if Jonathan had become ill in her absence? What if anyone rumbled us?

But in spite of all these vivid possibilities, in spite of occasional gloom when Helen would declaim on the impossibility of our situation, the necessity of ending it, we could not do otherwise than go on. Our relationship seemed charmed, as though blest from on high. There were no hitches. Helen was rarely unable to keep our appointments; she always looked incredible; we lived each moment fully, but we parted with increasing angst on her part and increased confidence on mine. In possessing her physically, in learning the subtle labyrinths of her being, I began to experience a new power, a new sense of stature.

This was reflected in my work. I was successful in the case concerning the djinn, basing the argument on the absence of *mens rea* – the intention to inflict injury – producing evidence as to the religious beliefs of the accused, harping on that and ignoring the patent fact that the accused must have known that injury would result to the woman, but had given it secondary importance. Common sense, in a court of law, can be trampled into the floor. A jury can be invited to share any perspective, and frequently will; such is the plastic nature of human reason when confronted, in an unfamiliar forum, by the persuasive power of those whose business is persuasion.

I won a rape case about this time, defending a man accused of a vicious assault. He had broken into the home of a deserted wife, raped and buggered her all night. If the accused is to be exonerated in such cases it must be shown that the woman was a consenting party to the activities complained of, that she, in effect, 'asked for it'.

Women, of course, never ask to be sexually abused, but a judge and jury are susceptible to all kinds of suggestion if the case before the court involves sex. Age-old sexual insecurities are easily played upon. I shut my mind to what I was saying; I had no business in objectivity; if there was any possibility of acquittal my business was to find it. My business was to win.

Even my marriage began to prosper. The silent impasse between Marion and me lessened. Being well catered for elsewhere, I could afford humour and consideration. Her foibles ceased to irritate. She went on the dry for long stretches. I accompanied her to her charity dos, felt her pride in me. I bought her a gold watch for her birthday. She reverted to calling me 'darling', with real affection. We began to make love again; she initiated it, reaching for me at night, slipping into my bed. It wasn't like the tempestuous journey I embarked on with Helen; but it was mildly carnal, and it eased the heightened sexual tensions the thoughts of Helen engendered. My marriage became my base, the certain place from which I executed my forays into other experience.

And I never bought the flat I had dreamt of for Helen and me.

Helen began to sound slightly desperate. She was well and truly hooked now; she had dared to give herself, dared to believe in a dream life. The solid basis to our relationship, our old friendship, had ensured trust; it had risen from its apparent ashes, fanned into flames we could never have envisaged as adolescents. Confounded and astonished by her own passion, Helen had trouble stabilizing her self-image which had begun to spin out of her control. Who was she, she demanded more than once, in occasional fits of dejection. No one: not a wife; not a power of any kind; only a mistress, a creature of deception, caught between two lives, the apex of the eternal seedy triangle, a tired cliché.

She wrote bright letters; she wrote letters heavy with melancholy. I stopped urging her to join me; I wanted her, of course, but the very momentum of our strange relationship began to impose a certain strain. The only way out of this, other than our making the break with our marriages, would have been for Helen to have had her own strong base, where her need for me would have been less. Only in retrospect did I examine the world from her perspective. She had no base that was not controlled by someone else. She was isolated in her domestic role, whereas I was part of a busy, challenging world. She had allowed passion to puncture the carefully nurtured shell of her self-sufficiency. She was being used by Kieran; she was being used by her son, who was as thoughtless of her as any spoilt child. Perhaps she began to suspect that she was also being used by me.

When I hinted to Marion that she didn't, perhaps, need me, being so busy with her charities and her friends, her response was acerbic.

'What are you talking about? Of course I need you. You're my husband. I'll never give you a divorce, so I hope you don't want one! You haven't encountered some silly passion and confused it with reality, have you?'

'No, of course not!'

The trouble was that there was a momentum in my life which was almost impossible to slow; I had a position to maintain now; Sir Billy Ryce held me up as the model advocate, the man who never blotted his copybook. Jeremy Witherspoon had been having a messy affair, and Sir Billy, who hated moral laxity, waxed wroth about the good name of Chambers being sullied when the tabloids got hold of the story.

If I broke with Marion, precipitated an untidy divorce, how would my position in Chambers be affected, my professional life which was the bedrock of my existence? If that foundered what would I have to offer anyone? And Helen had delivered no ultimatum. If she had, if she had forced me to choose between a void and an upheaval, perhaps the future might have been different.

Paris was our favourite haunt. We would stay in a hotel in the Ile St-Louis, wander around Notre-Dame, dine here and there, sometimes in the restaurant in the Eiffel Tower, once on board a *bateau-mouche* on the river.

I watched her face that night on the *bateau-mouche* as she gazed up at the floodlit monuments, the dream-like expression as though she had absented herself backwards into history. I loved to watch the impression she made on other men. On that particular night she wore a black velvet outfit over gold, and had drawn back her thick bright hair. She seemed exotic, foreign, even for Paris.

'Where did you buy that wonderful outfit?' I asked her that evening.

Helen pursed her lips and looked at me speculatively. 'You mean to say you don't recognize Dior when you see it?' She laughed then. 'For God's sake, Dan, I made the damn thing. It was a Vogue pattern

I bought in Arnotts and I got the material in a sale! You don't honestly think I could afford haute couture!'

'Tomorrow,' I whispered, into her ear, 'we will visit the Avenue Montaigne and you will choose something wonderful.'

'I can't take presents from you, Dan!'

'Why not? I love you!'

'I still can't take them.'

'Oh Helen, why not?'

'Don't be so cross. You know perfectly well why not!'

We got a taxi back to the hotel. I undressed this beautiful creature, divested her of her gold and velvet.

Later she said to me, lying in the dark, her voice full of the provocation she frequently adopted, stroking my chest with light fingers, tangling her fingers in my hair: 'Men have some kind of notion that a woman's passion exists for them, that it is generated by them! Such presumption!'

I recognized the signs. Helen wanted to challenge me, to shake me up a little. She often wanted to do this at three in the morning, when I had finally given in and was falling asleep.

'Well,' I replied sleepily, kissing her bare shoulder and feeling her shiver, 'is it not true that some well-directed male desire provokes a certain response?'

'Only evidence of what is already there,' she said, turning to me, and I heard the smile in her voice. 'A woman's passion is separate to anything she finds with a man; it exists in its own isolation!'

'Well, in that case, thank God it can be shared!'

She laughed. 'I'm being serious here. I have spent my life controlling my passions. You are the sole exception! I have kept them behind a great dam,' she added a little sententiously, 'like the waters of the Nile!'

'Some kinds of control,' I suggested, 'are just other names for death. We are born into this world in turmoil! I am glad you broke that dam for me!'

'I didn't,' she said seriously after a moment. 'It would be much too dangerous. I just dispense a little and then block everything up, which, I can tell you, is a considerable strain!'

'What would happen if you let it all out?'

'I would sweep both of us away! Would that frighten you?'

'No!'

'Well, that's categorical anyway! One of the reasons I so love you,' she added softly into my ear, 'is that you are not afraid of life! Another reason is that you are not afraid of me!'

Ah Helen, I thought, I am afraid of many things – failure, weakness, foolishness. But the self you reflect back to me is fearless and boundless. You have remade me in the image of your own power!

'You are a powerful, loving woman,' I whispered.

'I am a potentially ruthless woman,' she answered in a strange, thoughtful voice. 'It is something I am finding in myself, some kind of primeval defence mechanism, and I'm warning you about it now. It's only fair to warn you.'

I smiled in the darkness, feeling the silken skin against me and took this ruthless woman in my arms, but she stiffened and pulled away.

'I'm having a serious conversation here,' she said. 'I am trying to tell you of the strain I experience in juggling my own drive for life, even for transcendence, against your unquestioned perspective that I am your thing!'

'Helen!' I sat up, turned on the light. 'How can you even think like that?'

She pulled the sheet up to her chin in one of the automatic gestures of modesty which had never left her. Then she sighed. 'I live where I think and I cannot help the process.'

'You are not my "thing" as you put it.'

'Of course I'm not, but you have never questioned the perceptions which turn a woman into an object for the comfort of a man!'

I was silent. This was a Helen I did not know.

'Oh there's no doubt about my complicity. In apparently going along with your perspectives I can push back my own parameters, have forays into experience I can't otherwise lay hold of. But I am not and never will be your possession. Not my loneliness, not the domestic desert I inhabit, will bend me to that!' She sighed shakily. 'And I am afraid that ultimately I will have to make the sort of decision which will empty the present to serve the future.'

I tried to touch her, but she lay like something starched. I turned off the light. I could not untangle my bewilderment. Here we were, after a wonderful evening, a passionate lovemaking, and Helen, who knew she was the most important person in my life, was filled with some kind of fury, even oblique threats.

'Have I done something wrong?' I asked after a moment in a flat voice. 'I am very sorry if I have offended you.'

A moment later I felt her reach for my hand. 'Dan, you don't understand. I inhabit a tempest and am driven by it. I need an emotional home which is mine by rights . . .'

'I am yours by rights. I offered you my heart, hand, home . . . everything once, but you turned it down.'

She gulped in the darkness. 'What did I know? I was a child! A blind and angry child!'

'I know. But don't blame me for it now,' I said.

'No,' she said after a moment, 'but life is a dynamic, not something jelled for ever in amber. You cannot justify the mistakes of the present by the mistakes of the past.'

'You are chained yourself.'

'I know.' She giggled suddenly. 'It would be nice to have a change of chain.' I felt her warm body move against me. 'Anyway, kiss me, O Great Advocate,' she whispered, with the extraordinary emotional flexibility which apparently allowed her to shrug off the deepest angst with a flourish, 'and then I will tell you why I love you – assuming, of course, that I decide I still do.'

Eventually I fell asleep, the sleep that ambushed, that came suddenly and drew one down to cavernous depths of oblivion. But when I surfaced in the morning I knew, before I opened my eyes, that she was already awake. She was whispering something to herself. I looked at her through my lashes, curious to watch her when she thought I was still asleep. She was leaning on her elbow looking at me and, even with my limited vision, I knew that her face was tender.

'How do I love thee?' she was whispering in a voice so low it was almost inaudible.

> 'Let me count the ways.
> I love thee to the depth and breadth and height
> My soul can reach, when feeling out of sight
> For the ends of Being and ideal Grace.'

The verse was *Sonnets from the Portuguese*, written by Elizabeth

Barrett Browning for her husband. I listened, humbled by so much homage.

> 'I love thee with the passion put to use
> In my old griefs, and with my childhood's faith.
> I love thee with the love I seemed to lose
> With my lost saints, – I love thee with the breath,
> Smiles, tears of all my life! – and, if God choose,
> I should but love thee better after death.'

There was no answer to verse of such power. The sunlight streaming from the Parisian window across the tiled floor, the torpid languor of awakening, the woman beside me with a voice so low that any movement would have fractured it – had I not known already, I would have learnt then that the frequent brittle challenge in Helen's demeanour was only a shield guarding an acute vulnerability.

The next time we met in Paris Airport I guided her to Departures.

'Where are we going?'

'Rome, my darling.'

She turned shining eyes on me. 'One of the things I so love about you is your unpredictability.'

'One of the reasons everyone else finds me so boring is my predictability.'

She laughed. 'You are obviously hiding your light under a bushel!'

'I have no light without you.'

The plane swooped into Fiumicino. It was a warm night, and the Mediterranean air smote us like a warm blanket as we left the aircraft and walked down the steps to the tarmac. The taxi driver whirled us through downtown Rome, past the floodlight Colosseum, the floodlit Forum, the floodlit monument to Victor Emmanuel, before dropping us at our hotel in the Via del Corso. We surrendered our passports, were shown our marble-floored room, with the huge *matrimoniale*, the double bed so beloved of Italians. The air was full of warm, foreign scents.

'Are you hungry?' I asked, watching Helen hang her things in the wardrobe.

'Let's go out, see more of the city by night,' she said, eyeing her dresses critically. 'Which of these shall I wear?'

One was a black dinner dress and the other two were straight sheaths, one cream with a gold belt, one pale blue and white. I marvelled at her expertise, knowing that she made these herself, wondered how long it took her to make each garment, wondered if she invested each one with anticipation of our trysts. I was, in a way, subsumed with power. To have such a creature; to possess her; to call on her when I needed her; to love her as I did, to feel the fever of sexual passion which overwhelmed me even as I watched her standing there, considering her wardrobe.

'You're not going anywhere for the moment, young woman. Come here . . .'

Helen gave me an arch look. 'Oh, I don't know,' she murmured softly. 'You'll have to come and get me, if you can.'

I jumped off the bed, ran to her; she side stepped, ran to the bathroom with something in her hands, which I thought was a nightdress, shut the door. I tried the handle. The door was locked.

'Helen.'

'Mmn?'

'Come out of there.'

'Don't be so rude. I'm busy.'

I waited. I went to the window, put out my head and looked down at the bustling nightlife on the street below. The whole of Rome was out strutting its stuff; women in their finery; men escorting their beauties past the rows of eyes on the pavement terraces.

I heard a rattle in the bathroom.

'Have you gone down the loo?'

She opened the door. I caught my breath. The woman who stood before me was like something from a Cecil B. de Mille movie. She had piled her hair up on the top of her head and was wearing a clinging white gown, with a décolletage which left little to the imagination. She was wearing make-up, dark shadow around her eyes, red lipstick and I saw that she had painted her toenails gold. She sashayed past me on tiptoe, glancing at me from the corner of her eye, like a child who was still unsure if its foray into the world of adults was properly conducted. I caught my breath and let her walk across the room.

She stopped at the window, leant back a little as she turned to regard me haughtily.

'Well,' she said in a voice which belied the hauteur of her expression, 'what's the verdict? Is this a strap you see before you or the most delectable female in Italy?'

'If you wear that, you divine creature, you'll be kidnapped.'

'Oh I don't mean to wear it,' she said, looking down at herself in something like embarrassment, 'I just thought it would be fun to make it and model it for you.'

'Come here.'

She smiled, lowering her head. 'You're a slow learner. I never respond to commands.'

This time I was too fast for her, caught her before she could bolt again and the white gown slipped from first one shoulder and then the other and the coils of her chignon came adrift.

'I love you, Helen; I'm crazy about you,' I whispered in her ear as we lay entwined a little later. 'I would do anything for you.'

'Would you?'

'Yes!'

'Marry me.'

I sat up on one elbow looking down at her face.

'Nothing else makes sense,' she said. 'I'll get an English divorce. I don't like being a mistress.'

'You're not a mistress. You're yourself!'

The expression of defiant anticipation left her face, and slowly her expression changed. She turned away, got out of bed.

'Of course I'm a mistress,' she said. 'That's what the world calls it; the world is always right.'

'On the contrary, the world is never right; what can it know of the private agendas of the individual human heart?'

She began to put away the white creation, but suddenly changed her mind, slipped it over head.

'I may as well wear it,' she said in a brittle voice which I had never heard her use before. 'It's so exactly right for a whore.'

I made to speak, but she kept up a kind of chatter.

'Don't say a word ... just get dressed and take your mistress out.'

She dashed away a few surreptitious tears, but when I went to take her in my arms she backed away. She reached into the wardrobe and produced a black velvet evening cloak, part of the ensemble she had worn in Paris for our trip on the *bateau-mouche*.

'Just leave me alone . . . take me out . . .'

We went out; the whole of the Corso turned its head to stare at the woman on my arm. Her dreaming beauty, her colouring, riveted every eye.

We dined at a place called Tempio di Apollo, a terrace restaurant where the head waiter excelled himself in his assiduous attentions. Helen hardly spoke to me, cutting me short when I tried to make conversation. But I was a bad conversationalist; I needed to think, to find the vision with which I could put my life in order.

I saw how pink the whites of her eyes were and for the first time it occurred to me that she had had far too much to drink, an aperitif, half a bottle of white wine and half of red. This was unlike Helen. And I saw too that her whole being was stiff and chained with contained anger.

And I noticed that a man who passed us by on the pavement stopped, turned, and walked up and down several times trying to catch Helen's eye. He was swarthy, probably from the south. Helen glanced at him and turned her head away, but I saw how his eyes flashed as he melted into the crowd, turning his head just once more to look back at her.

When the meal was over I paid the bill, excused myself briefly to visit the loo. But when I came back to our table Helen was gone.

The head waiter shrugged when I asked where she had gone, flashed white teeth at me, showed me the palms of his hands, gave me to understand that Signora had walked off into the street. I asked him to try the ladies' room and this was duly attended to, but there was no Helen.

I set off in pursuit, but my lady was visible nowhere. The late night strollers did not number among them any lone woman in white. The Fiats tooted and roared around corners; the floodlights played on the monuments; the fountains gushed in baroque magnificence; but nowhere did I see the red hair, the white gown of a furious woman amid the rush of the warm night-time city.

I realized that she had probably donned the velvet cloak which was like the night itself.

I went back to the hotel, but Helen was not there and although I waited for more than an hour there was no sign of her. Anger gave way to anxiety. Imagination took over; I saw her beset by the Roman wolves, by the swarthy stranger who had paid her such attention from the pavement. Had he followed her? Did she even know her way back? Had she any lire for a taxi? Why had she done this? I had never known Helen to act capriciously, to play the prima donna.

I became alarmed, asked the management to contact the police.

Reception produced the passports; the weary policeman examined them, muttered lugubriously over Helen's photograph, '*Molto bella . . .*' as though her beauty were something on which I was personally to be congratulated, before turning to me with the question, '*Allora, lei è il suo marito?*' I confessed that I was not the signora's husband. We were *fidanzatiti*.

He gave me a knowing glance, a raised eyebrow, a slight purse of the mouth to indicate male felicitation, then assured me in broken English that the police would look out for her, but that she would probably be back under her own steam.

'Ze wimmin . . . zey are very . . . *come se dice . . . tempestose*? No?'

I disclaimed this, tried to make him understand that this lady was not like that, but my voice trailed off. I realized that she gave the term 'tempestuous' a new meaning.

'*La donna è mobile . . .*' the uniformed and avuncular member of the *vigili urbani* insisted with something approaching a wink, and I almost heard the orchestra for Verdi's *Rigoletto* in the background as a final touch of farce.

I thought too of how Helen, in her more sombre moments, would have hated it all.

I spent the night searching. Anxiety warred with anger. Could she possibly have gone off with that Lothario who had ogled her from the street? No, of course she couldn't. But Rome was not safe for a young woman on her own; what city was?

The taxi driver was patient, but in the end he suggested that the signora '*è forse andata via*' by which I understood that he thought she had scarpered. I also gathered from him that he did not think this reflected any great credit on me.

Towards dawn I returned to the hotel, but she had not returned.

Suddenly I imagined life without her; the aridity of it, the emotional mediocrity of it, the settled bourgeois complacency of it.

She had spoken the truth. Nothing made any sense except our future, full and free. I would have to face Marion, tell her the truth, face all the repercussions, cease the living of a lie. But thoughts of my wife's blame, her rage, her hurt, opened before me like a great pit. I thought of the fuss she would make, the vendetta she might well mount by coming drunk into Chambers and denouncing me, something she had once promised. For an unbidden moment I saw her dead, the victim of a road accident or some other fortuitous disaster; or indeed anything at all which would intervene and save me from the imperative of real decision, real action. My avoidance of decision, my longing to be absolved from responsibility, was a spiritual defeat.

But as the night wore on, I finally came to a conclusion. Helen, for reasons I did not comprehend, was my life. Without her, breathing or not breathing, I would be dead. Viewed in that light the choice was simple.

I returned to the street, the thoroughfare that would be alive again in an hour or two. The chairs were upended on the pavement terraces, the shops still shuttered, but already the early birds were up, preparing their premises for the new day. From somewhere came a deep throaty contralto singing '*O sole mio!*' and above my head shutters clattered open to the dawn air.

As the first sunlight woke up the faded ochre walls, Helen approached down the Via del Corso. She was wearing the black velvet cloak; her hair spilled over it. The sweepers paused to watch her, striding alone in velvet and white through the Roman dawn, like something from grand opera or a fable.

I watched her for a moment before she saw me, felt the relief, felt the tug at my soul of something more than passion. She was inspiration, what Beatrice was to Dante; the lost pilgrim's dream.

She gave me a half-apologetic smile, as though nothing much out of the ordinary had occurred.

'I'm very tired,' she said, taking my arm. 'I did not sleep very well!'

'Where were you, Helen? I have spent the night searching for you; the police have been looking for you!'

'Really? Am I that valuable?' She seemed reproachful. 'You

shouldn't have made a fuss. I'll tell you everything later. Right now I need to close my eyes and sleep for all eternity.'

She went up to our room, threw herself on the bed and slept almost immediately. I covered her with the sheet and lay beside her, watching her as her breathing deepened and small dew of perspiration appeared on her upper lip. Then, having contacted the police, I went out to the fresh heat of the morning. I found a jewellers, selected a ring, an emerald set in diamonds.

I woke her at twelve thirty and took her to lunch in Trastevere, the sleepy district across the Tiber where small, family restaurants spilt on to cobbles. Helen was not particularly communicative, deflecting my enquires as to her whereabouts the night before with good-humoured reticence, but she did any attempt to make conversation of a personal nature. It was as though she too had made a decision, as though part of her had deliberately withdrawn from me.

When the meal was over I put the box wrapped in gilt paper in her lap. She opened it almost reluctantly, saw the ring nestling on the satin, turned to me.

'I can't . . .'

'I know, I know,' I whispered. 'Read the card.'

She took out the small card from its envelope, read what I had written. She traced the words 'I love you and I want to make a life with you' with her finger. She closed the box, studied the tablecloth as though trying to sort through some private turbulence, reverse some resolution of the preceding night.

'Thank you!' she said very quietly, with a small sigh and her eyes filled with tears. She reached over and touched my lips. 'Say nothing more for now.' She handed me the box, took off her wedding ring, held out her left hand. 'The ring is very beautiful. Won't you put it on?'

It fitted. We sat in silence, smiling at each other. After a while she said with a low laugh, as though mocking herself: 'I'm sorry about last night.'

'I am too. I'm the one who's half dead from exhaustion. Where did you get to?'

'I spent the night in the Forum.'

'All night alone . . . in the Forum? The whole night? You could have been attacked.'

'Certainly not. I was invisible. I covered myself with the cloak. The bloody thing would hide the devil. I communed with ancient Rome, felt its stones under my feet, listened to its antique heart.'

'Why?'

She turned to me. 'I was fit for anything last night. You don't understand the ferocity that inhabits me. Sometimes it is strong enough to kill.' She glanced at me, raised an eyebrow in quasi-supplication. 'I had a decision to make, which was terrible . . . Don't look so woebegone. It doesn't matter now. I'm sorry . . .'

'We are betrothed now,' I said.

'Yes,' she said, 'however we manage it.'

'However we manage it,' I echoed.

'Thank you,' she said softly, laying her head for a moment against my shoulder. 'There's no need to say anything else.'

The night porter asked me later if Signora had recovered from being lost the night before.

'She spent the night in the Forum,' I said. 'She's all right now.'

His puzzled eyes dwelt on me for a moment as though I were the possessor of a madwoman.

Our second day was spent sightseeing. Helen bought a huge straw hat, flat shoes and we walked all over central Rome, from the Forum to the Colosseum, from the Colosseum to the Spanish Steps and the *pensione* where Keats had died. The Borghese gardens gave us a view of the whole city, the dome of St Peter's in the distance; the trees, the statuary, provided shade and elegance. We wandered down the Piazza del Popolo and eventually back to the hotel.

'I'm starving,' Helen said. But when we entered the hotel terrace restaurant, we looked at each other suddenly, returning without a word to our room, shut the door. She answered need with need. It was almost feral; I felt her teeth against mine, the tensile strength in her body. She made me crazed. She simultaneously yielded and challenged me, her breath coming in short accelerating gulps, beginning with a moan, ending in a long shivering cry.

'Did I hurt you, darling?' I whispered.

'Dearest, darling, Dan. I'm not made of thistledown . . . but I am reborn.'

Sleep came like a blanket, warm, and black and sweet.

Idylls end. It was raining when we got back to Paris. I saw a radiantly happy Helen to her departure gate, and as she passed out of my sight I saw her remove the emerald from her finger, place it in her bag.

I took my own flight to Heathrow, thinking of nothing but Helen and the weekend and the future.

I tried to work out the best approach to take in telling my wife that our marriage was over.

The house was silent when I let myself in; there was no response when I called Marion's name. I assumed she was out, went to the kitchen, poured a glass of milk, ate a biscuit, wandered upstairs with my bag. I had returned to normality. The mediocrity of my domestic life, the tedium, met me halfway to the landing. It was like returning to a cage. I turned over in my mind what I would tell Marion; she would react bitterly at first, but would accept it in the end. It was the only viable solution for her as well as for me; there could be no happiness for her with a husband centred on another woman. She would be better off without me. We had made a mistake with each other; having the courage to face it and remedy it was the only course.

The bedroom door was closed, prompting me to wonder if Marion was at home and had gone to bed early. I opened the door quietly.

She was sprawled across the bed, some of Helen's letters which I kept in my study scattered about her. One glance at Marion was enough; on her bedside table was her sleeping pill bottle, lidless, lying on its side.

They stomach-pumped her in hospital, brought her around. She hadn't really meant to kill herself, the doctor confided; it was a cry for help.

'But next time,' he said, 'she may just go too far.'

I studied my wife as I sat beside her, held the hand she stretched out to me. She was wearing hospital issue, a faded pale yellow nightdress which emptied her face of colour and made her eyes hollow.

'Forgive me, darling,' she whispered. 'I love you so much. When I read her letters . . . it was more than I could bear.'

I squeezed the hand in mine, looking for a moment at the long pale fingers, the polished nails, nails that had never been gnawed in passionate indignation. I saw her weakness and her neediness and her goodness too; for she had goodness, like all of us, and a certain neglected brilliance; but everything she possessed that had to do with thrust or vision was swamped in the midden of her insecurity.

She needed me, not as lover, not as friend, not as intellectual challenge, not as place of peace and laughter, but as a raft on this midden of her own making. She needed me as keeper more than husband, to prevent her from sinking into something that would not even exist if she did not permit it. Her emotional insecurity stemmed from a childhood without love; her social insecurity stemmed from an inferiority complex rooted in the British class system. But she lacked the means of confronting either the childhood deprivation or the class shibboleths which had so diminished her.

The prospect that had once risen unbidden now seemed cruel and frightening. I could not speak to her of Helen. When I got home I gathered up the letters in our room and put them away in a locked briefcase at the back of my bookcase.

I felt like the criminal of old, condemned to be torn asunder. I could not live without Helen; I was her addict; I needed her love, needed the terrible mauling she gave all the received parameters of my existence; above all I needed the constant dynamic that she represented, where nothing was ever stale or really known, but continued in a ferment of discovery, interlaced with peace.

But I could not destroy my wife.

I did not see Helen for some time. We kept in daily telephone contact, but I did not mention the future, nor did she. She was waiting for me to confirm the when and the how, but I could not. The time was out of joint for it; Marion was fragile; the spectre of expedient behaviour, rationalized through self-interest, disgusted me. Helen would not want me maimed, forever glancing back over my shoulder on the hurt I had dealt my wife. She told me that she was working on a novel.

'What's it about?'

'It's about a boy who grows up in an enchanted valley.'

'What happens to him?'

'Well, he has to decide that! The enchantment really resides in him.

He creates it, but he thinks it comes from outside himself. He's cursed with indecision. He lacks the courage, even the ruthlessness, to be who he is. He is a hostage, not to fortune, which is good to him, but to his concept of proud benevolence, to his pride.'

'Does he leave the valley?'

'Yes. But I think he will come back in the end.'

To tell the truth I didn't take this writing of hers very seriously. During this time, when I was retrenching my position, reneging not so much on my promise to Helen but my capability of acting, Helen never complained, never asked for anything. She seemed to accept it when I said that she was always with me. Things had somehow reverted to 'normal', which is to say they had returned to the old groove. I dreaded her reminding me of the content of that small gilt-edged card, waited for her to raise the issue of our 'betrothal', but she never did. Whenever I steeled myself to talk to Marion about our life I saw in my mind's eye her body sprawled across the bed, the empty pill bottle. And then, unbidden, would come the spectre of my mother's bloodied face on that terrible day when my father had left.

I did not discuss any of this with Helen. What went on below the surface of her thought she kept to herself. She let me see of her mind only what she wanted. What this cost her in terms of self-control I do not know. When she hinted, almost by way of reminder, that her son would be going to boarding school the following year, I did not take her up on it, although the silence which followed this announcement of hers was pregnant and waiting for my avowal.

When she failed to challenge me I assumed she was content to let things be as they were. After all, she knew that the parameters of our relationship were mapped and secure. But I did not really understand the pride I was playing with.

Professionally I could do no wrong at this time. The brief fees escalated. I realized one evening, with a sense of astonishment, as I worked on my private accounts, that I had become relatively rich. I had it all. I had Helen, sure that what we had was for ever. I had success. I had the semblance of a marriage and a wife who loved to spend and who seemed to have acquired a new contentment.

In the winter of 1975 Helen's mother died. Kieran phoned me to break the news and I spoke to Helen, offering my sympathy, telling her I would be there for the funeral. It was pouring rain when I arrived in Dublin that December morning. There was Requiem Mass and then the funeral to Mount Jerome cemetery. Helen was dressed in black and looked pale and drained, but she was poised as she smiled and kissed my cheek, with ostensible Platonic friendship when I presented myself in the porch of the church where people had come to shake her hand. Kieran was beside her, and Jonathan, dressed in a thick waterproof jacket under which could be seen his black school blazer, white shirt and tie, was tearlessly eyeing the mourners and fidgeting.

'I'm so sorry!' I said.

She smiled wanly. 'Don't be. She had Alzheimer's. She would have hated had she known. She's as well off out of it!'

She turned to take other proffered hands and I shook hands with Kieran. I had wondered how I would feel, taking his hand, now that I was his wife's lover. I had wondered if I would feel guilt or any stab of regret for what he would certainly regard as my treachery, but I felt nothing. There was no guilt; the old sense of friendship was there. I smiled at Jonathan and found my way into the church, sat in a pew and considered the stained glass. I felt very cold, despite my Crombie and sheepskin gloves.

Later, Helen read the lesson – 'The Lord is my shepherd; I shall not want . . .'

Her clear voice carried around the church. She was composed and elegant, standing at the lectern on the sanctuary steps, her hair a nimbus, like a being from one of the stained-glass windows above the altar.

This was the woman with whom I had touched eternity. But her eyes did not seek me out, and she returned demurely to sit beside her husband and her son in the front pew, directly behind the oak coffin. I saw Kieran quietly pass her his handkerchief and I knew from the set of her shoulders, that she was weeping, could almost taste the salty intimacy of her tears.

I suddenly felt an almost intolerable sense of exclusion. In this public forum I was nothing but a vague kind of mourner, present out of courtesy to my old friend and his bereaved wife.

This feeling of exclusion was intensified after the funeral when we returned to their house in Clonskeagh. A spread had been prepared; drinks were handed around. Helen talked with one guest, then another. Kieran, urbane and hearty, seemed genuinely delighted to see me and said how good I was to have come, how much it meant to Helen, drew me to one side and asked how I was.

'You're looking tremendous, old fellow. You are beginning to have that mien about you which has to do with power and success . . .'

'Don't be ridiculous.'

'It's true. And you're putting on condition,' he added, prodding me playfully in the tummy.

'So are you.'

I eyed his midriff, the white shirt with two straining buttons. I realized it was the first time I had seen Kieran formally dressed.

He regarded his stomach ruefully. 'What you're looking at there, Dan, is a slipped chest!'

I laughed, heard my laughter, knew it was hollow.

'Helen seems to be bearing up well under her bereavement.'

He turned to watch his wife who was offering sandwiches to her guests.

'Oh, Helen is made of stern stuff – or at least I think she is. But she has become very mercurial,' he added in a lowered voice, 'a bit unpredictable. She takes off for weekends here and there when I'm not at home. She seems to have friends all over the place with whom she stays . . . but I don't see any of them here today.'

He looked at me speculatively. 'You probably know more about women than I do, Dan, but do you think she could be . . . well, do you think it possible . . . that she might be seeing someone else? I know it's a terrible thing to suggest. But she's liable to inexplicable mood swings and things haven't been . . . well, quite what she might have expected. You know women – always looking for love's young dream and so forth.'

I muttered something, unable to look him in the eye. I listened to our exchange as though I inhabited a space behind us, where I overheard everything at one remove. But when I looked back at him I noticed how he frowned, how unhappy his eyes were, the sad staring look to them when his face was momentarily in repose.

'Of course!' he said. 'She is very important to me, even' – there he attempted levity – 'if she is a bit batty, but I sometimes think I should never have married her.' He looked into my eyes. 'She probably thinks the same. She doesn't even wear her rings any more.'

When I started he said apologetically, 'I shouldn't be bothering you with all this.'

'Not at all . . .'

He patted my shoulder. 'Well, never mind, it's good to have an old friend to talk to. But I won't bore you with any more of my problems. It's just that one likes to maintain the fabric of the family . . . and I suppose you have lashings of experience in all these human things.'

'I've done precious little Family Law, Kieran. But if you are so concerned, why don't you talk to Helen yourself. One of the principal reasons for marriage breakdown is lack of communication . . . or so I'm given to understand!'

'Yes,' he said. 'Of course I should; but, to tell you the truth, I simply don't know how. I don't know how to talk, to say what I feel. It's a language and, strange as it may seem, I've never learnt it.'

I looked at him, but his eyes did not meet mine and something like desperation hung about their fixed gaze on the carpet.

Then he asked almost abruptly, 'Do you ever hear from James these times?'

'Infrequently. You remember he's practising in California?'

'Yes. Which part did you say?'

I hadn't said, but I told him now. 'San Francisco . . . the Cranstein Clinic.'

Someone came to speak to him. I moved away and caught an unexpected glimpse of myself in the mirror above the mantelpiece. I looked drawn, almost old.

Kieran followed and introduced me to various people from the university; but I could hardly tear my eyes away from his wife, watching her out of my peripheral vision as she moved among her guests, hating the realization that the intense knowledge I had of this woman, of her body and her soul, was not something which conferred on me the right to monopolize an extra second of her time; remembering, with a curious sense of private privilege, with a sense of having lived in a dream, that I had seen this suburban faculty wife, this woman who was my mistress, walk to meet me, in black velvet cloak and plunging evening dress, down the Via del Corso in the Roman dawn.

For a moment I felt the whole fabric of my recollections concerning her to be a fantasy, insubstantial, a delusion. I had not expected her to wear the emerald ring, but its absence from her hand reinforced the sense of unreality. She hardly glanced at me and this fuelled my private, terrifying, suspicion, that I had imagined everything. It was a momentary thing, but it filled me with desperation and a fierce desire: to possess her right there, to push her against the wall, to bend that white neck, to feel the intimate, secret places in her yield and surround me . .

'. . . Even if she is a bit batty,' Kieran had said.

I thought of her disappearance that night which she said she spent in the Forum. I thought of the following night when we had almost devoured each other when she had finally lost the last of her inhibitions. I remembered the sense of privilege and elation at her comment, 'I am reborn . . .' She was not 'batty'; mercurial perhaps. Well, women were.

Before I left I cornered her in the kitchen.

'Helen, I have to see you soon!'

'You're seeing me right now!'

'Don't tease.'

She gave a wan smile. 'When?'

'Before Christmas?'

She frowned. 'OK.'

'I love you,' I whispered into her ear.

She touched my hand and shot me a look I could not interpret, before turning away to deal with Jonathan who had appeared at the door, handing him a plate of smoked salmon sandwiches.

On 21 December 1975 I met her at Heathrow. She seemed quiet when she arrived, a little remote, projecting the chill she could turn on at a moment's notice, but she responded passionately when I kissed her in the car. I was in a good mood; I had forgotten the sense of being the outsider in Helen's life; our phone conversations subsequent to the funeral had restored me to the old perspective. Helen was mine and I pulled the strings. I didn't think of it consciously in such terms; but I was, once again, in control.

We drove along the M3, and on to Winchester, stayed in a country house hotel outside the town, dined there. She purred at me through dinner; I marvelled at how yesterday's earnest ingénue had become the sophisticate, able to wield effortlessly the body language of desire. I felt a curious kind of pride in this metamorphosis. But, even though there was only ourselves to think of, she did not wear my ring and I dared not ask her why.

That night, as though impatient of my silence, she suddenly announced that we had to decide on our future. Jonathan would be going away to boarding school in less than a year's time. She would regard herself as free. She could no longer tolerate her life; the lie of it was unbearable.

'I want to be with the man I love!' she said, raising her head from the pillow and looking at me. 'I want a real life. I can't stand my Sundays or my Saturdays or my evenings; I can't stand living with someone who is utterly oblivious of my existence. It's an ongoing insult every day, every week, every year . . . It's driving me mad!'

'He's not oblivious of your existence. In his own way he cares deeply about you!'

'Was that what he was saying to you when you came to Mam's funeral?'

'Not exactly, but he made it clear.'

'And you feel a certain male solidarity with him; he has awakened the claims of old friendship?'

'Not exactly . . . but Helen, it's very difficult. What about poor Marion, as well as Kieran?' I said. 'They would be so hurt . . . and we would be damaged, we would be maimed, by hurting them! We're strong and we'll have each other for ever.'

Helen gave me a queer look. 'Do you think nobody is being "damaged" or "maimed", right now? Do you think the life I live is remotely bearable? I have to get out of it, one way or the other.'

'Oh Helen, we understand each other. We love each other. Nothing will change that! But how can we hurt other good people?'

'Dan, I can't buy into your domestic problems; nor do I expect you to buy into mine! Are you trying to manipulate me?'

'Helen, I'm trapped! Marion . . . tried to kill herself.' I glanced at her tight face and looked away. 'Forgive me for surrounding you in weakness.'

Helen sat up, put her head on her knees. 'You stupid man. You're not weak; you're actually supremely arrogant. You're assuming you can do the impossible – appease Marion and keep me. What sort of fool do you take me for?'

'You don't understand – '

'Oh, but I do. I understand, I see the dilemma, I see how you are blackmailed. You permit it. But I cannot allow it to become my problem! She doesn't want you for yourself, but she will never, ever, let you go.'

'I need and love only you!'

'Words, my darling, are only breath. Without action what earthly use are they to me?'

I tried to deflect what she was saying. I pulled her back, kissed her, stroking the silken throat. She moved abruptly away, observed me for a few minutes in silence, a sudden haughty cast to her face. I felt a *frisson* of dread; what if she were serious? What if she withdrew? The silence intensified; the sense of her ferocity, her terrible pride, filled the space around us. But when, without breaking the silence, I embraced her, she yielded.

But her response was strangely slow and deliberate. In retrospect it was as though each movement, each touch, was something she wanted to imprint on her memory.

Later, when perhaps she thought I was asleep I heard her whisper words with a recitational lilt, reminiscent, in a way, of the manner my mother would touch tentative keys when she was composing a new song.

> 'Will I recall the dark, the Christmas lights,
> The long year's longest night,
> The drive, the talk, the silence.
> Spilt laughter sparkling;
> The beacons on the M3
> Blazing into the dark?'

'Helen?'

'Mmn?' she responded, sounding wide awake.

'What are you saying?'

'Nothing . . . just rambling rubbish.'

I heard the ache, the anger, the sadness; I felt the premonition, but I sleepily shrugged it away.

Chapter Nineteen

My father became ill in March 1976. Flu had turned into pneumonia, and he was in hospital. He and Kelly were now living in Ottawa, where he had retired. Kelly had telephoned to let me know.

'They're giving him antibiotics,' she said, 'but he's not responding too well!'

I tried unsuccessfully to contact James. His practice in California was, or so he had given us to understand, colossal, but he was, in personal terms, an increasingly unknown quantity. He remembered birthdays and Christmas; wrote occasionally to my mother in loving terms; but he seldom came back and we were not encouraged to visit him. When I couldn't get him on the phone I sent him a telegram to advise him of our father's illness.

I phoned my mother in the South of France. She was now living in Provence with Charles, had retired from her singing career. Sometimes Marion and I visited them in their small château among the vines. I loved Provence, that land of the ever-present Middle Ages, where the villages pile up on the hills. Marion loved it too and was keen for us to buy a villa there, 'Something we could do up. We could instal a swimming pool . . .'

My mother had once, a few years before, asked me about Helen. 'What happened to that lovely girl? The one you were so fond of?'

'Helen. She married Kieran!'

'Oh him!' my mother had said and let the matter drop.

Now she sounded subdued, even shaken, at the news of my father's illness.

'Let me know if . . . he doesn't improve.'

'I will. Can I give him your love?'

'Tell him . . . I'm thinking of him. Tell him . . . I hope he gets well soon . . . that I'm praying for him!'

'Thanks, Mummy.'

'You needn't sound so surprised, Dan. I do pray sometimes, and your father and I made our peace years ago.'

'Did you?'

'Of course. He did the right thing, you see, and I told him so eventually. He set both of us free!'

'Mummy?'

'Yes?'

'Did you ever say this to James?'

'No.'

'Well, tell him now. Please phone him and tell him now!'

Ottawa was snowbound. I had been there before, in summer, but now it seemed, in its blanket of white, like a city belonging to another dimension. It reminded me of the old fantasy I had had, of a winter in the valley with Helen and I wondered if we would ever fulfil it. The snowploughs worked early in the morning and I found the Ottawa Civic Hospital on Carling Avenue, where my father lay, propped up to ease his breathing, an oxygen mask over his face. Kelly, looking pale and exhausted, was sitting beside him.

He was much thinner than I remembered and his once brown hair had become very white. But it was still stubbornly curly, its new whiteness seeming merely a temporary strange aberration. There was a drip fixed into his arm and the fluid in the plastic bag trembled as each drop was released to his vein.

I kissed Kelly's cheek and then approached my parent who had dared to sicken and age, feeling that he had been the victim of a gigantic mistake.

'Hello, Dad!'

He opened his eyes. 'Danny . . .'

'How are you, Dad?'

'I'm fine.'

He put down the oxygen mask, took my hand and held it. 'I'm fine,' he repeated. 'A bit tired, but otherwise A1. I'll beat you at tennis yet. But it's good of you to come.'

I looked at Kelly and she smiled at me wanly. There were creases in her face that had not been there when last I had seen her, but she had not really aged. Like Rachel, she had never thrown in the towel. Her face still bore the earnest, interested expression of the young.

'He's being monitored very carefully.' I saw the light in her tired brown eyes, and was struck again how much this woman loved my father. 'I'll go out for a bit,' she said; 'leave you two alone.' She picked up her coat and kissed my father's lips. 'I'll be back soon, darling.' She wriggled her fingers at me from the door and was gone.

I sat in silence, feeling strangely alien. My father said, 'Help me to sit up,' and I arranged the back rest and the pillows.

'It's this bloody wheeze,' he said. 'It makes one feel useless, tired, slipping in and out of dreams.' He patted my hand. 'But you're no dream!

'Not as far as I know, Dad!'

'How are you, my dear boy? You're looking very well! How is Marion?'

'She's fine.' Then I added, 'Mummy sends her best.'

His eyes lit up. 'Does she?'

'Yes. She said to tell you she was praying for you!'

'Prayers for an old fogey never went amiss!'

Then he asked me about her and Charles and I told him about their villa in Provence. 'And Charles has an apartment in Paris,' I added. 'In the Avenue Foch!'

He smiled. 'The Avenue Foch no less!' he said with a twinkle. 'Isn't it perfect for her?'

'James used to call it the Avenue Posh!'

He smiled sadly. I had said the wrong thing, reminding him of James.

But he rallied and launched into a barrage of breathless questions about London and about my work and about the erstwhile Head of Chambers. 'How's Billy?'

'Sir William retired a couple of years ago!'

'Oh. Why do I think that nothing has changed when everything is in metamorphosis? I've become old. It's so sly a process that one is not aware of it.'

'You're not old, Dad. Age is a matter of perspective!'

'It's also a matter of fact. I will be seventy soon! No matter what I do that fact remains.' I made some noise or other indicative of dismissal of these constraints.

'What age are you now?' he demanded suddenly. 'Let's see . . . you were born in 1940 so you're all of thirty-six! Still young, still time to do whatever you want!'

I felt suddenly absurdly youthful. I had been dreading the prospect of turning forty and now I felt as though I was surfeited in youth and opportunity.

'There are so many things I would like to say to you,' my father went on. 'Especially I may not see you again . . . well . . . not for some time.' His grip on my hand tightened. 'I can see that you are successful, but I would like to think that you are also happy!'

The statement took me unawares. He watched me search for a response. Then he murmured, 'The trouble with life is that is gives few second chances; we are generally left either to effect change ourselves, with all the suffering that may entail, or to abide by our mistakes. But if we abide by our mistakes we make the future hostage to the past!' He watched me from hooded eyes. 'Are you happy? Don't look so taken aback. The old can ask these questions!'

Suddenly the longing to unburden the true state of my life was overwhelming. I looked into the shrewd, sick eyes of my father.

'Actually, Dad . . . I . . . Do you remember me telling you about Helen? She married Kieran but it didn't work!'

'Ah,' he murmured after a moment. 'The lovely Helen whom I never met. So you are still fond of her? Not only that,' he went on in a note of sudden discovery while he regarded me closely, 'you are actually involved with her?'

'Yes.'

'Can I ask what you're going to do?'

I sighed. 'I don't know, Dad. I just don't know! I know what I would like. But it's not easy. Marion is vulnerable . . .'

He regarded me in silence for a moment and then said, 'To tell you the truth I did not expect that marriage of yours to work. Your wife struck me as a haven seeker – if you'll forgive me for being blunt. But better late than never to tell you this – if your marriage is not a success, if you have found happiness elsewhere, sort things out and put your life where your love is! The matter is too important and the years will mock you. You may owe Marion many things, but not your life's happiness! How often do you think chances of that repeat themselves?'

He became breathless, resumed the oxygen mask.

I looked at him, so faded, so pale, so diminished in the steel hospital bed with the medical apparatus all around him, and the spirit in him burning as strong as I had ever seen it, the candle flaring brighter at the end. But what did he know of my life?

'She'll kill herself if I leave her!' I wanted to scream at him. 'She'll bloody well kill herself . . .'

I was ashamed of my self-centredness. But my father was oblivious to my turmoil and my shame. He had closed his eyes.

'There's a line from Swinburne,' he said after a moment when I thought he was asleep, 'which sums it up: "Keep silence now for singing time is over." We have a little time here; we have one life and then "singing time is over."' He opened his eyes and looked at me. 'Don't waste it . . . the singing time.'

While he slept I thought of my last meeting with Helen in Winchester. I had driven her back to Heathrow. After she had questioned our future and I had not been able to answer her, she had not mentioned the subject again. But she had been graver than I had ever seen her and had kissed me very slowly at her departure, touching my face with tentative fingers, as though she would imprint on them every lineament, like a blind woman.

I put my head in my hands, tracing the memories, wishing in a sudden fit of weariness that I had Helen to go home to, that we had a house and could shut the door, draw the curtains, build up the fire and I would put my head down on her breast and let the world go away.

I hardly heard the door opening, and I hardly recognized the man who entered. He was fortyish, dressed in cashmere overcoat, scarf, gloves. I watched him half turn to close the door, saw, as he removed his hat, that he was balding in a pattern similar to my own; he wore horn-rimmed spectacles and he smiled at me with a caustic familiarity in which sudden suppressed emotion warred with his old search for sarcasm. It took me only a microsecond to recognize my brother.

Sarcasm evidently failed him for he clapped me on the back in silence and as he stood beside the bed my father opened his eyes, cried, 'James!' and put out his arms to draw his elder son to his paternal embrace.

I dined with James at his hotel, the Château Laurier in Rideau Street, that evening, passing the Parliament Buildings on Wellington street en route, remembering them from my childhood when my father had pointed out to James and me the architectural features of the city. It was Saturday; a blizzard was descending on the city. It was bitterly cold, the sort of cold which is incomprehensible to someone who has never known it, and the warmth of the Château Laurier was more than welcome.

James and I discussed my father, whom the doctors said was now rallying. It was a strange dinner; each of us was tense with sudden, unbidden emotions, which we tried not to show. James had the settled air which arrives in mid-life, the air which announces that challenge is over and certainty has arrived. A slight paunch had made its appearance on his midriff. He seemed prosperous, expansive, strangely American, as though he had decided to take as his own the accent and body language of his adopted country.

'Well, Danny boy, you've got all grown up!'

'I was grown up when you left!'

'No way . . .'

We talked a great deal about old times, but when I tried to mention Helen he changed the subject. I quickly realized that he wanted to skirt around anything that would remind him of Kieran.

I thought of Kieran's suddenly sensitive face when I had last seen him and he had asked me about James. So I said straight out, 'Kieran was asking about you the last time I saw him . . . not long before Christmas!'

'Was he indeed!' he muttered, with the air of a man upon whom an unpleasant topic of conversation has been foisted and who is looking around for an escape.

'Did he never try to contact you, James?' I persisted.

James's face darkened and he looked away. 'He did, actually . . . recently. He wrote – oh, to say several things, one of them being an apology. Some matters – pertaining to long ago – had evidently preyed on his mind. When I didn't answer he had the temerity to phone me!'

'Did you talk with him?'

'Oh yes. But I pretended I didn't know who he was!' He smiled at me with the old grim smile he had used when talking long ago of his father.

'When did he phone you?'

'Recently.' He shrugged. 'It's not important! It's not important any more.'

'Are you sure?'

'Good heavens, do you take me for a child?'

Then he promised he would visit me in London within the year. He was the same James; and, in some strange way, he was not anyone I had ever known. He had grown away from me and the knowledge of it was lonelier, having met him again after such a lapse of time, than if I had not met him at all.

The whole flight home was an exercise in a private stock-taking as to what my life was about, how I was to make sense of it. I heard my father's words: 'If we abide by our mistakes we make the future hostage to the past!'

By the time we were making our approach to Heathrow I could not wait to talk to Helen, find the nearest phone box.

I got through at once. She answered as though she had been expecting my call. But her voice was very quiet.

'Is something wrong, darling?'

'Yes,' Helen said slowly. 'I've been trying to reach you.'

I waited. My mind scanned the horizon of possibilities.

'This will come as a dreadful shock, Dan – something terrible has happened!'

'What? What has happened?'

Her voice wobbled and broke. 'Kieran is dead!'

My stupefaction must have reached to her across the long distance line, for she added shakily, as though she was about to burst into tears, 'It was an accident!'

'When?'

'Three days ago. We had his funeral yesterday!'

'Where?'

'He was drowned in Lough Corrloch!'

'How did it happen?'

'He was fishing, fell out of the boat!'

I felt the shivers caress the back of my neck. I thought of Jasper Malcolm, who had met the same fate so long ago, of Helen telling me that the spirit of the drowned boy was said to be seeking revenge, of everything which conjured up the contradictions surrounding the valley, its people, and even Ireland itself.

'I'll come over at once!'

'There's no need!'

'But there is need, darling! I want to look after you!'

'You can't look after me,' Helen said coolly, 'you have made it perfectly clear that you can't! Your first loyalty is elsewhere. That is very proper of you. I'll be all right; I have friends! You don't need to worry about me!'

'Please don't be like that, Helen. I'm sorry I wasn't here when you phoned. My father is ill in Canada and I went to see him.'

Her voice softened. 'I'm very sorry, Dan. I know how much he means to you! Is he OK?'

'Yes, I think so. At least for the time being.'

'I have to go now. God bless you always.'

'Helen . . .'

The line went dead in my hand. I did not know it then but the nightmare had started. I did not know that the option was already gone from me. I suppose I had expected due warning, time to work on solutions. But I had had that time, and had failed. And now the 'singing time' of which my father had spoken, was over.

I could no longer contact her on the phone. I cursed her phone line which seemed perpetually engaged, until I was informed by the operator that the line was disconnected.

For days I was stuck in the Court of Appeal – a case which I could not leave. But I wrote, assuring her that I was coming, assuring her of my love. When my case before the Appeal Court finished, I flew to Dublin, took a taxi to her house in Clonskeagh, but the house was silent and there was a FOR SALE sign outside. The neighbours I questioned said she had gone away and had left no forwarding address. I telephoned the estate agent and he said his only contact with her was through her solicitor who had power of attorney. I went to see the solicitor and he said his client's whereabouts was confidential. He did, however, promise to forward any correspondence. And then he said he was glad I had called because he had something for me which his client had asked him to send me.

I hoped, expected, a letter. But the packet he took from his safe was nothing of the kind. I recognized its shape and knew the contents before I opened it. There on the satin lining was the emerald ring; there too was the gilt-edged card with the legend I had inscribed, 'I love you and I want to make a life with you.'

I went to the valley. The house was boarded up. I walked as far as the lake, retracing my steps of former times, imagining the girl with the long titian hair beside me, imagining Kieran picking up bits of moss to show something esoteric and remarkable.

I visited the Grehans in their cottage. Sean Grehan told me a little about the accident. Kieran had fallen from his boat while out fishing on the lake, and drowned.

'There are some pretty bad currents out there, you know.'

'When was the inquest?'

'The other day . . . Death by misadventure.' He sighed. 'Helen was very cut up, the creature; but Mr Malcolm was very good to her!'

'Mr Malcolm?'

'Yes. Mr Joss Malcolm, the new owner of the valley. He's an American. He was in the lodge at the time of the accident and tried to help.'

'Helen told me about him. Is he still there?'

'No. He's gone. He comes only once a year, you know. He's a busy man – a doctor, in New York. He's gone home.'

I looked at Sean, at his tweed cap, at his weathered face, at his worn hands, the same leathery fingers which had shown me how to milk a cow one long ago summer.

'Where has she gone?'

'She didn't say. Isn't she back in her place in Dublin?'

'No,' I said. 'She's gone away!'

'The creature!' Sean Grehan muttered. 'It's the poor woman's way of coping. She needs a break!'

'It's not a break, Sean. She has sold her house!'

'Is that so?'

I thanked the Grehans, and Sean walked me to the gate. As I was about to take my leave he added, 'I can tell you this, but no one else. I saw the accident – or almost did.'

'What do you mean?'

He pointed. 'I was on the side of the mountain beyond, above the lake. I heard the splash – you know the way sound carries near water.

I turned and saw him in the lake, in difficulty, and then he was gone. I could do nothing. I was too far away.'

'Of course you couldn't. Did you tell Helen?'

'Yes. She was walking with Mr Malcolm at the time and I ran down the hill to tell them to get a boat. We got out the small boat with the outboard motor which Mr Malcolm keeps. Funny thing, though,' Sean said, dropping his voice, 'when we got his body out she didn't cry at all . . . just stood there staring at him like a woman in a dream! I think they had their troubles – she and Kieran.'

'What do you mean? What troubles?'

He looked at me meaningfully. 'Whatever they were they've gone with him now! But I heard him one night not long before he died, stumbling through the heather above the lake and he was in a bad way!'

'How do you mean?'

'He was terrible cut up,' he said looking at me squarely. 'He was drunk and sobbing.'

He touched his cap and moved away.

I drove to Glendockery, walked the main street, stared at the stone basilisk, read the legend about its erection by a grateful tenantry. The demon's eyes leered into mine and its bat's wings raised themselves as though to daunt me. I already knew the strange forces which inhabited Ireland, but I felt them that day as though they had singled me out, singled Kieran out, and Helen too, wherever she had gone. I could not help wondering if we had, unwittingly, challenged a tragic, vengeful spirit of the valley.

As I passed the post office I decided on impulse to go in, buy some stamps, anything for the pleasure of being in a place where I had once stood with Helen. Mrs Cafferty was there, chatting to a customer. She was quite grey now and was knitting what looked like a pink jumper. Her eyes met mine as I was about to slink away. She started with recognition. Before I could move she called out, 'Is it yourself that's in it, Daniel McPherson? I haven't laid eyes on you these umpteen years! How are you at all?'

And then of course the talk was all of the tragedy in the valley.

'That lake is a good place to keep away from!' she announced grimly, as though privy to some juicy piece of arcane knowledge with which she would tantalize us.

The other customer nodded. 'Terrible strange things have been happening there down the years. It's not the first drowning.'

I felt a shiver climb my backbone. Fiddlesticks, I thought. Pure fiddlesticks.

I asked the estate agent if I could view Helen's house, but I felt like a trespasser as I was shown over the four bedroom semi. It was pristine; all signs of family life had been almost erased. Except for the few scribbles on the wall of Jonathan's bedroom, one would not have suspected that the house was the same one as the moderately untidy home I had visited on the occasion of Mrs Fitzgerald's death. I stood in the sitting room where I had had my last conversation with Kieran, saw my reflection in the mirror, noticed the silk cushions on the settee, the porcelain centrepiece on the mantel, the items of Waterford crystal in a glass case. On a small side table there was a picture of Helen holding Jonathan in her arms. She was smiling.

'What will happen to the furniture?' I asked.

'Any of it that a purchaser doesn't want to buy will be sold.'

I looked in on the dining room, saw the sewing machine in the corner, the means by which Helen had assembled her exotic wardrobe. But the portable typewriter was gone. There was a wicker work box on a shelf and, propped beside it, a half-finished tapestry.

One of the bedrooms had been given over as a study. There was a desk with an anglepoise lamp, bookshelves filled with scientific publications, drawers filled with sheafs of papers. The agent indicated the latter, 'These will be removed, of course.'

I sat at what had been Kieran's desk, swivelled his chair, trying to imagine life at number 3 The Glade, with Helen downstairs. It was here that Kieran had elected to spend his time, indifferent to the woman who filled my senses and my dreams.

But as I moved a scientific tome, a sheet of paper, which had been hidden underneath, came into view. It had some scientific legend on it and something else. Across the bottom of the page there was a scrawl in Kieran's writing: 'Fuck you, God, for this torment. Fuck you!' As I thought of all this afterwards, thought of Kieran, thought of Helen, thought of what Sean Grehan had said to me, the words Helen has whispered to me in Rome when we lunched at the little restaurant in Trastevere, returned with sudden force: 'You don't understand the ferocity that inhabits me. Sometimes it is strong enough to kill.'

It was a force she shared with Kieran, but his was covert. Was it possible that he had turned it on himself?

I went to see Kieran's mother and pay my respects, but she was disjointed and wept easily.

'Helen?' she said. 'Helen's gone off for a while with Jonathan. She needed to get away, but she'll be back. She'll stay with me when she comes back!' She sounded so certain that my fears began to subside. She gave me tea in flowered china cups and thin slivers of fruit cake.

'Where is Jonathan at school?' I asked her. She looked blank for a moment, as though the effort to deal with memories, other than those concerning Kieran, was too great a strain.

'Oh yes ... He'll be starting boarding school ... a place in Limerick.'

'Which school in Limerick?'

'It might be the Jesuits ... or maybe the Benedictines. I can't remember.'

Then she asked: 'Do you remember the night we drove into the valley on your first visit there?'

'Yes. We got out to look at the stars!'

'Did we? Kieran was always fascinated by astronomy. He was brilliant at everything.' She lowered her voice. 'Did he ever tell you he thought the valley would bring him bad luck?'

My mind reverted to a day in Walton Street, Kieran sitting on his bed, photographs of Lough Corrloch scattered between us on the bedspread. 'Not lucky for me ...' he had said.

But I did not want to become involved in this typically Irish foray into superstition, this search for predestined causes for life's calamities.

'Ah no, he was happy there.'

'I know he was happy there, especially when you came. He often said you were his greatest friend!'

She smiled wanly and asked if I would like another slice of cake.

I visited Kieran's grave in Mount Jerome. The mound was fresh, the wreaths withering. I stood for a long time. I did not pray; I had not prayed for years. But I thought of many things, of the past, of what could have been, of his life and his charm, and his faults and his suffering.

'Goodbye, old fellow,' I whispered as I turned away.

My last port of call was Rachel. She was in bed, suffering from a chill, propped up with pillows, reminding me of that Easter in Walton Street when I had come home from Cambridge. She was wasted compared to her old self, but the indomitable spirit that inhabited her was unabated.

'Oh Holy God, will yez look what the cat's brought in!' she announced with a chesty chuckle. 'If it isn't the great important barrister come to see the poor old biddy in the bed.'

I laughed for the first time in what seemed a long time. 'Rachel, you're a tonic.'

'Yeh look as though yez need one. What's been after happening?'

I told her.

'Say yer prayers,' she advised. 'Yeh need the bit o' comfort from the good Lord. That lassie is free now. But sure what bloody use is that, with yez all tied down in holy deadlock?'

The matron came in, took Rachel's temperature, reached adroitly into the bedside locker and removed an almost empty baby Jameson, turned baleful eyes on Rachel and tucked it into her pocket.

'This is Mr Daniel McPherson, a barrister, I'll have yeh know,' Rachel informed the unyielding bosom before her. 'He's goin' to be a judge and he'll fire the whole bloody lot o' yez into jail for larceny.'

The matron smiled thinly, glanced at me and said something about taking her chances.

'Jaysus,' Rachel said when she was gone. 'That oul' faggot has a nose like a bloodhound. She's on to me now. But what'll I do without me little drop?'

'Fear not,' I said, producing from my briefcase the two small bottles I had had the foresight to purchase. 'Never let it be said that I would fail you, Rachel.'

Her eyes lit up. 'Yeh were always a good boy. Now, where'll we stash it?' And she ordered me to find her handbag and to put the bottles into it. 'They'll hardly go pokin' around in me bag.'

I told her I had been to see my father.

'Will he be all right?'

'Fine, Rachel. He's being well looked after! And James came to see him. All he had was a touch of pneumonia!'

'Ah,' Rachel said, 'pneumonia! The old man's friend!' She added musingly, 'The old woman's too!'

She seemed suddenly tired, but I held her hand for a while and talked about London and St James's Park and how we used to feed the ducks together so long ago. I knew before I left that I would never see her alive again. It came to me very quietly, this knowledge, so I lingered, watching her doze, and kissed her carefully before I left.

She died a week later, slipped away in her sleep.

Chapter Twenty

Helen's absence, once it was clear that this was not a temporary excursion, nor time taken out to sort through private trauma, became a torment. How could a woman amputate the one passionate relationship of her life? She had told me she was ruthless, but, secure as I thought myself, I had not believed her. And while the memory of what we had been to each other was still warm and stubbornly reassuring, I had to confront the cold prompt that I had taken too much for granted. If anything her decisiveness gave her a challenging dimension, increased everything I felt for her, now that I knew it was not there for the taking. But she was gone. Her disappearance was a statement, a seemingly final one.

Jonathan was not at boarding school in Limerick. I tried them all. Helen never returned to live with Mrs Fitzgerald. The world did not, after all, wag according to the requirements of Daniel McPherson.

In the ensuing desperation, I decided to find her. She would be easily traced, unless she was deliberately trying to cover her tracks.

And so, to put my domestic affairs in order first, to have a life to offer her, I finally asked Marion for a divorce.

We were in the kitchen, after dinner, putting things away. Marion had had too much wine. Her voice was a little slurred and her co-ordination slightly off target. She dropped a glass as she was loading the dishwasher and it smashed on the tiles.

'Dan, stop staring at me with your godawful, silent reproach. I don't know what's got into you lately.' She clicked with her tongue and raised her eyes in mute invocation to whatever powers dwelt beyond the ceiling. 'It's as though you always think you're in some blasted court,' she went on, 'that you have to be eternally playing to an imagined audience. And I can't stand your bloody awful measured patience!' She bent to sweep up the pieces.

'This can't go on.'

She turned to stare at me. 'What can't go on?'

'We're living a lie. We're both in limbo, Marion! We tolerate it from cowardice, or a combination of cowardice, laziness, pride.'

She turned back to loading the dishwasher. I handed her a casserole dish. She put it in, closed the machine door carefully, turned to look at me. Her eyes were full of tears.

'Is there still . . . that woman?' she asked then, in a low voice.

'No . . . and yes. It's a long story. I don't want to go into it right now! You and I are all washed up anyway. What is the point of continuing the charade? Surely you see that the best course is to end it? To end it amicably, generously.'

I heard my voice, courtroom precision, cold, disembodied, wishing there were some better way, wishing I were capable of empathy with her, wishing for mutuality of understanding. But I had left this moment too long for it to be anything other than one charged with explosive tension.

'"Surely . . . surely . . ."' she mimicked. 'I'm sick to death of all your self-serving certainties. You think you can muck up someone's life and then come along with "surely this" and "surely that".'

She tried to leave the room; I took her arm.

'Think about it, Marion. What earthly use is continuing it?'

She burst into tears. 'You're hurting me!' shook me off and headed for the door.

It was later that evening that I found her in the bath with her wrists slit. She had lost a lot of blood, but was alive.

I stayed with her in the hospital until she came around. She was muttering incoherently, groaning a little, moving her arm and causing the transfusion bag hung up beside her to shake.

'Oh Dan . . .' she whispered, staring in horror at the crimson plastic which was feeding someone else's blood to her. She closed her eyes again as though to blot out the memory of what she had attempted, but wept silently.

'I'm sorry,' she said through her tears. 'Don't hate me, Dan. Dump her! I'll make you happy, I swear it! I'll stop drinking. I'll be a good wife . . .'

She tried to put her bandaged arm around my neck. I saw how the transparent tube was affixed into her vein through a 'butterfly' and replaced her arm on the bed before she upset the hydraulic balance of her transfusion. But I saw the fear and the desperation in her and kissed her on the forehead, as though this small gesture would chase away the accumulated pointlessness of our shared frustration. The nurse who had entered smiled discreetly, deposited the cup of tea and the biscuit on the bed trolley, and withdrew.

In that moment I wished that the corrosive angst which had us in this place, might disappear forever, and, most of all, that my heart was mine for the giving. I also saw, in my mind's eye, my mother's bloody, tear-stained face on the day my father had left. It rose, an accusing spectre, like the Ghost of Christmas Yet To Come.

The letter I sent to Helen, care of her solicitor, was silent on my wife's attempted suicide. But I did indicate that I feared an absolute relationship between us would create frightful damage.

> I am yours, but I am chained. You must decide the future on that basis. The decision rests with you. If you despise me for this you will be perfectly right. But never doubt my love for you; it is not negotiable, although I have a duty where I am and I must carry it to the end.

Her solicitor acknowledged receipt of the sealed missive and said he would forward it. I waited, but Helen did not reply.

Marion came home from hospital, watched me, was careful, cajoling, as though I were a dangerous child. Four weeks later she told me she was sure she could become pregnant if I would make love with her. She was desperate to make something which would secure me for ever. I distanced myself even further. I had no alternative. It had to do with survival.

Time rolled on. I immersed myself in work, and in the cultivation of a stubborn endurance, lost wide spectrums of belief, but gained, perhaps, something of wisdom.

Marion, as though chastened by her brush with death, tried to turn over a new leaf. She became careful, once more, with her drinking, and kept herself so busy with her friends and her charities that she invested less in me and was therefore less fixated on the impasse between us.

A year after Helen disappeared I began an affair with a barrister from another set, but after the initial excitement, it petered away. She had red hair and was beautiful, but she was a million miles from where I stood, forever guarding an abiding, impotent, regret. She was not Helen.

I tried to put my relationship with Helen behind me, to let it go. Sometimes I thought I was succeeding; my work would go well; another case would be won; another client was pleased, or ecstatic, depending on the nature of the case. But I was secretly sick of criminal advocacy.

'The trouble with criminal work,' Catherine said to me from her vantage point as a fully fledged tenant, 'is that if you lie down with dogs you get up with fleas!'

Was this true? Was there a subtle hardening of the conscience at stake in defending those accused of crime? Some of them were innocent, the victims of police blunders, or their own stupidity. Some even confessed to crimes they had not committed. Many, I suspected, were guilty as sin; but they were as entitled to my best efforts as those I believed to be innocent. It was not my business to make judgements; so long as they did not confess their guilt to me, I was free to defend them. Of course I occasionally also acted for the Crown, was the prosecutor. But I was tired of the hustling involved, of the slightly soiled feeling I sometimes brought home with me, and began to hanker for more civil law work, and appraised our chief clerk, Mr Sam Bushwell, accordingly.

One fiercely windy day I had my own brush with mortality.

As I was waiting to cross Fleet Street opposite the gateway to Middle Temple Lane a young boy, striving against the gale, suddenly lost his balance on the edge of the footpath and fell on to the road into the path of an oncoming bus. I reacted without thinking, rushed into the street, threw the child to the pavement. The screech of the great red leviathan was the last thing I remembered for some time. I had taken a glancing blow, which hurt my back and had chipped the bone in my left knee. There was surgery and a doubtful prognosis as to whether I would walk again without a limp. I pondered ruefully how all this had happened courtesy of the bus to Hackney. In such manner are we reminded of our importance.

Nearly three years after Helen had walked out of my life I saw her photograph in the Times Literary Supplement. I chanced on it by accident one Sunday, as I read the papers after lunch. First I saw the photograph, glanced at it. Marion who was making a list for a party she was throwing, looked up and demanded, 'What are you so galvanized about, darling?'

'Nothing. Just a new book which might be interesting.'

'Oh, what's it called?' she asked without much interest.

'*The Hidden Valley*.'

'Who wrote it?'

The phone rang. Marion went to answer it. I returned, mesmerized, to the paper.

'Helen O'Callaghan, author of *The Hidden Valley*', said the paragraph beside her photograph. The accompanying review was about the novel. I read the thing in stupefaction. The review said the book displayed an unusual insight into the contradictions of the human psyche, 'a remarkable debut for Ms O'Callaghan'. I took the page of the newspaper upstairs, folded it and put it away. But first I kissed the smiling face, Helen, in white shirt, sitting near some shelves lined with books. Her face seemed thinner and the eyes graver. I looked at her for a long time, feeling the old knife twist inside me, feeling alive, feeling desire, storming at the gates of my prison, blind with hopes which had not been fulfilled.

Next day I bought the book in Hatchards in Piccadilly, turned hastily to the flap where the same photograph was waiting.

'Helen O'Callaghan was born in Ireland and now lives with her family in New York,' was all the niggardly snippet of information was able to tell me.

The novel was the story of a young boy growing up in an enchanted valley, where his early idealism becomes tainted by a gradual loss of innocence. In this loss the valley itself changes, at first imperceptibly, becoming a threatening place, its beauty hiding agendas he could not once have imagined. Seduced by forces which represent themselves as holy, which manipulate his idealism, whose true nature he does not have the ability to recognize or, when he does recognize them, does not choose to control, he is led away from the path of his peace. He leaves the valley, but finds that on his return, the one place in which he expects to find absolution has altered, has lost its serenity, is cynically measuring him.

It was a disturbing book; it was not a book I would have thought

Helen capable of writing. It was a comment upon human experience, seduction, through folly, into pain.

Oh Helen . . . where did you learn this? Who are your 'family'. Are you remarried? Are you happy?

I could write to her, I thought, care of her publishers, and started a letter. But after the first sentence I put down the pen. What was the point? The time had gone. What could I offer her? Could I even bear to see her, or she me? No. Writing to her would be an exercise in presumption. It was too late.

'Leave well enough alone,' the serpent said in my ear. 'She has found a new world. Why rake up the past? Exercise control.'

But I did not want control. If the book said anything it told me to have the courage of my convictions. Helen was still alive. There was still a chance. I should go to her and find out what she wanted, tell her that the future was ours at last if she wanted it.

I showed the novel to Marion.

'My God,' she said, 'the little Irish girl. You're not over her even yet.'

'It's not a question of getting over her. She wasn't some kind of illness. It's a question of trying to live without her. That's the truth, Marion.'

A short time after this Marion overdosed again on sleeping pills and had to be rushed to hospital to have her stomach pumped. When she recovered she told me in tears how much she loved me, how she couldn't live without me.

'You mucked up my life from the beginning. Don't make it worse. Don't leave me. If you do I can't go on!'

Later, having slept, Marion picked up the threads of discourse: 'She never loved you anyway. If she had she wouldn't have buggered off and married someone else. There's no point in staring at me like that! She's living with her family in New York . . . that's what the book said. And she'd never look at you now, Dan, not since you had the accident. I know you were once a great stud,' she said this bitterly, 'but you're not so gorgeous now. Well, none of us is, including little Miss Hot Pants who probably thinks she has the literary world at her feet. Do you imagine for one moment that she would be bothered with you now?'

Chapter Twenty-One

Thirteen years passed, hounding each other in hot pursuit. Discipline, control, were now the staffs of my existence. I had stayed with Marion, fearful of the terrible weapon with which she ensured my obedience. I had forgotten Helen in the way that you forget the beating of your heart. It's there all the time; you are seldom conscious of it; but it remains the corporeal centre, the *sine qua non* of existence. Sometimes it will flutter; occasionally there will be a sharp sting through the ventricles to remind you that it stands between you and the grave.

Helen had published two more books, both of them well received, but neither of them so full of penetrating anguish as *The Hidden Valley*. Then a film based on it made its appearance. She had become a success.

I was making a lot of money; Marion was spending it. With the years, with the acceptance that she had the upper hand, we had lost the impetus required for separation. It had really come but once, as important things tend to in life; one chance, no more. I had failed to seize the moment; Marion had out-manoeuvred me. I had not known how to proceed thereafter. I was really something of a wimp; a conscientious, courageous advocate, but in my domestic affairs I was feeble. Marion had learnt how to circumvent the strength in me; she used tactics which played to every ideal I had ever embraced, and used them to secure what she wanted. She had an ally in me; she was able to mobilize my guilt.

It hardly mattered now anyway. Our life together had its own momentum, its own inertia, which I no longer had the will to break. I had no home, not in the full sense of home as spiritual and emotional sanctum, but my life with Marion was still the only home I knew. We acquired a villa in the South of France, not far from the one owned by my mother and Charles, and she went there for lengthy spells in summer. Feeling the emptiness at my life's core I increasingly chafed at our childlessness and discussed adoption with Marion. But she was no longer really interested: 'What on earth would we do with children now? We'd be in our sixties when the child was graduating,' and the adoption people, when I made enquiries, told us we were too old. If we had had children, I thought, our villa with the pool might have resounded to the splashing and the laughter of youngsters, rather than the clink of cocktail glasses. I could not bear the empty social round which was the breath of life to my wife. During the Long Vacation, when I might have joined her, I stayed behind working. I now had developed a civil litigation practice, which grew so fast that I had trouble containing it. I took silk and became a Queen's Counsel. I looked at myself in the mirror on the day I was admitted to the Inner Bar and thought how Helen would have smiled at the wig. I was a grey man, I thought, a fixture in Chambers, an urbane lawyer, sharp and encyclopaedic from the neck up; but from the neck down I was a human parody, a tin man.

Marion evidently thought so too, for she flew back one day from our French villa to tell me she had met a retired English colonel and that she wanted a divorce.

She seemed triumphant. 'You were no use to either of us, neither to that little piece from the bogs, nor to me! How could you be when all your thought was with her? And you were no use to her because you were tied to me! Do you think I didn't know that she had stolen away your soul? You should have had the guts to stand up for what you wanted!'

'You used to say you loved me, Marion,' I said mildly. 'I thought it might have been true!'

'Oh for heaven's sake! Love may withstand many things – time, distance, even neglect – but it will never withstand indifference. It has been a kind of torture, Dan, to be the real Other Woman, the one you didn't want. In the end I went for therapy – no I didn't tell you; there are lots of things I haven't told you. But the therapist helped me to understand that I was wasting my life trying to resolve something insoluble; that I had chosen you because, in some subliminal way, I needed to repeat the denial I experienced in childhood!'

When I was silent she went on: 'Oh, I know I've done some idiotic things. That's all behind me now!'

'I'm sorry, Marion. But I was never able to be the custodian of your fate!'

She sighed. 'Semantics again! You're good with words, Dan, but you're as cold as a stone!' She paused at the doorway, looked back. 'You should take a good look at yourself. You sold out to compromise; and compromise has sucked the life from you!'

When she was gone I went to the mirror. The face that confronted me was indubitably my own; I saw it every morning without taking much heed of it. But I examined it now relative to the reflection I used to know in the past. I saw my steel-rimmed glasses, my greying hair, my shrewd, prudent, lawyer's face. The *joie de vivre*, the sap that had once given such life to those lineaments, where were they now?

Marion was right. My father had been right. I had played both sides against the middle and I had lost.

It was August when the curtain rose on the final act in the drama.

The receptionist had phoned up. 'A lady to see you, Mr McPherson, a Ms Bouthemy. She doesn't have an appointment, but she says she's an old friend.'

'Show her up,' I said. I was curious as to who could be claiming the kindred of old friendship. The name Bouthemy meant nothing to me, although it had an echo like something once known and forgotten. I went into the corridor to greet her at the top of the stairs.

She was wearing a straight off-white skirt and jacket. Her hair was cut to shoulder length. She was slim, and she smiled a little coquettishly. For a moment I didn't know her; then recognition came and I struggled for her first name. She preceded me into my room with the provocative walk I had once thought deliberate, narrow hips swinging. I closed the door and we stood looking at each other in silence.

'Sit down, Monique,' I said, indicating the leather armchair by the window. 'I didn't think we would ever see each other again!'

She sat.

'Would you like some coffee?'

'Some of that water would be nice,' she said, indicating the carafe on my desk. I poured her a glass, watching, as though at one remove, the effect her presence had on me. There was a rush of old teenage perspectives, as though the world was still out there and still worth the toil.

'What have you been doing with yourself?' I asked, drawing a chair up beside her. My mind scanned the reasons for her visit. Perhaps it was professional. Perhaps she was seeking advice. Perhaps it was just an impulsive social visit because she was in London. 'It doesn't seem very long since we met at Lough Corrloch!' I went on. 'Are you still living in France?'

'No, in London. My husband is in the wine business. We've been living here now for five years!'

Her French accent was strong, but her syntax had strengthened, was almost perfect.

'Your English is better than it used to be,' I said, 'if less colourful.'

'How dare you!' she said with a laugh. 'But you were always provocatively direct – when you weren't pretending to be innocent!' She put her head a little to one side, an old gesture. 'You're not as colourful either – you've gone grey!' She said this almost accusingly, and I smiled.

'I know. I'll soon be fifty!'

'I'm grey too!' she rejoined ruefully, 'although, of course, I will never admit to a day over thirty!' There was a slender swatch of silver at her temples and a small sprinkling through her fair hair.

'You look very well, if I may say so!'

'I don't know what you mean by that!' she said with a small *moue*. 'Englishmen are always awkward with compliments. Frenchmen, on the other hand, are natural liars, which is why women love them so much!'

'I'm not an Englishman!'

She inclined her head, smiling. 'I'm sorry; I forgot. But you don't seem Canadian!'

'I've been here for too long, become imbued with the spirit of the place that is England.'

'Very lyrical,' she said with a hint of mockery. 'You became imbued with the spirit of another place, once,' the tone of her voice had changed, 'a place we both knew!'

She was looking at me keenly. Her face had become serious. I thought of the valley and Monique's teenage whisper, '*Mon Dieu, il y a quelque chose là-bas qui me donne des frissions dans le dos!*'

'Have you heard from Helen?' I asked.

'Yes.' Her face expressed a certain relief, as though she had been waiting for me to ask and was afraid I would not. 'We have kept in touch down the years. We have visited each other.' The smile died on her lips. 'You know about her books, I suppose?'

'I read them all! I saw the film.'

She was silent, watching me, sipping water with the studied languor of the French woman who is alluring because she believes she is, because she knows that the feminine principle takes no second place. The rings on her hand flashed fire; the small pearls in her ears were exactly right.

'Did you try to find her?' she asked softly. 'Did you ever try to contact her?' She emphasized the word 'ever' with a presumptuous sternness.

'I did,' I said, suddenly irritated at being interrogated. 'As a matter of fact I also sent her a letter, through her solicitor, after she disappeared. She did not favour me with a response!'

Monique gave me a sharp look, and a low deprecatory laugh. 'And so you are piqued. You would have kept her on the end of a string indefinitely, and you were piqued when she changed the rules. I suppose your letter did not offer her anything, did not propose a life together? You expected her to answer you; you wanted things back the way they were. She could continue to prop you, while you were a prop elsewhere!'

I was too indignant to reply. I was angry that she should even know of my relationship with Helen, angry that Helen should have told her, incensed that she should dare to refer to it in such terms. It touched a vulnerability I could not endure; it was possessed of an impertinence which was hardly credible. I stood up to indicate that the interview was at an end.

'Is there some way I can be of help to you?' I asked, to change the subject and to disguise my anger. 'You'll forgive me if I seem rushed, but . . .'

'Oh no. I didn't come here seeking advice, or anything like that,' she said, unperturbed, without making any attempt to bestir herself.

I contained the urge to be peremptory, leant against the desk, picked out a dead leaf from the potted camellia, a present from Catherine, a thank you for recently helping her out. Catherine wasn't a neophyte any more; she was on course for the top.

Monique sipped her water and looked around the room. 'But it's been very nice to see you again!' she said in a softer voice, as though aware that she had overstepped the bounds of tolerance. I waited and when she did not volunteer anything further, I made another attempt to indicate that the interview was over and that the door was within easy walking distance. Her presence was becoming unendurable. She brought with her too many memories, too much misgiving.

The affable inclination I made towards her sprang from the condescending urbanity I had watched myself adopting over the years. It was a shield, fostered to save time, to protect me against the world's legion time-wasters, to forestall any possibility of self-disclosure. 'I hope you'll forgive me now, but I have another appointment shortly.'

Monique did not budge. She took another sip of water. 'You've become so pompous,' she said in tones of asperity. 'So English! But I'm not going just yet, Dan. I have come here to tell you something important.'

My patience was exhausted. I began to dislike this woman who had intruded herself into my personal sanctum, on the pretext of a very nebulous, and very old, acquaintance, and had then proceeded to dish out recriminations about something which was none of her business. I heard a footstep outside in the corridor and then the door opened and Matt Hartley's face appeared. Matt was now the Head of Chambers.

'Oh sorry to disturb you, Dan. I didn't know you had company,' and his face disappeared.

'What is so important?' I asked, turning back to my visitor.

But even as I spoke, as I looked at her strangely uncertain face, the face of someone who did not know how to impart the news which she carried, I was filled with a premonition as sharp and immediate as revelation. All the postures of my profession, the confident, superior, demeanour which was second nature, suddenly seemed attitudes struck against the wind; as though the safe habitats of the decades were only houses of cards. There was something wrong with Helen. I knew it before she could speak.

'Helen is not well,' Monique said. Her voice trailed away and she looked from me to the plane trees outside. The room was suddenly filled with stillness. 'She has contracted a blood disorder,' she went on after a moment, 'a variety of leukaemia. She has been fighting it for the past two years, but I'm afraid the battle is almost over. The enemy has won.'

'Will you be specific?'

'It's a matter of days.'

In the ensuing silence I heard every sound in Chambers, the shrill of the telephones downstairs, the clatter of the photocopier, the bleep of a phone next door, the footsteps on the stairs, the sound of voices from the courtyard outside.

'Where is she?'

'She's in the valley. She's alone there; she will leave tonight for the hospital! She should be hospitalized already, but decided to spend a day at the old house to say her goodbyes!'

Monique looked at my face and her own softened. 'I won't answer any questions,' she said, widening wet eyes to forestall the tears. 'I have no permission to tell you anything. Perhaps I shouldn't have come to see you at all. But it seemed so ridiculous, such a waste. I once thought – was I mistaken? – that you loved her as much as she did you!'

I could not answer. I was a shadow in a grey world. In the silence I heard Time snickering in Fountain Court.

My mind began to calculate coldly the appointments I had, the work on hand, what could be delegated, what could be postponed.

'I'll go at once!'

Monique stood up. 'Remember, she is still angry with you. You must not expect immediate understanding or forgiveness.'

'For God's sake, Monique,' I burst out in anguish, 'Helen could have come back to me any time she wanted – or made me come to her. All she had to do was raise her little finger! So what are you talking about?'

She gave me a pitying look. 'You really don't know? Men are such fools!' She sighed. 'Well, it's not for me to say!'

I tidied my desk, escorted her downstairs, told Janet to cancel any appointments for the next week.

'When will you be back, Mr McPherson?'

'I'll phone.'

I drove to Heathrow, flew to Dublin, hired a car and went to the valley.

It was evening when I got to Lough Corrloch. A Toyota was parked in the yard. The kitchen door was open and Helen came out when she heard me arrive.

She leant against the door jamb. She was wearing jeans and a pale blue cotton sweater. I got out and approached her. It was clear at a glance that she was very unwell; she was much thinner and her face was almost impassive, except for her eyes, which seemed deeper. She had the fragility, the aura of someone touched by eternity. She held her hand out, as though she had been expecting me.

'I suppose Monique has been to see you?' she said. 'I told her not to. But I knew that she would! What has she told you?'

'Just that you are here and that you are ill.' Her eyes were enormous. There were shadows around them and hollows under her cheekbones. But her youth had not deserted her; her beauty had come from within and now it imbued her every gesture with even greater poignancy. The lushness of the flesh had gone, but its memory hovered, and its grace.

As she turned to precede me into the kitchen I saw that she closed her eyes for a moment as though she were in pain.

I followed her, sat at the old deal table. The sight of her aroused such turmoil that I felt like the boy I once was, emotionally charged and uncertain, desperately and irrevocably in love.

'What happened to you? Are you lame?'

'An accident. I hurt my back.'

'I just came to say goodbye,' she said in a tone of careful pragmatism. 'I got here six hours ago and was on the point of leaving. I'm afraid there's no tea, no milk, nothing to offer you!'

'Oh Helen . . .'

'You've changed. You look older,' she went on in a musing voice, 'older and disciplined and rich and all the things you wanted to be. Although I never imagined you lame.'

'No, Helen. Not all the things I wanted to be . . .'

'Well, that's life I suppose. Disappointing in the end! Did you read my books?'

'Yes. I thought they – '

'Don't dare say anything complimentary. They were middling . . . poor things but mine own!'

'They made you quite famous!'

She put her fingers through her hair, pushing it back with the old movement, the unconscious seductive, grooming gesture of the female.

'There was luck involved. The critics didn't understand the first one, but they suspected it meant something. As a result I got some decent reviews! And after that I was more or less launched.'

'How's little Jonathan?'

She seemed amused. 'Nothing "little" any more about Jonathan! He's an aspiring stockbroker in the Big Apple!'

'Ah . . .'

She smiled in the silence, the first smile she gave me. 'Have you become boring, Dan, or are you just overwhelmed to see me?'

'I've become boring!'

She laughed. The tension broke and her face lost its hauteur. 'I deserve that.'

'I'm overwhelmed,' I said, trying to school my voice. 'Since when do I need to tell you, Helen, what I'm feeling?'

I waited. I drank her in, her tired elegance against the wooden chair, the burning hair, the old impish expression as though challenging me. But her eyes expressed things I had never seen in them.

'God, stop looking at me like that. Is it so obvious? That I'm dying? Queer, isn't it?' She regarded my desperate face almost dispassionately. 'So are you, for that matter, so you needn't look like a sick sheep! I'll just beat you to it, that's all!'

'What happened to you?' I whispered. 'Why . . . ?'

She shrugged. 'The slings and arrows of outrageous fortune. Why not?' She lowered her voice as though someone were listening. 'At first I reacted violently. There was so much I wanted to do with life; I could not believe I had been singled out for this execution. Eventually I learnt acceptance. It was the hardest lesson. It meant that it was definitely too late, that certain dreams were over!' She looked at me, sighed. 'But I'm glad to see you, Dan. In fact I need your forgiveness! And I want to ask you something!'

'Forgiveness for what, for God's sake?'

'You'll know soon enough! But I want it in advance!'

I took both her hands. 'Helen, there is nothing to forgive, except what you have to forgive in me. What did you want to ask me? My poor darling!'

She withdrew her hands. 'Don't! No pity!' She turned her head away. 'I wanted to ask you if you ever tried to find me.'

'I did. I went to Dublin, down to the valley, but you had covered your traces.'

'Is that all?'

'I hired a private dick. When it was clear that you had left Ireland I decided to respect your need for privacy, your decision. What could I give you? I had problems with Marion. She slit her wrists. I wrote to you.'

'Yes . . . essentially telling me I was second best.'

'No! Never!

'And when my first book came out did you read it?'

'Of course.'

'Did you think of writing to me again or perhaps you had nothing to say?'

'I started a letter. But I saw that you had a family in New York. And Marion had another go at killing herself. We had lost the chance, Helen. I saw that the time for us had gone.'

'Is there intelligent life on earth?' she asked the opposite corner of the room. 'How could the time for us ever be gone? The people we have shared our lives with – could they even guess at what had been between us? Would they have been capable of even imagining it?'

Through the open door we heard the shiver of the wind in the leaves, watched, in mutual melancholy, the shifting light across the yard.

'Come into the avenue. It was the first place I saw you. This house is mine now, you know, until the lease runs out.' She stood up. 'Are you coming? I have no time to waste, you see, so I have to be bossy. People never appreciate time when they have it!'

Outside we stood for a moment, looking into the green tunnel where the branches reached across above the avenue. She walked slowly down the driveway, paused by the gate where the dog roses still bloomed.

'You were playing at Tarzan, that first day!' I said.

'I was!' she admitted, breathlessly. 'I was absolutely thrown by your guessing it!' She looked at the boughs above her head, raised her arms, dropped them in a gesture of defeat. 'I can't play at Tarzan any more, or anything else for that matter! Crazy, isn't it? I never took it seriously – death, I mean. I thought it only happened to other people, victims of accidents, or people who were ready, old fulfilled people. But life's lessons are real; it isn't kidding.'

'And you beat Kieran at chess and he was livid!' I said, clutching at memories to contain the ferocity waiting to burst in me.

She was silent for a moment. 'Yes. I don't want to talk about him! You were right, you know; he was gay. He was in torment; how much I didn't realize until he was gone and the unspoken weight of his suffering was lifted.'

'Yes . . .'

'I wouldn't have minded his homosexuality so much if he had even been capable of a relationship. You know – just common or garden friendship. But he required me only as a kind of wallpaper, a blind. He was really quite ruthless; I learnt it from him. He was so afraid of his own truth that he didn't care what he did, until Fate turned its jaws on him. He was having some kind of relationship with one of his students, who had threatened to expose him. And I think there was something else . . . something from the past, because not long before he died he lost that careful bonhomie and I saw glimpses of where he really lived.

'And you – you wanted everything; you wanted me and the self-image to go with both. And I was a fool, initially all dewy-eyed with innocence and good intentions . . . the paving of the road to hell . . . and then with passion and, latterly, sick with the affront you offered me, the terrible presumption of it!'

'Don't say that, Helen.'

'You even loved me – at least I believed you did. That belief kept me bound and chained to you. You would have manipulated me until you destroyed me.'

'No!'

'But yes. Not deliberate, I grant you, but still the only reality you could give me!' She shrugged, as though throwing off sorrows.

'How did Kieran really die?' I asked abruptly. '*Was* it an accident?'

'When we pulled him out we found that his pockets were full of stones! I removed them for Johnny's sake and never told the inquest.'

I held her head against me. 'What should I have done, Helen? About us?'

'You mean – from my perspective?' she said against my chest. 'I think you should have come after me, Dan, found me! You should have had the courage to allow your wife to face her own demons, without making you – and me – eternally pay for them. I hadn't disappeared off the face of the earth. But because you didn't I have kept something from you; you will find out what in due course. I was too proud to tell you at the time, in case you thought I was trying to force your hand; and I'm not able for it now . . . And if I told you, you might try to upset the stability of things which have acquired a *modus vivendi* over the years. You'll find out and you'll just have to understand and forgive, if you can!'

She looked at me, put up her hand. 'Don't ask me any questions. I am not the woman you knew; I am very tired; I have lost my elasticity. I am not able for recrimination or any of those nauseating last journeys into regret.'

She glanced at me again. 'All that idealism is gone, you know. All that belief!'

I searched her for what she felt for me, alert to the nuances of her tone and her expression. I remembered what Marion had said to me: 'She never loved you anyway . . .' I knew it was a lie.

'You haven't told me anything about your life,' I said after a moment. 'Did you remarry, have other children? What have you been doing for the past thirteen years?'

'I have been living with a good man, who is kind and who loves me and who is companionable. Mind you, he doesn't know the full story about you and me, only that we were childhood friends. But despite his kindness, despite everything, I have been, on a level which no one but you ever touched with me, the loneliest woman under the sun!'

'Who is he, the man you are living with?'

'Joss Malcolm, the guy who owns this valley. You remember I mentioned him in my letters? He used to visit the Lodge. He was here when Kieran died. He was the one who fished him out. I went back to America with him. I have been living with him ever since!

'I didn't marry him,' she added defensively, glancing at me for a moment and looking away, 'though he asked me often enough. He does not know where I am now. I refused that awful, useless treatment and signed myself out of the clinic, leaving him a note to say I was going away for a while. He's probably worried sick, but I'll phone him tonight. I've come home because I wanted to see this place once more! I wanted to see it alone. And I wanted you with me at the end.' She looked at me with sudden sarcastic enquiry, the brittle mask designed to hide the true Helen. 'If you wouldn't mind, that is. If you have nothing better to do. If there isn't something else which has first call on your duty.'

I released her, turned and walked away, put my arm across my eyes, unable to hide from her any more. But she followed me and took my hand, leaning her head against my shoulder in the old gesture.

'You can't stay here,' I whispered eventually. 'You need medical attention!'

'I'm booked into St Michael's Nursing Home in Dun Laoghaire. They were expecting me this morning, but I phoned to tell them that I'll be very late. There's a room there, overlooking the harbour. It's the one I had when Jonathan was born. I'll be able to see where you used to arrive on the mailboat!'

We moved down the avenue together, paused at the outer gate to the boreen. I knew that the pool was lying a few hundred yards away under the evening sun. The sheep were bleating on the sides of the mountains; the light of evening played on the west-facing escarpment. If I closed my eyes I could imagine the open back door, the smell of turf smoke, the sound of a girl's laughter: 'Ah Dan, you are letting your ambition cloud your common sense.'

'It reminds me of that first day,' I said. 'Nothing has changed.'

She looked around, then back at me in gentle compassion. 'But on the contrary! Everything has changed! We have all moved away down our own personal valleys of no recall. The gorse may still be bright, the heather purple, but there is that small nip in the air which tells us it is the end of summer.'

I tightened my arm around her, felt her spareness. She coughed, glanced up archly and recited:

> '. . . this nipping air,
> Sent from some distant clime where winter wields
> His icy scimitar, a foretaste yields
> Of bitter change – and bids the flowers adieu.'

She waited, but I could not speak. 'Wordsworth,' she said. 'Sure you've only half educated!'

That evening she insisted on walking along the pier at Dun Laoghaire before I took her to the hospital. The mailboat was in.

I noticed how rapid her breathing had become and, alarmed, drew her down beside me on the seat. She lay back on the stone bench beneath the empty bandstand canopy, where her eleven-year-old self had once sat. She put her head on my lap.

We talked. She put her hand up to take off my glasses and drew my head down until our foreheads touched. I told her of my love. I whispered it as it was, something I had lived, absolute, irrevocable; I told her of my life since she had gone. She listened in silence, although now a few tears slipped from under her lashes and down the side of her nose. I wiped them away.

In the white-blue light from the mercury vapour lamps of the harbour I saw the grey in her still luxuriant hair. Her face was lifted, the chin pointed, eyes closed. It did not seem to me then that it had changed, except for the maturity, the small lines of having lived, the pallor of illness, but I felt the vitality burning there yet. I had never loved her as I did at that moment, knowing the parting coming, knowing her with all the fibres of my life, of the past and of the future I had once thought to plan.

There were two sudden, short booms from the mailboat before it slipped its moorings and left soundlessly for the sea. She did not move to watch it or give any indication of having heard its farewell.

* * *

When it was over I went back to the valley. She had given me the keys and I opened up the house, went to her old bedroom, lay on her bed.

'I've left the house to you!' she had said at one point, before she slipped into unconsciousness. 'There's a few years left in the lease. Go back there after I've gone. I'll join you,' she added with her old quirky smile and a breathless laugh, 'if I can.'

The room was maidenly as ever, although a little mustiness filled the air, despite the open window. I did not sleep, but waited in the darkness, but the night wore on into morning and nothing disturbed the peace. I began to realize that it was the peace which was remarkable, the old serenity I had always felt near her. The room was heavy with it, wrapped me in it.

Before dawn I lit the lamp and, on impulse, went to her small deal wardrobe. There on the shelf was the copy of *King Solomon's Mines*. I took it down, dusted it, found that the pages of her old journal were gone. But something else lay among the pages which had not been there before. It was a fresh white envelope with my name and the date I had last met her in the valley. Inside was a piece of flint with a small carved heart. It was folded in a sheet of paper, with a handwritten poem.

LONDON REVISITED

(Written on return from London, January 1974)

A young man, once a strange boy at the lake,
Patina of ambition, calm, restrained,
Stands by the hotel window pen in hand,
Less young, but vibrant now with adult power
Mature agendas – triumphs, conquests, gains,
Life's prized impedimenta.
Behind him the domes and misty spires,
Of a great city in a grey-blue haze,
The green expanse of Hyde Park's winter sward,
White horse and rider viewed from sunlit tower,
The Serpentine in frigid wintry calm.

Roll back the years,
The boy, freckled, stranger by the lake,

Still lives!
No power or purpose can erase that yesterday,
No attrition of the years,
Austere pathways to influence and gain,
Or reputation's splendour;
Wigs, gowns, fine points, subtle thrusts,
Love lost and found;
No matter what life's onward rush will yield or lose
The crystal love, the innocence remains.

Epilogue

The Lodge,
Lough Corrloch
24 April 1993

Dear Mr McPherson,

Thank you for your letter. I remember you well from Helen's funeral.

I know the lease on the gamekeeper's house at Lough Corrloch is due to expire next month, but you are, as a childhood friend of Helen's, welcome to use the place whenever you want. I intend to do it up and let it as a summer cottage for tourists. Mrs Grehan has kindly agreed to look after it for me. So any time you want to come, just let her know.

As you see from the address, I'm back in Ireland. It's the first time I have returned since Helen's death. I've really come to get restoration work on the Lodge under way. Most of the work will be carried out during the next few months while I'm back in the States. But I'll return in the summer with my daughter.

The Grehans tell me that you like to visit the valley during the month of August. Although the lease expires next month I hope that you will come back in August this year, if such is your wish. I'll be here then and would be mighty pleased to shake hands with you again. It will be time enough for you to hand over the keys when you have had your vacation.

It would be nice to talk to someone who remembers Helen. I miss her greatly, although I suspect that she was restless, as though hankering for something she had left behind her. It must have been this valley, of course, and now that I have spent some time here I begin to understand why.

But I console myself that her spirit, at least, is free and I like to imagine that she comes here sometimes and wanders with me by the lake shore.

Sincerely yours,
Jocelyn Malcolm.

I tried to recall Jocelyn Malcolm. I had met him at the funeral, a grieving man, grey-haired, taciturn and talkative by turns, wearing an American macintosh over sombre clothes. We had spoken briefly.

He had seemed dazed at the time: mentioned something about troubles coming in multiples; that his daughter had suffered a fall in a riding accident on the day that Helen had left secretly for Ireland, was hospitalized and in plaster. She would be all right, but he wanted to hurry home to New York to her.

At the time I thought what an anodyne it must be, having a loved one to rush home to and comfort, someone with whom to share the grief, and I envied him this, particularly in thinking of the girl, wondering was she his and Helen's daughter, but unable to ask, the time being less than appropriate and my own susceptibility fragile.

Helen had been laid to rest in the small graveyard in Glendockery, where she and I and Kieran and Monique had rambled after Mass one Sunday to read the legends on the tombs. Standing among the other mourners – Joss Malcolm, Jonathan, good-natured and friendly, who did not remember me, Monique who shared her umbrella – I had noted in a detached way, as though the proceedings were remote, how stony the soil was, and how the rain formed small puddles on the new mound.

A week ago I went back to the valley for the last time. Yesterday morning I went in search of my landlord to hand over the keys.

I chanced to meet him as he came along the boreen from the lake. He did not look like a man in his late sixties, was younger, more affable and talkative than I remembered. He gave me a truly American handshake, a robust movement of the arm straight from the shoulder, took the keys from me, reminding me of his offer for me to continue to use the house whenever I wanted.

I was about to decline politely. It was time for me to go. Helen had been dead for four years. Her ghost did not walk in the valley, nor in the house, although I had waited every night I was there in some kind of stubborn and insane hope.

But even as I was about to refuse the kindly offer, I heard the girlish voice call from the slopes above us. I looked up, saw the dark red hair, the form and, as she came closer, the face. My hand went instinctively to my heart to still its suffocating leap of recognition.

'It's my daughter,' my landlord explained, smiling fondly up at her. 'Did she startle you?'

'Your daughter?'

'Well, she's not really mine, but I look upon her as my own. She loves it here and I'm going to give the valley to her someday! She missed her mother's funeral and is thrilled to be here at last.' He glanced at me. 'Helen was pregnant with her at the time her husband died. Did you know that?'

I stood rock-still. My mind was in overdrive. 'Are we safe?' I had asked her that last time as she lay silken white beneath me.

'Yes,' she had said after a second's hesitation. 'Safe as houses, my Daniel.'

'Yeah,' Joss Malcolm continued, 'about three months pregnant at the time of his death. The baby was born in the States; she's an American!' He laughed, his eyes following the girl on the slope above us. 'She thinks that's neat, although she's sorry she never knew her real father!'

'You'll have to forgive me if you can,' Helen had said. 'I'm not able for recrimination.'

'What's her name?' I asked. 'What's your daughter's name?'

'Danielle . . . Nice name. Helen was particular about names!'

I turned to watch the form, the red hair tumbling in the sunlight, the laughing teenager whooping towards us through the heather.